MYSTIC LAKES

MYSTIC
LAKES

A NOVEL

Damian Musello

DONALD I. FINE, INC.
NEW YORK

Library of Congress Cataloging-in-Publication Data

Musello, Damian.
Mystic lakes.

I. Title.
PS3563.U8347M97   1987   813'.54   87-45106
ISBN 1-55611-046-4

Library of Congress Catalogue Card Number: 87-45106
ISBN: 1-55611-046-4
Manufactured in the United States of America

10 9 8 7 6 5 4 3 2 1

To my parents
with my love and admiration
and to Patricia,
a valued friend, an encouraging voice

Part One

I

"YOU CAN'T STAY HERE," I said to Marion. She was sitting at the desk in my office on Moody Street, smiling, pleased at the look of surprise that must have shown on my face.

"Aren't you even going to say hello?" she asked. "It's been a long time."

"Hello, how are you? Now we've got to get you out of here," I said. I went out into the anteroom and looked through the blinds, then returned and sat in the visitor's chair. It was nine in the morning and I'd just arrived for what I'd thought was going to be a normal day's work. I had a one-man detective agency with a steady list of clients I'd worked ten years to develop, and when I walked in the door and found Marion I felt all that begin to evaporate. It was the feeling of coming across some person or situation you've been avoiding for years, that you know will alter the precarious balance in your life. "What are you doing here?" I asked. "Did the FBI start to get close?"

Marion nodded. I thought I saw a subtle shift in her eyes, a moment of worry maybe, or sadness. She had cool gray eyes, the iris metallic like burnished aluminum, the pupil, jet black. Emotion rarely showed in them—it was carefully concealed, strictly controlled. The moment passed quickly, but now her smile looked forced. "They started showing my picture around the neighborhood. Some friends tipped me off and got me a car. I've been in Boston a week."

"Great. They're going to start checking everyone here you've ever been involved with. They followed me for a month last time."

"I didn't realize . . ."

"What the hell do you think? You think they leave me alone? Every time something happens that has even the slightest whiff of political activity I've got someone knocking on my door, 'Derek, where were you last night?' Goddammit Marion, coming here is crazy."

"Sorry," she said. "I thought you might not mind seeing me again."

"Whether I want to see you or not is irrelevant. That's not the point."

"You've gotten nervous in your old age."

"Smart is the word."

"Whatever."

My anger began to subside. I looked her over, this woman I'd hoped never to lay eyes on again and had waited ten years to see. She was still beautiful, with her high Cherokee cheekbones and the shiny black hair that hung straight to her shoulders. She was inordinately proud of her one-sixteenth or one-thirty-second share of Indian blood: she thought more of that one renegade Wilson who had bedded down with an Indian woman than all the other Wilsons put together. She had told me once that she felt his blood in her veins, giving her the strength to do what she wanted or had to do, no matter what. Her full lips still formed a firm line, betraying a tendency toward stubbornness, and she held her shoulders and back straight, with a stiffness I always associated more with nineteenth-century explorers posing formally in seal skins and mukluks for their group picture, or with that Western settler she admired, than a woman who was raised in a split-level ranch in a western suburb of Massachusetts. Wall-to-wall carpeting. Extravagant TV antenna. Two cars on an asphalt driveway running directly from street to garage, past clumps of decorative juniper. A life Marion had fled.

I got up, went to the window of the anteroom again and peered through the blinds, looking for signs of someone watching the entrance. A brick building faced me from across the street, five stories of windows shining in the early sun. Clandestine surveillance. I would have to check my rearview mirror now, listen for a certain hollowness on the phone line, regard strangers I met with increased suspicion.

"We've got to get you out of here," I repeated, more quietly this time.

When I turned she was staring at the desktop. "Derek, I . . . I'm thinking of turning myself in. I'm tired of being a fugitive. I've become an icon for the movement, the longest-running show, still playing after fifteen years. I'm an object of curiosity and perverse pride for the people who keep me free. It's become a game, 'How long can we frustrate the FBI?' "

"Is that why you came back to Boston?"

"I didn't think so until now." She stood up and began a slow turn around the office, looking blindly at everything I'd used to fill up the room—the photographs of Venus, Mars, Jupiter and Saturn I'd hung methodically along the walls; the lithographs I'd printed; the books I'd collected, all the means I'd used to fill up what I'd thought was a new life. She made the rounds pensively, walking in her masculine way, heavy-footed, her boots sounding loud on the wood floor. She was dressed in jeans, a gray sweatshirt and a dungaree jacket.

"Derek," she continued, "I've lived in a dozen cities the last fifteen years, none of which I chose for myself. They were places to escape to: New York, Chicago, New Orleans. I can't even name them all without thinking hard. You know them. I wrote to you. You never answered."

"I know them." I continued the list for her. "Detroit, Newark, Los Angeles." I stopped to remember. "London, Johannesburg, Athens." We were fifteen feet apart, making a slow approach with words and a careful shifting of bodies. I followed her restless movement.

She smiled. "It wasn't London, actually. It was Belfast. Importing money." The memory pleased her. "Five hundred thousand dollars for the IRA."

"Half a million for guns and murder," I said.

She frowned. I was supposed to be impressed. My response seemed to sap her energy and her shoulders slumped a little. "Have you changed that much, Derek? Is that why you never wrote back? Did you ever try to contact me?"

I didn't answer. It was one of the reasons. I wasn't sure of the others. Since I'd gotten out of Walpole, after doing five years for the "political action," the bombing of a Brighton bank that had killed my partner Richard Del Tredia and sent Marion into hiding, all I'd wanted to do was take care of myself. My own business. Before, I'd been willing to do anything for what I thought was right, but in jail I had time to wonder where my acts of violence stood on the moral spectrum. I couldn't decide. That scared me. It still does. Marion's letters always made my doubts resurface, so I would read them, burn them, then try to put them out of my mind.

"Why didn't you try to contact me?" Marion asked again. "It wouldn't have been difficult."

She had turned away from me and was assessing one of my lithographs. She was withdrawing into her hard shell again, regaining the energy she'd momentarily lost. I watched, a spectator to some interior struggle.

She pointed to a print and said, "Signed by D. Anderson. You're doing art now?" She stepped back and held up her thumb like a dilettante in a museum. "Clever use of mass and space, dark and light. Very . . . pretty."

"You don't approve?" I asked. "What's the matter? No time for art in the trenches?"

I saw a smile play across her lips. She moved over to a framed photograph on the wall, her direction taking her a few steps closer to where I stood.

"What's this?" she asked.

"A picture from *Voyager*—the moon and earth together."

A planet and moon surrounded by deep, black space. Two small, illuminated crescents of light. Black interstices. Galactic emptiness. "Everyone should be required to carry that around in his wallet," I said. "It would give some perspective."

She looked at me over her shoulder, her lips still curved in a smile, her eyes amused. "You're looking for comfort in science and the arts now? We could have fed a thousand people with the money they spent on that picture."

"Somehow I knew you'd say that."

I moved behind her and put my hand on her shoulder, rubbing the smooth cotton, feeling tense flesh and muscles, stroking as if to prove she was really there. I couldn't make the connection between Marion's presence and my office, the warm June sunshine and images rising from the past, the desire to talk to Marion and the urgent need to get her away, for my safety and hers.

"Why didn't you contact me, Derek?"

The question startled me this time. "Because . . ." I let the sentence trail off.

"You can do better than that."

"I know," I said, then went on, quickly, "we don't think the same way anymore, Marion. I don't buy the old arguments. I don't believe you have to meet force with force."

"Tell that to the Irish," Marion said. "Tell that to the Israelis and the South Africans. The only ones who can stop fighting are the winners, and then they'll fight to keep what they've won."

"Why did you come back to Boston, Marion?" I asked. "You didn't come here to trade political banter, did you?"

Her body tensed, then relaxed. "I don't know," she said, "I wanted to see you. I had some vague idea of how our meeting would go. I thought it would be good. I even imagined that we could pick up right where we left off." She let out a short laugh. "Pretty ridiculous."

I put my arms around her waist and clasped my hands over

her stomach. She put her hands on top of mine. I smelled her scent, the oils of her hair and the sweat on her skin. For a moment I could almost believe the years hadn't passed or that we hadn't become separated by more than time, but the feeling lasted only seconds and suddenly I knew we were in my office in Waltham and that I had been listening all the while to the footsteps on the sidewalk outside, waiting, half expecting to hear an authoritarian knock on the door, official, insistent.

"It was just a dream," Marion said, "a vague dream of settling accounts and having a normal life . . . whatever that is. How long do you think they'll give me, if I turn myself in?"

"I got seven years. They paroled me in five," I said. "They'd probably give you less since you were only driving. You might do only three years, unless—"

"Unless they bring in all the nasty, terrible things I've done since?" Marion asked. She pulled away from me and walked over to a heavy canvas bag on the desk, jerking it open and pulling out a pack of cigarettes. She shook one loose, put it between her lips and lit it. All business again.

"Do they know what else you've done?"

"I don't know!" She waved out the match and threw it in the desk ashtray. "They always seem to catch up to me. They keep tracking me. They never give up." She blew out a cloud of blue smoke. "Fuck them," she said.

I watched her complete the transition to tough Marion. We were far apart again. I went over and sat in the visitor's chair.

"I'm disappointed in you, Derek," Marion said. "You saw Ray get shot in Dunn County just for registering voters. You got your head cracked in Chicago. You saw King murdered and Bobby Sands starved and now . . . how can you forget all of that?"

"Marion, it's not just a matter of forgetting. I turned thirty in jail, Walpole. All metal and concrete. Metal bars, metal beds, desks. Concrete floors and walls. Cold, always cold. Cold people with their lives on hold. At thirty-five I was hanging on by the skin of my teeth, barely making a living. Now, at last, I have a life for myself."

She looked disgustedly around my office. "A life for your-self," she said. "Wonderful."

"We can't all be martyrs."

"No," she said, "I suppose you don't have it in you."

"Not fair."

She inhaled again, the deep draw of a heavy smoker. She considered me through the smoke. "You're right. Sorry. I just . . ."

"Just what?"

"I don't know."

I wanted to go to her but I held back, listened to the cars rolling past outside and thought of bright sunshine.

"I suppose you want me to go," Marion said

"I don't," I answered.

"That's not what you said when you first came in."

"You surprised me . . ."

"I trust what people show me when they're surprised."

I shook my head. "It's not you I didn't want here. It's what you represent."

"And what's that?"

"A lot of things," I said. "My past. The way I used to live. I need time to think before I can spell it all out for you. You've come in here like a stampede, just like you did in the South. Tact was never your strong point."

She smiled and took another long drag. "No, I suppose not. And you always needed a long time to think. It's a way of putting off hard decisions."

"You always went off half-cocked. Snap judgments. You considered that a strength."

"I just trust what I feel," Marion said. She dropped the cigarette into the ashtray, looked coolly around the room. "I'm going to be around for a while. You'll have time to think."

"Are you going to turn yourself in?"

She let out a short laugh, but it sounded hollow. "I don't know. For the first time in my life I need time—like you. Maybe it's your proximity. You're already rubbing off." She shouldered her bag and moved toward the door. I followed and stopped her, turning her around to face me. I kissed her, brushed my hand over her cheek.

"I've toyed with coming to see you a hundred times," she said. "I got your telephone number and didn't call and didn't call. I kept all the men in my life an arm's distance away." She put on her sarcastic smile again. "They must have thought I was a cold bitch."

I laughed. "What, you? Marion Wilson? Never."

She tilted her head to the side. "What do you mean?"

"You were a hard nut when you wanted to be."

"Is there something wrong with that?"

"No, I think it's part of your attraction." I kissed her again. She put her head on my shoulder.

"I'm not such a hard case anymore," she said. "I'm fedup . . . tired. You turned thirty in Walpole. I turned thirty in a tenement in Newark. Plaster walls with holes in them . . . it looked like Beirut. Garbage, rats, rats the size of armadillos . . . sometimes the electricity would go off for no reason at all, and there was never enough heat.

"I celebrated number thirty-five in a safe house in Bottineau, North Dakota. Beautiful place. Cabin on a lake near the Canadian border. Fishing for my dinner, reading by lantern light, a woodburning stove to heat the cabin. I chopped the wood myself. Actually learned how to use an axe without cutting my foot off. The air was fresh, pure."

"Sounds good," I said, stroking her hair.

"It was. I wanted to stay there, in Bottineau, on that lake. I sat for hours and watched these birds paddling across the water, diving under, coming up an incredible distance away, and tried to imagine what it would be like swimming submerged in that clear water. I could see bears on the opposite shore. They'd stare at me and I'd stare at them. We left each other alone. That's what I wanted to be, alone, chopping my wood and reading by lantern. Then Danny came and took me to Oakland. That was just over a year ago. Now I'm here. The FBI caught up to my last move pretty fast."

"Why didn't you stay in North Dakota?"

"Because it was a dream, some kind of fantasy. I'd just be running away from everything like everyone else does, or wants to do, anyway. It would be denying what I think you have to do with your life." She said this as if she were trying to convince herself or bolster her own spirits. I held her tight, wanting to comfort her, but feeling as if hiding was what I'd been doing since I saw her last. I was what Marion didn't want to become. I lived watching out for myself. She couldn't accept that and, probably, couldn't accept what I'd become. I pushed that out of my mind and held her.

After a while she shook her head to dispell her thoughts and then drew back to look at me. "We have some time," she said. "Let's spend it together. I haven't been here in years. I want to go to Rockport and the Gardens and Castle Island. Remember when we use to picnic on the Island?"

"Of course I remember."

Her eyes shined. "Let's go there again."

There was something unreal about her lightness, out of synch with where she was, her precarious situation. I went along with her though. "Picnic at Castle Island. Okay," I said. "But first we've got to get you to a safe place." I thought of what might be waiting outside. "I should leave first," I said.

She looked at the door.

"I'll see if I'm being followed. If I am, I'll call just so you know to watch out. Let the answering machine take it. If you haven't heard from me in an hour it's probably safe to leave, but use the back exit."

She dropped her arms from my shoulders and walked slowly back to my desk. She threw her bag down and sat on the corner. When she looked at me her eyes were angry. "Fuck," she said. She folded her arms tightly across her chest. "Well? Go."

"Where are you staying? Where can I call you?"

She gave me a short, frustrated wave. "I'll get in touch with you. Now go."

I stepped from my office into sunlight, letting my eyes adjust and trying to look unconcerned, but I immediately felt as if I were being watched. Paranoia. My office was on a busy main street crowded with stores and restaurants, heavy with pedestrian traffic. Everyone who approached was a potential agent, spy, cop. I hated the feeling. I got my sports car from the parking lot across the street and headed out into traffic, keeping an eye on the cars behind me. I spotted him after a few quick turns. He was alone, driving a foreign model sedan. He was a good tail and I wouldn't have spotted him if he hadn't had trouble with one of the red lights. I've been followed before and it usually doesn't bother me, but this time, with Marion waiting, I wanted to lose him and slip away in the heavy traffic. I wanted to pick up Marion and go to the ocean, watch the on-shore wind pull at her hair. Instead I let him follow me to a restaurant in Watertown where I ordered a late breakfast. Then I called my office. After the beep I said two words, "Got company," and hung up. While I picked at my watery eggs and butter-soaked toast, I fought an urge to go out and confront the man waiting for me. Instead, I ordered a second cup of cast-iron coffee. I read the paper—headlines: "PASTORA BLAMES CIA FOR ASSASSINATION ATTEMPT," "IRAQI JETS BOMB IRAN." In Switzerland, Botha was working to "improve South Africa's image."

When I returned to my office Marion was gone and the room, which had never bothered me before, seemed an empty place.

II

────

I OPENED THE BLINDS and let the late-morning sun pour into my office. "Have you changed that much?" Marion had asked. I had. I had changed the moment the bomb went off in the Brighton National Bank. Richard and I had set the charges before a long row of teller's windows. This was our political statement, our attack against the "Imperialist Infrastructure." We talked in large nouns then. Our enthusiastic, educated minds were filled with grandiose concepts begun with capital letters and taught to us as children in school: Liberty, Independence, The Fraternity of Man. The young think in grand terms, single words, broad concepts. As we grow old we become more concerned with nuances, the adjectives and adverbs of life, the structure of sentences—commas, semi-colons, periods. Richard, Marion and I were dangerous, armed with large words and big ideals. It was late at night, only a few streetlights illuminated the offices. I was backing away towards the side door and Richard was coming towards me, having set the timer. I could see his white teeth shining in a smile. I smiled too—at that moment it was a game to us. Blows against the Empire. Then I was lifted off my feet, thrown against the rear wall and knocked unconscious. I woke up in a prison hospital. Richard had been killed. But it wasn't his death that changed me, it was the thought that, if the timer could go off too soon, it could also go off too late, and it might have killed innocent people. We'd already talked about that, but only in abstract terms. Rich's death made it real: his back torn open, his spine exposed by the concussive force—our cool dogma turned into bloody flesh. I realized he could have been someone innocent and unaware of our jargon, the first teller to arrive, a young girl perhaps, paid minimum wage, struggling to make ends meet, thinking about what she was going to do that night or on the weekend. Richard was willing to take his chances, but what right did we have to involve her? That imaginary girl became a symbol in my mind. No matter how good my motives were, what right did I have threatening her life? None. That was my limit and that's what separated me from Marion.

I was unsettled by Marion's visit and not up to doing work, so I left the office and drove around the city aimlessly, my mind a jumble of thoughts that didn't quite coalesce into anything coherent. I had lunch somewhere out in Holliston, twenty miles west of Boston, and I still don't know how I wandered out that far. When the sun was starting its plunge to the western horizon I was back in Brighton so I stopped for dinner at Kiernan's Tavern.

Kiernan's was an Irish pub, as Irish as Paddy's pig, serving only the biting whiskey and thick, dark stout of the motherland, with nothing but Irish ballads on the juke box and meat and potatoes in the kitchen. It was the kind of place where the descendants of tenant farmers and day laborers who had fled famine and the hard life in Ireland could come and drink away the evening, throwing darts and sipping their beer as if outside the door there was not a blacktop avenue and a mall, but emerald green fields marked by low stone walls. They could come and feel some semblance of their heritage by looking at the life of their father's father through safe, distant memory.

I sat on a stiff-backed stool at the bar and ordered a beer from the old codger who manned the tap. He was short and bent, with a shiny bald head, a long sharp nose and a mouth turned down as if he were tasting every bitter memory that had plagued his life. When he brought the pint to me he held it away, croaking irritably, "$1.75."

The bar was narrow and dim, the walls sheathed in dark mahogany and decorated with overly ornate lamps that cast more shadows than light. The wall behind the bartender was stacked with bottles set before a mirror that gave an illusion of greater space. Above the mirror was a row of aged photographs—turn-of-the-century portraits of rough-looking men dressed in unaccustomed suits and looking like tough boys decked out for the Sunday choir.

A young voice beside me said, "You know who they are?"

I turned to see a man in his mid-twenties leaning against the bar, partly as if sharing a confidence and partly because he was three sheets to the wind. He had long black hair parted down the middle and swept back behind his ears, and an open, expressive face.

"The Invincibles," he said proudly. "Is that right, Jimmy?" he said to the shrunken bartender.

Jimmy wiped out a pint glass with a white towel. "That's right," he said.

"Defenders of the Republic."

"Defenders of the Republic," Jimmy repeated.

The young man turned to me and said, tapping my shoulder for emphasis, "They shot Cavendish and Burke in Phoenix Park." He nodded to the bartender. "Didn't they, Jimmy?"

"They did." The old man reached for another glass.

"Got hung for their trouble."

"That was a long time ago, John," the bartender answered.

John considered the pictures as if searching for an answer. He couldn't come up with one. He was momentarily distracted by a loud whoop from the rear of the pub as someone playing darts struck the cork, then he turned to me again. "It wasn't that long ago, was it?" he asked.

I shrugged. "No idea. When was it, Jimmy?"

"1882," he said quickly. Some dates people never forget. I remember November 22, 1963; August 26, 1964; April 4, 1968;

October 12, 1969. Small ripples in the eternal pond. Jimmy slung the towel over his shoulder and started rinsing glasses. He kept a wary eye on the young man beside me.

I said to him, "That's a long time, John."

He studied the grim-faced men. "Still got the British sitting on their face," he said. He pounded the bar. "Jimmy! Another stout."

"You've been drinking since five, John."

"Com'on."

The old bartender served him another beer, muttering under his breath, his face cramped with a sour look.

"Thanks, you old fart." John smiled.

"You watch yourself."

"I am, Jimmy, I'm watching myself all the time."

Two men—look-alikes—wandered over from somewhere in the crowd and stood behind John. They were both about six feet tall, with the solid look of having spent a lot of time in the gym. They had short black hair and wore imitation leather jackets, the kind that look expensive but cost forty dollars at Bradlees. It took a while for John to notice them perched behind his shoulder and when he did he turned with exaggerated surprise.

"There you are!" he said. "I was wondering when you'd show."

The two leaned in and spoke quietly to him like undertakers addressing the bereaved.

"Sure, come on," John answered with excess pleasure. "Let's go talk someplace more private." He lurched unsteadily from the bar.

Jimmy watched him go. "I'll expect you back," he shouted, more to the two men than to John, I thought.

I ordered another stout which the crotchety old man brought and held out of reach while I fished for my money. He watched the door nervously and glanced around the room as if looking for reinforcements.

I sipped the beer. After a while I asked, "Want me to take a look?"

He shrugged grumpily and busied himself with an order, but he didn't say no.

I went out to the front steps and stood scanning the sidewalk. There was a dark parking lot across the street but I didn't see any movement there. I watched a flat-bed trailer pass by and was getting ready to head back in when I heard the scraping and shuffling of struggling feet, then a strained breathing.

The pub stood by itself, with a closed gas station on one side and a two-family house on the other. I looked into the alley separating the house and pub and saw John pressed up against a wall with the two men moving in on him. One of them took John by the shoulders and threw him down. There was a flurried scramble and then the two men jumped back. I moved into the alley and saw John pull himself up, holding a flimsy piece of wood that looked like a side support to an orange crate.

"Com'on, make my day," he said to the two. They laughed. He laughed too. If he didn't have the sense to be scared at least he had presence.

The man closest to John stepped in towards him and John swung the strip of wood like a baseball bat. The blow glanced off the man's shoulder and he pulled back his right hand for a punch.

I grabbed the outstretched arm at the wrist and elbow and jerked it back, cantilevering the man off his feet and to the ground. Then I braced my left foot and drove my right shoe into his partner's stomach, shoving him against the pub wall. I ended up with my forearm pressed to his throat. We stood like that, looking into each other's eyes. I waited patiently until he got the message and then I stepped back.

The man on the ground came up in a hurry. "Who the hell are you?"

I didn't answer but reached for John's shoulder and dragged him toward the street.

"We're not through with you, Spenser!" one of the men yelled.

Jimmy and two men in their mid-twenties were just heading

outside to help when I steered John Spenser back to the bar. The three of them checked him for damage.

Spenser smiled at them as if the whole thing was funny.

"You all right?" Jimmy asked.

Spenser smiled crookedly. "I'm great. I was saved by my buddy." He tapped my shoulder like I was a faithful dog, then said, "That was pretty good. Are you a cop or something?"

"Private investigator," I said. I sat down and ordered shots for both of us. Jimmy set up two glasses in a rush, like a buck private jumping to a command, and when I reached for my wallet he stopped me with a wave. All of a sudden I was his best friend. I watched the two other men move over to Spenser. One of them had limp blond hair and a chunky body—a high school athlete going soft. The other had a narrow, crafty face and had the thin look of someone who ate poorly and not often. They spoke quickly with Spenser, looking agitated.

"Wait a minute, wait," Spenser said, waving his hands. "Relax. Let's find out who the cavalry is." He extended a hand to me. "I'm John Spenser." He waved to his blond friend, "This is Mike MacDonald, and the skinny guy here is Len Clausen."

I told him my name. "What was that all about?" I asked.

Spenser smiled again. "This and that. Business." He thought for a moment whether to go on.

"More trouble from McGuiness," Clausen said.

"Who's he?"

"President of the Local," Clausen answered, looking around angrily, as if the man might be close by.

"Union business," I said.

"That mean something to you?" Spenser asked.

I shrugged. "Unions and trouble are synonymous."

"They don't have to be," Spenser said quickly, as if covering well-traveled ground. "This one wasn't when McGuiness first came in—he's gone bad."

"He's a pimp, he sold out," MacDonald added.

"He's a goddam Scotsman, that's what he is," Jimmy said. He had moved to within earshot, his hands still busy.

"What does that mean?" MacDonald said to him.

Jimmy flushed slightly. "Sorry. I just mean . . . you give a Scotsman an inch—"

"Yeah?" MacDonald interrupted.

"Never mind that," Spenser broke in. He turned his attention to me. "Well, no matter what you think about unions, thanks for helping me."

"No problem."

He considered me for a moment. The adrenaline rush from the fight had sobered him up and now he looked tired. Whatever else he was going to say he decided against, saying instead, distantly, "Well, thanks."

"It's okay," I said, and added, "Make my day?"

He let out a short, self-deprecating laugh. "It's the only thing that came to mind. They thought it was funny." He stood up to leave. "I'm beat, time for home, TV, something." He motioned to Jimmy. "Give Anderson here anything he wants."

Clausen stood with him. "I'll go with you."

"I'm all right."

"Good, I'll go anyway. They might be outside."

Spenser nodded to me and left, leaving MacDonald standing beside me.

"What's the deal?" I asked him.

He leaned on the bar with both elbows and ran a hand through his blond hair, as if he too were exhausted. "John's running against McGuiness. It's a tough fight."

"I noticed."

"That's not the first time either," MacDonald said. He looked down the bar and called out, "Hey, Jimmy, can a Scotsman get a beer here?"

I went back to my house in Watertown feeling as if I'd spent the day plowing the fields, except that I'd done little more than drive and run through my conversation with Marion over and over again. The tussle at Kiernan's didn't count for more than exercise.

I owned a two-story Cape then, located on a low knoll near

the Charles River. I'd lived there for five years and had grown into the neighborhood, a maze of short, narrow streets with one- and two-family houses with postage-stamp lawns. If I were suddenly struck blind I could still live here, still find my way to the corner drug store and to Halston's Market (owned by Tony Voccella, who kept Halston's name on the sign when he bought the place), and I knew that the neighbors would keep an eye on me and would help out in small ways. That's what a community is for, in the old sense, surrounding yourself with people who will leave you alone, mostly, but who'll be there when crunch time comes. That sense of belonging was the reason I'd stayed here for so long, when there was nothing and no one holding me in Watertown and I could have gone anywhere. Sometimes I thought the feeling of community was more in my head than a reality, more something I wanted than really had, but still I stayed.

My house was a small place, but when I walked into the dark living room it felt as wide and empty as a barn. It made me think of Spenser: "Home, TV, something." I like my job to keep me busy; that's one reason I took it on—long days, nights, weekends. Tonight I had nothing to do.

It was too late to go to a movie, there was nothing I wanted to watch on TV, and after a half hour I found myself wandering around the house, turning on lights, turning them off, opening the refrigerator and finding nothing to eat—restless as a cat in a cage. I tried mulling over what Marion had said but it left me with nothing but questions.

Finally I went up to the second-floor porch where I have my ten-inch Meade telescope set up. The Meade is a fine piece of equipment, the amateur astronomer's Porsche. It has a stubby, blue-black barrel mounted on a precision, worm-gear electric drive that will glide smoothly to any coordinate. Using a well-oiled Meade is like flying in an ultralight aircraft: there's just you and wherever you want to go—the North American nebula in Cygnus, the Great Spiral in Andromeda, just set the coordinates and go.

I hunted down Jupiter in Boötes and swiveled the Meade,

the electric motor humming faithfully. From the cabinet I have set up for spare equipment I took out my observation diary and scribbled in the date, seeing conditions, the temperature. Then I pulled a stool over and hunched over the lens. The huge planet, even with the Meade, was little more than a bright dot with a yellow tinge against a field of white, swarming stars. But it stood out in relief, palpable, seeming almost to breathe or hum. Four white moons were set nearby: Io, Europa, Ganymede, Callisto. I drew their position in my notebook, comparing their movements from other observations. The last time I'd looked all four moons were on one side of the planet, so what I saw looked like a tennis ball followed by four golf balls. Now Io had moved to the other side; an inch in my telescope, a million miles in space. As I made my ritual observations I began to relax, calmed by the routine. Jupiter had a faint red band I could just barely make out and as my eyes adjusted to the dark I thought it became plainer, but still it was almost a mirage, a suggestion of color, a hint of the violent storms racing across the planet. Looking at the night sky is an exercise in what you can't see. For all the planets, constellations and nebulae you struggle to discern, you know there are a million times that number beyond the limits of vision: spiral galaxies churning glacially; supernovas exploding and falling to ruin; great clouds of dust being pulled by gravity into new planets.

As I stooped over the lens, I heard the voice of the widow next door, Mrs. Krazesky, talking in the high voice she reserved for small children and animals. "We have to go in now, mommy's tired, yes she is, mommy's tired, she's had a long day." I knew she was addressing her old spaniel, who would be looking up at her hopefully, tail wagging, knowing it was time to go in and that the evening's investigation along Winter Street was over. The first year I lived in this house I noticed that Henrik Prokop, a stern gentleman from two houses down, would shovel the widow's sidewalk after each snow and rake her yard in the fall. When he died, I took over the task. I dragged her garbage cans out to the street on collection day and early on the morning after a snow (she was a poor sleeper, awake at the first hint of daylight, anxious to be out), I would clear off her steps and sidewalk from the streetlamp by the Harlows' to the fire hydrant just past my house. She made me pies on Thanksgiving and fruit cakes at Christmas.

I leaned over the porch railing. "I'll let her in later, Mrs. K, if you like."

Her porch was dimly lit by a streetlamp, bathed in a faint gray light. It took her a moment to figure out where my voice was coming from.

She finally saw me up on the porch. "Looking at the stars again, Derek?"

"Jupiter, Mrs. K. Clear as day."

"I must take a look sometime." The spaniel turned at the sound of my voice, knowing what was up. Her tail wagged faster. The widow bent over her, "Do you want to stay out?" The tail wagged furiously. Mrs. K called up, "Not too late, Derek."

"Half an hour."

The old woman scratched the dog behind an ear, murmured something and went inside. The spaniel sat contentedly on her haunches, hind paws splayed out and glanced up at me.

"Not too far, Floppy," I said.

The old dog bobbed her head, which might have meant consent, then ambled off into the shadows.

I swung the Meade away from Boötes, down a few degrees into the section of sky bounded by the Coma Berenices and Virgo constellations. This is nebula territory, a dense graveyard of suns that you don't so much look for as sweep through, gawking like a tourist walking through Mt. Auburn cemetery, thrilled by famous names: The Sombrero nebula, the Black-eye nebula. I'd been trying for years to find an unnamed nebula known only as M 100, of which my guide book says: "You can be proud of your skill if you can pick out this faint nebula." So far my skill has been outmatched by this dim luminescence and I kept after it for nearly forty minutes before I remembered Floppy. I packed up the Meade clumsily, still caught in the concentration of looking deeply into the night sky, as woozy as a lover coming up for air.

When I made it to Mrs. K's, Floppy was waiting obediently on the porch. She thumped her tail and dipped her head towards me, then turned to the door. I let her in and set the lock, closing the door quietly but knowing the old woman was still awake, listening for the pad of her companion's paws, reassured that all was well.

I stood on the porch for a while, watching the Harlows' teenager skulk home, late again. The blue light of a TV set flickered in Al Brobesky's livingroom. I took a last deep breath of cool night air, decided that I could finally get to sleep and went off to my own house.

III

I HAD A PREMONITION about John Spenser and I was
right. The next day, as I sat in my office, filling out final
reports and writing up the next week's schedule, he came
by.

He wore a white, shortsleeved shirt, corduroys and white
running shoes. He looked nervous, undecided about coming to
me. Somehow he seemed younger in the daylight, without the
drugged melancholy I'd seen in him the night before.

I sat him in the visitor's chair and he crossed his left leg over
his right, a knee pointing towards the ceiling. He played with
the lace on his shoe.

"How are you feeling this morning?" I asked.

He smiled in that self-deprecating way he had. "A little sore.
How about you?"

"Not bad."

He was going to say something and then suddenly, to cover
up, reached for his shoulder and made a windmilling motion
as if loosening muscles. "Stiff as a bastard," he said. "I think
I landed on my shoulder."

"Take a hot shower."

"I did."

I nodded, waiting for him to come out with it.

"I'm not quite sure why I'm here," he began finally.

"Try telling me about yourself first," I suggested.

"Oh, right," he said. "I'm shop steward over at National Trucking, just over in Watertown." He jerked his thumb in what I took to be the general direction of the company. "It's one of the biggest parcel delivery services in the country."

I told him I'd heard of it.

"We're having kind of a hassle over there now," he continued, "because our contract is coming up for a vote. I think we should strike but I have a feeling the union's going to recommend approval." He stopped uncertainly.

"And?"

He rubbed his forehead with a thin but strong hand. His whole body was like that, thin and wiry, with a look of sinewy toughness.

"It's confusing to explain. I've been trying to form a new union at NTS. Part of a nationwide movement called Teamsters For an Open Union—TOU. I've been at it a couple of years and I'm starting to pick up support. I think that after this contract, which is sure to screw the membership once again, that I'll have enough votes for a decertification. Every contract we lose more rights, rights to object to conditions and treatment. The union tries to make it up with more money or benefits, but the rights are slipping away."

"So you're trying to decertify the Teamsters?" I asked.

He nodded and smiled again. "That's right. And everyone thinks I'm crazy."

"I don't think you're crazy," I said. "But I find it hard to believe you have enough members willing to vote against them."

"Believe," he said. "You have to work there to know how they've fucked around with us the last few years."

"Okay. What can I do for you?"

He paused and rubbed his chin. Although he looked tentative, it wasn't from weakness. He was hesitant, but self-assured at the same time, as if he was only debating bringing a third party into his trouble. He could handle himself, but he wanted an outsider as a sounding board. Finally he reached into his back pocket and pulled out an envelope that had been folded in half. He handed it to me.

"I got this in the mail a few days ago," he said.

I opened the envelope and pulled out a single sheet of white typing paper. Standard watermark. There was one word in block letters cut out from a magazine. "SCAB." It was signed, again in block letters, "A UNION MAN."

"Pretty vague," I said.

"But I get the point," Spenser said.

I nodded. I do bodyguard work. In fact it's where I make most of my money. But I was sure John Spenser couldn't afford my prices. I told him that.

He shook his head. He seemed angered by the suggestion. "I'm not looking for a bodyguard," he said. "I can take care of myself."

"Then what do you want from me?"

"Advice," Spenser said.

I folded the paper, put it in the envelope, and gave it back to him. "My advice to you would be stay in the system," I said. "When unions get nasty, they get very nasty."

He looked disappointed.

"Why do you want to decertify? The Teamsters have unionized half the shops in this country. Won concessions that their members never had before."

He shook his head, frowning. "You don't understand."

"I understand," I said. "I've done this kind of organizing myself."

He looked surprised. "Union organizing?" he asked.

"Union, voter registration, political demonstrating, you name it."

"When?"

"A while ago," I answered. Although I'd only known Spenser a few minutes I found myself pulling for him. He had a vitality and sureness that would win people's trust. It was probably one of the reasons he was running a successful decertification campaign. But he was operating on very dangerous ground now and I wasn't sure he fully realized it. I wanted to pass on my experience to him, an old veteran to a new recruit. "What I'm saying is, I know the frustration you're feeling. But listen, one thing I learned is when to cut your losses. Instead of starting a new union, why don't you change this one from within? Vote in your own members?"

He shook his head quickly as though he'd heard this before. "The elections are a joke. The union slate wins every time, except for a few token offices. I think they do that just to make everything look like it's on the up and up. When a union wants to vote down a contract they hold a roll call vote. When they want to make sure a contract is passed they vote by mail. With office elections, we vote by mail." He made a motion like crumpling paper and dumping it in a trash basket. "All our votes just go down some damn black hole somewhere. It's all rigged."

I knew I wouldn't be able to convince him otherwise. I wasn't even sure I thought he was wrong.

"Okay," I said. "So if you want to go through with the vote, are you sure you've got the muscle?"

"I think I might now," he said. "Not muscle exactly, but leverage."

"What kind of leverage?"

"I want to show you," Spenser said. He looked down at his watch. "We have time. I want you to drive over to the Mystic Lakes with me." He looked as if he wasn't sure this was a reasonable request. It wasn't, really, and I should have put myself on the time clock as soon as we walked out the door. But I was interested in him and, for reasons I wasn't sure of, I wanted to help him out.

"You can't just tell me here?" I asked.

"I want to show you."

I shrugged my shoulders. "All right, John, let's go."

We got into my sports car and Spenser made noises of appreciation for it. As I turned onto Moody Street and headed for Watertown, he said, "This is a top of the line model. You must do okay in your business."

"Fairly well."

"What kind of stuff do you do mostly? Divorces and such?"

"Mostly I do bodyguard work, but I also do missing persons—some ETP's."

"ETP's?"

"Employee theft programs." I watched a frown cross his face and I smiled. A shop steward wouldn't like that. I said, "The people I catch are just thieves, John, there are no politics involved."

He nodded slowly. "I suppose you could think that way, but people act the way you expect them to. The way you treat them. If you treat them with respect, they respect you back. Theft is a symptom, it's not the disease." He said this evenly, in the tones of dispassionate appraisal. "Where I work," he said, looking at the road ahead, "we have production quotas. So many parcels sorted or loaded per hour. That's all well and good. But the quotas are pushed a little higher every few months. After you've been through that a while you realize that the quotas are based exclusively on numbers generated in some office somewhere. At NTS it's in the IE, industrial engineering. Those numbers have nothing to do with what a man can do reasonably in an hour, with the equipment and materiel at hand. They're purely profit/loss numbers. They have nothing to do with how you feel that night, good or sick, whether it's December and cold, or July and broiling hot. It's just production and you have to keep up."

"And when you get a raise the numbers go up to cover the increase," I said. "Catch-22."

Again, Spenser nodded. He could discuss something he felt strongly about without getting emotional. I respected him for it.

"It's like a lie," he said. "We're given the quotas as if they're the result of careful study—you know, 'by skilled professionals using the latest scientific equipment'—when actually it's just some guy upstairs asking himself, 'How much do I have to get out of Spenser here to retain my profit margin?' But that's never stated. Like I said, it's a matter of respect."

"Except that the workers know what the real story is, and the supervisors know," I said. "So there's an unspoken agreement that this is how it works, right?" I turned onto Fresh Pond Parkway and we drove under the thick leafy arms of the roadside elms.

Spencer thought for a minute, staring out the window.

"I suppose you could say that," he said, "but the trouble comes when the system is breaking down. When it's ninety degrees in the hub, or the feeders are overloaded. Packages everywhere. Chaos. We still have to stick to the numbers and we can't talk about what's going on in a real way because everybody is supposed to believe that IE took everything into account. So it's our fault. Then everyone starts talking past each other. That's where the union is supposed to step in."

"And it doesn't."

Spenser snorted in disgust. "Right. I've got grievances up the fucking arm," he said, making a chopping motion with his right hand above his left elbow. "The business agent never does anything with them. 'Just keep the guys working,' he says to me. 'Quit bellyaching.' And then I have to go back to the guys with egg on my face."

"So with your new union you're going to win back respect?" I asked.

"I'm going to damn well try."

I pushed the car along the Parkway, a highly improbable road that wound through residential neighborhoods, yet carried all the traffic from Boston's western suburbs into the city. The road turns into a parking lot at four o'clock. But it was midday now and traffic was light.

We drove to the northern edge of the urban center, to where the Mystic River formed the town boundary between Arlington and Winchester. When we came to a sign that read, "Mystic Valley Recreation Road," Spenser told me to turn in. We followed the road, with the river to our left. The city traffic fell behind us and soon we were driving on what felt like a quiet country lane. It was hard to believe that we were fifteen minutes away from the docks of Chelsea or the tenements of Dorchester. The land along the river had been set aside as a public park and we passed open meadows and thick forest.

Spenser had a smile on his face. "I'll give you the grand tour," he said. "This place is amazing."

A half mile further he pointed toward a spot where the river broadened into a wide lake.

"This is the first lake," Spenser said. "There are three in all. They're man-made with a series of locks and dams. At the turn of the century this was supposed to be a canal system connecting Boston to Lowell, but the project fell through. Now it's all public swimming, boating. People come here from all over to picnic and just hang out. Get the fresh air."

He gave me the promised grand tour, following a circle around the chain of lakes. He told me that he jogged around this route, a five-mile run, and that he called it his "Little America Run," and he showed me why. On the eastern shore there was a small, middle-class black neighborhood, on the western shore a cluster of middle-class whites, and on the northern rim an exclusive district dominated by sprawling Tudor houses with carefully managed lawns that spread to the water's edge.

"Everybody grabbed a little of the tranquility the lake has to offer," John Spenser said. "A piece of the American Dream." I found myself smiling. He had a romantic's vision.

"On the weekend," Spenser went on, "people come from the city and barbecue out here and picnic. The Haitians have their little spot, the Islanders their favorite fishing banks. Two or three universities have sailing docks and the college kids come out and party. I jog around here and it's like running through the neighborhoods in Manhattan. You know, where one block is Greek, the next is Irish. It's great." He settled back in his seat and watched the lakes sweep by, smiling, with a happy look in his eyes. I know I wouldn't have seen the Mystic Lakes that way if John Spenser hadn't been there.

"There's one private boating club," Spenser said. "That's where we're going."

We looped back to the second basin, driving by way of the northern shore where stately Victorians painted in seven carefully chosen colors watched serenely over deep, healthy lawns. As we passed a grove of slender birches, Spenser pointed to a dirt lane that plunged off from the main road toward the water.

"Pull over a sec," he said.

We looked down the narrow lane to a spot not very far away where a chain-link gate restricted access to the club beyond. It was an unpretentious gate, meant not to broadcast its purpose too loudly. The gatekeeper was a clean-cut teenager with sandy blond hair cut in a boy's regular, who wore an Izod sportshirt and white tennis shorts and shoes. He looked like the kind of kid you'd call "lad" and flip a half-dollar to as you sauntered by on your way to a quick sail and a tall gin and tonic. No, that was too much. You'd never flip him a half-dollar, because he'd glare back at you and jack up the volume of the Walkman he'd stashed somewhere, raising the decibel level of a Motley Crue ballad that happened to be playing. But he fit the image this club wanted to project—wholesome, genteel surroundings that were private. Very private.

Spenser told me to park beside a brick pumping station that was across from the entrance, hidden from the main road. It was a little bit of skullduggery that I didn't understand, but I went along with it anyway.

"Our timing is perfect," Spenser said, looking at his watch. "He'll be here any minute."

"Why?" I asked.

"Richard McGuiness, the esteemed president of Local Nineteen."

"He comes here?"

"Every Friday, like clockwork, to the Mystic Boat Club." Spenser nodded in the direction of the gate. "Here he is."

I looked across the street and saw a black limousine with tinted glass windows turn off the main road and pass through the gate in a cloud of dust.

"Come on," Spenser said, climbing out of the car, "there's something I want to show you."

Spenser headed with a quick, athletic step down a path that ran beside the lake. We walked under swamp maples, their fat leaves all but blocking out the sun. It was ten degrees cooler in the shade. The dirt path was right on the water and small waves lapped against the shore.

"Like I told you," Spenser said, "I jog around here every Friday and on the weekends. It's an ideal spot. Lots of shade and nice soft paths.

"One day I was running here and saw that limo go through the gate. I could tell who it was from the license plate—'President One." He shook his head. "What a pretentious bastard. Anyway, I thought, what's our Pres doing at this exclusive club? So I decided to stop and have a look-see. I never overlook the value of coincidence."

I followed Spenser along the narrow path, having to walk fast to keep up with him. Whether he was excited or just naturally a fast walker I didn't know, but I had three inches on him and still had to hustle to keep up. I told myself it was my street shoes. We crested a small rise and looked down into a secluded hollow below surrounded by a copse of birch trees.

"Down here," Spenser said.

I slipped and skidded down the slope behind him and bumped into him at the bottom. He put up his arms protectively and kept me from falling on my face.

"Take it easy," he said.

The lake was to our right and he pointed out across the water. "There's the rear deck of the club," he said.

Across an expanse of windblown waves I saw a two-story, gray-shingled building with a painted wooden deck that extended out over the water. There were tables and lounge chairs on the deck, the tables covered with multi-colored umbrellas. A flag pole stood at center deck, with a flag luffing in the breeze. Even though it wasn't a particularly windy day it seemed as if the cool water and hot land had combined to create a steady on-shore wind. Sailboats at the dock twisted with the wind, their halyards banging against their masts, sending out lonely tones like church bells. There were a few couples seated at the tables.

"He'll be out any second," Spenser said.

We waited, for what, I wasn't sure. Soon, though, we saw a tall, fair-haired man in his early sixties come out on deck accompanied by a slightly younger woman who moved with a nice swing to her walk. McGuiness was wearing a short-sleeved sportshirt and tan chinos. The woman wore a red tartan shirtdress and tassel flats. McGuiness treated her with courtly manners, drawing her chair out as they sat at a secluded table.

"That's McGuiness," Spenser said, "and that is not his wife."

I gave Spenser a surprised look. He was staring fixedly at the couple. "That's the leverage?" I asked.

He nodded.

"You're going to blackmail your Local president?"

"I'm going to suggest he not contest a decertification vote," Spenser said. His slim face had tightened and he looked unsure, as if he was fighting with the idea, balancing what he hoped to achieve against the extremism of the move, the danger and simple dirty politics of the scheme.

McGuiness and his lover ordered drinks and leaned close together, talking animatedly. They looked happy together. That would raise McGuiness' stakes.

"Look at them," Spenser said. "McGuiness, the leader of working men who have to bust their asses all day for a buck, fucking some WASP bitch who's getting thrills from working-class muscle. Doesn't look like he's working too hard on the contract, does it?"

"Who is she?" I asked.

Spenser shook his head. "I don't know. They're nervous about meeting here even though they must have checked it out. They usually have one drink and then she leaves in the limo. I've never been able to follow it. It must take her to wherever her car's parked."

"Should be simple to check her plates."

"For you. I wouldn't know where to start."

I nodded. "You don't just want advice, do you?"

Spenser smiled. "I do and I don't. First, what do you think?"

I looked at McGuiness and his woman. Spenser could corner him, and that would make him a very dangerous man. "I think you've got him by the balls."

Spenser laughed.

I went on, "You could do it one of two ways. Find out who she is and put the pressure on her, and, indirectly, on him. Or you could go directly to him." I stopped and gave Spenser a slow once over. "Either way, John, you'd lose."

The smile left Spenser's face. "You mean, so long as I dick around through normal procedures and don't become too much of a threat, McGuiness won't bother with me." His voice sounded bitter. "But as soon as I start playing hardball, being effective, getting to where I might actually win, he'll get mean and stomp on me."

"I mean you'd be no different from him."

"Yes I would."

"How could anyone tell?"

"From what I do."

"Like blackmail."

Spenser's face grimaced with annoyance. "It's a one-shot deal," he said. "I wouldn't make it a normal procedure, for Chrissakes."

I shrugged my shoulders. "You do it once and what's to stop you in the next crisis?"

"I'm not that type."

"I wouldn't be able to tell."

Spenser made a gesture of frustration, no more then the flick of his hand.

"And besides," I added, "the first meeting could get pretty dicey. They might just decide to do cosmetic surgery on you."

Spenser stared at me and then looked back across the water to the club where his president sipped his drink and laughed with his lover.

"That's what I wanted you for, to go meet him with me. In some neutral place," he said.

"And afterwards? We don't know how McGuiness will react. You'd need a guard everywhere you went. I couldn't do it, because you couldn't afford it. Do you have some supporters who'll protect you?"

He shook his head. "They're all working men. They can't afford to ride around on my coattails all day."

"Then some time, if he wants to, McGuiness will get you. He can pick his spot. It wouldn't necessarily be right away, it could be a few days, a week, a month. You'd have to be on guard all the time. You'd have to think twice whenever you started your car, took a walk at night, entered your apartment. Do you have a girlfriend? You'd have to watch her too."

"I get the picture," Spenser said. "I should let him," he pointed across the lake, "get away with the shit he's been pulling because he's got the power and is not afraid to use it. But when I've got power I should just let it ride."

"You've got some power, but not enough. Look, I may be all wrong about this McGuiness. I don't know the man. But you're the one who's going to force the issue, and not in a very smart way."

"What about, 'right'? I've got the moral high ground. I'm right and he's not. Doesn't that count for something?"

"You give up the high ground if you use blackmail."

Spenser turned away and walked a couple of paces along the brown, dirt path. The white trunks of the birches swayed gently around us.

I said to him, "You told me this new contract will be worse than the last. There's your power, John. Let enough people become unhappy and they'll vote out McGuiness without the blackmail."

With his back to me he shook his head. "I know what you're saying but it just doesn't happen that way. These people can withstand a lot of abuse. It's almost as if they're penitent, as if they believed they deserve it because they aren't white collar go-getters or something. They believe that they're not as de-

— 41 —

serving as the college grad, the office manager. They half believe the garbage tossed out in the media that unions have destroyed American industry, that the workers are overpaid and lazy. The old-timers remember all the good the union's done and see anyone who wants change as anti-union. They think these are just hard times. The young guys worry about their families or are just plain apathetic. Then there are the defeatists, who think we can never win, who give in to power before they even fight." He turned to face me from ten feet away. "I've got to make it happen. This is my chance." He was talking himself into it. He'd been frustrated too long and had now caught a glimpse of light.

"Will you help me?" he asked.

My mouth was dry as I shook my head. Turning him down would be tantamount to sending him out alone. "It's foolish. You just have to have more faith in the men you work with."

His young face dropped into a frown and I hated the disappointment I'd made him feel. I hoped my refusal was enough to stop him but, I was almost certain it wasn't.

We rode back to Waltham in silence. It was a long ride. When we got back to the office he asked me again to help him and again I refused. I could have gone with him on that first meeting—it would have been like any other job. But I don't usually have a stake in my cases and whether I think they're mistakes or not I take them, it's a job. This was different, and I wanted to warn John Spenser off. But he was young, idealistic and determined—the holy trinity for all movements.

"John, why'd you come to me?" I asked.

He turned at the door with a sly smile across his thin face.

"Because I know who you are. Or I thought I did. My brother was one of those draft dodgers who passed through Day Street. He had a lot of respect for you." Spenser shrugged. "I guess I was expecting something more."

"That's all history." I said, and added, "Think this one through. Think about where you want to be in five years. Will all this be important? Mean anything to anyone? You're wrapped up in it now. Think it through. You'll go through all this bullshit and trouble and in five years no one will give a damn."

"So that's where you're at?" he asked.

I nodded.

He gave me a long look that I couldn't read and went out into the sunlight. I thought that was the last I'd ever see of him.

IV

THREE DAYS PASSED without word from Marion. I'd get home, hoping for a note in the mailbox or slipped through the door slot, or I'd arrive at my office expecting a message on my answering machine. Nothing. I had no idea what I was expecting to happen between us, but everytime I found no message at home or at the office I felt let down. I wrapped up an assignment for a local department store—their security guards were stealing stereo equipment and selling them at nearby colleges from the back of a rented truck (at a very special, low, low discount rate)—and then I had time on my hands to sit and stew.

Monday night, after three days of hearing nothing, I was frustrated and on the verge of going out to look for her. Instead, I took a fifth of Johnnie Walker, the seltzer bottle, a big, heavy tumbler, and sat out on my porch. I eased down into my wicker chair and put my feet up on the short railing that ran across the front of the porch. The FBI was still watching me, and I saw their man in a car down the street. The end of his cigarette glowed red everytime he took a drag.

"Now you can watch Derek get pleasantly potted," I said to myself. I toyed with the idea of walking down and offering him a drink, then I toyed with the idea of just going and giving him my two cents' worth, then I decided both ideas were stupid. I took a drink and enjoyed the slow burn as the Scotch did its work. It was a warm night and the air felt like satin and the traffic on Orchard Avenue sounded muffled and distant. The ivy on the trellis at the end of the porch rustled from random night breezes. I heard voices from the house next door and the sound of a TV across the street. "From Lebanon today . . ." an announcer's voice said.

The night reminded me of the first time Marion and I had worked together. We were two college students who'd volunteered to register black voters in Dunn County, Alabama. The year was 1966 and it was summer, like this, only the air was dry and seemed to suck water right out of the soil. The roads in Dunn County that summer were dry as a bone and it seemed like all day, every day, I was washing dust from my mouth. The dust and the smell of Sweet Gum I could remember clearly—that and other things. The drive for volunteers was organized by a local church in Burlington, Vermont, where I was going to school as a pre-med student. All the college kids who had volunteered were to meet for the bus ride down South, so it was early one Sunday morning when I first saw Marion. She was wearing blue jeans cut off into shorts, rubber thongs, and a two-strap top without a bra. She carried a canvas pack on her back.

The reverend who was running the show took one look at her and said, "You can't travel dressed like that, Miss."

She glared at him. "Why not?"

"Because we're going into a sensitive political situation," he said patiently, "and we have to conduct ourselves in a manner above reproach." He was a young clergyman and he made the mistake of being condescending to Marion.

She glared at him again for some time, then took off her back pack and drew out a gray sweatshirt. Right there, with ten volunteers and the reverend grouped before the bus, she pulled off her top and stuffed it in the pack, her breasts swinging free as she bent down. Then she wiggled into her sweatshirt and spat out, "There, how's that?"

The reverend turned red, but not with embarrassment. "We're not going to Alabama for fun or to exercise our rebellious hormones," he said, his voice shaking. "You've heard about Mrs. Liuzzo. The Klan doesn't like us white northerners butting our nose into their lives. They mean business, and so do I, and your swinging your breasts in their faces isn't going to help any."

"I'm not going to let some redneck asshole tell me how to live," Marion said.

"Then you have a choice, Miss. You can dress the way you want and stay here, or you can dress appropriately and help people who need you."

That was the first lesson Marion learned in the South. You have to sacrifice bits of ego, parts of your constructed self-image, adapt yourself to your cause, if you're serious about what you're doing. This was hard for Marion to swallow at first, because she was at that headstrong age when she couldn't stand anyone calling the shots. What she did was, from then on, come rain or shine, was to wear that bulky sweatshirt. She wore it when it got dirty or smelled of days of sweat, after the sleeve was ripped in a downtown scuffle. It became a trademark, and people looking for her could simply ask for that girl in the gray sweatshirt.

"Hey, Marion, when are you going to take off that shirt?" other volunteers would call out to her.

"When we win the battle," she'd say.

I took another sip of my drink. Marion had been wearing a sweatshirt when I saw her Friday. No doubt the FBI had notes about her in their files that read, "Often wears gray sweatshirts." I looked at the dark car parked down the street and watched as the cigarette was tossed to the sidewalk and broke into a mass of glowing coals.

The reverend was right about the atmosphere in Dunn County. The local whites viewed us as invaders, as unwanted as carpetbaggers after the Civil War. Their resentment spanned a hundred years, generations of fathers and sons. It had an intimidating validity to it, this issue of decades, a familial solidity that made us feel insubstantial. The South then was a fortress, surrounded by a strong wall of hatred, and we entered observed by hostile eyes. You can bet we kept together wherever we went—venturing out only in groups or assigned pairs.

Since I was impressed by this Marion girl, by her self-assurance and almost brusque manner, whenever I could I teamed up with her. But at the same time that I admired her style, what I interpreted as her cosmopolitan self-assurance, I thought she was going about our job all wrong. Our sole purpose was to convince the black sharecroppers that voting was the way to make their lives better, but they were scared, or a lot less naive than we were. Most of them lived on land owned by whites and they knew they could be evicted on a day's notice. They knew that when they went downtown to register, the registry would be filled with whites, and when they went out to vote the polling hall would be filled with whites, whites who would take down their names and remember their faces. Their hesitance frustrated Marion.

"Voting is the way to beat the bastards!" she ended up yelling one day.

I laughed. These people didn't know what to make of Marion. Here was this tall, big-boned, outspoken woman who could swear like a ditch digger, who came down from the north and tramped into their lives. She was all force and no subtlety.

One day I said to her, "Marion, you're coming on to these people like a pushy New Yorker getting on the subway. You're the very image of a self-righteous northern liberal."

"I don't understand them," she said. "Here's a clear opportunity for them to get some real power and they're not taking it."

"They know what's at stake," I said. "They also know that when the voting's over, you and I and all our friends are going back north to our comfortable homes and leave them with whatever comes next."

That struck home. The idea that people didn't really trust her or believe her sincerity had never crossed her mind.

"I'm serious about this work," she said after a while. "I'm not just talking. I'm putting myself on the line here."

"And that's why we came," I said. "We're a show of hands. Numbers, bodies in support. We're just support, Marion, the rest is up to them."

She changed after that. She was polite and almost girlish, and suddenly the men who had stood with their arms folded across their chests, giving her short answers, dropped their hands and invited us to sit down on their unpainted porches and gave us cool lemonade to drink, telling us stories about landowners and the troubles of farming too little land. Just enough land to put food on the table and maybe make the rent. That's how the system worked, Marion and I learned. So all through August we drove the narrow back sharecropper lanes to the shacks with hollow front porches that made your footsteps sound like a drum beat. The sharecroppers started to come around and began to register in small numbers, but it was a long, slow process.

Towards the end of the month Marion and I were out late every night, moving through the black Alabama fields, our headlights showing the ruts in the unpaved lanes. I was nearly always tired, from a combination of nerves, long hours, and hard beds. Marion would want to press on.

"One more house," she'd say.

And I'd answer, "It's ten o'clock (or ten-thirty, or nine-thirty). Everyone's in bed and it's a long way back to town."

But we'd go on.

One night, August 26th, Marion and I were out making the rounds with Ray Leiberman. Ray and Marion were too much alike—both determined to get their own way. They bickered constantly over little details, which road to take, which house to stop at, when to take a break for dinner. Around nine-fifteen we were stopped at a crossroad, a place where two dirt lanes intersected, with broad fields stretching away on all sides.

"Car lights coming towards us," Ray said.

I looked ahead and saw twin beams advancing on us.

"He's moving slow," Ray said.

"Too slow," I added.

"So what?" Marion said from the back seat. "Take a left."

Ray turned to her. "Let's check out who this is first."

"What for?"

"Because I don't like surprises."

We'd been told to keep an eye out for suspicious-looking cars, because there were rumors that the Klan was going to cause trouble before the end of the month. Registration was coming to a close and they wanted to discourage the blacks who were beginning to sign up in growing numbers. Everyday in our headquarters in the cellar of the local church we heard rumors, new rumors, variations of old rumors, rumors based on hearsay, slightly reliable sources, impeccable sources. "The sheriff said . . ." The talk dealt less and less with registration and more often with rumors of Klan meetings, meetings in back fields, cross burnings, night riders. Men with shotguns looking for volunteers on roads too secluded, vulnerable. There was a siege mentality in our cellar, and each night when we went out it was like heading off on patrol in a strange land with the enemy lying in wait.

"Let's see who it is," Ray said.

I kept the engine running with my foot on the gas. The car came slowly, not like someone driving home after a night in town.

"Can you see how many are in there?" Ray asked.

"Looks like two," I said, "but the others could be slouched down."

"Slouched down?" Marion said. "You two are paranoid. You're making me nervous."

"Good," Ray said.

I strained to peer into the oncoming car, trying to see beyond the figure bent over the steering wheel. The person beside him disappeared, becoming nothing more than a shadow.

"That's the Rev's car," Marion said.

We all laughed as our tense muscles relaxed. The Reverend pulled beside us and rolled down his window.

He smiled when he saw us. "You all look like you've seen a ghost," he said.

"You had us going for a minute," Ray said.

We sat for a moment with our engines idling. I could hear the night peepers again and I wondered if they'd really stopped as the Reverend's car had approached, or whether the pounding in my ears had drowned them out. The night seemed peaceful again.

"Are you out alone, Rev?" I asked.

He nodded. "I took Jamie back into town. He wasn't feeling well."

"It's getting late," Ray said. "Should we head back in?"

The Rev sighed. "Let's do a couple more. I'll take Marion. Hop in, girl."

"I'm not a girl, Rev," Marion said.

"Hop in, Miss Marion."

I said, "Marion and I make a good team, Rev. Take Ray."

The clergyman shrugged. "Makes no nevermind to me."

"See you, Mata Hari," Ray said.

Marion climbed into the front seat. "Mata Hari?"

The Rev spoke before he left, "More bad rumors. Keep a sharp eye, hear?"

"Hey, Rev," Marion called out, "you sound more like a Southerner every day."

"Must be the grits."

Overhead the night sky had a seamless depth. It was filled with so many stars the constellations were lost, suspended in galactic swarms. Only Vega stood out from the background, a blue-green star in bas-relief. Somewhere east of it was Cygnus.

I said to Marion, "Let's go someplace where we can put our feet up on the railing and sip Old Granddad."

Marion lit a cigarette. "I told myself I'd have a mint julep before I left here. Haven't had one yet."

"No time."

"No time." She exhaled. "It's okay, having no time. I like being caught up, feeling the pressure. Time becomes something else besides just minutes slipping away. It becomes an opponent, a deadline to beat, a challenge. The commonplace becomes important. I haven't washed my hair in a week. Do you care?"

"No."

"If I were in school or back home I'd have to concern myself with social amenities. They're unimportant here. All that matters is the issue at hand, the job to be done."

"So I can't convince you to go for a mint julep?"

"One more house."

We turned right at the crossroad and headed east along a lane that became more and more remote—no houses, no lights. Just the cold stars overhead and our headlights on the brown dirt.

We came to a one-story shack with a single light shining from the front window. The sound of our car doors closing echoed across the fields, our footsteps on the porch were muffled concussions.

"Who is it?" a voice called out.

"We're with the National Coordinating Committee, sir, here about voter registration," Marion said.

A tall, stern, black man with gray hair opened the front door. He'd heard of us and he wasn't happy that we'd come to his house.

He said, "I started farmin' this land in forty-six. Right out of the army. Mr. Hollowell, he owns the land, Mr. Hollowell and me, we never had any cause to fight and I don't aim to start it up now."

"You're not starting trouble, Mr. Brown," Marion said. "Hollowell has no business considering your vote as a threat."

"*Mister* Hollowell," the old farmer answered, "knows what's going on as well as I do, Miss. You people don't just want us to vote, you want us to vote the white folks out of office. They don't go for that." He wasn't looking at us as he spoke. His red-rimmed eyes panned up and down the lane. I turned and followed the direction of his eyes, expecting to see something, but the road was dark.

We heard the car before we saw it. We heard the race of its engine, roaring flat out on the trunk road that intersected our lane about a mile up.

"You'd better leave," the farmer said. He turned his back to us and slipped quickly into his house.

Marion started to say something but I grabbed her arm and led her quickly to our car. I started it up and backed clear across the lane, our tires spitting dirt.

"What's going on?" Marion asked.

"I don't know," I said. "Nothing, I hope." But I didn't believe it. Something in the man's eyes when he heard that engine put the fear of God in me.

I pushed the car back down the lane, skidding along the uneven ridges of the tire tracks. Marion saw the other car and watched as it hurled through the intersection up ahead. When we reached the crossing we stopped.

"What the hell was that?" Marion asked.

"I don't know, but it scared that farmer and spooked me."

We sat with the engine idling. A slim breeze crept through the car on a black cat's feet. Our breath laid clouds of vapor on the windshield.

Marion asked, "Which way did the Rev and Ray go?"

"I can't remember."

"Down there? Should we check?"

"Do you want to?"

"I don't know. Maybe. Maybe we should."

We drove a short distance down the road.

"How far should we go?" Marion asked.

"I don't know."

"I'm scared," Marion said. "The Rev said we should be careful. Should we turn back?"

We turned around, and when we got back to the center, the cellar of the church, there was a feeling in the air. At first I thought it was because everyone was tired and running on nerves, but there was more to it. Ray and the Reverend hadn't come back yet, and they still hadn't come back by midnight. Usually everyone had left the church by then, but we all hung around without stating the reason. We were just waiting. Finally we all went home to the families we'd been boarded with, and it wasn't until morning that we learned that Ray had been shot dead and the Reverend had given him the last rites, his body folded up in the front seat of the car, not two miles from where Marion and I had turned around. Marion never forgave herself for not checking further up that road.

I took another drink of Scotch and poured more from the bottle. Goddamn, here I am getting drunk with that son of a bitch staring at me, I thought. The surveillence had begun. Now, in the interest of national security, my mail would be screened, my phone tapped, my movements noted. I was a category: "Known Radical Agitator." Probable underground contacts. "Detain in the event of a national emergency." There was nothing I could do about it. I was duly recorded, filed in a manila folder in a gray metal filing cabinet, the subject of periodic review. My feelings about the official designation were irrelevant. We live forever with the consequences of our acts.

The Dunn County vote that September was for seven offices, for everything from Sheriff to tax assessor to coroner. The blacks hoped to gain just three of these offices with their new-found power, but when voting day came the whites won every office by clear margins. What had happened was simple. The plantation owners had brought their own "niggers" in and registered them, confident that when election day came they'd stay with the boss's ticket. And they did. The boss is the boss, and one vote is just a lot of trouble. Consequences.

Marion and I heard the results when we were back in Vermont. After registration we'd headed north, sure of victory. The election results cured us of our naiveté, but Marion learned another lesson. She hadn't finished what she'd started in Alabama and the words I'd spoken to her, how we were going to pack up and leave the sharecroppers behind, left a bitter taste in her mouth. That's what we'd done and she couldn't reconcile it. She no longer fit in at school. Everything seemed banal and irrelevant. She couldn't see the purpose of studying social reform when the work was out there to be done. Why read great philosophical pronouncements (John Marshall Harlan, Supreme Court Justice, Sole Dissent, 1896: "The law regards man as man and takes no account of his surroundings or of his color when his civil rights, as guaranteed by the supreme law of the land, are involved") when we knew it wasn't true—that they were just nice words on official documents? A headline, "Two Civil Rights Workers Slain," meant more to Marion then the combined works of Lincoln and Jefferson or the grandiose text of the Civil Rights Act. Those texts meant nothing when a black couldn't register for fear of his life, or a northerner help him.

She dropped out of the University and left Burlington, and I didn't hear from her again for over a year.

I set my glass down hard and stood up. Fuck it, I thought, I'm not going to sit here with you watching me. As if to comment in response, the man in the car lit another cigarette with a flaring match.

I took the glass and bottle and went inside. From the cupboard underneath the TV I took out three automatic timers. I set up one each on the TV and the livingroom lamp, both to go off at eleven o'clock. Then I set the other in the bedroom to go on at 10:55 and off at 11:30.

The Cape had a coal door in the cellar that led onto an alley. I slipped out there and crossed through back yards to Maple Street.

V

M Y FIRST THOUGHT WAS to go by Bill Stacom's house, then maybe head over to Jeremy
Richards' or Robert Glazier's. All three had
lived with Marion and me in the years before the Brighton
bank bombing. They didn't have anything to do with the attack and although the police hassled them for awhile, they'd
managed to lead normal lives afterwards. Bill was a social
worker for the city of Boston, Jeremy was a musician who'd
had a moderately successful band and now made lots of money
recording advertisements, and Robert was a dishwasher part-
time and a publisher of a socialist newspaper full-time. We all
kept in touch in fits and starts. Touched base every few weeks
or so. Bill lived in Cambridge, so I took the 57 bus to Harvard
Square, then headed to his house.

I cut across the Cambridge Common, underneath maples in
full leaf. It was busy there, for ten o'clock at night. Kids decked
out in their punk regalia sat under the trees and hung out on
the paths. They had hair shaved in more different styles than
a topiary and wore tough-guy sleeveless shirts, twenty-year-old
army pants and paratrooper boots. Day-glo painted skate-
boards seemed to be in style and they showed off their stuff for
their friends who sat on the back of the park benches, smoking

cigarettes. The girls too, looked rough and tumble, like they had a chip on their shoulder.

I walked down Walden and turned onto Otis, a block of rent-controlled apartments with the cheapest rents in town. Cambridge has tough rent-control laws and long ago Bill had been lucky to snag an ordinanced apartment so although he was paid the ridiculous wages of the social services industry, he was able to live on a Cambridge side street that young urban professionals would kill to buy into. Rent control, that anathema to free marketeers, was the only way people on Bill's salary could live in decent housing in Cambridge. Bill lived in constant fear that his landlord would eventually find the right pocket to line and turn his building into condos.

When I got to his house I found Bill under his old Volvo, his size twelves protruding, toes pointed towards the clear sky. The light from a work lamp illuminated the undercarriage.

"You're just in time," he called out. "I'm about to drop the gearbox."

"Trouble?"

"No, I just like crawling around on my back."

"I'll rephrase the question. What's the problem?"

"No second gear. Can you give me a hand?"

I gave him a round of applause.

Bill's feet wiggled as he laughed. "Are we finished? I've got three bolts in the bell housing. You take them out and I'll hold the transmission."

The car was up on ramps. I crawled underneath.

"I get twenty bucks an hour."

"How does that translate into Bud's?"

"Becks."

"Like I said, Bud's."

I unscrewed the bolts with a ratchet and we lowered the gearbox to the ground.

"What time is it?" Bill asked.

"Ten-thirty."

"Fuck it. I'll leave this here for the night. Think anyone will steal it?"

"I'd give him an A for effort if he did."

Bill stood wiping his hands with a rag. He was tall and round shouldered, his blond hair cut unevenly by his wife, Margaret. He carried a lot of weight on a bulky frame and was the kind of man who seemed to displace an excess of space when he entered a room. When you stood next to him you felt crowded.

"I love working on this thing," he said. "It makes me feel *so* self-sufficient, you know what I mean?"

We went up to his apartment. In the kitchen Margaret was attacking a pile of dishes, water running full blast from the faucet. Her dishwashing philosophy was to let the plates and glasses soak all day so she could rinse them with scalding hot water at night, wearing rubber gloves. Steam collected on the window over the sink.

She brushed a strand of graying hair from her forehead. "Derek, have you eaten?"

"Yes, mom."

"There's chops."

"I've eaten. Thanks."

Bill took two beers from the refrigerator. "It's after ten, if he hasn't had dinner by now he doesn't deserve to."

"He's a bachelor, Bill. You'd starve if you were by yourself."

Margaret viewed my single life as a physical ailment, an ongoing tragedy. She and Bill had two little girls, Jody and Marion, and she believed that everyone wanted children, that they were all just in various stages proceeding to procreation. To Margaret the highest form of human expression was raising the next generation successfully. Other concerns, like "career" and "personal growth," were merely interesting diversions from the primary task. She was very hard headed about this and thought anyone who believed otherwise was being naive.

The doorbell rang and Bill buzzed the ground floor lock. A minute later Jeremy Richards sauntered into the hallway. Margaret rolled her eyes ("Him!") before he entered the kitchen. Jeremy wore his aviator sunglasses. He leaned against the kitchen table and waved a limp hand in greeting.

"Don't everyone collect here, I'm busy," Margaret said.

We reassembled in the livingroom, which was filled with the odds-and-ends furniture Bill and Margy had accumulated over fifteen years. Nothing matched, except in the context of having been bought second hand. Bill sat in the recliner they'd found at a yard sale five years ago.

"What's new in the music business, Jeremy?" he asked.

"Nostalgia," Jeremy mumbled from the back of his throat.

"Nostalgia?"

"Sixties. They're back, or in, as the case may be. Cover songs of old Byrds' tunes. Stratocaster rediscovered. Remakes of 'House of the Rising Sun.' Have you seen the new Prince video?"

"Missed it," Bill said, snapping his fingers.

" 'Lucy in the Sky with Diamonds,' psychedelic, cartoon graphics. Prince grinding his pelvis against a montage of slides. Very 'I am the Walrus' oriented. Interesting. And Prince is always ahead of his time, the others will follow. Punk bands are doing Beatle remakes reverentially, like paying homage to masters of the long gone past."

"They've taken on a golden sepia tone," I said.

"Yeah. The kids are interested, like, what happened back then? What was that Woodstock stuff all about? It's gratifying, isn't it? Reaffirms something."

"Don't fool yourself," Bill said. "They're just interested in a generic sense. How we got away with everything we did. They don't want to know what we were about, just how we went about it. All those slogans have a romantic feel to them, 'Free love,' 'Tune in, Turn on, Drop out'. 'Make love not war'. Wow. Sounds like fun."

Jeremy sniffed and rubbed his nose. He had the habitual running nose of a dedicated cocaine user and showed off his infirmity proudly, as if to say he was too sensitive to survive his competitive, back-biting business and this dull, mundane world, without a mild depressant, and he had enough cash to escape in style. "It *was* fun."

"It was," Bill said.

"Better then the fifties, slash, eighties."

"Be Here Now, Jeremy," I intoned, pointing my finger for emphasis. "Make do with the present."

"He sounds bitter, doesn't he?" Bill said to me.

"Structurally bitter."

"Who is?" Margaret asked. She came in with a glass of red wine cut with soda water to make it last. She slipped her bare feet under her as she sat beside me on the couch.

"Jeremy's having an adjustment reaction to the times," I explained.

"Who isn't?" she said. "I was just getting used to my twenties when I turned thirty." She sipped her wine. "Now I'm comfortable in my thirties and I only have a few years left. Suddenly I'm middle-aged and I find myself screening the videos that Marion and Jody watch. Makes me feel like I should have my hair up in a bun, walking around with pursed lips."

"No one's ever ready for what comes next," Bill said. "You're lying in bed one morning and suddenly you realize that kids have been calling you 'sir' for five years. You think maybe its time to readjust your self-image."

"Tell me about it," Jeremy said. "Every time some kid calls me 'sir' I want to look over my shoulder. Gives me the creeps."

Bill nodded in sympathy, then continued, "I'm trying to get ready for the next surprise. When I was young I just slipped from one thing to the next. Now I'm saying, 'What should a thirty-seven-year-old man be ready for? What comes next?' I've become more self-conscious."

"We were brought up to avoid being self-conscious," I said. "We thought it was important for a person to live outside of himself, to expand his consciousness. He was supposed to put himself at the service of some grand scheme, some overall good."

"But what have we got now?" Jeremy said. "A generation of Harvard Business School graduates hustling to get on Wall Street, juggling adjustable rate mortgages for their condos."

"Look who's talking," I said.

"I make good money, but I'm still doing music," he said.

"How's the Porsche?"

Jeremy brushed aside any suggestion of extravagance with a wave of his hand. "Hey, that's how I relax. Take it on the Pike and watch the stripes turn solid."

Bill gave me a look, a smile on his lips. He was going to add something, but caught himself.

"What am I going to do about those videos, Jeremy?" Margaret asked. "Some of them are too much. Sex and violence. Violence and sex. All parents are fools. 'Hey, that's me they're talking about,' I want to say."

"It's the same old story," Jeremy said. "When we were young they burned Beatles records. Rock and roll was a tool of the devil. We were against censorship then. Are you ready for it now?"

"No, just confused," Bill said. He gestured toward me and Jeremy. "Look at you and Derek. Still single. Half the people I know, even in couples, are either unmarried, married but floundering in the process of getting divorced, or divorced for the nth time. Nobody seems to be propagating the species. Nobody seems capable of the job of creating a home and raising a family. Something's wrong."

"Raising kids is your province," Jeremy said. "Don't lay it on me."

"Right. Raising kids is my province and helping the ones who end up in court and out of school and out of jobs on the way to nowhere is my job too. And I should be exercising some control over how they're influenced."

"You can't control change," Jeremy said. "It happens all on its own, by forces we'll never understand. We set up rules and systems to try to channel the power but it's like a dike on a river, eventually a flood comes that wipes the whole deal out. I just wish there were more changes. I want craziness, a sense that anything can happen, creativity unleashed."

"Hippies running naked down Boylston Street," Margaret said.

Jeremy waved a hand at her. "There was force then. Power. Unexplained energy. But it's dissipated. Everyone's waiting for the next breakout."

"You are," Bill said.

"You want to live in Florida of the mind," Jeremy countered. "Temperature ninety-eight point six, blue sky, not a cloud in sight."

"I want to deal with real life, sustaining life, not fantastic notions of the creative urge."

As Bill sparred with Jeremy I had to smile. It was so familiar, this verbal battle back and forth. We'd been arguing this way for years and we'd always taken it seriously—too seriously at times—but I couldn't help thinking that it was better than not giving a damn. I shifted slightly in my seat and listened as Bill refined his argument.

"Change happens in small increments, a millimeter per generation, in each person born. A slight shift in attitude from one's predecessors, a greater depth of knowledge, a more refined sensibility. But for every two feet we go forward, we slip back one. We slip back, push forward, slip back. It's slow, painstaking and it can't be done all at once. You're impatient, Jeremy."

"Maybe," Jeremy said. "But there have been times—the sixties, for example—when the rate of change accelerated. That's what I miss."

The conversation rambled on and I listened with half my attention, basking instead in the dim light of the room, the lingering smell of dinner, watching the gesture of hands, the movement of limbs. Margaret refilled her glass, unfolding her legs in a supple movement, padding barefoot to the kitchen, returning, carbonation bubbles rising from her wine, hissing faintly. She repositioned a lampshade before sitting down. Bill held his bottle up to the light and checked the remaining wash of liquid. In the hall outside, a neighbor's door opened, closed with a solid thump. Jingling keys. The point of the evening became these isolated perceptions, superimposed on a flow of words in a warm room, an apartment, a home reconstructed daily by Bill and Margaret.

"So, have you saved any juvenile delinquents lately?" Jeremy asked Bill.

Bill smiled at his sarcasm. "I got a kid into a voke-ed program. He might amount to something."

The doorbell rang. Bill looked at Margaret, lost the toss and got up to answer it. He returned with Robert Glazier.

"This is turning into old home week," Bill said.

Glazier stood in the doorway, taking stock, then he sat in the remaining arm chair. He was a small man with short black hair parted on the side and black, plastic-framed glasses taped together at the bridge. He wore faded jeans, a T-shirt and had a worn backpack slung over his shoulder. He carried himself with an air of what he hoped was noble poverty, a life dedicated to ideals and purpose. As soon as he sat down he pulled a tin of tobacco and papers from the pack. With stylized care, calculated to focus attention on him, he rolled a cigarette.

"My office is being watched again," he said. He licked the seam and lit his cigarette.

"Hell," Jeremy said, "are they going to start hounding us again?"

"Could be," Glazier answered, "or if no one else has noticed anything, it could be just me."

"Your highly successful Socialist activities," Jeremy said. "Dangerous to the Republic."

"It must be Marion again," Margaret said.

"Probably," Glazier said. "Anyone else notice an escort?"

Bill said, "I've been out of that whole scene for so long I couldn't spot an FBI agent if he sat on my front porch."

"Derek?"

"Nothing, but I'll keep an eye open. I don't have anything to worry about."

The tenor of the evening changed perceptibly, became tense. We were reminded of past associations, commitments to purposes that for a long time had been forgotten, that had ceased to be as important, lost in the minutia of daily existence. As I had been aware since Marion's visit, the others realized again that there was an arm of the government, in a building of gray corridors, florescent lighting, metal desks, that would forever hold them accountable for things they did in earlier, reckless years. They didn't know who reviewed their file coolly, calculating, or what he would assume, consider, finally decide. They didn't know what he was made of—what kind of person works for a government? What are his biases, his vested interests? What must be protected, in this person's eyes?

"Well, *we're* clean," Bill said, looking at his wife, "unless they consider the Phoenix a radical newspaper these days. What about the rest of you?"

"I've got some controlled substances I'll have to stash," Jeremy said.

"Don't leave anything they can use to harass you with," Glazier said.

"I know, I know."

"Derek?"

"Clean."

Marge asked, "You're not still on probation, are you?"

"That was over years ago. I even got the okay for a gun permit."

"Robert?"

Glazier tapped his glasses back up on his nose with an index finger. "I'm always open to review, just because my paper has incendiary words like 'Worker's Revolution' in the banner."

The room fell quiet as everyone went through a mental checklist of their lives, homes, searching for anything, a book, a letter, magazine, a device, a substance, that would lay them open to questioning, provide a wedge for agents of the government to make life tougher, more uncomfortable.

"Poor Marion," Margaret said after a while. "Why doesn't she just give up?"

"Not Marion, never," Jeremy said.

"I feel sorry for her," Bill said, "caught in her own trap. I've always believed she had nothing but the best intentions, but somewhere along the line her ideas got twisted. Now she doesn't have the clarity of mind to know when she's doing more harm than good.

"When we worked with her we had a clear-cut issue. End the war. Something that was close to home. Then I knew we were right. Other things get foggy, full of political nuances. Is there really such a thing as institutional racism? I've seen kids, real disadvantaged kids, who've worked their way out of the ghetto, and I've seen others who never felt like they had a chance. You can see it in their eyes when they're giving you their cynical number. Who do we blame for their failure? Someone like Marion is always blaming some 'system,' and attacks it, but that's just destructive. It doesn't lead anywhere. The problems are too complex for anyone to take the high ground and proclaim that they have the answer, demanding their own solutions."

Glazier took a drag from his cigarette and looked at Stacom through a cloud of smoke. "What if no one is even bothering to look at a problem?"

"Like what?"

"Like South Africa," Glazier said. "We've ignored apartheid for years, and by ignoring it and financing companies working there, we're supporting the white power structure."

"I don't support apartheid," Bill protested.

"What have you done about it?"

"South Africa's fucking three thousand miles away!" Jeremy said.

"I have kids in Dorchester killing each other. That's enough for me," Bill said.

"Your neighbor down the hall could tell you that Dorchester is ten miles away and that they've got their own problems too." Glazier answered, "They'd consider you a meddling liberal."

Bill smiled. "A meddling liberal?"

Glazier nodded. "It all depends on where you decide your front step ends. For some people it's their own lives. They can't see beyond their own needs. For you, Bill, it's your city, for others it's their state or their country. For people like Marion, wherever they see something going wrong they feel obliged to help out."

"She reminds me of the anti-abortion people," Jeremy said. "They feel it's their duty to stop all abortions, as if it's their own personal sin if they don't. There are limits to what someone's responsibility is."

"Said like a true Yankee," Glazier answered. "Good fences make good neighbors."

"Damn straight."

Glazier stamped out his cigarette and laughed to himself. "What about you, Derek? You've said before that you're just trying to get by."

"That's right," I said, "just making a living. But I think you try to live as you want others to and hope everyone falls into line. It's all we can do, really."

"That's a cop-out."

I smiled. "Just a simple truth. They always seem too simple."

"Bullshit. Nothing happens without direct action. People would forget about the situation in Northern Ireland overnight if there wasn't a bombing every other week. Same in South Africa. Or, closer to home, would the nuclear movement have stopped one power plant if people hadn't marched in the streets?"

"That was nonviolent protest," Jeremy said.

"So what?"

"There's a difference," Bill said. "I tell my kids every day, fighting isn't a show of power but a sign of weakness. True moral strength doesn't need violence. I tell them about Gandhi resisting the British."

"Gandhi succeeded because of the implication of violence," Glazier said. "What worked was the threat of all those people behind him running wild. If he had only ten followers the British would have laughed in his face."

"The point is he didn't," Marge said, "and he didn't resort to violence. I don't think he ever would have."

Glazier objected. "The man said, 'Between violence and cowardly flight I can only prefer violence to cowardice.'"

"He was talking about sticking to principles," Margaret responded. "He knew that at some point armed force would have to be faced squarely and he rejected running from it."

"Well," Glazier said, taking off his glasses and rubbing his face, a habit he had when he was becoming frustrated, "the point is that sometime force has to be met, questioned, challenged. Marion just circumvents the sitting duck stage and goes straight to active response."

"What a nice way of describing murder," Margaret said.

"It's pointless to argue, anyway," Jeremy said. "If there were ever four people who will have little or no effect on the world it's us."

"Speak for yourself, Jeremy," Bill said.

"We just talk and talk."

"You just talk. Marge and I are doing the best we can. All you could expect. So is Robert."

"What about Derek?" Jeremy asked. "Sorry," he said apologetically to me.

"It's all right."

"You said yourself that you're watching out for number one. After your experience in Walpole, I don't blame you."

"That's no excuse," I said. "I feel like I've been on hold for years—and I have, I know it. Either you're part of the solution or you're part of the problem."

"Testy," Jeremy said.

"Yeah, well," I answered, "this is the second time today I've had to justify myself."

"Really?" Glazier said. He gazed at me, his small eyes intent.

I held off saying more because Glazier seemed too interested. Since he'd come in I'd had a feeling he was looking for something from us, a sign that we'd heard from Marion too. Which meant either he thought she was around and wanted to see her or they had already met and he wanted to know who else she'd talked to. That raised all kinds of questions in my mind and I felt a sudden oppression, realizing that I didn't trust him enough to sound him out. The room was becoming too small, too intimate for what I was holding back from these people I'd known for twenty years, and I let the conversation drift around me. They'd want to know about Marion and I couldn't risk telling them. That's the kind of garbage Marion had created finally, driving wedges between people. I hung around another half hour, then said goodnight and stepped out into the cool night air.

Some clouds had moved in from the west and a light drizzle had started to fall. As I stood on the steps, Glazier came out beside me. He took off his glasses and wiped them with a handkerchief, carefully, because of the broken stem. Finally, he asked, "You haven't noticed anyone watching you?"

This was the point where we would either level with each other or not. I decided I couldn't trust him. "No one. But I'll keep my eyes open. You think it's Marion?"

"Undoubtedly," he said, nodding, and then added, "It sure isn't me they're after." He put his glasses back on and blinked as his eyes readjusted. There was an expectant air about him, as if he was waiting for something from me, or was debating telling me something. Our mutual hesitation had a palpable, electric feel. He hedged. "When was the last time you heard from her?"

I waited a moment, watched him shudder when a wet gust of wind hit him. "A long time . . . months," I said.

He blinked and lowered his glasses, rubbing his eyes, showing some frustration. As soon as he realized nothing useful was going to be said, he wanted the conversation over.

"I'll let you know if I hear anything," I said.

"Do that. I want to talk to her. I'll do the same for you."

"Great." He went back inside and I walked back through the park, which was deserted, the teenagers presumably back home with their books, and I felt as wooden and cold as the empty benches.

VI

I T RAINED FOR THREE DAYS, each day the rain coming down harder, more steadily, so that today, on Thursday, all Boston was awash, the storm drains flooded, the sidewalks new-formed rivers. Water stood three inches deep on the back streets. There probably wasn't a dry pair of shoes in the city. It was near five o'clock and I was watching the fat droplets pour down, bouncing off the asphalt like silver ball bearings. On Tuesday I'd done my bodyguard bit for the concert promotion agency that kept me alive and thriving. My golden goose. It was an outfit with Old Boston ties that had at one time handled all the cultural events in the city, booking highbrow acts like the Bolshoi, the touring symphonies and opera stars like Maria Callas. But in the sixties, about the time I was marching in the streets, they'd seen the light and had moved into the popular market, beginning with rock bands and branching out into the dinner circuit performers from the forties and fifties. I got a job with them because the lawyer who'd represented me after my big mistake had blue-blood ties that rivalled anyone on Beacon Hill. He got me an entree into the Charles Street Promotion Agency and they've since paid me very well, embarrassingly well, to escort their clients, to hold doors, create avenues through crowds, stick a heavy hand in front of overanxious fans and persistent journalists. Why are your concert tickets so expensive? Because the promoter pays guys like me a premium rate. Why do they pay me a premium rate? Because I look good in a suit and my manners suit their clients. On Tuesday night I'd done my bit with a rock star whose hair was cut into an interesting herringbone pattern and shaded three different colors. His head looked like the weave of an expensive sports coat. On Wednesday I'd taken a Las Vegas regular to perform at the Chateau DeVille in Framingham. I had my week's pay and anything else would be a bonus, but I'd felt lousy after both assignments and was down on the uselessness of the job because I kept thinking of Marion. It was as though she were standing behind me, smirking at the lunkhead who held doors for crooners and hoofers and pushed his way through the inevitable knots of excited fans who blocked the stage entrance. (One of her letters came to mind in which she called rock music "kiddy porn.") I kept telling myself, "This is just a job, clean work," and asking myself, "Why should I care what Marion thinks?" but the answer was it wasn't Marion's approval that worried me, it was my own dissatisfaction that I was recognizing. She was just a catalyst. I was belatedly turning this over in my mind, not particularly in the mood for self-flagellation, when I was saved by the phone ringing. It was John Spenser.

"We've got the summary of the new contract proposal," he said after we'd barged through the formalities. He sounded pumped up, like a man who sees the field of battle at last.

"Not so good?"

He laughed. "We only get the 'abridged-for-morons' version," he said, "but even that doesn't look so good. They're asking for a two-tier pay scale. All the new guys make three bucks less an hour than the present employees. You get what that means, don't you?"

"Yeah," I said.

He told me anyway. "It means the guy working next to me

will be making less money. He'll resent it. And it means that the company will have an added interest in getting me out of there."

"And the union will go for this?" I asked.

"Of course," he said, "because there's a pay increase tied into it. That's the sweetener for us."

"So what are you going to do?"

"We're having a meeting tonight. Can you come?"

"Why?"

"Do you really have to ask?"

"I did, didn't I?"

"Okay," Spenser sighed over the phone. "I'm hoping you'll change your mind about helping me. That you'll be convinced that what I want to do is necessary."

"I'm convinced that it means trouble."

"If you just see how hungry these guys are . . ." He sounded frustrated.

"Sure, they're hungry," I said, "they're starving. That doesn't mean you have to serve yourself up as the main course."

He laughed. "For chrissakes, lighten up. Nothing's happened yet. I haven't even called McGuiness. Ease up."

He refused to take the situation seriously, which is the simplest way to continue forward when all the red warning flags are up and the alarm bells are ringing. Ignore them and laugh.

"All right," I said, "where do I go?"

The meeting was in the cellar of Kiernan's, where I'd first met Spenser. I got there at seven o'clock and ran in from a driving rain, shaking the water from my hair as I went through the door. The room was crowded, mostly from the men playing darts and their friends, and I pushed my way through to the bar and ordered a quick Jameson. The whiskey took the chill off my bones in a hurry and I looked at the pictures of the Invincibles and smiled. Spenser knew how to organize, right down to the place he chose for his meetings. Even if his followers didn't know who those Irishmen were, and some of them undoubtedly would, Spenser knew who they were and as he spoke tonight in the cellar he would remember them and what they'd meant to others.

I asked Jimmy the bartender how to get downstairs and he pointed to a door to the right of the dart boards. I went through to a set of narrow steps with old boards that creaked under my feet. At the bottom I was met by a husky man with a black beard who wore a faded T-shirt and jeans. He was probably the biggest guy Spenser knew and the job of bouncer had fallen automatically on his shoulders. He took the position seriously.

He put a heavy hand to my chest. "Who are you?" he asked.

"I'm Derek Anderson," I said. "Spenser invited me."

He nodded and looked me over carefully, sizing me up. "What's he want you here for anyway?" he asked.

"If he didn't tell you, I don't think I should."

He stood in my way for a few seconds longer, then stepped aside.

I went by him into a room that was narrow like the bar above but was furnished only with chairs facing the rear wall. The room was filled with about sixty or seventy men and women who looked like they'd just gotten out of work, or at least hadn't gone home to change after their last shift. They still wore the worn clothes of factory workers: T-shirts or sweat shirts, jeans or corduroys, orange leather work boots. I was wearing a grey wool summer suit and felt as conspicuous as a dandy at the stock car races. I searched the room and saw Spenser in the first row of seats, talking with Len Clausen and Mike MacDonald. I caught his eye and he waved me over. Clausen and MacDonald looked like they were having a grand time, looked as though they enjoyed being in the center of the action, the Man's right-hand men. Seeing them this second time, I got the feeling that they were inexperienced at organizing and that they probably didn't have much of an idea what waited for them. Spenser stood up energetically, with a smile on his face, and shook my hand. He had changed his clothes for the meeting and was wearing blue cotton pants with a white shirt. "Have a seat. I'll get started," he said.

MacDonald gave me a good long once-over. Obviously Spenser hadn't said much about me. That was a good idea, since there was no reason to create a stir if I wasn't going to help him.

MacDonald leaned over across Clausen and asked, "Why'd he ask you here? Are you a lawyer?"

"Yes and no," I said, and left it at that.

There was a microphone at the front of the room and Spenser took it from its stand so he could walk around freely. He called for order and waited for the noise to stop.

"All right, everybody. Thank you for coming. First order of business. This room costs a hundred bucks, so cough up."

Spenser warmed them up slowly, taking his time getting down to business. He cracked jokes with people in the audience, spreading his attention evenly through the crowd. He called everyone by his first name, pointing at them, directing everyone's gaze around the room so they could see their own numbers. He worked around the room, drawing a ring of attention around the crowd and bringing it back to himself. By the time he started in on the contract the crowd was loose. He began by taking jibes at the union.

"When we go to the hall to 'discuss' the contract," he began, "well, you know what that's all about. Max Bruner, the business agent, will get up there and blow his own horn, saying how tough he's been on John Reed and all the managers at NTS." (This brought sarcastic laughs from the crowd.) "He'll tell us how great our jobs are, right? And how rotten the economy is and how lucky we are, right? And what a bunch of shits the supervisors are but how he's stood up to them, right?" There were answering jeers and laughs from the audience. Spenser moved back and forth as he spoke, looking restless, toying with the cord of the microphone. There was no hesitation in his voice.

"He'll say, 'I work so hard for you.' " Spenser theatrically beat his chest with a fist, then straightened. "Yeah, right!" he said. "He's been driving around in that limo of his, drinking from the wet bar." He paused for a moment. "Did you ever notice how, when ever you need Bruner he's always busy?" Catcalls rose from the crowd.

Spenser raised his voice over the noise, "Then Bruner's going to get down to his real point, which is going to be, 'Geez, you guys are makin' too much trouble. You're filin' too many grievances. Lay off.' "

Spenser let that sink in for a few moments, then went on, "You know how many grievances we have pending?"

"Too fuckin' many!" MacDonald yelled.

"Too fuckin' many is right," Spenser said, "and no goddam action. Pete Delmonico gets more action from his ex-wife. How busy can Bruner be? He's never around."

"Maybe he's jazzin' Delmonico's ex," someone yelled. The crowd laughed.

Spenser laughed too, then went on, "I'm serious now. Bruner hasn't seen John Reed in four months. Count them," Spenser marked the months with his fingers, "February, March, April, May—four months! He's our business agent all right," Spenser said. "He's giving us the business!"

The crowd loved it, they clapped, shouted back.

"Then," the young man said, "then we'll get McGuiness himself up there. He'll have that tired look on his face, with his shoulders stooped like he's got the weight of the world on them." Spenser hunched his shoulders in a pantomime. "He'll wheeze a little bit, like, 'my emphysema is killing me,' then he'll tell us how long he's been struggling over this contract. All the months of strenuous effort." I watched Spenser pause here. "Strenuous effort," he continued, "Uh huh." He stopped again and seemed to consider what he would say next. "The only strain he gets is a sore elbow from lifting martinis." The audience laughed.

Spenser went on, "McGuiness will also tell us about all the other contracts he's had to negotiate for all the other members in all the other companies this spring, just so we'll remember what an important man he is and how small we are. Well, we're not small, are we?"

Shouts, "No!"

"And we deserve all of his energy, right?"

"Right!"

"We're not talking about some piddling little three-member shop here. We're talking about the first national contract with the second largest freight hauler in the United States. What happens here will have an effect on contracts all over the country for the next three years. These negotiations will either stop the union giveaways of the past or let them continue. These negotiations will either reestablish the union as a strong force for us or as an obstacle against us."

Spenser was on a roll, heated up, a film of sweat beginning to form on his forehead. He strode to Clausen and grabbed a thin sheaf of paper from him. He marched back waving the papers in his hand.

"Then McGuiness will come to this," he waved the paper. "This is the contract." He looked at the papers sullenly. "Our version of the contract.

"Do you know how many pages a real contract is?" he asked. He waited for an answer.

"A real contract will run over thirty single-spaced pages," Spenser said. "With microscopic little print. You can't even read it. That's the National Freight Master Agreement. What have we got here?" he asked, and began to go through the pages one by one.

"First page, a letter recommending passage, from Bruner. Second page, a letter recommending passage, from McGuiness. Third page . . . Ah hah! At last, the first summary page of the contract." He counted out the last three pages. "Three pages of the contract. Boiled down from thirty!" His dark eyes scanned the room.

"What the hell are we voting on?" Spenser asked. He answered his own question. "A few major provisions. What will McGuiness say? He'll say, this is all *we* need to know." Spenser pointed his finger to a place somewhere far outside of the room. "McGuiness—yeah, he knows what's good for us, he wants us to trust him. Remember what happened with the last contract?

Remember how out of the blue we learned that we'd voted for a reduction in the minimum hours required? Now they only have to work us for thirty hours and they can send us home. Does anyone remember that being discussed last time? When I asked Bruner about it he said, 'NTS is under a lot of pressure. Deregulation has increased competition in the industry.'" Spenser looked around the room, bent over intensely, his hand tightly gripping the microphone. His knuckles were white.

A man's voice called from the audience, "To hell with him. NTS made four hundred million dollars last year."

Spenser acknowledged him, pointing, "Thank you, you're right. Damn right. Four hundred million." He let the numbers sink in. "Why are we being forced to make concessions? Are we gonna be fools like the auto workers and make sacrifices and then watch the company officers take home million dollar bonuses?"

The room had begun to heat up, the air dense with humidity from sweaty bodies, the evaporation from wet clothes growing opaque with cigarette smoke. The stale atmosphere intensified the closeness of the workers sitting shoulder to shoulder in their uncomfortable chairs as they concentrated on John Spenser, each one of them following his rapid, wound-up tight movements, his clipped speech. It reminded me of the church cellar in Dunn County, all the focused energy, building from one person to the next, adding to itself and becoming more than the sum of its parts—becoming, finally, intoxicating, drowning out caution and reason. I knew that feeling very well, knew where it had taken me, from my small core of friends, my network that I considered blood-family—Bill, Jeremy, Marion, Richard and Robert—to the Brighton National Bank, to a row of tellers' windows, to a place that was just one room in one building in one city but had somehow come to symbolize more, everything we'd experienced together and fought against. A building—one story, flat roofed, concrete-block walls covered with a skin of plasterboard, linoleum floors. Tellers' windows. Pine and mahogany veneer. My life had become a dream that only I and a few others shared, and no one else could possibly understand what we thought we were doing. I watched John Spenser working himself into that dream state, watched the people following him, being drawn in, all that they'd experienced together a common bond, and John Spenser telling them what they'd already thought, telling them what they wanted to hear.

And he told them what they wanted. He ripped the papers in his hands in half and tore the contract apart verbally. No one took issue with what he said.

"And what's going to happen after all the useless talk about this piece of crap is over?" Spenser went on. "You're going to get a ballot in the mail. Make an X and send it away. To some garbage dump in New Jersey. No one counts those things. You know it, and I know it."

He slowed down and looked as if he regretted what he had to say next. "Let's face it, this union is a great union. It's done a lot over the years. But the people running the union now have lost touch with what's happening on the shop floor. They've been in the executive suite too long. It's an old story, but it's true. They've gotten used to their limos and their private jet trips to Atlantic City and Las Vegas. They've come to think that they know more than we do. McGuiness and Bruner, they tell me they've got the inside info. That we out here don't know enough to make up our own minds. That's an old game, friends, and it may be true, but only because we aren't told enough. McGuiness and his friends have started to think like management, to see their own members as not smart enough to run their own union, and that, friends, pisses me off. It makes me mad and makes me think its time for a change."

"Bullshit, Spenser." The voice came from the rear door and we all turned to see a group of six men standing on the steps. They were all big and stood loose and ready.

The man who'd spoken stood on the bottom step. He was about six feet, with short blond hair parted on the side, a thick mustache and a red, mottled face. He might have been forty, or forty-five years old, with the rough build of someone who'd done physical work all his life. He wore jeans and a T-shirt and a blue satin baseball jacket with "Local 19" stitched on the arm.

"What are you doing here, Packy?" Spenser asked.

Packy smiled and stepped into the room. The bearded guard moved to cut him off and Packy stared at him for a second, then walked around him to the last row of seats.

"We're union men, too," Packy said, still smiling. "We just came to hear what you've got to say." He glanced slowly around the room. "And check out who's here."

"And disrupt the meeting."

Packy waved a hand. "No disruptions, promise," he said. He turned and waved the others in. They fanned out around the room. They didn't do anything, just spread out along the walls, but it was enough. Packy said, "You were saying it's time for a change."

Spenser watched the whole operation and after Packy told him to go on he did the right thing—he smiled. Then he addressed the crowd.

"I should have said this at the beginning," he said, "but Packy just reminded me. I knew already that there would be spies in the audience. Not just for NTS but for the union too. For one thing, I can't say anything that sounds like I'm calling for a wildcat strike or encouraging work slowdowns or stoppages or anything like that. Reed will hear about it and I'll be canned. Now we know that McGuiness is listening too. Fine." Spenser stopped. People were looking out of the corner of their eyes at the men who stood like guards beside them.

"This is something we'll have to get used to," Spenser went on, "intimidation." I watched one of the invaders smile. "The people in power will always resist change, in any organization, started for any purpose. And what I'm calling for, and the reason you're here, is change of a big order." His eyes scanned the crowd. "And we can't expect McGuiness and his friends and supporters to welcome us with open arms. We can expect, in fact, them to fight us tooth and nail. But that's what it's come to. We find ourselves in a union that not only doesn't support us, doesn't talk to us, doesn't give us a fair hearing, doesn't even give us credit for the brains God gave us, but threatens us when we try to help ourselves."

Spenser was gathering steam again and Packy moved to slow him down a bit. "Who's threatening you?" he asked. "Not Rick."

Spenser fought back an urge to answer directly. He resisted it. I walked to the back row and sat down beside Packy. I wanted to crowd him a little and give him something extra to think about.

He looked at me as I sat down and worked over a stick of gum thoughtfully as he looked over my suit, placidly considering who the hell I might be. The formal get-up worried him.

I said quietly, "Let the man speak, sir. You'll get your chance." I didn't know if he would, but I didn't care. I'd decided to play a lawyer's role. A man dedicated to due process, etc., etc. Packy considered for a moment and decided to keep his peace. He had been sent to make McGuiness' presence felt and he'd already done that. He kept quiet.

Spenser went on, detailing what course the union should take. They should reject the contract. If the union failed to do that, and failed to give the membership a say in any new proposals, the members should vote to decertify. He told them that the same issue was up before members around the country. That now was the time for them to speak up, to make their move. What happened with this contract and the Teamsters for an Open Union would send a signal not just to NTS but to all companies around the nation that were working to break their unions. Companies in every industry. In steel, in the airlines, in trucking, in the coal fields.

"Workers have taken it on the chin for the last ten years," Spenser said. "We've been blamed for everything from the collapse of the auto industry to the last two recessions. We're greedy, lazy, inefficient. We're the new niggers on the block. We need our union officers to speak up for us and fight, not roll over and stick their legs up in the air like dogs. They haven't done that and it's time we did it for them."

I felt Packy tense beside me, so I turned sideways, rested my arm on the chair back and smiled at him. I was still throwing him off.

Spenser concluded the meeting by calling for a vote on a motion to send a letter rejecting the contract to McGuiness. It passed. As the meeting ended Packy asked me, "Are you working for him?" with a tone suggesting he thought I was buying the Brooklyn Bridge.

"What do you think?" I said, choosing to be cryptic.

I stood up and walked away, up to Spenser. He was nursing a long-necked Bud. He didn't look satisfied.

"It ended flat," he said.

I nodded. "But it could have been worse. Packy and the boys were sent here to intimidate but they didn't. In a sense they did you some good."

"How's that?"

"You came out of the first minor skirmish intact," I said. "Now you've got to finish the job."

"What do you mean?" he asked.

I waved him to stand. "If there's going to be trouble it'll be outside while the crowd is leaving." I turned to his two friends. "Lenny, Mike, now you get to do some real work," I said.

"Like what?" MacDonald asked.

"We've got to make sure everyone leaves immediately. No hanging around to shoot the breeze . . . okay? Let's hope it's still raining."

The rain had stopped. The crowd had broken up into small groups and was clustered in the parking lot across the street. Packy and his men were standing by the lot entrance and looked like they were considering something. That made me nervous as I stood with Spenser, breathing in the damp night air, talking over what we should do. The four of us split into twos and went through the assembled groups, telling them it was time to go. We worked at it until everyone had left. It wasn't easy, because not everyone was aware of the potential for trouble, and it took us a half hour to clear the lot. When the last car had gone Packy and his men were still at the entrance.

I held MacDonald, Clausen and Spenser back. "Packy's

—— 79 ——

standing up by the main gate," I said. "If they wanted to mess with us they'd have met us further back in the lot." I turned to Spenser. "That means he just wants a couple of last words with you. Let him say his piece and then let's get the hell out of here."

Spenser looked relieved. "Far out," he said, looking from Packy to me. "Intimidation psychology." His gray eyes were bright with amusement. "So he just wants to talk with me. Okay." He laughed.

I was getting impatient with him. "You really don't understand how serious this all is, do you?"

"I'm taking it seriously."

"No you're not," I said. I waved towards the men at the gate. "Come on. Let's go up and see how much it takes to push them over the line. I want you to see how funny it is to fight when you're outnumbered and overpowered." I moved off to the gate. Spenser stopped me.

"Relax, Derek. I won't bait him. I'll be on my best behavior. Promise." He turned to MacDonald and Clausen, both of them pale and jumpy. This wasn't as much fun as standing before the adoring crowd. Spenser said to them, "Do you two have your cars in the lot?"

Clausen shook his head. "We're out in the street."

"Okay," Spenser told him, "you just kind of wander past them when Derek and I stop to talk. Got it?"

The two nodded and we walked towards the men assembled at the parking lot gate. Packy took a step to block our path. He was smoking a cigarette which he threw down on the ground and crushed under his heel. He looked calm and relaxed and I decided that if Spenser kept his head we'd be through with no trouble.

Clausen and MacDonald kept walking past Packy and one of his men blocked them.

I called out, "See you guys later," and looked at Packy. He watched the two men pass him and nodded. I let out a deep breath.

Packy said to Spenser, "You had a good crowd tonight."

"A lot of unhappy people," he answered.

"Those people will always be unhappy," Packy said. "They think the union can solve all their problems."

"Just some of them."

Packy nodded grimly. "And you think you can do better than Rick McGuiness? You're just a kid, Spenser. You know your company but you don't know what else that Rick has to put up with. If you were a local president the companies would eat you alive."

"That's your opinion."

Packy took a step closer to him. "That's right. Me and a lot of other guys. We've been with the union for years. Long before you were off your mother's tit. We remember what it was like driving trucks with bald tires and bad brakes. When a supervisor could fire you without blinking an eye. We remember that."

"Good for you," Spenser said. "It's not enough now."

"Not enough? You little shit."

Spenser started getting angry. "That's right, not enough. See, you think that you really don't deserve everything the union's got out of the company, like the union stole it for you. We deserve it, and more. Your thinking is backwards, Packy. Your mental processes are fucked up."

I stepped between them. "Let's not get personal, boys." I said. I nodded to Packy. "You did what your boss wanted. Let it go."

Packy gave me a blank look. "Who the fuck are you, anyway?"

"Derek Anderson."

"Mind your own business, Anderson."

"I am."

"You a lawyer or something?"

"That's none of your business."

He pointed a finger at me. "I'll give you a warning. Hang around with this guy," he pointed to Spenser, "and you're asking for trouble. Because he's asking for trouble." Packy gave Spenser a long look, his eyes sharp and menacing. "I'll be seeing you later," he said.

He moved as if to walk away, and then changed his mind. He turned back and motioned for me to follow him. I did, and when we were a few steps away he bent his head close to mine, confidentially, and said, "Look, no matter what you think, we don't want trouble with this kid. He's just young." He looked at me to see if I was following him. "This is family trouble and there's really no need for interference from outside."

"Great," I answered, "if there's no trouble, there'll be no interference."

He considered that for a while, bobbing his head as he thought. It wasn't exactly what he wanted to hear, but he decided to leave it there. "Well, all right." He tapped my shoulder like a buddy. "Keep your nose clean," he said, and walked away.

As he and his men walked off down the street Spenser asked, "What did he say?"

"He explained that this is a simple domestic squabble."

"It is, huh?"

"That's what he said." I looked closely at Spenser, noticed the determined look in his eyes. "Packy's one of the guys you have to watch out for."

"I know."

"And not just because he's on McGuiness' payroll," I said. "Because he's loyal to the man. For men like Packy loyalty is the most important thing in their lives. It's like an oath of fealty. Ideas don't mean much to them, but they'll put their lives on the line for a man they trust and respect. But there's more to it than that. If my guess is right, Packy is one of those people who grew up on the bottom of the pile, with no breaks, no college education, no easy money. Life has been tough for him and he's come to expect that's the way things are. He grew up fighting for everything he's got and that's his attitude toward the world. Hard nosed, fight for everything. You don't believe that. You're telling him that he can expect something better and in effect you're telling him his life didn't have to be as hard as it was. He can't get that time back so he doesn't want to feel that it was all for nothing."

"It wasn't all for nothing," Spenser said. "In his day the union did its job. He benefited. All I'm saying is it's time for more."

I shook my head. "Maybe from where you're standing, but he'll see it differently. It's almost a matter of jealousy, that you can have this innocent view of a rosy, prosperous future, full of employer-employee mutual respect . . ."

"You think I'm naive?"

I stopped for a moment, wondering if that was true. I didn't want to tell him I thought he was being simplistic, but images flashed through my mind—the futility of Dunn County, the foolishness of Brighton. It wasn't right for me to discourage him just because I had become as jaundiced as Packy. "I respect what you're trying to do," I said. "I just want you to see Packy and McGuiness in three dimensions rather than just as cardboard heavies. They have a vested interest in their union that involves their whole lives. That's what you're fighting, John. The people at that meeting tonight liked your ideas, but that won't carry them when the hard times come. Ideas don't pay the rent or buy the food."

The minute I'd finished speaking I'd regretted what I'd said, because a stubborn look came over John Spenser's face, and I thought for all my talk all I'd probably done was push him closer to carrying out his foolish blackmail plan. He didn't say anything for a long time, looking off the way Packy had gone.

I went on hurriedly, "That's why I'm telling you to wait until after the contract. Let the people get really frustrated, so all you have to do is lead, not prod, them."

Spenser smiled, and a questioning look crossed over his face. "Derek, you've been trying to put the reins on me from the start. What's with you? I expected someone more willing to take chances."

I looked at him. The warm front that had moved in and pushed out the rainclouds had brought fresh winds from the south that smelled pungent and sweet. The breeze pulled at the ends of his long black hair. He stood straight and strong, full of the drive of youth, the determination of people who haven't met all the failures that dog us through our lives. And I knew that no matter how determined he was, how careful or smart or cunning, that the battle he'd chosen for himself was against things that were out of his control, that he had about as much chance of defeating the union as he did of stopping the wind that surged up from the Carolinas. I couldn't tell him that, but I tried to explain.

"The reason an entrenched organization like your union lasts is because it's something real, it has an everyday effect on people's lives. Right or wrong, good or bad, it's something palpable. It's the pay check and the food and car and the medical benefits. When those things are in line people don't even want to see what else is going on. They don't want to be confronted by it. They look past the little abuses and wrongs until those things hit them over the head. I don't see that happening here. Your people are dissatisfied, slightly angry. They probably all think McGuiness is a crook. So what? Most Americans' believe their Senators and Congressmen are crooks. But they've come to accept it. They even find it slightly amusing. People have to be personally stressed to change, and yours aren't. You've got an uphill battle convincing them they need change. Whether they came here tonight or not."

I had made matters worse and I knew it. Why does the truth always push people like John Spenser to higher extremes?

I said to him, "If you're still hoping I'll meet McGuiness with you, forget it. You have only one real option here, John. That's to win fair and square at the ballot box."

He reached out and put his hand on my shoulder, smiling as he did. "Okay, Derek," he said. "I'll get off your case. You don't want any part of it, fine. Thanks for helping tonight. It's too bad, we could have worked well together." He started to walk away.

"John, for chrissakes," I called after him.

"So long, Derek." he said.

VII

T HE SUN WAS UP EARLY THE NEXT DAY, or, that is, I got out of bed late, so the morning was hot and humid by the time I got moving. I was feeling slow, almost hungover from worrying about Spenser—his mulish determination to oust MacGuiness—and the heat didn't help matters. I got out of the stuffy house, taking my breakfast onto the front porch, and lingered over coffee and bagels smeared with cream cheese, enjoying the air's hothouse feel, breathing in the aromatic sweetness of the pine just to the right of the porch. The deluged earth sweated moisture that a faint breeze swept up and collected. Somewhere, in a few days or weeks, this dim evaporation would coalesce into dark clouds and fall again as fat drops, disgorging, as they struck the ground, a brief exhalation of New England air. Not very clean air at that. Then again, the rain that had washed down on us in torrents hadn't been too clean either, full of acid, if the scientists had it right. In the last century people only had to worry about their neighbors downstream, now smoke stacks in Ohio send plumes of sulfate ash to Massachusetts, where it falls like toxic snow.

Why the hell am I thinking about this? I wondered. I slathered more cream cheese on a half-bagel and sipped my coffee.

Colombian coffee from South America. Underpaid bean pickers and ravaged rain forests. Capitalist pig American megacorporations exploiting Latin America. Even a simple breakfast was fertile ground for knee-jerk liberal guilt. If one had a mind to he could trace the route of something like this coffee and see within it the entire history of human exploitation, greed, social conflict, reform; a blueprint of theory and debate: Locke, Burke, Mill, Marx, Engels, Keynes. At the docks: containerization (union struggle, labor obsolescence, unemployment). On the seas: foreign registration (corporate unaccountability, unsafe ships, underpaid sailors). On shore: U.S. supported oligarchy (suppression of democratic institutions, maintenance of rigid class system). On the plantations: worker exploitation (maintenance of impoverished underclass, destruction of ecosystem). How far you wanted to go is a matter of choice. I chomped down on the bagel and followed the bite with a swig of steaming coffee, as if to show some silent observer that I didn't care, that, okay, my morals were lax.

When I finished breakfast and was headed across town I checked in my mirror for signs of the tail from yesterday. No one. If the Bureau stayed true to form I would be under spot surveillance, followed on random days, the odd evening or afternoon. The randomness made it harder to keep an eye out—you were lulled into a false sense of security and then one day, a week or three weeks later, you felt a tingling on the back of your neck and you spent the rest of the day looking over your shoulder, checking the reflection in shop windows.

The air in my office was thick and heavy, like wet cotton batting, so I left the street door and the door to the waiting room open, hoping for a little circulation. I'd had an air conditioner once, but my office building was built in 1910 and the electrical wiring couldn't handle modern conveniences. End of air conditioner.

I took off my sportscoat, got more coffee going in the automatic coffee machine, sat down behind my desk and waited for something to happen. The lulls in my business were like pregnant pauses. I could almost feel, somewhere out there, beyond the oak door and glass windows, a sequence of events being played out that would send someone to me, Derek Anderson, P.I. If I dwelled on it, the anticipation could become a physical sensation—a concentrated waiting, like a sentry at his post. Bad metaphor—a sentry protects something. What was I protecting? The public good? No, even if I waxed poetic I couldn't buy that. What is the public good? Leave the noble reasoning to fictional characters. Better to say I was a force, a force for some good. No—still too high-minded, exaggerated. Leave it that I do a good job that helps people . . . Even as I thought this I realized that I was constructing an argument for Marion, for her inevitable question, "Derek, what the hell are you doing as a P.I.?—a bodyguard?" I realized I didn't have an answer, except at the bottom line: easy money.

There was a loud, rapid knock at my office door and I looked up to see a well-dressed man in his mid-twenties standing silhouetted against the sunny street. His hair was slicked back like the male models in Gentleman's Quarterly and he wore black-rimmed aviator glasses. He had a neatly trimmed mustache.

"You keep banker's hours," he said.

I looked at my watch. Nine-fifteen. "I'm not a farmer," I said, "I don't get up with the roosters."

"Apparently not," the man said. He closed the office door, crossed the room without making a sound, and looked pointedly at the visitor's chair.

"Have a seat," I said, on cue.

He sat down and took his time looking around the room, like a real estate agent pricing the value of a home, tallying up square footage. His eyes rested momentarily on the coffee maker.

"Help yourself," I said.

"I only drink decaf."

After he said this he took an envelope from his inside pocket and placed it on my desk, at the same time placing a finger over his lips and motioning me to read. I took out the letter: "Quiet. Room may be bugged. Marion wants to see you. 8:00 P.M. 132

Chaney Street, Mattapan. Ring bell for Dalton." While I was reading he said, "I think my wife is cheating on me."

I glanced at him over the page. "Really?"

"Yeah. I want you to follow her." He pointed to the letter and raised an eyebrow as if to say, "Well?"

I put the letter back in the envelope and placed it carefully on the desk.

"How long have you suspected your wife?" I asked, keeping the charade going. I rose and went to the coffee machine, filling a cup. From my vantage point behind him I looked the man over. He sat straight with his back just touching the chair, his arms folded across his chest. Muscular. Trim. His suit was a light wool, gray, and he looked comfortable wearing it, like he wore suits often. Not my image of someone active in the Underground, but what the hell did I know? My knowledge of clandestine organizations was fifteen years old, from another time, and my knowledge of what they were about now was as informed as the average certified public accountant's. My image of an activist was of someone like Robert Glazier, thin and pale from working in the restaurant and spending long nights putting together his labor of love, his *Worker's Revolution Weekly;* his face pinched from dedication to a hopeless cause, his skin splotchy from extreme diets (No meat! No dairy products!). This man didn't fit the bill, unless the underground had gone the way of organized crime, complete with legitimate businesses, board meetings and lunch at the Plaza.

"I've felt like something's been going on for about six months," he was saying. He hadn't turned to look at me, instead his eyes scanned my desk, coming to rest on some papers I had there. The print, from his vantage point, was upside down. "She's been acting strangely, distracted." Now he turned slowly to me. "I don't trust her."

"That's too bad."

"Yes." His voice was expressionless.

"It's usually too late when a man and woman no longer trust each other."

He nodded faintly, as if the mistrust was a heavy burden.

"That may be, but I need to know." His sunglasses stared blankly back at me, a stolid front, impenetrable, the glassy eyes of a dull, heavy animal. I sipped my coffee. "I didn't catch your name."

"Franklin. Thomas Franklin."

"How'd you come to choose me, Mr. Franklin?"

There was a moment's hesitation. "From the Yellow Pages."

"Not many people pick me out of the Pages," I said, watching him carefully. He merely shrugged.

"I take it you're local."

"Of course, Boston. Newbury Street."

"I have friends down there. What number?"

He made a vaguely impatient gesture and pointed to the envelope. I ignored him again and kept prodding.

"What number?" I asked.

He shrugged again and then bobbed his head with a frustrated, okay, if-you-want-to-keep-playing movement. "Sixteen."

So he wasn't from Boston. That part of Newbury was strictly boutiques, furriers and art galleries. No apartments. (Which proved exactly nothing. I was going on the assumption that he was either with the underground or the FBI, and in either case he wouldn't necessarily have to be from the area. But wouldn't it be likely that an agent from the Boston Bureau would be working my case? And wouldn't Marion depend on someone from wherever the radical hotbed was now? The ramshackle backwaters of occupied Cambridgeport, where aging hippies carry the torch for Hampton? Or the housing projects of Roxbury, always good for dissatisfaction and dissension? In any case, I was still groping in the dark.)

Franklin, or whatever his name was, was getting impatient. He grabbed the envelope, crossed quickly over to me, again soundlessly, almost as if he didn't disturb the air, and stuck the envelope in my hand.

I put my cup down and held the envelope in both hands, trying to make up my mind. What the hell, take a wild shot: "This is entrapment," I said.

His face remained blank and immobile, as if set in plaster.

"You've got wandering eyes," I continued. "You notice too much. I think you must be too proud about it. Do they grade you in FBI school? Have classroom drills? Find the Missing Evidence? Who would guess that my coffee was regular, not decaf? How did you know?"

He stood unmoving, and I watched my reflection for a while longer in his aviator glasses. I had a pretty convincing look of anger on my face.

Finally he smiled and took the glasses off. "It's the smell."

"The smell."

"Yeah," he stuffed the glasses into his breast pocket. Decaf's not as heavy as regular. Congratulations, you picked me up on it. I'll remember that. I suppose I was showing off."

"And don't read upside down either. It's a dead giveaway."

He nodded, still smiling like a boy caught in a harmless trick. "You noticed that too." He sounded disappointed in himself and I realized just how young he was. Mid-twenties and new to the Bureau, no doubt. Marion was just a fugitive to him, no different from an axe murderer or an embezzler. Her motives would have no context for him, no meaning. He was three years old when Martin Luther King said, "I have a dream."

A hundred thousand of us had marched on Washington that day and stood and listened and felt as though we would burst, filled by King's words and pride that, yes, we were on the side of right, that we were going to march with King and bring injustice to an end. This FBI boy would have no memory of that. The whole business of civil rights and antiwar demonstrations was something he'd only studied in high school and seen in films. It was history, fading fast. He probably wondered what all the fuss had been about. He was just doing his job, one of his first assignments at that, and he was doing everything to shine. It occurred to me that this whole charade was probably his own idea, done without anyone else's okay. I had an over-achiever on my hands.

"Let's see your ID," I said.

He took out a leather wallet and tossed it to me. His name was Paul Newman.

"Your folks like the movies."

He took the wallet back and read his own name thoughtfully. "Yeah," he said. "Used to be people named their children after saints. Now they name them after 'stars.' I think I actually disappointed my parents when I went into law enforcement. They wanted me to do something more chic—something they could brag about at the country club."

"Fascinating. What the hell is this?"

The way I cut him off snapped him back to business. For a moment, when I'd caught him in his act, his lean face had taken on an added flush and he'd let his guard down in confusion. Now he slid back into deadpan, which fit him about as much as clown shoes would fit Fred Astaire. That's what had bothered me about him; for all his nonchalance, he was trying too hard.

"We have reason to believe that this Wilson might come this way. She might try to get in touch with you."

"If she does I'll have to call you. That was part of my release agreement."

"Sure." He didn't believe me and smiled to let me know.

"Hey, I promise," I said. I went around my desk and sat back in my chair, relieved that I hadn't accepted the letter. That would have put me in deep. I waved at the visitor's chair expansively, saying, "Let's talk."

Newman hesitated, caught between an official circumspection and his natural curiosity. He hadn't been on the job long enough for everything to have become routine. There was still interest in every phase of the operation; in fact, I might be the closest he'd gotten to a "subject." Newman thought for a moment, his right hand unconsciously patting his suitcoat, as he constructed a rationale for staying. He couldn't come up with one. "I've got what I came for," he said. "I better go."

"What'd you get?

He smiled slyly, shrugged noncommittally. "You didn't leap

up and shout, 'Take me to her!' I'm not sure what that proves, except maybe you're careful."

"You realize that I could raise hell for you over at the Kennedy Building?"

He was unperturbed. "They would put on a big show of reprimanding me, but nothing would come of it. Tight-ass guidelines. The senior agents hate them, bend them whenever they can. Go ahead, call the Bureau. They'll be real sympathetic to you." He smiled smugly, the smile of a man who enjoyed the perks of staying on the law's good side.

I grinned back at him, although I wasn't finding anything funny. It was just a Mexican stand-off kind of grin. See? My smile is as wide as your smile.

"Make your parents happy, Newman," I said. "Go to Hollywood. You seem to enjoy role playing."

As I spoke I noticed something odd. I always turn my answering machine on when I leave the office, and as I looked at it now the red "on" light was not lit.

"I'll be seeing you around," Newman said, stepping back slowly toward the door.

"Great, fantastic." I gave him a dismissing wave. When he'd gone, padding in that soft-heeled, agile way they must have taught him in Skulking 101, I turned to my answering machine. There was a feature on it called "announcement check," by which you played back the recorded message that callers heard. I punched the message and heard Marion speaking drolly, sarcastically.

"How's this?" she said. "I could have left a note, but this was more fun, safer too, seeing how you never know who might be spying on you, right, Derek?"

She went on to ask me if I would meet her that afternoon by the kiosk in Harvard Square at four. She ended with her mocking tone, making some comment about being too cautious to meet in public. I erased her instructions and replaced them with my usual message, then sat back to think. I didn't mind her sarcasm, because my case of nerves, which she found so humorous, was well founded—I was being followed at odd intervals and I had just received a business visit from the local Bureau, albeit from an over-enthusiastic kid like Paul Newman. I was right to be careful, and Marion knew it. That wasn't important. What was important was the stupid way she'd left the message. (What if I'd turned on my machine without noticing she'd altered the recording? What if the FBI had my phone tapped?) It showed me her state of mind. Her cynicism wasn't so much directed at me, I thought, as at herself, her situation, a sign of a general fed-up attitude towards the state of things. It was a further reflection of what I saw going on in her the first day she came in. Marion was like that—any conflict in herself she turned out to the world at large because she saw herself only in relation to others. Marion constructed herself entirely by a process of comparison. She emulated traits which she admired and rejected those she thought were weak, or selfish, or, by virtue of not being ambitious enough, ignoble. In that sense Marion was the complete political person. All that she was came from give and take, interaction, a constant mechanical, radar-like reflection of her personality onto others—the dense vibration of will and thought echoing out and coming back, altered, from which she sensed strength, weakness, the validity of thought or emotion. She could not live, did not exist, alone.

Marion was political, and hence, judgmental, and it was that unyielding, critical eye of hers that I wasn't ready to face, to have trained on my life, to take the measure of my last ten years, if only because I wanted to judge myself, and even as I thought this I knew the process had already started, had been going on, in fact, since I walked into my office and found Marion seated at my desk. And it occurred to me, as I got up and absentmindedly reopened the doors leading to the street, letting a blast of hot air surge into the stuffy room, bringing a faint smell of auto exhaust and melting tar, if Marion's return had started some mental reorganizing or reassessment in me it was because I wanted that change, and if Marion was unsure of where she was, now, midway through her life, long past resilient, dogmatic, self-possessed youth, then I was too, and if there was ever a moment when I should see her and take stock, cover the ground I'd been avoiding for years, now was the time.

But it was only nine-thirty and I had the whole day to kill. I opened up my directory of Massachusetts manufacturers and called up a few, explaining my ETP services to them, something I do regularly to expand, as the current lingo has it, my "client database." After five calls I scratched out three companies—two had agencies on the job already and the other (the only one of five) had no theft problems. I noted one down as a possible, and wrote down a definite call back on the last. So much for that. I got up and paced. That wasted another two minutes. I went outside and stared at the traffic. Main Street in Waltham has a turn-of-the-century feel to it, a street lined with brick buildings, not one over five stories, and each with an awning shading the sidewalk. You half expected a butcher sporting a handlebar mustache to step out to the sidewalk, cleaning his hands in a white apron. But the butcher on this street had followed the Edsel into history, replaced by more *au courant* specialty stores: Ted's Cookies; Marianne's (imported olive oil, condiments, a deli counter with plates and cold salads, none for less than five dollars a pound); Computers 4 U (Apple, IBM, DEC and Kaypro); and Century Lights, where you could buy a reproduction of any Victorian lamp ever made. Stores for people with large amounts of expendable cash. Discretionary funds. My office was the only one that seemed out of character, although I'd done my best to match the ambiance, using cool, austere, stencil to write: D. ANDERSON . . . PRIVATE INVESTIGATIONS . . . PERSONAL SECURITY. Bonnie, who owned Marianne's, thought at first that I was out of place, until I explained to her that the people who used my services were the people who bought her overpriced quiche—the white collar professional, the up and coming or the already up and over. Sheet metal workers do not use PIs. Plumbers don't use them either, and I've never done business with a bus driver for the MBTA. But I have done jobs for most of the high-tech companies along Route 128, or for the VPs who run them.

I walked down toward the drugstore on the next block. At Marianne's Bonnie was bagging croissants for a customer. She looked up and waved merrily. Everything is okay in Gourmetland. Booming business.

Unfair, Derek. She's running a good shop and making a decent living—no more to it than that. She has her ups and downs. She has to juggle debits with receipts, arrange daycare for her youngest, make sure the oldest is going to school and not skipping classes (smoking joints behind the gym). No basis for cynicism here, even if you think that what she does just perpetuates conspicuous consumerism—more rhetoric, catch phrases. Is there anything wrong with selling pint bottles of virgin olive oil at prices that only five percent of the population can afford? Is there a moral law that says people in an affluent society can't indulge themselves? No, but I've always sneered at the wealthy, the well-to-do who made their money at jobs I considered unworthy—professional athletes, TV personalities, prepubescent rock stars with empty heads. Is this plain envy or do I have a Puritan streak, a real belief that you take what you need and spread the rest around? If I won the lottery tomorrow, would I keep twenty or twenty-five percent and give the rest away? . . . or, when the government took its half of the money, would I suddenly get sweaty palms, watching my fortune sink from taxation, and run to the nearest investment counselor, Liberty Mutual Investment Corp., John Hancock Securities? I pictured myself walking into the cool lobby of that glass tower downtown, taking a quiet, smooth-riding elevator to a top floor with a panoramic view of Boston Harbor: the ships at anchor on blue water, jets lifting off, arching towards the cloudless sky, heading to Europe, Africa, Asia. A young secretary with shining hair would take my name, "Yes, Mr. Anderson," reach out with painted fingernails to a Trimline phone and whisper a few words. I would be ushered down a deep-pile carpeted hallway to a tastefully decorated office with a picture window overlooking that same spacious view, seeming to encompass the entire world, and an efficient young man in a tailored suit would reach across his desk, obsequious, fawning, and shake my hand, "Yes, Mr. Anderson." I would look at my Swiss watch, sculpted from Alpine granite with two simple gold hands showing the time (late morning) and I would say, "I have a flight in an hour . . ." and he would hurry himself, reaching for my file, saying, "We have some CCD's that might interest you, or an IED, or perhaps a PPP . . ."

I bought a *Globe* at the corner drugstore and wandered back to my office, tapping the window lightly at Marianne's as I passed. Bold headlines dominated the front page: MONDALE TAKES NJ, WVA, CLOSES IN ON NOMINATION . . . There was heated speculation as to his running mate, possibly a woman. President Reagan was in London meeting with Thatcher. The accompanying article lingered, with what could be liberal self-righteousness, on what they had for dinner: Lobster mayonnaise, *noisettes* of lamb with rosemary and oranges in caramel. The article said demonstrators marched outside the state reception. The Iran/Iraqi war had taken to the air, jets had entered the fray. Beyond my doors the Waltham traffic noise rose and fell like waves rushing a beach and I heard snatches of conversation from pedestrians hurrying by, the high lilt of women, a jeering outburst from a group of teenage boys. The newspaper seemed to bring word of events happening in a separate zone not quite connected to this life, fictional reports from some long-running, late-night soap opera. It didn't seem to have anything to do with me, but that was only because I'd made it that way, training my indifference in a mental gymnasium, flexing my detachment like engorged muscles in the face of a bombardment from radio, television, the daily press. Who cares what Ronnie and Margaret say to each other? Central America is four thousand miles away. Let the Moslems turn the Middle East into a slag heap with their Islamic jihad. Leave me be, let me live my life and get on with your own.

I didn't do much the rest of the day, except to postpone an afternoon appointment, and when three o'clock finally came I locked up the office and got my car out of the lot. The first thing I had to do was lose Newman or whoever might be following me. I drove around Waltham for a half-hour before deciding I was clear.

The way to Harvard Square seemed to be one long traffic jam, or that's how it felt because I was anxious and in a hurry. The sun was still high, turning the June afternoon to a Turkish steam bath, so I took off my jacket and tie and rolled up the sleeves of my shirt. It didn't help. Sweat trickled down my back where it pressed against the car seat. I started to think about what Marion and I should do. We'd have to go someplace safe; somewhere secluded and quiet. She wanted to go back to Castle Island, but I thought it was too open. I decided on a drive out west, to Sturbridge.

Marion had told me to pick her up at the kiosk in Harvard Square and as I drove down Boylston Street I remembered that the kiosk was next to the Tasty, a coffee shop that was a favored hangout for the Cambridge police. When I arrived, moving slowly past the Garage and the last block of record shops and clothing stores, four cops were lounging on the corner, watching the crowds, shooting the breeze. A squad car stood by the curb. I pulled over and saw Marion flipping through a magazine at the newsstand. She was dressed smartly, like a college professor's wife, in ankle-length peg pants and a pearl-colored, oval-necked sweater. Standing fifteen feet from the police, she looked cool and serene, as if she had nothing more on her mind then a short ride home and an evening dip in the swimming pool. I signaled to her and she smiled, waving, before she put the magazine down and sauntered over to the passenger's window.

"Quick, get in," I said, glancing in the rearview mirror. One of the policemen looked our way, probably getting ready to wave me from the curb.

"What's the rush?" Marion said.

I nodded towards the cops.

She looked over at them nonchalantly. "That must be where they get their free coffee."

"That's very astute. Come on."

Marion smiled and got in, almost laughing as I lunged out into traffic. I cut off a swarm of pedestrians crossing against the light . . . they're fearless in Harvard Square . . . and I looked in the mirror and saw that the patrol car had stayed by the curb. I thought we were clear—then the cops pulled out after us.

I watched him in my mirror and swore under my breath. Marion looked back, the smile on her face freezing.

"This was a bad place to meet," I said. "You take chances."

"They're not chances," she answered. Her hand crept to the opening of the large cloth sack she had strung over her shoulder.

"Never mind that," I said.

We headed out towards Concord Avenue, taking the left fork before the Harvard Science Center. The police car followed us, nonchalantly, not in a hurry.

"Probably just a coincidence," Marion said, but the color had left her face.

I looped around the Cambridge Common onto Concord and now the car was right behind us. Marion had a hard time not looking back. He gave us time to get past the bus stops that run along the Common and then he gave the siren a short burst.

"Take it easy," Marion said, more to herself, I think, than to me. It sounded like something she'd said to herself a hundred times before.

They took the regulation positions, one officer behind us with his hand on his pistol, the other approaching my window at a sharp angle. He scanned us before leaning in.

I put a shocked, innocent look on my face. The surprised, upstanding citizen. "Problem, officer?"

He had white hair sticking out around his temples from underneath the black baseball caps the Cambridge police wear. "License and registration," he said.

I shuffled through my glovebox and got out the registration, then pulled out my license. He took them both in hand, standing back, then he bent down and looked across to Marion. She turned full face to him and smiled. My stomach did a flip.

The elderly cop said, "I'll be right back," and ambled to the cruiser. I watched him radio my license plate in and wondered if Newman had put a notice on me. I didn't tell Marion about that. Buses pulled out from the curb behind us and swooshed by with engines sounding like jet aircraft. The cop behind us looked bored, staring out over the Commons, scratching at his bicep.

"Happens all the time," Marion said, now under control, looking ahead unconcerned. "Cop looks at you on the street, maybe because he thinks you're pretty, or he wishes his wife would cut her hair like you, and it sends shivers down your back. Cop steps out off the sidewalk and stops your car . . . then lets some grandmother cross the street. You were ready to run him down and he was just being nice. You see two cruisers parked near your apartment and you wonder, 'Is this it?' " She turned and gave me a weak smile. "Sometimes you hope it is."

Overhead a pigeon slid past with outstretched wings. I watched a preoccupied Radcliffe coed walk hurriedly down the sidewalk, lost in thought. Marion shifted in her seat and muttered something under her breath. The wait was interminable.

We heard the patrol car door slam and I watched the cop walk towards us, splay-footed, like someone with a sore back, a man who spent too much time sitting on soft car seats.

He gave my papers back. "You took off right through that crosswalk," he said, sternly, like a grandfather lecturing an irresponsible teenager. "Harvard Square is the busiest Square in Boston. Ten thousand people pass through it everyday. You've gotta be careful."

"Sorry."

"Sorry won't do," he said, waving a finger. "It won't help after you've knocked someone down. We have fatalities there every year." He handed me a written warning, then left gruffly, without pleasantries, to show how serious he was.

The police swept by us as Marion and I sat motionless by the curb and Marion watched them leave, shaking her head. She took a theatrical deep breath and let it out, "Whewww."

"Sorry," I said, "that was my fault."

"Nobody's fault," she said, repeating again, like an incantation, "happens all the time."

I didn't make any move to start up again, letting the car just idle, my nerves settle, my body temperature, raised and ready for flight, to cool down.

"Where were we going?" Marion asked.

"I don't know, but now I'm in the mood for something undeniably secure."

She nodded agreement. "Head towards Brighton."

She told me to stop along the way so we could stock up for dinner, so I pulled into the parking lot of a local supermarket chain that sold everything from haddock caught off Nova Scotia to egg warmers made in Taiwan.

"You shop here?" Marion asked.

"No, I thought I'd admire the scenery. Look at the pretty mercury-oxide lamps."

She returned my smirk. "These chains are consolidating the distribution of food in this country."

"I love talk like that. 'Consolidating the distribution . . . Monopolizing the exchange . . . ' "

She pointed towards the street with exaggerated seriousness, "Go."

I put up a hand. "Wait a minute . . ."

"Forget it," Marion interrupted. "Everything I do is a political act. You know that. And not just me, everyone, whether they want to believe it or not. We live in a society, a collection of individuals . . . it's politics from word go . . . a fact of modern life. Not just who you vote for, who you give donations to to absolve your guilt. It's the little things too. You buy hamburgers at MacDonalds and you're partly responsible for the destruction of rain forests in South America, because *that's* where the beef is. You buy Granny Smith apples and you're supporting the South African regime. Simple economics. Have you ever crossed a picket line? Walked by striking flight attendants because you didn't want to change your schedule? You were pressured by a deadline, you had no choice, right? That's not just a practical decision, it's political too. Have you gotten lazy, Derek?"

"Not lazy. You're just being unrealistic."

She nodded. "Right. Unrealistic. How stupid of me." She pointed to the road. "Go."

I glared at her, ready for an argument, and then the moment passed. "You always were a hard woman to live with," I said, suddenly laughing.

"You're not the only man who's said that." Marion said, smiling back at me.

We did it her way, stopping at small specialty stores all over Brighton, and everywhere we went it seemed that Marion, although she'd been in Boston for scarcely a month, knew everyone as old friends. I remembered that about her, the way she could develop friendships easily, share confidences within an hour of meeting someone she liked.

We bought vegetables from Theo Constantelos—he had a cramped store with a five-ton truck parked out front, piled high with crates of tomatoes, lettuce, cucumbers, strawberries, watermelons. Theo was stocky, as short and powerful as an Ionian wrestler and looked most comfortable holding a forty-pound box in his thick, meaty hands, his hairy forearms stiff as metal bars. He slapped Marion on the rump and, without preamble, thrust two heads of lettuce into her hands, saying, "Just in today." We bought milk from a spa in Waverly Square where Louise, whose red hair was puffed up on her head like a rising cumulus cloud, stood behind the cluttered counter smoking a menthol Virginia Slims, watching "Days of Our Lives" on a portable TV. She took a puff, coughed, and before Marion could say anything, as if they'd been through this before, said, "Any time you're ready to quit yourself, I'll join you." We stopped for fresh cod at Hannon's Fish Market, run by Hannon himself and his two dark-haired, teenaged sons, who looked sullen, like all kids helping their father after school, wearing stained, white aprons as they slapped the cool bodies of fish onto butcher blocks, slicing and peeling the skin back in one bored, deft motion. We walked down the block to where Marion had somehow ferreted out a bakery that brought out soft, hot, french bread everyday precisely at four-thirty. Two industrial electric fans blew gusts of air down the narrow aisle before the cash register, attempting to counteract a blast of heat from the rear kitchen, damp hot waves of air sweeping out into the store and carrying the overpowering aroma of fresh baked bread.

When we were finished at last, and wound through the tense rush hour traffic (but we were calm, a serene island in the confusion, sipping fruit juice from Louise's spa) I said, "I feel holy, so self-righteous, helping the little man."

Marion laughed. "Be snide. See if I care. Everything I told you is old hat anyway. Everyone knows about chain stores and lettuce from California, but they choose to ignore it. It makes their life inconvenient or too complicated to deal with. They prefer to think that they have no choice, it's all too big for them, but really they're making a conscious decision not to bother. You're just as bad as the rest of them."

"*Mea culpa.*"

It was a small thing, our back and forth about the politics of shopping, but for Marion and me it reestablished an old way of being, of working together, from when we used to argue everything, from buying leather sandals or the relevance of Marx in a postindustrial society to who was responsible for birth control. When we were lovers we couldn't let anything lie without debating it to the nth degree. Sometimes we argued when we agreed, like ballplayers practicing their fielding. It was a habit I'd gotten out of, having grown lazy, as Marion said. But, riding in the car on our way to her Brighton apartment, it felt as though we were picking up exactly where we left off, as if nothing had changed at all.

We stopped for wine, then drove along Chestnut Hill Avenue until we reached the block of apartments where Marion was staying. There was a massive silver birch in the courtyard of the brick complex and after I parked my car on the street we walked along the sidewalk under its leaves, moving from sunlight to cool shade.

"I could learn to love this place," Marion said, stopping to look up through layers of branches and leaves. The sky was shut out, hidden by the dark green hood.

"How long can you stay here?"

"How ever long I need, I guess," she said. There was a note of dissatisfaction in her voice. She turned and went into the entryway, slipping her key into the lock and saying, "The man who agreed to put me up, Ron, he and I have our differences, but he puts up with me, probably out of revolutionary fervor." We went into a dingy hall and started up a stairway with walls dented and scraped where furniture had cut into the plaster. The hall was illuminated by a bare light bulb and had a medicinal, musty odor. "Ron's trying to unionize the projectionists in Boston," Marion said as we climbed, "so he feels like he should be sympathetic towards me." She smiled over her shoulder. "But in the end he's uneasy, like you. You should have seen the look on his face when he found out who I was. He must have been told that I was just some itinerant socialist." She let out a short laugh. "God, he went pale." We came to a door on the third floor landing. "All you Sunday afternoon activists. Committed so long as it's convenient."

"I'm not so sure I'm committed anymore," I said.

"I know," she answered. "Somewhere along the line you just gave up, Derek."

It looked like a bachelor's apartment, with a bachelor's attention to comfort, like the single armchair placed before the TV, with a small table in front of it for anyone who wanted to eat in front of the tube, and a bachelor's lack of concern for the mess: magazines piled high on the shelves by the window, newspapers on the floor, a jacket slumped over the couch. There was a main hall with a coat closet at one end and a kitchen at the other, overlooking a backyard. Next to the closet a door let on to one bedroom, then an entry to the livingroom, and after that a door to the bathroom and a second bedroom. I saw in the first bedroom an unmade bed and clothes heaped on the floor. There was a dresser with the two top drawers open and socks sticking out like they'd been jammed in impatiently. The living room was furnished haphazardly, with mismatched and worn furniture. A lumpy couch with an Indian-print cotton blanket draped over it, probably hiding torn cushions, sat against one wall, and across from it was a string of bookshelves heaped with books, records, pamphlets, a stereo and a black and white TV set. An overturned wooden box served as the coffee table. The apartment looked out onto the central courtyard and through the large picture window I saw the birch leaves shaking in a light breeze. The shade made the apartment dark, so our eyes had to adjust as we entered.

Marion called out to the empty rooms. "I'm home!"

We made dinner slowly, giving our nerves time to settle down after the scare on Concord Avenue, the image of the police car pulling behind us still fresh. Slowly the memory of the cop's slow walk from behind us receded until it became something that could have happened long ago, harmless now, a bad dream remembered in daylight.

And there was something else, in the ritual preparing of the meal, the intimate ceremony of readying the vegetables, frying the red perch in fragrant olive oil, the kitchen filling up with the aroma of spices, the stove's heat, we talked quietly about nothing, the sunlight growing dim, the rush hour traffic dissipating, a restless energy dissolving to calm. I made a huge salad, an abundant salad, more than the two of us would ever finish and I looked up to catch Marion smiling.

"What?" I asked, looking down at the bowl piled high with lettuce, radishes, cucumbers, olives, chunks of feta cheese, a mound like something spilled from the Horn of Plenty.

"Nothing," she said, turning back to what she was doing, but I knew that what she'd been smiling at was simple: an apartment, usually empty, now full.

I watched her, noticing as though for the first time all of her features, the way she was aging in fine increments, the gradual addition of shallow lines around her eyes, of extra padding on her shoulders and waist, of heavier skin on her hands, still slim, but the mature skin of her mother, and I felt the loss of not having shared the years of those changes.

I opened the wine and poured it into two glasses. Marion came over and we lifted the glasses together. She was smiling like someone had just told her a very corny joke. Maybe she thought I was going to make an ornately romantic benediction. She was right. I tried. "Here's to a quiet night at the old homestead," I said. We clicked our glasses to toast. "Just you and me."

I wrapped my arm around her waist and led her to the porch that lead off the kitchen. The backyard it overlooked had a sorry strip of lawn and a small overgrown garden that someone had once tried to cultivate and then abandoned. There were woods beyond the yard and another apartment building past them. Sunlight filtered through the trees and seemed to become moist on the passage, turning amber and thick. The evening air was heavy with the smell of earth and the decay of last year's leaves. I heard the thump of a small foot hitting a kickball, followed by squealing voices.

Marion raised her glass. "To the lower forty. May our riches increase."

We ate dinner by the light of an ancient railroad conductor's lantern that Ron had stashed in a corner, and afterwards we cleared the table and washed the dishes. Simple pleasures.

Afterwards we went out for more wine, walking up Chestnut Hill Avenue towards the reservoir, the night air around us warm and heavy like a familiar coat.

Up ahead of us a Suburu station wagon parked at the curb and a couple, in their thirties, got out, taking a load of groceries from the back. They hurried up a path to a single-family house set a short distance off the street. When we got to the house Marion stopped and looked after them. The inside of the house was brightly lit and Marion watched the two as they set their bags down on a kitchen table, talking to each other, unloading groceries, all habitual movements. The woman went into the next room where her four-year-old son watched TV. She said something and the boy turned, answered—we couldn't hear what they said.

Marion said, "I used to hate people like that. Just a knee-jerk contempt."

"Not anymore?"

She smiled. "Now I'm just confused."

"Is it so terrible to want that for yourself?"

"Depends. Depends on what you have to do for it." She tugged on my arm. "C'mon."

We worked our way through the second bottle of wine, lying on the livingroom floor with the lights out, watching the birch leaves move to a weak breeze.

Marion lit a cigarette and blew smoke toward the ceiling. "Did I tell you I went home to see my folks?"

"No. When was this?"

"A few years ago."

"How was it?"

"Bad. Pretty bad. They were scared the whole time I was there. The house felt like a bunker. My mother refused to go out the whole time." She stared a moment and then shook her head as if dismissing an unpleasant memory. "I did a good job messing up their lives."

"Did they tell you that?"

"Do you think they had to?" she asked. She stared at the end of her cigarette, then took a drag. "Remember how much of a hard time we used to give my father?"

"He supported the 'fascist war machine,' I think we said."

She nodded. "A designer of death, I called him once." I saw the end of her cigarette heat up as she inhaled. "What snot-nosed asses we were," she said.

"We had a cause. We were right, too . . . we just shouldn't have given him such a hard time."

"That's not it," she said. "I found out years later, from my mother, not him, that he'd become an engineer because when he was a kid he read science fiction—he was a real science nerd, she said—and he wanted to build space ships." She looked at me. "I never had any idea. Suddenly I got this image of him as a skinny, gawky kid, all ga-ga over Buck Rogers, dreaming of elaborate space ships with hydroponic gardens and complicated warp drives or whatever the hell he thought would move them. I never knew that side of him. I never knew that he joined his company to work on the space program, or that when the war geared up and the company shifted its whole program . . . him too . . . that he considered quitting."

"He could have."

"That's what I told him. He just looked at me and said, bitterly, I remember, 'You really think so?' That's it. That's all he said, with this awful look on his face." She got up on an elbow, looking for the ashtray. She found it and flicked away an ash.

"He stayed in the job just long enough to get his kids through college, to pay off my school loans and my brother's loans. Then he quit." She lay back again, eyes open, staring at the ceiling. "My goddam HELP loans."

"There're other things he could have done."

"Get the point, will you? We would gang up on him—you and me, and our holier-than-thou friends. He would rant and rave and support Nixon and Vietnamization and 'peace through strength.' Christ! All he really wanted to do was help *me*, and he ended up making excuses for himself."

Smoke from her cigarette curled in lazy spirals towards the ceiling. She took another drag. Exhaled, lips pursed.

"Anyway, he was wrong. I know that," she continued, "making 'smart bombs' . . . jesus . . . and despite all the noise he made he hated the work, but he was stuck. He did his work and paid our bills and who would blame him or anyone? Would those two we saw down the street? They've got their little son watching TV. What would they do for him?"

"They've got their priorities," I said. "Doesn't mean they'd do what your father did."

"No," she agreed, bitterly, "they'll just do the little things . . . ignore the hungry, the corporations, ignore the land going to hell."

"Marion . . ."

"I know, you're right, that's tired old crap . . . tired, used up, impotent. Hollow phrases . . . absolutely not a grain of truth."

"You have to give people some slack. You're just too hard . . ."

"I have to be," she cut in, "someone has to be. Everyone thinks the world is put right by large pronouncements and great movements. Wide-screen historical dramas. It's not. The world is made day by day by what we do. Would the death camps have been possible without train engineers? Right now everyone is bitching and moaning about Star Wars, but the physicists are lining up for their government grants and more men like my father in little high-tech companies are designing components telling themselves this is how it goes. 'I'm doing this for my children.' " She mocked them, beating her closed fist against her heart, reminding me of Spenser's bitterness. "The price of sanity is eternal vigilance." She stopped and rubbed her forehead with the palm of her hand.

"Is what you do sane? Giving money to extremists so they can terrorize women and children?"

"I don't know." She leaned over and stubbed out her cigarette. "That night you and Peter were in the bank, the explosion was incredible. The doors and windows blew out in a million pieces onto the sidewalk. I was sure you were dead. Positive. The alarm shrieked over the neighborhood. I started to get out and go to you when a car came down the street. The driver didn't stop—he took off. But while I waited for him to leave I felt the police must be on their way and I was scared, terrified of being caught. There was no sign of anyone moving in the bank and I knew I should go help you, but then I saw blue lights flashing down the avenue and I panicked and started up the car. I rolled past the bank, the police coming closer, and I felt them at my back. I drove off. Half of me screaming to turn around and half of me screaming to get away."

"I never blamed you for leaving."

"Thanks," she said with a wan smile. "I never blamed myself

for being scared. That's natural. But I did blame myself for giving up on you. I said, 'They're dead, that's it,' when I knew there was a chance you were alive, needed help. But I gave up and ran. It was like that night in Dunn County—you and I gave up too. That was two strikes against me, Derek. I've never given up on anyone or anything since.

"I monitor everything in my life to make sure it's correct—what I eat, buy, wear." She rolled over and propped herself up on her elbow. "The utility that supplies electricity to this place uses oil from Saudi Arabia and power from the nuclear plant on the South Shore. Assad is an Arabian Nixon, a conniving politician. Nuclear power is nuclear power: dangerous, dirty, and a stupid way to boil water. So I don't use any electricity that isn't absolutely necessary."

"That's absurd."

"You would think so."

"How do you know this? Keep track?"

"That's what I do. Do you think I spend all my time in dark cellars making pipe bombs?" She laughed again. "I spend most of my time tracing people, industries, distributors, getting the information to people who care. Sending out lists to those newspapers no one reads. You won't find what I do in the *Globe.*"

"Is that what you're doing here, now?" I asked.

She lit another cigarette and didn't answer. She went on as if I hadn't asked a question. "There's only one gasoline company that's okay, although they're all less than perfect. There are only certain beverages you can by, mostly fruit juices, some seltzer waters. Even books; most publishing houses dip into the defense pot of gold. Every aspect of daily life has to be scrutinized." She looked at me, smiling at my face, which probably showed confusion. "Sound compulsive to you, Derek? Extreme?"

"Sounds impossible. Nuts."

She laughed again, and I realized how little happiness there was in her laughter. It sounded instead like an alternative to something else, tiredness, entropy.

"It is impossible," she said. "But it's the only joy . . . no, that's not right . . . happiness . . . satisfaction, that's it, satisfaction I feel." She stopped abruptly.

I thought back to the couple that Marion watched. "Listen," I said, "you deserve something for yourself. You have to think of your own life."

"There's enough people doing that already," she answered quickly. She got up and stood before the open window, feeling for stray wisps of night air. I moved behind her and wrapped my arms around her waist, looking out with her. The birch's broad, flat leaves moved as if underwater, brushed by sluggish currents. A car drove by, its tires a shush on the pavement. I could make out a short stretch of sidewalk illuminated by the yellow glow of a streetlamp. It was a night that could have belonged to any time or place; the quiet streets, the warm night air. The automobile passing might have been a carriage and horses; the lone man sauntering towards the reservoir, a gentleman of the last century. The wind was the breeze that made candles flicker on café tables in Fiesole and the clouds obscured the moon above St. Mark's. Marion's body was warm against mine.

I put my hands on her shoulders and began to knead the muscles I knew would be tight, tensed. "What are you going to do?" I asked.

"I don't know," she answered.

I turned her around and pressed her against me, feeling her breasts against my chest. "Let me give you something else to think about," I said.

A smile curled her lips. "What would that be?" I kissed her, an awkward kiss because we were both smiling. "As if I hadn't been thinking about it already," she said.

I brushed my lips across her forehead, under the dark widow's peak. "You've got too much going on in there," I said, "I want to take you away from it for a while."

"Think you can?"

"I'll give it a try."

She raised her lips to mine. "Yes, try," she said.

I slipped my hands under her sweater and ran my fingers over her flesh. I could feel that her body was still tense, that all that was running through her mind still had hold of her. I took her to her bed and we lay together as I stroked her hair. We held each other, arms wrapped tight, then began to slip our clothes off, slowly, as if shedding the years we'd been apart, stripping to the skin, so that finally, when I pressed her white breasts against my chest, the dark nipples erect; when I pressed her soft stomach to mine, and traced patterns on her thighs and when I kissed her lips and chin and collarbone and circled her breasts with my tongue; when I entered her, her flesh hot and moist; Marion murmured my name, once, and she had forgotten what had brought her here and we were together again, for a time.

VIII

―――

"**I** DON'T BELIEVE THIS," Marion said.
"What?"
"The U.S. has invaded Grenada," she said.
It was ten o'clock the next morning and we were still in bed.
I was lying on my back and Marion was sitting up, cross-legged, reading the paper.

"We invaded Grenada?" I said, repeating the information.
"What the hell for?"

Marion's attention was focussed on the headline story. She said, absently, "Because Reagan's dying for a chance to flex his muscles."

"He picked a tough country."

"Mmmmm," she said. When Marion was engrossed in something it was next to impossible to get her attention. I settled into the sheets and admired her shoulders. Her skin was naturally a light brown, the light color of freshly baked bread. I leaned forward and smelled sweet sweat and salt. I put my lips to the ridge of her spine and reached around to fondle her breast. She slapped my hand away.

"I'm reading," she said, shortly.

I stared up at the ceiling. The plaster was cracked and gray, looking a little like the moon seen through a telescope. It wasn't very interesting. I pulled the ends of Marion's dark hair. It was thick and full, weighted down with natural oils. Even in the morning it fell neatly into place, as if she'd brushed it a hundred strokes.

"I don't see one gray hair on your whole head," I told her.

"Derek."

I ran my hand lightly across her back. The room was dark, peaceful. My body felt as if I was immersed in a hot, oily bath, my tired muscles buzzed with electric energy, sore and satisfied, but ready for more. We'd made love until dawn was just a suggestion of light, a fuzzy whiteness like a TV just after you turn it off. I'd had only a half-sleep, conscious always of Marion beside me.

I made my roving hand a touch light enough to tickle. Marion arched her back away.

"In a minute!" she said. She took another section of the paper and plopped it on top of me. "Here."

I looked at the paper. "I don't read the sports."

"Then wait."

"Okay," I said, giving in, "what do they say about Grenada?"

"Not much," she answered. "There's a news blackout. Can you imagine that?"

"No, I can't," I said, sitting up. I read over her shoulder. "Where is this place, anyway?"

"The Caribbean."

"Are we making the world safe for tourism?"

The paper gave the particulars of the invasion, or what was possible from second hand sources.

"That's almost as ridiculous as England going after the Falklands."

Marion cast a glance out of the corner of her eye. "You seem to find it amusing."

"It's asinine."

"Derek, we just overthrew an independent government."

"I didn't say I supported the thing."

She went on, exasperated. "We didn't approve of Adams, so we just walked in and kicked him out."

I dropped down on my back. "Let's form a committee. We'll march on Washington."

Marion laughed and threw the paper aside. She lay on top of me with her legs straddling mine. "You think you're funny?"

"I'm not interested in Grenada at the moment."

Her wide mouth parted in a smile and she kissed me with her lips open, her tongue searching for mine. She shifted her hips so that she was open to me and I started to adjust my position.

Marion raised up on her elbows and looked thoughtfully at the wall behind my head. "What kills me is he'll come away a hero. Like he did something great."

I wrapped my arms around her shoulders and pulled her down.

IX

―――

"I T'S NOON FOR GOD'S SAKE," Marion said.
"We should get up. Don't you have work to do?"
I told her I had to shepherd a performer from
Logan Airport to the Chateau DeVille dinner club that night.

"Strange work."

"It pays."

"Derek in the entertainment biz." She looked at me as if she
expected me to explain myself. Tell me about this, her look
said.

I wasn't ready to defend myself, so I changed the subject.
"I'm free for the day."

It was her turn to hesitate. She pulled absently at the hairs
on my chest and I saw her carefully choose her words. Something that had stood silently between us returned. The unspoken truce we'd accepted the night before, the unspoken
promise not to press too far, now became a wall between
us.

"I have some things to do this afternoon," she said carefully,
her voice a warning. "Maybe we can meet later," she said.

"What things?"

Her gray eyes were deadpan. "Don't ask."

"What things?"

No answer.

"What the hell are you doing here?" I asked. "Maybe it's time you told me."

"Maybe I don't want to . . . yet," she answered. She pulled the covers off her and went to wash, leaving me trying to pull information from silence. I listened to the water splash in the bathroom.

I got dressed and waited for her in the kitchen. She came in moving briskly, with business-like motions, rummaging through her shoulder bag for keys or something. The night before was forgotten. "Can you give me a lift to the subway?" she asked.

Her hair was brushed back, still wet from her shower. I saw a few drops of water that she'd missed with the towel gleaming on her collar bone.

"Sure," I said.

I dropped her off in Kenmore Square and then got on Storrow Drive heading west towards Waltham. I needed a shower and shave. Beside me the Charles River flowed sluggishly, broad and flat, an ancient river that in its day had worn down mountains. For thousands of years it had been clean and fresh water, and in just a few decades we'd turned it into an open sewer. Maybe that means something, I don't know, but it struck me that it takes a long time to build something pure and good, and it takes no time at all to destroy it. I turned off Storrow Drive at the Mass Pike cloverleaf and took the turnpike to Waltham. It was the fastest way home.

X

———

ISTOOD ON MY FRONT PORCH and stared at the front door. It was opened an inch. There were faint scratch marks around the bronze lock. As I thought about what might be waiting inside I heard footsteps coming up the walk. I turned and saw Newman ambling towards me like someone visiting friends on a Sunday morning. He wore a gray-blue suit and a red tie. His white shirt looked crisp, as though he'd just taken it out of the wrapper.

I turned away and opened the screen door. Then, gently, I pushed the front door open. It was dark inside and I waited for my eyes to adjust.

"Morning, Mr. Anderson," Newman said behind me.

My eyes adjusted to the dark room mechanically, from front to back, so the mess of the living room was revealed in order: the tipped lamp by the door, the upended arm chair beyond it, and further in, the strewn cushions of my couch. My mouth went dry and I stepped into my house, prepared for the worst. I knew that whoever had done this was long gone, but still the room had a foreign presence. When you live alone the slightest intrusion into your home is discernible, the buzz of a fly by the window, the hand of the postman by the mailslot. The intruders were long gone but I could feel them as if they were still there and I could tell you there had been, probably, two of them, not one or three.

Books were thrown from the shelves, pictures torn off the walls, plants ripped from their clay pots and left standing, their roots showing.

Newman stopped behind me and whistled.

"You people didn't do this, I hope," I said to him.

"No way. We don't operate like this," he answered.

"No, you just bug offices and tap phone lines."

He didn't answer that, he just followed me into the wrecked room. I went to the windows and opened the blinds.

"Mmmmm," Newman said.

"What?"

He surveyed the room cooly, taking stock. "Nothing's really damaged, just messed up. Upended."

He was right. Everything was tipped and turned, but nothing was smashed.

"What are you into these days, Anderson?" Newman asked.

"You mind?" I said, "I just got here."

He smiled. "Sorry."

I went to the kitchen and stopped short in the doorway. All the cupboards had been emptied. They'd been less careful in here. The floor was littered with broken cups and plates. The table was turned over with its legs pointing straight up. The chairs were placed around it upside down too. They looked like they were set up for an ersatz Lewis Carroll dinner.

I mumbled, half to my self, "Looks like Packy has a sense of humor."

"Who's Packy?" Newman asked.

"Never mind."

I waded through the broken crockery and made for the coffee maker. I hunted up two unbroken cups from the floor and went through the business of making coffee. It's the only way to face a ransacked house. Newman righted the tables and chairs and sat down.

"Invite yourself in," I said.

"Thanks," he said. He ran a hand over his carefully combed hair, stopping to scratch the hairline on his neck. He was still smiling. "I was going to ask you where you were last night, but I'll hold it for a while."

"It's none of your business, anyway."

"Let me remind you," he said, mildly, "that one of the conditions of your parole is that you cooperate with the authorities."

"A nice word, 'authorities,' full of dark implications, the heavy hand of the Law."

"Just the same . . ."

"Let me get my coffee first, will you?"

He let out a short laugh. "I take mine with milk, no sugar."

With that we both looked at the refrigerator. Nothing was spilled from it. Packy didn't want to spoil my food. Newman and I looked at each other and laughed.

"Nice guys," he said.

While the water was spluttering out over the coffee grounds, I took the opportunity to look Newman over. There was something old-fashioned about him—maybe his polite way didn't suit him. He seemed like he belonged to another era, the fifties or even earlier, the Hoover heydays.

"What's up, Newman?" I asked him.

He searched in vain for something for his hands to play with. "Well," he began, "I just wanted to ask you a few more questions—"

"Uh, huh," I cut in. "When did you join the FBI, Newman?"

He smiled when I cut him short. "Three years ago," he said. "I graduated from college with a B.A. in nothing in particular. I was in ROTC, though, and that got my foot in the door with the Bureau. Seemed like it would be exciting."

"That's a good reason to spend your life putting people in jail."

"You mean I should have some real moral fervor?" he asked, getting annoyed. "Maybe I do. Maybe I think that society benefits from the work I do. The people I 'put in jail' deserve to be in jail."

"People like Marion Wilson?" I asked.

"She's a criminal. She breaks the law every day she doesn't turn herself in."

"Whose law are we talking about?"

"The law of the United States."

"You're more idealistic than I thought."

"Okay, I'm following you," he said. "Law is relative, etc., etc."

"Something like that."

"But you deal with what you've got."

"Okay."

The coffee maker gurgled as the last water dripped through the grounds. I poured out two cups and passed one to Newman, then I sat down. The remains of a cup crunched under my feet.

"What's the story here?" Newman asked.

"It's not an FBI matter."

"Maybe we can help."

"I doubt it."

He passed his hand over his hair, stopping again to scratch at his collar. He was getting frustrated. "Look," he said, "I'm trying to be friends with you."

"Why?"

"Because, well, here's how it works. I'm sitting in the office on a quiet Tuesday. No cases floating around. We get a call from the Oakland bureau saying they got close to a Marion Wilson, one-time mad bomber, self-styled revolutionary. They suggest we look up certain people. We draw lots. I get Derek Anderson, Wilson associate, presumed lover, partner in crime, now turned model citizen. Somehow even managed to wheedle a PI license, gun permit . . . why are you smiling?"

" 'Presumed lover.' We were kids. Teenagers. You're not lovers then, just fellow experimenters."

"You over it?"

"Of course."

He glanced around the room, seeing the whole, small house. "You married?"

"No."

Newman nodded.

"Don't jump to conclusions," I said. "I'm not pining away."

"Okay," he said. You could see him filing something away in his mind. He went on, "The older guys are excited. Marion Wilson. Wow. They're like bloodhounds on the scent of a big, big fox. The energy level of the office picks up a few notches . . ."

"Should you be telling me this?"

He waved a hand. "Not to worry. I know what I'm doing. Anyway, where was I? Yeah, memos are passed, interoffice meetings held. Protocols discussed. Guys start going to the gym. Pumping iron. Guys who haven't seen the range in six months take target practice. This is real energy, excitement, and I'm wondering, 'What's happening here?' Everyone's all smiles. Lean and mean. Determined. I check out this Anderson and I don't see anything special. Unimpressive little office in Waltham. Getting a little thin on top, a little thick around the middle."

"But not bad for an old man."

"You could use some gym work," he said, and then went on, obviously enjoying himself. "I check out the Wilson file and see some interesting stuff. She's got a fairly serious felony-murder on her, some other warrants that tell me she's pretty much a moral low-life, and she seems to have her hand in some 'subversive' activities, but all in all she seems low rate."

"Low rate?"

"Yeah. 'Power to the people,' etc. Corny. Old-fashioned."

I laughed.

He smiled with me, raised his fist in a mock power salute, "I mean, struggling for the oppressed masses? C'mon. Give them jobs. Send them a few billion from the World Bank. Let them work for a living. DeLorean did more for the Irish than the IRA ever has. He fucked up but he had the right idea."

"I see your point."

"No you don't, but that's all right. Anyway, I don't get all the excitement. I feel like I'm missing something."

"Nothing much. Maybe some of your older guys feel like they have something to settle. Or finish off."

He considered this. "I feel like this is how it must have been when the Bureau was after Dillinger and Floyd and all those gangsters."

"Close, I guess."

Newman took a sip of his coffee and stared at me thoughtfully. "So what do you think?"

"About what?"

He took another sip. "Think we'll catch her?"

I shrugged. "Probably. She'll keep on doing what she's doing. You'll keep on doing what you're doing. Eventually you'll run into each other."

"You think we should keep after her?"

I laughed. "How am I supposed to answer that?"

"Anyway you want."

"Go for it. Be all that you can be. I think that everyone should do whatever the hell they please. That's my philosophy."

"You're never going to be serious with me, are you?"

"I find it hard to take you seriously, yes. It's nothing personal, I just don't know what to make of you."

He liked that. He liked being unpredictable. Maybe that explained his visit.

I looked at the mess around me and glanced at my watch. I had to get ready for my evening job with the Charles Street agency.

"Want to help me clean this up?" I asked Newman.

He smiled. "Outside of Bureau guidelines."

"Now you're worried."

He tried to look apologetic. "Everything strictly by the book."

"Then beat it. I've got work to do."

He got up and made for the door, all kinds of smashed glass crunching under his feet. "Jesus, what a mess," he said. At the door he turned. "I'll be stopping in again."

"Can't wait."

"Right." He put an open palm up in mock salute and sauntered out.

I was telling the truth when I told Newman I didn't know what to make of him. All the time he was being ingratiating and frank I felt like I was being set up for something, like he was wired for sound and baiting me. At the same time, whenever I talked to him I got a sense of the great gap between us. In terms of age it was only ten or twelve years, yet he seemed as if he came from a different country, or culture. When he left I tried to put the conversation into some kind of perspective but it wouldn't fit anywhere. He made me uneasy.

I put the house together, which amounted mostly to turning everything I owned right side up again. Was it possible that Packy was capable of symbolic gestures? "Anderson, I'm going to turn your life upside down, then tear it apart." That's what he seemed to be saying over and over again as I flipped the chairs, lamps, tables back on their legs—at least, that's what it seemed to me, but I'm susceptible to symbolism. I had studied Joyce and Eliot, practiced the art of political "demonstration," learned the use of gesture. This was effective stuff. Who'd ever done this to me, following whatever reasoning, had given my active mind plenty to worry over.

When I was through I had just enough time to grab a quick supper, change into a light suit and head to Logan Airport to meet my client. I wasn't in the mood to face the jam at the Callahan Tunnel, so from Waltham I took the 95 by-pass to Rt.2, then the Mystic Valley Parkway through Revere to East Boston. I parked in the central lot and was ready for another boring evening and fat paycheck, when the limousine for Jerry Vane arrived at the TWA terminal at precisely six o'clock. I talked to the driver for a while, then took my place by the door, ready to swing it open with that certain flair the Charles Street agency likes to show all its clients.

Mr. Vane came out of the terminal with his Boston booking agent, Joanne Smythe, followed by a porter rolling a carrier stacked with suitcases. Vane was medium height, about five-six, which made him half a foot shorter than me. He was pudgy and soft, a man entering his late fifties who made it—for thirty years he'd been singing sentimental love songs, recording an album a year, doing Las Vegas, the dinner club circuit. His loose skin was tanned the deep, even tan of golf courses and swimming pools. He signalled the porter to put the suitcases in the limo's trunk, using a brief, authoritative wave. He looked like a man used to having people wait on him.

Joanne Smythe worked for Charles Street, and though I'd never asked her, I'd always assumed she got the job, as I had, by taking advantage of Boston society's inbred parochialism—through some kind of blue-blood ties. She was short, slim, dedicated to aerobics, the kind of woman who wore matching tights, leotard and headband and looked great in them. She mingled in party crowds with a kind of desperate efficiency. Tonight she was dressed conservatively for Mr. Vane, in a simple white blouse and white linen skirt, but I'd seen her in black leather pants and a motorcycle jacket for rock stars, Norma Kamali sack suits for avant-garde performance artists, and homespun, flowered dresses for country western singers. She pulled off each incarnation with equal facility.

Tonight she was formal and demure. "Mr. Vane, this is Derek Anderson," she said, smiling at me as if to share the secret of her latest pose. Joanne worked by sharing select confidences geared to the preferences of whoever she wanted to impress. To me she said once, in an intimate lull in one of our jobs together that she dreamed of showing up some night in her old beat-up Volkswagen, wearing jeans and an old sweatshirt and bringing some famous client to eat at McDonalds. This was supposed to appeal to me, the Ancient Hippie.

We climbed into the oversized Mercedes, Joanne and Vane sharing the back seat, me up behind the driver.

Vane settled back professionally—a man who liked chauffeurs, the star treatment. We were to drive directly to the Chateau, arriving at about seven. Vane would do two shows, at eight and ten, then we'd head back to Boston. Easy money.

Vane sighed theatrically, with a smile, and said, "I only had time for one drink on the Shuttle. I need to lubricate the old vocal cords. How about a drink, Derek?"

There was a bar between the seats and I mixed a dry martini for Vane, a gin and tonic for Joanne and a Scotch and soda for myself. I passed them around.

Joanne was saying, "I have to admit, Jerry, that I have a soft spot for your music. It's so hard to find romantic songs these days."

"You flatter me," Vane said. "My music is really meant for your parents."

Joanne turned a little to face him and crossed her legs, showing a length of muscular calf. "I know," she said, "but I find that I get more and more like my mother every day."

"She must be very pretty," Vane said. They laughed together.

I looked out of the smoky gray windows of the car. We were on the Turnpike, passing behind the two Hancock Insurance buildings. The oldest of the two was once Boston's tallest building, constructed in the Empire style, a rectangular block of soft granite with vertical grooves, now heavy shadows in the evening light. It looked aerodynamic, ready to lift off at any moment. Beside the old edifice rose the new Hancock, a glass tower, angular, sharp edged, inpenetrable, reflecting back the inquiring eyes of the city with a sheath of a thousand mirrored windows. The old granite building was reflected in the new— short, stunted, like a mother beside her mutant progeny. Two generations of architectural theory, products of the pompous scramble by richly endowed companies to claim supremacy of the air, conspicuous monuments to money and power. Yet they were beautiful too, because they could be built, because they were constructed for no better reason than to show off—beautiful in their irresponsible flamboyance.

Vane followed my gaze and said, "They are something, aren't they?"

"Yeah, and down in the streets around them the homeless live beneath heating ducts."

"Derek, you're such a poop," Joanne said.

I shrugged and smiled because she was right. It wasn't what I'd been thinking; I'd just answered Vane with tiresome liberal cant. What I'd said was true, but it's possible to be right and tiresome too. Would Marion agree? No, the Hancock buildings would be enough to set her off for an hour.

I said, "I travelled in England once, the southeast corner. That was the dairy center of England at one time . . ."

Vane added, "Beautiful country. Flat and green. A lot like the mid-western states."

Joanne egged him on, trying to steer away from my conversation. Nothing disruptive for the clients, please. She asked if he'd given concerts in England.

"Oh, yes," Vane said, pleasantly, "England, France, Germany. All over. But I think we interrupted Derek."

I went on, ignoring the strained smile on Joanne's face. "I was just thinking about how something, some engineering feat can be beautiful, no matter what else it symbolizes. That area of England I was talking about is now the nuclear power center of the country. They have huge complexes, not like here, where there is just one of the conical cooling towers—their plants have as many as six. You'd be driving along the M1 or M11, through, as you said, Mr. Vane, a flat plain, and in the distance, against the horizon you'd see the sweeping curves of those towers, fluted and almost delicate, like a glass vase. They were graceful—beautiful. But at the same time I knew it meant that land once used for farming had been taken over by an industry capable of poisoning the entire countryside in one accident or, as is probably more likely, destroying the surrounding fields and water slowly over decades. It also meant that farmers were being forced off their land the way they are here. I thought it probably wasn't a coincidence, this concentration of nuclear generators, that for some reason, politically, that area had been chosen as the site for London's power. But even with that in mind, those towers were magnificent in an eerie way."

"I know what you mean by eerie," Vane said. His face had the bland look of someone who never troubled himself to look under the surface of things. "They struck me the same way. They were forbidding."

"Forbidding, yes," I answered.

"I'd love to see them," Joanne chirped, determined to keep the conversation light.

Vane said to me, though, with mild curiosity, "What makes you believe there was some kind of concerted program?"

I shrugged. "I don't know, it was just a guess."

"I've learned over the years," Vane said, in a fatherly tone, "that looking for a hidden, guiding hand behind everything just causes you a lot of needless worry."

"Words to live by," I said.

"Oh, let's get off this dreary subject!" Joanne said. She asked Vane about his program for the evening and the conversation veered off to hit tunes of the forties.

I stared out the window. We were passing through Newton and I remembered a stint as a house painter I had done there. Before that I'd worked in a bottling plant and before that as a materials handler at a stereo assembly plant—some of my own incarnations. I wondered if there was any organizing principle behind all that I'd done and could find none except maybe some vague belief in the sanctity of manual labor. The influence of Kerouac and London. I had fooled myself, I thought, that I was staying my own man.

We came to the tollbooths in Waltham and then began to climb the long last hill that would take us out of the Boston Basin. At the crest I had a last view of the city, an image of hard towers sitting in a yellowish haze, the color of tobacco stains. Marion was down there doing something, pursuing some dream that somehow she'd kept alive for twenty years. The city drifted from sight and I felt acutely my own diminished expectations, as I listened to Joanne and Vane's polite banter in the limousine, speeding westward.

XI

I RETURNED HOME WITH a restaurant dinner sitting in my stomach like a sack of rocks: tough steak, dish-water potatoes, vegetables drowned in butter. The only true remedy for hard-boiled stomach is soda water, so I fixed myself a drink garnished with Johnnie Walker. Then I walked gingerly around my lately vandalized apartment and just managed to keep from checking the closets. I prowled around the place, going to all the windows, hoping for a trace of a breeze. Nothing stirred. The night was as hot and heavy as a steam boiler.

I changed into rugby shorts and tennis shoes without socks. My yuppie uniform. I plopped down on the L-sectional couch that had cost me nine hundred dollars and tried to relax after a job well done. Instead I was bored and restless. Vane's show had taken forever. Not to say he was bad, it just wasn't my music and I had other things on my mind. Marion and John Spenser. I hadn't had a chance to call Spenser before I picked up Vane, so after winding down with my drink I dialed his number.

I'd forgotten the time—it was almost midnight. He was groggy when he answered.

"Jesus, Derek, some people have to work in the morning," he said grumpily. I heard bumping and scraping as he stretched out to check the time. "Jesus. Wait a sec." The phone dropped on a table. Spenser was gone about half a minute and he sounded just as bad when he came back.

"Sorry," he said, "I had to get the brain cells firing."

"You still in one piece?" I asked.

"Sure, why?"

"Any threats? Anymore letters?"

"Not recently. No. Why? Have you had some trouble?"

"Someone broke into my house and rearranged the furniture."

"Anything stolen?"

"No. It was more like a performance piece. 'Life Upside Down.' "

Spenser was quiet. I heard him breathing. Finally he said, "I feel really badly, getting you into this. Sorry."

"Don't worry about me," I told him, "think what it means to you. They're going to try to isolate you. Has anything happened to those two friends of yours?"

"Mike and Len? Not that I know of."

"Ask them. Tell them to keep their eyes open."

"Okay."

"Have you thought any more about what you want to do with McGuiness?"

I heard him sigh, the kind of sigh someone makes when, yes, he's been thinking about something for a long time and still haven't made up his mind. "Yeah," he said simply.

"I still think it's wrong."

"I know," he said, glumly.

"You've got the moral high ground. Keep it. Don't bring yourself down."

"Yeah, yeah."

It was my turn to sigh. We were getting nowhere. I asked about the contract.

That made him sound even more frustrated. "McGuiness called for a mail-in vote, so the thing is as good as done. Two-tier wage schedule and all."

"That's good. That gives you ammunition."

"I've already got ammunition," he answered, leaving off that he thought he just didn't have the guts to use it. That's where he was now, berating himself for lack of courage, which was beside the point.

"You've got the ammunition and you could use it if you wanted to," I pressed. "But you're going to decide not to. It's a complete, considered decision on your part, based on values. It's not a defeat."

I heard him laugh, a sarcastic, jaded sound. He said, "When we had the full membership meeting at the union hall, McGuiness raked me over the coals, without once mentioning my name. He spent most of the time in a detailed history of Local 19, complete with stories of people who tried to break the union. Most of them turning out to be working for management. He lumped me in there with all those flacks and stool pigeons." He said this, his voice round and throaty, full of hurt. "There was no way for me to answer. I couldn't even get the floor. His people kept hogging the microphone. Asking him slow-pitch questions like, 'President McGuiness, what have you done to increase the medical benefits of your members?' " He laughed bitterly. "Quite a performance."

"You've got to expect that treatment," I said.

"What? Yeah, right." He went on, not really listening to me or his answer. "I just sat there and took it. People started looking at me, like it was a game and they were waiting for my move. But I was stuck. It was his show, his territory. I was helpless. Finally I stood up and shouted something and gave him the chance to rule me out of order and jump on my case. A fiasco."

"That was just one meeting. Learn from it. There'll be others."

"Others? Right. And pretty soon I'll become the quack with his inane comments who keeps trying to interrupt the noble president at every meeting. I saw guys like that when I first signed on. They looked like nuts to me. Frustrated outsiders. I remember thinking they should just shut up and let McGuiness speak. That's when I still trusted him."

I sympathized with him, but his pessimism was starting to get to me. I told him about Dunn County, all the months of organizing, the careful planning for car pools on voting day, the detailed assignment of observers and voting assistants at all the polling sites and how even then we'd lost the election. "But that was just round one, John," I said. "You're not even there yet and you're starting to get down. They kept after it down there."

"How is it there now?"

I stopped. His question froze me because for all the years of effort, Dunn County hadn't really changed. The power still belongs to the whites. The blacks are still the majority and are still without a voice. What has the entire civil rights movement accomplished? There's talk of a "structural underclass." Compared to white kids, twice as many black males never finish high school. Never work a regular job. I remembered what Bill Stacom said, about change being slow, taking place in increments, over generations. John wouldn't want to hear that.

I said it anyway. "Real change takes time, John. You're laying the foundations now. That's enough."

He answered, without conviction, "I envy your patience. I don't think I've got it. I can't accept just laying the foundation. You know that. Listen, I've got to go. Sorry about the trouble." He broke the connection.

And I was left feeling as helpless as Spenser probably felt because I'd done nothing to change his mind. I was beginning to feel useless all around, to Marion, John, neither of whom I could convince or help, and I mixed myself another stiff drink. I needed to get away.

I went up to the roof and took out the Meade. The Orion constellation was up, the Greek warrior frozen against a backdrop of stars like a man caught in mid-stride. A snapshot of past, outmoded history; the ancients' trust in the divinity of stars, their revered Olympus. I looked at it now as a modern; certain of the galaxies hidden in the warrior's sword, sure that if I set my motor drive to 0534 right ascension, -0524 declination, the hazy diffusion of the Great Nebulae would appear before my eyes, a sight of greater history still; light millions of years old, a nova long since cooled, dissipated. I bent over the eyepiece and sighted through shimmering waves of heat rising from the observation deck, making the image float, mirage-like. The dark cloud seemed to move before an intense nova glow, but I felt nothing. The image was as unreal to me as the newspaper reports of presidential primaries and battles in the Persian Gulf; it said nothing to me, gave me no direction, was as mute to me as the Grecian gods. Patience is needed, Bill Stacom says. Patience, I said to John Spenser, time moves slowly but steadily, and good does rise from this mess we make, shining like the clear light from long dead suns.

XII

I CALLED MARION THE NEXT DAY. It was about two in the afternoon and she sounded dazed, as if I'd woke her up or caught her in the middle of something, or maybe I just imagined it. The temperature was climbing into the eighties again but at last the air was moving, coming in off the ocean.

"A good day for Castle Island," I told her.

"Castle Island?" she repeated, as if she'd never heard of it.

"You remember, picnic tables, fields of clover, sailboats in the bay."

There was a momentary silence from Marion's end. I imagined her, her eyes squinting from sleep, absently pushing the hair back off her face.

"I don't know, Derek, I don't think I can."

"Why? Are you worried about the police?"

Her voice was distant. "No, it's just that I got in late last night and I'm tired and I've got stuff to do later."

"When, later?"

"Later."

"So we'll go in the afternoon, stretch out, take it easy."

I knew it sounded like I was trying too hard, being stupidly "up", but I wanted to see Marion as much to get her away from whatever she was doing as anything else. Suddenly I felt like I was competing with her, taking sides in the battle she was fighting with herself. "You looked a little pale the last time I saw you," I plunged on, "You need sun."

"Work on my tan?" she said. I heard the first signs of humor return to her voice.

"A touch of UV poisoning."

"Catch up on my skin cancer." She laughed.

"Like that."

I felt her deliberating. "Okay."

We made arrangements and I hung up the phone. I assembled everything we'd need for the outing, sweaters in case it was cool near the ocean, a blanket, an ice chest with food, all the time enjoying the feeling of thinking for someone else.

When it was time to move everything out to the car I thought about the possibility of Newman waiting outside. I went to the screen door and glanced up and down the street. I couldn't see anyone so I casually strolled down the walk, then ambled both sides of the street. Still, I didn't see anyone so I walked two houses down to my car and almost got in. There was one more possibility. I checked the under carriage and wheel wells, then the front bumper. Under the back bumper I found a donut-shaped hunk of metal—an electronic transmitter. I smiled and carefully pulled it off. If I moved it a few feet they wouldn't detect the motion. I found a suitable clump of bushes and laid the transmitter down by the roots, then loaded the car and drove away.

When I reached Marion's she was sitting on the steps of Ron's apartment and when she saw me she picked up her bag and approached me without a smile or wave. She got in and leaned deeply into the seat, distant, preoccupied. We didn't talk much as I headed to South Boston.

Castle Island is an oceanside park on the easternmost tip of South Boston, in a blue collar neighborhood where three-decker houses are clustered around factories. South Boston is a no nonsense town and Castle Island is one of its main attractions. It's not really an island, but a peninsula—a drumlin connected to the mainland by a narrow beach. The peninsula juts out into Boston harbor and from the hill that rises in the center you have a clear, windswept panorama of the bay with islands scattered around like a herd of sleeping whales. The skyline of Boston lies due west with a glass and metal forest of skyscrapers looming over the rotting wooden piers of the waterfront.

It seemed as though most of Southie had turned out to take advantage of the clear day. Strolling with us along the narrow path were dawdling elderly couples, lovers arm-in-arm, packs of teenagers hooting and hollering, young parents herding their preschoolers and pushing infants in carriages. A toddler broke away from her mother and made a break for the beach, flailing her arms and giggling with newfound motor control over arms and legs. To walk unaided! Marion intercepted her and swept her off the ground. "Where're you going?" She laughed as she hauled her catch back to her mother, who had her hands full with a baby in diapers. While she and Marion talked I turned my face to the ocean and the onshore wind, letting it blow my hair back. The bay was dark blue and choppy; catspaw gusts made white caps on the rolling waves. The bay seethed with sailboats: single-sail dingies; day-sailers with jibs unfurled; slow, comfortable sloops and sleek wood-hulled racers. Bowing with the wind, slicing deep through the waves, the boats tacked and jibbed, racing before the wind. Marion gave a wave to the young mother and came back, slipping her arm through mine. We headed off the path and struck uphill, walking over long, green grass and clover heavy with fat white and purple blossoms. We found a low-limbed elm almost at the hill crest and I spread out the blanket in its shade. Marion stood and took in the scene, a smile turning up the ends of her mouth. She laughed.

"What?" I asked.

"It's just as I remembered it," she said. "This place was always hopping." She lowered herself beside me and stretched out, her gray eyes no longer inpenetrable, but bright and liquid. She was free again. "What have you got in that cooler?" she asked.

We popped juicy grapes into our mouths and took in the scene, vignettes appearing like short slices of a play: two sailboats off-tacking to avoid collision, the dangerous heel of a day-sailer under a sudden gust, a teenager dancing to a song on the radio, skip, jump, a two-step.

Far out in the harbor a cargo ship lay at anchor with another beyond it. Behind that one too, there would be more ships, tankers waiting for entrance to the inner harbor, a chain of ships curling around Winthrop Head. Just below the Head was Logan Airport, festooned with jetliners: L-1011's, sleek as greyhounds; mammouth, mesozoic 747's. From our perch under the elm we watched them taxi, lumbering heavily along the concrete runway until, with surprising grace, the nose lifted, then the entire sleek body, lifting off the ground with engines whining in increasing pitch, the craft ascending, cushioned by air, attaining the impossible, tons of metal and nervous passengers rising up and sweeping over our heads as we craned our necks, rising into the sky, reaching thousands of feet into the fluffy cumulous clouds in seconds. Seeing all this, the ships, the aircraft, the tall buildings beyond the wooden piers angled like bad teeth in murky, dank harbor water, you could feel the rhythm of Boston; commerce, industry, flowing in, out, a pulsing, tidal machine. Marion and I took all this in with the leaves of our elm a canopy from the sunlight.

Marion was happy here—being a spectator where there was a mix of humanity like this around her was the only way she could allow herself to slow down.

She glanced at me out of the corner of her eye. "How was the crooner?"

"Okay. A paycheck."

"How can you stand it?" she asked.

"What?"

"Working at something not particularly interesting, just for a paycheck?"

"That's how nine-tenths of the world lives, Marion."

"I'm asking *you.*"

"It's not all terrible," I answered. "Some cases are interesting, particular problems that are difficult to fix."

She nodded silently, her eyes studying my face. "I've worked some crummy jobs too . . ."

"I just said it was all right."

She smiled and ignored my protest, ". . . busy work, secretarial work, factory-piece work. I made decent money but found it nearly impossible to get out of bed in the morning. So then I took other jobs in day-care, social services. Rotten money, but it felt better. It reminded me that anything we do feels better when it helps someone else."

"That's you . . . and Bill," I said. "He keeps trying to explain that to Jeremy but it never sinks in."

Marion looked out to the harbor and watched a sloop tack to starboard. "Jeremy," she said, "he's a survivor. I suppose he's well-off by now."

"Comfortable."

"He never gave a damn about what we were doing. He just wanted to be 'in.'"

"Didn't we all?"

She smiled. "I suppose. I suppose that's how it happens. We start out playing kid's games and somehow they stick with us, become adult games."

"What you do has a little more impact than a kid's game."

She nodded and raised a wry eyebrow. "King of the Hill on a big scale."

"You can't call it a game."

"I know." She stretched out on her back. "Just being cynical. I'm not good at it. I'm too sincere." She chuckled. "Cynicism is your province."

"Thanks."

She reached out and touched my hand. "I meant it as a compliment. I've always thought that cynics are nothing but ruined romantics."

"That's good."

She squinted at me with one eye. "It's true. But you affect a calm detachment. That always helped me, really, before—we made a good team."

"Still could."

She closed her eyes and smiled. "Maybe."

I watched her, seeing the young woman I'd met in Vermont years ago. What had I been attracted to then? It was an air of completeness, an internal confidence—she knew what she was about. The uncertainty I was seeing in her now was new.

I asked, "Why don't you just stick with your social work and quit everything else?"

"Don't start," she said, "you'll just get us into troubled waters."

"I'm serious now," I pressed on, "why can't you go after what that couple we saw last night has? Isn't that enough to work for?"

Marion pursed her lips and squinted at me again. "You're determined to pursue this, aren't you?"

"Who, me?"

"Yes, you." She sat up. "Let's take a stroll," she said.

We started off down the hill and I saw the mother whose toddler Marion had hauled in, so I steered us in that direction, filled with half-formed schemes. The woman and her two children were sitting on a flower-patterned blanket, and as we drew near I heard her say to the oldest, "Now that you've stood up, how are you going to get back down? You're on your own, kid."

Marion called out, "Jessica, how's it working out?"

Jessica looked up at us, smiling wearily, "I need four hands," she said.

Marion introduced us and I looked at the toddler, a skinny baby for her age, with pink cheeks, blond curls as fine as the down on an ear of corn, and a wild look in her eyes as she prepared to charge off towards the beach again.

I said, "Amy seems determined to strike off on her own."

"She's a wanderer, all right," Jessica said.

"Can we take her for a walk, if we stay close?"

Jessica looked grateful. "Tire her out, will you? And stay close."

"Come on, Marion," I said. We each took one of Amy's hands and walked her between us. Marion walked stooped over, slipping naturally into baby talk. Amy wore a look of splendid ecstasy.

"Let's take her over by the water," Marion said.

At the railing overlooking the bay, Marion hoisted Amy to her hip. Down below us waves struck the riprap wall and the little girl was fascinated by the slap and foam. Marion pointed out the sights: sailboat, cargo ship, airliner, island.

"She's not getting any of this," I said.

"You'd be surprised," Marion said.

We took Amy for a long walk, winding along the path that followed the bay. We gave her a real naturalist's tour, explaining about trees and clouds and flowering clover. She listened to us with exquisite uncomprehension, pulling pea petals off the clover with exacting concentration, poking the elm's ragged bark with a stubby finger. Marion handled her with that intuitive feminine ease that men know they'll never possess. Whenever we handle a child it always seems to be a special deal, out of the ordinary, and we're as self-conscious as boys at their first dance. I hung back, letting Marion do everything, hoping that balancing Amy on her hip, holding her out for an up-close inspection of maple leaves, would tip the scales away from her life in the underground.

Amy began to wind down and look worriedly for her mother, so Marion said, with what I hoped was regret, "We'd better get her back."

Jessica was in the middle of a messy diaper change when we returned. "Great," she said, "we're down to our last diaper here, time to go home." She pressed her nose into her baby's stomach, "Time to go home, isn't it?" She packed Amy and everything else into an old, worn stroller and marched off, waving goodbye. I don't know what Marion was thinking, but she watched for a long time as Jessica wound her way through the afternoon crowd.

When we returned to our blanket the sky was filling up with dramatic, extravagant cumulous clouds in constant motion and changing shape before high-altitude winds. As we watched, the clouds billowed, lobes of shining vapor striking higher, foaming upward in streams of sunlight. On the horizon the white clouds turned to black in an approaching storm front, and the wind about us picked up in intensity, the harbor waves becoming more violent. We followed a wind gust as it blew past our tree, ripping off leaves, hurtling down the hill and raising dust on the walk, the skirts of women, speeding out over the water, visible as a dark spread of ripples, heeling the sailboats on the bay.

Marion leaned back and cradled her head in her hands. "Feel that storm coming. The change in the air."

I watched her fall into a light sleep. The smile on her lips faded as her face relaxed, her eyelids fluttering with the reading motion of the eyes beneath. I studied her high cheek bones and the soft skin stretched taut over them. All the years between us and I still felt protective of her, despite her confidence, her self-assurance.

After the defeat in Dunn County Marion had packed up and left Vermont for Boston. She moved into a loosely organized commune, an antiwar group, in a down-at-the-heels neighborhood in Mattapan, in an apartment where rats scrabbled ceaselessly between the walls. She immediately began planning rallies, marches, sit-ins. This was 1967 and the antiwar movement was picking up steam. From my secluded campus in Vermont I could feel the tempo of protests growing stronger, more urgent, and in January of '68 I was no longer able to ignore the issue. By then everyone in the country was taking sides, polarizing like metal to opposite ends of a magnet. I still felt the flush of my experience in the South, felt like a veteran, mature, seasoned, and I thought I could do Marion's outfit some good. Lend a sense of professionalism. Besides, I missed her. I headed for Boston.

I reached Mattapan after an all-day marathon hitch-hike and stumbled into Marion's neighborhood after dark. Marion's street was in a hollow between a high ridge and a narrow, sluggish river. There were warehouses along the river, most of them abandoned, with shattered windows that looked like jack-o'-lantern teeth. Across from the warehouses a row of tenements sat dwarfed by a black forest that climbed the ridge behind them. It was a bitter night when I arrived and no one was on the street, just me and two starved dogs who eyed me speculatively. When I got to the number Marion had mailed to me, I thought there was a mistake. The building was flanked by two burned-out hulks and was unlit in front. The windows were smashed, the front door ajar. I walked up the broken front steps and peered into a black hallway that looked like it led to the bowels of the earth. Incredibly, I heard voices, loud and happy, from somewhere in back. Watching my footing, with a hand touching the wall for direction, I moved through the hall, bits of plaster and broken glass crunching under my feet. I saw a light from a crack under the rearmost door. When I got there it was opened slightly and I gave it a light shove and stepped in.

An envelope of warmth swept out to surround me and I stood stunned momentarily by the heat, blinking in the yellow light. The talk in the room stopped and I was aware that all eyes were turned on me. I felt like a person who had stumbled on stage by accident during a performance.

When I managed to regain my wits I began to make sense of the scene and was snapped to focus by Marion's voice: "Derek! It's about time!"

She was in the center of a cluttered, littered room, standing before an ancient press, the kind operated by turning a handle. She had on the inevitable sweatshirt and jeans, her hands smeared with printer's ink, a streak on her chin. She was smiling at my confusion. "It's about time," she repeated. "Get over here and work this crank."

I was still stunned and feeling awkward. "Give me a moment to thaw out, for Christ's sake," I said. "I'm frozen solid."

I dropped my shoulder, slid my pack to the floor and took in my surroundings. The room was furnished with tables and chairs that looked like they'd been picked up off the street before rubbish removal. The table was peeling several layers of paint, the armchair disgorged a disreputable looking stuffing and the lone book shelf was nothing more than a few boards held up by concrete blocks. There were half a dozen people in the room, none of them over twenty, surveying me with varying degrees of interest. Before I could respond to Marion's injunction, one of the men came up to me. He was shorter than I and had shoulder-length brown hair parted in the middle. He had large round eyes that were always, I learned, filled with mirth, as if he were perpetually observing some astounding event. He was, really, because he found life a source of constant amazement. He was Richard Del Tredia.

Richard introduced himself, shaking my frozen hand enthusiastically. His hand felt like a red-hot poker in mine.

"Wow. Cold hand, warm heart," he said. "You're nearly frostbitten. Let's get something warm in you. I think there's some stew left."

Marion wiped her hands on a soiled rag and hurried over to throw her arms around me.

"You made it! I wasn't sure you'd come. Are you going to stay? Have you left school?" She was full of questions.

"Yeah, I'll stay, probably," I said, with what I thought was admirable bravado.

"Great!" she said, and turned to the group in the room. "People. Another soldier."

She introduced me. At the table, sorting leaflets, was a girl named Margaret, a homey-looking sandy blond with a big-boned face of innumerable freckles. Across from her was a pudgy kid, big and clumsy, named Bill, and in the armchair, strumming an expensive Martin guitar, was Jeremy. He waved at me when we were introduced.

"The rest of the people are upstairs," Marion said. "We've all got crazy hours, working stupid jobs, mostly, and handing out leaflets when we can."

"Give him a minute to catch his breath," Rich said. He tapped my shoulder. "Let's get some food in you."

We went out into the dark hall to a stairway with Rich talking like a tour guide.

"We've got the whole back of the building, three floors. The bottom floor's the shop, the second floor is the kitchen and common rooms and the bedrooms are on the third floor. We sleep communally."

"Sounds good."

"It works out okay, so long as everyone cooperates."

There was a door at the head of the stairs, closing off what was once the main hallway. When we passed through it everything became a little more normal, the adjoining hall was heated and lighted and the smells of cooking, a pungent meaty smell, wafted in the air. Rich led me into the kitchen where two teenagers sat at a metal table.

"Have a seat," he said, motioning to the table. He went over to the stove, lifted the cover off a ten-gallon pot and said, "You're in luck."

I sat down with the kids at the table. They both looked bummed out, arms crossed over their chests, staring vacantly at the table top. One had long, reddish-blond hair that hung down over his shoulders and a thick mustache that covered his lips. The other had black plastic glasses and springy black hair that was coerced into a ponytail in back.

"You guys work here, too?" I asked.

The black-haired one answered, "Just passing through. On our way to Canada."

"The draft?"

They nodded simultaneously.

"Where're you going?"

They looked at each other as if it was a matter of debate. The black-haired one said, "Montreal, probably. Maybe Toronto. We hear the music scene's good there."

His partner snorted. "Maybe we can join Jesse Winchester's band. Call ourselves the Dodgers."

Rich placed a steaming bowl in front of me. "The sarcastic one is Jimmy Hersey. The optimist is Robert Glazier."

Glazier asked, "You headed north?"

"I got myself a deferment. Family contacts."

"Did you register?" Hersey asked.

"Of course."

He shook his head with disgust. "Registering is as bad as going over and fighting. You're still supporting the war."

Rich sat down with us. "We've held a couple of draft card burnings. That's why we're a way station for people like Jimmy and Robert heading over the border."

The way he said it, it seemed that Hersey and Glazier occupied some exalted, noble status and suddenly I felt embarrassed for my smugness at having some political pull.

"I refused to register," Rich continued. "To do so would be implicit support of the whole system. And even if any of us do manage to duck the draft, it doesn't mean we're absolved of resisting an immoral war."

I was caught off guard, plunging from what I thought was a daring act of joining Marion and her group to being placed in an uncomfortable position. The daring ex-civil rights worker had taken the lazy route and evaded his responsibility. The price of freedom is eternal vigilance, Jefferson had said. I learned that all over again. As I plunged ravenously into my bowl of stew I had my first inkling that my comfortable college days were over for good.

I heard Marion's rapid footsteps coming up the stairs as I was finishing the last piece of stew beef in my bowl. She tromped into the kitchen and threw herself into a chair beside me.

Her eyes were bright and cheerful. "We're going to have a meeting soon. You'll see how we operate."

"Great."

"What do you think of the place?"

"It's a rathole."

She laughed. "It's not Simpson Hall, but what did you expect?"

"Four solid walls. A roof. Not much."

"You can always go back."

I shook my head, although the thought had crossed my mind.

I wanted a chance to adapt to the haphazard surroundings. "No," I said, "we've got business to do."

Marion nodded with a satisfied gleam. "That's right. It's like the South all over again, Derek. Only this time we're going to finish the job. Right?"

"We did everything we could, Marion. We were just volunteers. There's only so much a volunteer can do."

"You're wrong," she answered. "We let those people down."

"They let themselves down."

She shook her head, her mouth a thin line of tightly drawn lips. "You've got it wrong. You'll see," she said.

We went into the common room, where the meeting was to be held. The room was once a dining area for another apartment that Marion's band had walled off and made their own. There was an odd conglomeration of doors leading to plywood boards. There were no windows and no furniture, just overstuffed pillows thrown along the baseboards. The room had the musty, damp smell of a place that never saw the sun. The only light came from scores of candles set up everywhere. The place felt like the church of some underground sect.

I sat against the rear wall and watched a motley assortment of teenagers straggle in: the boys with long, unkempt hair and faded bellbottoms; the girls in baggy jeans or overalls, although some, like Margaret, favored long print dresses. The hubbub of conversation died down when Marion took the floor.

"We've got a new member, people," she told the new arrivals. "His name's Derek and he worked with me down south." This brought admiring applause. I waved like a ballplayer being introduced before a game.

Marion went on: "And staying with us for a few days before heading north is Jimmy Hersey and Robert Glazier." Again applause.

"Right on!" someone shouted.

"Right, fucking on," Marion said. She collected her thoughts. "You all know about the rally," she said. "Rich will cover that in a minute. We need more help printing leaflets and especially more help getting them circulated around the city.

I want everyone who goes to work to take ten of them everyday and post them before they get to wherever they're going. And we need more paper. Anyone have any ideas where we can get some cheap?"

"Rip it off," a voice called out.

"Good idea," Marion said, "but we don't want anyone busted for common theft."

"Try the colleges," I suggested.

"The school newspapers?" Marion asked.

"Right."

"Great idea. You've got yourself your first job."

Having made a contribution I felt better, slightly more comfortable, and I settled back to listen.

"Posters," Marion continued, "I have some ideas for posters but I don't want to hog the whole process. I think everyone should make their own. But I was wondering if all slogans should be approved first."

"Bullshit!"

"Hell, no!"

Marion smiled. "That's what I thought. But let's try not to be too flip, this is serious stuff. No, 'Ho, ho, ho, Ho Chi Minh.'"

Marion finished up saying she was wrangling a parade permit from the city and then she handled some of the more mundane details of running the commune: cleaning assignments, shopping duties, a request for someone to try and fix a leaking faucet. Then she turned the meeting over to Rich. She came over and sat beside me, slipping her arm through mine.

Rich got up slowly and entered the circle with his head down, taking his time to collect his thoughts.

I settled in, lulled by the candlelight, enjoying the feeling of being involved again, to be with people serving a common cause. I took Marion's hand in mine and gave it a light squeeze which she returned. It's all we needed to do.

Rich's glasses caught the candlelight as he tapped his lip with his index finger. He had a faint smile on his face, like he was preparing to tell a joke.

"Well," he began, "I've been talking with the other organizers of this rally." He pointed his chin at the ceiling as if the other organizers might be hiding in the rafters. "I don't really know what to make of them." He paused again. He was a slow talker. "I don't know if we're really compatible. The Weathermen seem a bit wild-eyed. A bit too much of the nihilist in them. They want to tear everything down. I'm not too sympathetic to that." He lowered his head and his lanky brown hair swung off his shoulders. He scratched his ear. "The SDS are more in our sphere. They're more focused on stopping the war, which is where our main concern is now. They're a bit too snobby, however. They're college brats when you get down to it. Changing the curriculum is high on their list."

Hoots and whistles from the assembly. I knew what he was talking about, but weren't we really college drop-outs, college brats, too?

Marion seemed to know what I was thinking and pulled me close to whisper, "We prefer that everyone who joins us leaves college completely behind. College life is irrelevent."

"It is?"

"Completely."

I thought I'd bring that up with her later and turned my attention back to Rich.

"In any event," he was saying, "in this action we're going to work most closely with the SDS, for one simple reason. They're dedicated to nonviolence, and we are too. You don't fight aggression with aggression. Then you're just playing the enemy's game. And in that case the enemy will always win. You don't stop a war by beating on your own people. No. We intend to lead by example." Rich was smiling now, a broad, prideful grin, and it seemed to me that in the candlelight his skin glowed, heat emanated from the tight flesh on his cheekbones and from the starburst shining of his eyes behind his glasses. The kid beside me was rocking back and forth, listening to Rich.

"If there was any group you could identify us with in history," Rich said, "and comparisons like that are important, they're like guideposts on the road for us, if there was one group I would match us with it would be the early Christians. Not," he put his hand up, "not that I believe in that Westernized, bastardized, monolithic, multi-national corporation that exists today. We are offering our actions not for some removed God in a fairytale heaven, but for peace here on earth.

"So at this rally we're going to march, we're going to speak and *be heard*, we're going to sing, we're going to show the people that they don't have to fight, that they don't have to kill the people of Vietnam."

Cheers broke out as Rich finished speaking. Marion took her hand from mine and clapped. The kid beside me raised his arms and waved them over his head. They all believed Richard . . . he got me going too.

He went on to lay out the details for the march and rally, which were to take place in a week. The rally would take place on the Boston Common and from there we would march to city hall, where six draftees would burn their draft cards. "Hopefully," Jeremy called out from a corner, "for the waiting eyes of the news cameras."

Marion tugged my arm, "Jeremy's our media specialist."

"Media specialist?"

She nodded. "We don't mess around. If you've got a message you have to use every means you can to get it across."

Rich was running his eyes over the kids assembled around the edges of the room. "Okay," he said, "anyone else want to speak?"

The big, pudgy kid named Bill raised his hand.

"Okay, take the floor," Rich said. He went over and took Bill's place beside Margaret.

Bill ambled awkwardly to center stage, more shyly than either Marion or Rich had, and I guessed that he wasn't used to being the focus of attention. He stood with his shoulders hunched, the way big people do to make themselves smaller. His hair was long but it was still cut in a traditional style, something like a boy's regular with a side part and the back cut straight across the neck, the resulting combination as awkward as his movements. He looked to the girl, Margaret, before speaking, with a shy smile that looked like an appeal for help.

"We all walk in and out of this neighborhood every day," he began, "and a lot of us have mentioned that we don't feel particularly safe. Margaret, for one, has talked about this." He smiled at the girl. "It's tough on the girls," he said. "Now, we can either organize some sort of patrol or we can try to win over our neighbors, which I think is more in keeping with our ethics. It's something we should do anyway, I think, otherwise we risk becoming like Mrs. Jellyby in *Bleak House,* who focuses her help on people far away and forgets her own home." He smiled apologetically for the literary reference. "We shouldn't forget our own back yard."

"What have you got in mind?" Rich asked.

Bill brushed back his blond hair, which had a habit of falling over his eyes.

"Well," he began, "there's a park, Dooley Park, at the top of this hill behind us." He jerked a thumb over his shoulder. "It's a mess right now. Broken glass, broken basketball rims, stuff like that." He took a deep breath and gathered his momentum. "I propose that we go up there and clean the place up. Maintain it."

"Great idea," Marion said.

Rich added, "We can post a sign saying 'Cleaned by the Day Street Commune.'"

Bill's face contorted in disagreement. "I think we should do it anonymously. I mean, the word will spread anyway, and it will look better if we don't trumpet what we do. Too showy. We're doing this because people should help out their neighbors, not for self-advertisement."

This set off a spirited debate among the commune members and even the draft-dodger, Robert Glazier, got involved.

"I agree with Bill," Glazier said. "You folks want to be a sort of center of correct thinking. You want your ideals to kind of emanate out into the streets. Advertising makes you seem self-serving."

"But we want people to know who and what we are." Rich said.

"They will," Glazier said. "but who you are will spread by word of mouth, which is much more effective."

"I don't really care if the word spreads anyway," Bill said. "What we are isn't important. I just feel that if we improve the conditions in this neighborhood the people will improve too. They're good people at heart. It's the conditions that make them steal."

Margaret spoke up, "Bill, it'll take forever for us to feel safe unless the kids around here learn about us right away."

Bill gave her a sympathetic smile. "It won't take all that long, Margy, and the effects will be much more lasting. Do we want to be the good people who keep doing nice things around the streets, just to do them? Or do we want to be the do-gooders who are always looking for a return on their investments?"

I could feel Marion tugging with excitement on my arm. She could hardly wait for Bill to finish before she broke in, "It's not self-advertising, Bill. We'd just be announcing ourselves to our neighbors. It's a pointed gesture, sure, but it doesn't diminish the effect."

The big kid sighed. "Well, I'll leave it up to a vote, but I really think we should just be a positive force and leave it at that."

The vote was in favor of posting a sign, which clearly disappointed Bill, but he took the defeat with a shrug and a smile.

Robert Glazier had watched the proceedings stoically, with his legs stretched out straight before him and his arms folded calmly across his chest. Now he pushed up his black glasses with his index finger and said, "I think Bill has a really valid idea and you folks should expand on it. Don't stop with the park. Do other things too."

"What else should we start?" Rich asked, not just to Glazier, but the group in general.

A redheaded girl with a narrow, serious face, who had her arms wrapped around her knees, said, "The women in this area have to work during the day. That's why there's so many kids running loose with no one watching them. Maybe we can offer to watch them during the day."

"I'm not taking care of some of those hoods," another girl said.

Marion jumped in, "We could limit it to young children, infants to ten years old, something like that."

"Do you think the mothers would really trust us with their kids?" the girl answered.

"We'll have to win them over," Marion said.

"I think we should try it," Rich said. "What else?"

"I know a lot about cars," Jeremy said. "Maybe we could do repair work at cost."

"Or just offer help," the kid beside me, who was still rocking, said.

"That's good, too," Rich said, turning his broad face to Jeremy. "It'll take work. Some investment. Let's think about that and watching the children."

It was decided that the park clean-up would start after the rally, and the meeting began to wind down. It ended, as usual, I learned, with a song, led by Jeremy. When it came time to sing he grabbed quickly for his Martin, as if this was what he'd been waiting for all the time. He gave the strings a quick, forceful strum and then picked off a set of dazzling notes.

"We'll do 'The Times They Are A-Changin',' " he said.

Everyone knew the lyrics to the Dylan song, and in the dark room, pungent with the smell of liquid wax, I felt I was in a chapel, a small corner of a vast church, as a congregation sang together:

> Come gather 'round people wherever you roam,
> And admit that waters around you have grown,
> And accept it that soon you'll be drenched to the bone,
> If your time to you is worth saving,
> Then you better start swimmin'
> Or you'll sink like a stone,
> For the times they are a-changin'.

Their voices rose, getting stronger with each line, Marion's soft, breathy voice, Rich's low, hesitant bass, growing more sure:

The line it is drawn
the curse it is cast
and the slow one now will
later be fast
As the present now will
later be past
The order is rapidly fading
And the first one now will
later be last
For the times, they are a-changin'.

There in the dark room, the young voices rising around me, the words seemed to be true.

"That was well done," I said later to Marion. We were lying in the dark of one of the private rooms reserved for special occasions on the third floor. Everyone else slept four or five to a room.

"It's a good group," she said. "At least we've got a good core—Rich, Bill, Margy, me, Priscilla . . ."

"Who's that?"

"The red-haired woman who suggested taking in the children."

"Ah." I bent down and kissed Marion on the lips, the forehead, her high-boned cheeks.

"I didn't think you'd leave Vermont," she said.

"I thought I'd had enough after the County, but I guess it's gotten into my blood. I felt at a loss in the Green Mountains."

I slipped off of her and lay on my back. I took her hand and put it on my stomach. The house was quiet, except for the sound of sleepers turning over in the next room.

"Is that the only reason you came down?" she asked.

I smiled. "I thought about you and what you were doing all the time I was up there. And I wanted to do my part in stopping this war. The two thoughts somehow merged. I wanted to do my part and I wanted to do it with you." I squeezed her hand. "I kept thinking about your shiny black hair."

I heard a chuckle in the dark. "Is that all you thought about?"

"Do you want to hear all of the erotic details?"

Another chuckle. "Yes."

"You would," I said. "What about you? Have you got anyone down here?"

"Everyone and no one."

"I'm not sure I like that."

"Don't be possessive, Derek."

I turned on my side and caught her eyes in mine. Her face was firm, immobile, warning me that she meant what she said.

"I'm a free person," she said, "I belong to no one and no one belongs to me."

"I'm going to change your mind on that, Marion Wilson."

Her face softened, but her eyes remained cool. "You are?"

"I am."

We made love again that first night, but it was different for me because I felt a weight, as if other men were watching me, waiting for a wrong move, for their chance to take my place.

My first assignment for the commune went well. I found a sympathetic ear at every college newspaper office I went to looking for paper for our leaflets—every campus in the country was radicalized in those days—and at the same time I allowed myself to be interviewed as a representative of the 'Day Street Commune.' Free publicity for the rally. I was happy because I'd landed on my feet in the organization and had come up running. And because Marion was pleased. My experience at organizing in the South had paid off—I was helping people again . . . kids my age in the States, people I'd never see or know in Vietnam. It felt good . . . right.

But my success didn't win Marion's full attention. She and Richard Del Tredia had been lovers since she'd joined the commune and they continued with my arrival. Spending time with Marion became a matter of circumstance—whether whatever job you were doing happened to throw you together. I started juggling my schedule so that as the evening came Marion and I were somehow together. But I didn't like the feeling, this covert campaign of mine which ran counter to the ideals of the other members. I felt like I had a secret from the rest. At least Bill and Margy were open about their feelings—about staying faithful to each other. I would have been too, but my problem was that Marion would have none of it. She said she didn't understand what their idea of being 'faithful' meant. That there are a thousand ways to be faithful.

Preparations for the rally began to accelerate. We stopped printing leaflets two days before the event and concentrated on getting them hung around the city, on lampposts, in laundromats, in coffee houses, dormitories, in the subway, anywhere we could think of. Jeremy was doing his job as media representative—he gave interviews to *Boston After Dark*, the *Globe*, the rock and roll radio stations. He had a natural gift for separating himself from the innumerable radical groups that filled Boston, making our hodge-podge band of some twenty-odd people seem like an established voice for the antiwar movement. The rally became an event put on by the Day Street Commune and the Weathermen and SDS.

We heard one of his radio interviews during an evening meeting.

"Music is an integral part of our method," he told the radio reporter. "That's why we'll be having music between all the speeches. Our music carries our message as well as any one speaker."

"We are going to have music?" Rich asked him.

Jeremy swept back his long, thin, black hair with both hands in a quick movement. "That occurred to me as I was talking to the reporter. It's true, isn't it? Our music is our message."

"I don't disagree," Marion said. She was sitting next to Richard. "But you should have spoken to the group, first."

Jeremy did his best to look contrite. "I know. But it felt like a revelation when we were talking. I thought you wouldn't object. It is a good idea."

"Who's going to do the singing?" Rich asked drily.

"I thought I would," Jeremy answered, looking at the tops of his sneakers. He looked up, "That is, if we can't find someone better known."

Rich said, sarcastically, "Oh, yeah, we could get Tom Rush at the last minute."

"Or Joan Baez," I added.

"Or Bob Dylan," Marion said.

"I'm sorry," Jeremy said, "I wish I'd thought of it sooner."

"Well, you can handle it," Rich said. "It is a good idea. But let's vote anyway."

After the meeting I caught up with Marion.

"Let's go for a walk," I suggested.

"I can't," she answered. "Rich and I have some things to talk about and then we've got kitchen duty."

"Who arranged that?"

"Arranged what?"

"That you'd have the kitchen detail together."

Her mouth turned up in a smirk. "No one did. It rotates on a system all on its own." She fingered a button on my shirt. "Derek, you're here, I'm here. Isn't that enough?"

I didn't answer. I wanted to say no, but thought that it would be the wrong thing to say. Instead I said, "Maybe I'll see you later."

"Maybe."

But I was sleeping alone in the communal room when I heard Marion and Rich come up the stairs much later. They laid down in a far corner and I listened as they stripped off their clothes and settled together.

The day of the rally the commune was up and active at six in the morning. No one ate anything, we were too nervous and eager to get going. Instead, most of us slurped down a cup of coffee while preparing for our assignments. Marion, Margy, Priscilla and the rest of the girls were in charge of getting the posters and banners together and to the Common. Rich, Jeremy and I were to go and pick up sound equipment and haul it over before the rally.

I stood in the downstairs shop and watched as Marion made

last-minute preparations. She was in her gray sweatshirt again, and the only thing that had changed with her was that she'd forsaken her boot-leg jeans for a pair of bell-bottoms. The pants were snug around her waist and hugged her thighs and calves. I went up to her and wrapped my arms around her shoulders. She gave me an excited hug.

"Are you ready?" she asked.

"Ready," I said.

Priscilla came over, her freckled face pale with nervous energy. She was smiling. Marion reached out an arm and pulled her into our embrace. I noticed for the first time that Priscilla's eyes were an electric green.

"You must be Irish," I said to her.

"You guessed," she said.

I gave both Priscilla and Marion a kiss on the cheek. "Gonna be a long day."

"A good day," Priscilla said.

"Come on, Derek, time to be motorin'," Rich called.

Marion gave me a long, hard kiss on the lips. Priscilla's lips brushed cheek. "Good luck," she said.

I marched out through the hall feeling like I had springs on my feet. Action. I was energized, a ready soldier, a soldier for peace. I met Rich and Jeremy at the door. We gave each other the power hand shake, our faces wide with smiles.

"Wahoo!" Rich yelled.

It was early February and the day had that kind of cold that has a snap to it. The air as brisk and clear as glassy ice. A bright, blue, bottomless sky stretched endlessly to the heavens above us. It was the kind of day where anything seems possible.

The three of us climbed into the commune's VW bus, an old van whose dark green paint had faded to a dusty finish. The door on the passenger's side was wired closed with a clothes hanger, only the driver's windshield wiper worked, and the rear fender had been crushed in by some previous owner. Rich drove. The bus started hesitantly with a sputter and plume of blue smoke. Rich ground it into gear and we lurched forward.

"We're off!" I yelled.

As we drove to the rental store in Brighton, Jeremy pulled a mouth harp from his dungaree jacket and began to play a rapid, breathy blues tune.

"You're good," I said.

He took the harp from his mouth, leaving it cupped in his hands. "Chicago blues," he said. "I heard this great band the other night at Paul's Mall. The Butterfield Blues band. Outa sight. Horns. Electric guitars. Tight stuff." He put the harp to his lips again and played something low and mournful. "Charlie Musslewhite," he explained.

Rich looked over his shoulder. "Jeremy knows all the bands, don't you, Jeremy?"

"Yeah." He took a deep breath and blew a staccato "Train Time."

To the sounds of Jeremy's ragged tune we bumped through the quiet, dirty streets of Mattapan, through a short stretch of fashionable Brookline, where proud Garrison colonials were still decorated with Christmas lights, across the city to Brighton. The rental outlet was not yet open, so we grabbed a cup of coffee from a donut shop and huddled in the van, which was cold because the heater wasn't working. They never did in Volkswagens.

The shop opened at eight and we went in. There was a kid of about eighteen behind the counter, looking as if he'd just gotten out of bed and had only just made it to the store. He wore a plaid shirt with most of the checks worn off and old corduroys with the cheeks worn out. His brown hair was pulled back in a ponytail. He took his time shuffling papers behind the counter while he got his mind in gear. We didn't hurry him.

Rich pulled Jeremy over to a bank of equipment. The shop was just one room with a counter in the rear and it was full of amplifiers and speakers of all sizes, their fabric-covered faces staring at us blankly.

"What should we get?" Rich asked.

"Big mothers," Jeremy said. "We want to blast the Common."

"Do we have to match outputs and all that electrical stuff?"

"Of course," Jeremy answered.

"I thought you guys knew all this," I said.

Rich grinned. His eyes sometimes got a wild look, bright and amused behind the thick prescription of his glasses. "You could fill a thimble with what I know about sound systems," he said.

"Then why didn't you leave it up to the other groups?"

"Sound is power," Jeremy said. "We got the sound, we run the show."

"There won't be a show if you don't get it right."

Rich laughed. "We'll figure it out. Keep the faith, Derek."

We went up to the kid behind the counter. His face was pinched with the pain of a late night. "What can I do for you brothers?" he asked, rubbing his forehead.

"We need sound. Big sound," Jeremy said.

"What for?"

We told him about the rally on the Common.

His face lit up. "You brothers running that? Outa sight. My friends are going." He clenched a fist and raised it over his head. "Stop the war!"

We smiled in unison and raised our fists too.

We followed the kid, whose name was Paul, into the low valleys between the walls of equipment and he matched up a powerful amp with four speakers that stood five feet tall.

"I'll give you an Altec dynamic range microphone so you don't have to worry about wind pick-up," he told us. "You don't have to worry about frequency response." Rich and I nodded as if that meant something to us. Jeremy looked pleased.

"Yeah, that's okay for the speeches, but we're going to have music too."

"Music? Far out. I'd give you a ribbon mike but it's not good for outdoors." Paul tugged thoughtfully at his ponytail. "Tell you what," he decided, "I'll give you a cardioid mike. It's got a heart-shaped pick-up pattern and it'll reduce wind hiss."

He hurried behind the counter and came back with a box

still stapled closed for shipping. "We just got this one in, brand new. I'll check it out for you first."

He set up the equipment we were going to use, the four speakers, the amp, the two mikes, and showed us how to patch them together with a confusing array of electric cables.

"What are you using for power?" Paul asked. Rich and Jeremy looked at each other.

"Man, the Common doesn't exactly sprout electrical outlets," Paul said. "You need a gas generator."

Rich's face broke into his wild grin. "I didn't think of that."

We stood in a tense silence until Paul started laughing. "No power, too much," he said. "You guys are lucky. You came to the *right* place." He went back to the counter. "I've got a friend that works in a power tool rental store."

Paul made arrangements with his friend and helped us load the equipment into the van. When we were finished Rich started back into the shop for a receipt.

Paul put up his hand. "No charge, brother."

"No charge?" Rich said. "Don't you even want a deposit?"

"I trust you man," Paul said, and he made a V with his fingers. "Peace." He started to walk away and then turned back. "Don't forget gas for the generator!" he yelled.

We drove off laughing.

"Good vibes," Jeremy said, throwing his head back and shaking it with amazement. "Good vibes."

Paul's friend gave us a generator free of charge too, and when we left his store we felt like some benign deity was watching over us. "Our Lady of the Peace Marchers," we called her. Just to see how far we could go, when we stopped to buy gas for the generator we looked for a place where another long hair was working and told him what we were about. No charge. The vibes were definitely good.

When we got to the Common the other two groups were hammering the last boards onto a makeshift speaker's platform. Rich brought us over to the SDS leader, Robert DuBois, and pulled him aside. DuBois was tall and malnourished looking, as if eating was one of life's inconveniences he usually forgot. He had the intense piercing stare and pale, sallow skin of the college radical.

"Did you bring the bullhorn?" he asked Rich.

Rich's wild grin spread across his face as he led DuBois to the van.

DuBois' eyes widened. "Far out!" he said. "When you guys do it up, you do it up right."

The three of us were smiling, but we tried to look nonchalant, as if this was the way the Day Street Commune always operated.

"I'll get you some help," DuBois said.

Rich put up his hand. "We'll do it. Patching everything together is a bit confusing."

We hauled everything on stage and we were surrounded by curious onlookers when the rest of the Commune arrived. I didn't see them come, so it was Rich who greeted Marion. He was watching for her.

"Everything set?" she asked as Rich helped her onto the platform.

"Lights, action, camera," Rich said lightly.

Marion gave the setup a cool appraisal. "Will this stuff be loud enough?"

"They'll hear us in Quincy," Rich said.

"They'll hear us in Los Angeles if we get on the news," Marion answered. "Jeremy!" she called out. "Any reporters here yet?"

Jeremy looked around from behind a set of speakers. A crowd was beginning to gather already, a knot of fifty people standing in the cool February sunlight. They had begun to arrive in two's and three's, a slow accumulation like grains of sand carried down a river. When Jeremy looked around I followed his gaze and realized the rally was really going to happen. People were coming to hear us out, to support us, coming from Boston, Cambridge, Jamaica Plain, Somerville, to hear the Day Street Commune and the Weathermen and the SDS. They were going to march with us. Sing with us. Cheer with us as six boys burned pieces of paper. The fire and smoke would join us together.

"I don't see any reporters here yet," Jeremy called out to Marion.

"There's a pay phone in the hotel at the other end of the Common," Marion said. "Call them."

"From the Park Plaza?"

"Why not?"

Jeremy put down the cable and headed off.

Marion turned and looked out over the growing assembly. For the first time she smiled. "It's going to work," she said.

It did work and that day I felt for the first time the antiwar movement gathering like pressure in steel boiler. More than five thousand people joined us on the Common, stood in the winter sun and urged us on. That day was the moment when I felt myself caught up in something bigger than myself. I felt I had become part of an extended family, that, as Paul had said, we really were brothers and sisters, that everywhere I turned would be someone I could trust and understand. It was a feeling you don't forget.

Long after the rally had ended, in the late morning hours, I lost track of Marion and found myself in the common room, alone with Priscilla. Her red hair was a tangle and her face was pale, her freckles standing out all the more for her weariness. We were slumped on the pillows against the wall, lax from exhaustion. All we could do was laugh at how tired the other looked. Her thin body rested languidly on the pillows and I felt as though time had stopped and that we could lie in that splendid stupor forever. I moved beside her and took her in my arms and she raised her face to mine. The idea that we wanted and could have each other entered my mind like a cool breeze issued through the leaves of an elm tree outside a bedroom window, filled with relief and sweet fragrance. Marion was off with someone else and for the first time I recognized that she was free, and I was too and that this freedom was all right. We were free then, but that kind of freedom never lasts.

* * *

"You're frowning," Marion said.

I opened my eyes and saw her leaning over me. "I was just thinking about Day Street."

"Why the dour look?"

"Because we were so naive and full of ourselves. Because those days are gone, done, over."

"For you, not for me."

The sky overhead was now full of black, heavy clouds. When I turned my head I could see gray bands of rain slanting to the ground across the bay in Quincy.

"The rain's going to reach us soon, maybe we should head for the car," I said.

She smiled. The bitter mood that had infected me hadn't touched her and she was still enjoying the Island. "Let's wait until the last moment," she said, rolling onto her back again, grinning up at the clouds, "I want to feel the cold air that comes just before the rain."

I don't know exactly what I was feeling, a combination, maybe, of envy for her happiness and annoyance because she was pointedly ignoring my mood, but I said, still staring skyward, "As long as you're happy, everything's fine."

"I know what you're thinking, Derek," she answered. "You're bitter because nothing turned out the way you wanted it to. You had a rotten experience in jail so you've drawn in your defenses like some medieval city. You're safe, but you're walled in. The community we had in Day Street is over for you, but only because you ended it yourself. You gave up on it."

"It never existed. We were just a bunch of kids sleeping together."

"Watch out folks. Derek's bitter and isolated, so he's going to cut down his entire past. I know where you're at, Derek, I see it everywhere I go. People who couldn't live up to their own standards so they have to reject them to get by. Those are your issues, not mine."

I didn't answer because I knew she was right. All our sour, bitter emotions that we blame other people for come from who we are. Bitterness is nothing more than anger at yourself, turned outward. Cynicism is doubt of your own motives projected onto others. I was bitter and cynical and I wanted to pull everyone else down with me. Marion was free from those feelings because she had never abandoned her most naive, idealistic dreams. That was what I saw in her, the part of me I saw alive in her and the part of me I wanted to protect when I wanted to protect her. And yet Marion was an extremist, and it was that part of me that I rejected, that I wanted to reject in her, and in John Spenser.

I asked her, "What's your problem, then?"

"Exhaustion," she said, with a faint smile, "I'm tired of running the world's errands."

We watched the clouds roll swiftly past.

"But I don't really have a choice," she went on, "I've got to keep going."

"No, you don't," I said. "You can stop all your plans and programs and 'actions' and melt into the backround."

"You keep saying that," she answered, with that amused upturn of her lips. "Are you sure you're saying it for me, or for yourself? You'd like me to become model citizen Marion because it makes you feel better. Eases your guilt for not doing anything, eases that suspicion that you're really powerless."

"I don't consider following the law inaction or powerlessness."

She laughed. "You sound so prim, Derek. What about the companies that do business in South Africa? Do you know that they have to maintain a racist hierarchy? How do we deal with that? Forget about it? Is sending guns to Ireland worse than the English sending soldiers? Is supporting the PLO different from supporting the Israelis?"

"You steal."

"Give me a million dollars and I'll never steal again."

"There's no right or wrong, is that it?"

"From whose point of view?"

"From no one's, it's an objective value."

She laughed. "We'll go in circles, Derek."

"That's okay, I've been going in circles ever since you came back." I swatted at a fly hurrying for cover from the rain. "You must believe in some great right, that's what you're fighting for."

"I don't know what 'right' is," she said. "I don't fight 'for' anything, I fight against wrong. I'm a fireman, always looking for the next fire."

"The tired fireman," I said, feeling a trace of bitterness entering my voice, "you have a very romantic image of yourself."

"No, I don't," she said. "You do, and even you don't believe it. You're just mad. Don't take your frustration out on me."

She turned on her side and put her hand on my chest, her fingers working under my shirt. "Don't be angry with me, Derek. I just want some peace. A few days to be with you without recriminations."

"She wants peace," I said, the anger taking over me. "What peace have you given all those people you're supposedly helping?"

She took her hand away, suddenly, like I'd stung her with electricity.

I said, knowing that my voice would still be hard, as my face must have been, pointed up towards the cloud, "And with all that, I think I still love you. It feels like Vermont, the South, Day Street all over again."

She laid her head on my chest. "Be careful, Derek."

"What do you feel?"

She answered quickly. "When I saw you that first day in the office it was as though not five minutes had passed since Brighton." She glanced up briefly and smiled. "Oh, you've changed, your hair's shorter. Thinner. But it was still Derek who walked through the door. And it was like a part of me that had been missing was replaced. It scared me because there is so much that can come between us and I don't know what's going to happen. And . . . I don't know . . . if it doesn't work out, that part of me may always be empty . . ." She stopped for a moment. "Even when I wrote to you and you didn't answer I felt you with me. I knew you read my letters and that was enough.

I'm with you now, and even though not everything is right, it's enough. Is it enough for you?"

I reached out and slipped my fingers through her hair. "It will have to be, for now," I said. The clouds overhead swept in low and at last the air turned cool in a sudden, damp, fresh gust. The last sailboats in the bay heeled and headed for shore, and the bows of the outlying tankers turned towards the wind. I thought, in a perfect world we could choose the people we love, but the world is far from perfect and one day someone walks into our life and a void is filled, and if we drive them from our lives an emptiness will remain, like a weakness in the bones, or a faintness of breath. With Marion lying beside me I felt whole and strong again for the first time in years.

XIII

====

I DON'T KNOW WHAT would have happened between Marion and me if events hadn't accelerated and taken a course of their own. But by the time I'd dropped her off downtown I'd admitted to myself that I didn't want us to be separated again. I couldn't see beyond that—I had a half-formed idea of taking her away to Vermont or Maine or some place where it was green and cool and calm, but I didn't know how I could convince her to go or what we'd do when we got there. What I had to do first was find out exactly what she was doing in Boston.

I drove back to the Brighton apartment and rang the bell. It was early afternoon, and I hoped that Ron, the man fighting a useless holding action against the computerization of movie theaters (trying to unionize a technology already dead, as hopeless as Pittsburgh's workers trying to force out cheap Korean steel), wouldn't be home. He wasn't, or he wasn't answering the door. I jimmied the lock on the outside door and went up to the second floor. If I remembered correctly, Ron's apartment had a dead bolt. Hard to force. There was a hallway that led beside the apartment to a rear fire exit. A window at the back looked out onto the worn yard that Marion and I had raised our glasses to, and when I stuck my head outside I saw

I could step across to the porch. I looked around for signs of life. The woods were quiet, senseless, with the unused look of leftover city woodland. The only stuff back there would be stray cats, bald tires and beer cans. Over the rise I could just make out the top of an apartment building. To the left a short section of parking lot was visible where a dusty VW sat looking as though it hadn't been driven in months. I took a deep breath and stuck a foot outside the window, then my head and shoulders, all the while composing excuses as to what the hell I was doing jumping to a porch in broad daylight.

Gingerly, with an eye to the garbage cans below, I stretched a foot to the porch railing and eased across. The kitchen door was locked but the window beside it was open. I stepped in and stood still. The apartment was quiet, with no sign of sonorous breathing from Ron's bedroom. I went to the front door, snapped open the lock and swung the door open. If Ron was there I'd tell him Marion had given me the keys.

"Hello?" I called out. No answer. I peeked into his room. He was out.

Marion's bedroom had the feel of a crash pad. There was a mattress on the floor and an empty duffle bag beside it. Three books and a newspaper were stacked neatly against the wall. One title read, "Alternative America." I flipped through the pages. It was nothing more than a computer print-out of legal-aid associations, halfway houses, community programs and various and sundry collectives. Everything from abortion clinics to zen meditation centers. The book was at least ten years old and there were heavy red lines drawn through the names of many of the listings, presumably those out of business. At least a third of the names on some pages were crossed out. Marion's alternative world was shrinking. Another of the books was Ropke's "A Humane Economy," an attack on national socialism, and the last book, judging from the condition of its cover, was new, "Gaia," by J. E. Lovelock. Marion had underlined in the preface, "From this has arisen the hypothesis, the model, in which Earth's living matter, air, oceans and land surface form a complex system which can be seen as a single organism and which has the capacity to keep our planet a fit place for life." I put the books back. I had a brief glimmer of how Marion must feel coming back to this bare room every night. She had no home, no stable center for her life, except perhaps a collection of books, an abstract ideology, a calling as isolated and harsh as a monk's.

I glanced at the paper and then picked it up hurriedly. It was Glazier's *Worker's Revolutionary Week*. Following a hunch, I flipped the pages and found a column entitled, "FYI" by one "Margaret Richards," listing the New England companies with investments in South Africa. It was a regular feature, "a weekly column for our readers' information." Glazier had known all along where Marion was and he hadn't told me. I held the paper, feeling cheated and knowing there was no reason to be. Glazier didn't trust me and I supposed I'd never given him reason to. There was a gap between us that I hadn't seen before. I threw the paper down in disgust and searched the room, angry, pissed off at what I supposed I would find. I found it in the closet, where I pulled out a sturdy briefcase, the kind a Wall Street lawyer might carry. I snapped it open. Laid out neatly in rows were stacks of twenty-dollar bills. I counted fifty thousand dollars.

I went out to the living room and sat in the single, unsteady armchair, wondering what to do next. Marion was either delivering the money somewhere or buying something, probably small arms, with it. My stomach started to go sour and I began to sweat. I felt a disconnected outrage at the stupidity, the small-mindness that would keep Marion playing out this cycle, begun when the first pleistocene thug picked up a long, heavy tree limb. Why do we keep making the same mistakes?

I sat there until the apartment began to go dark. From somewhere in the building rock and roll reached me through the soles of my feet, thumpbadumbump, like an arrhythmic heart.

Marion came in about half past six. She swung the door open and stepped wearily across the threshold, letting her heavy shoulder bag slip to the floor. She looked like a mountain climber who'd just reached base camp after a perilous descent.

Her face looked strained, preoccupied. When she finally saw me, sitting in shadows, a brief flash of panic crossed her face— then she recognized me.

"What are you doing here?" she asked.

"Waiting for you."

"How'd you get in?"

"It's not important. What's the money for, Marion?"

She didn't answer, or rather, stood composing one of several answers that came quickly to her mind. I watched her consider each one, and it seemed important to me, to us, maybe, which one she chose. (What were you doing searching my room, or, It's none of your business, or, a lie, something sugar coated, aid to struggling independent political parties.)

She avoided the question, choosing instead to cross into the room and slump onto the couch. "Don't start, Derek."

"Why not?" I asked with too much force. "You gave me the impression that you came here to see me, or maybe to turn yourself in and start over. Or maybe you're just passing through on business. Which is it?"

"All of the above," she said.

"This isn't multiple choice."

She smiled. "I know."

I watched her stare down at the tops of her shoes, answers swirling around inside her but bottled up, none of them presenting itself clearly, "This is what I want." She wasn't sure what she wanted.

"I'll help you," I said.

She looked up, her eyes wet, glassy. "I have to do it myself."

"You can't. You don't always have to depend on yourself."

"On this I do," she answered. She stood up abruptly and began to pace. "On this I do," she repeated. She walked in long, slow circles, snapping the fingers on both hands, crackling sounds coming from her fingertips like electricity arcing in a short circuit.

"Face it, Marion, you're wrong here. Stick to your column. 'FYI.' I like that. Gives people the information to make their choices. That's good."

—— 169 ——

"It's clever, but it's not enough." she answered. "It's just not enough."

"It's plenty," I said. "With this other crap you go too far. There're limits, Marion, limits to everything."

"Where? Where are they? Show me where they are and who follows them?" she said.

"Right here, they're right here, with you. Each person alone sets his limits and follows them."

She stopped and smiled. "Christ, you are a romantic."

"Spare me the one about the harsh realities of life. They're for people who don't have imagination or courage."

"You're telling me this?" she shot back.

We stared at each other like fighters across the ring. Then we both jumped when the sound of the phone blasted through the apartment.

Marion turned quickly and went to the extension in the hall. "Hello?" she said, with the voice of someone expecting bad news from a hospital.

"Now?" she said. Her voice dropped down a notch. "You said tonight." I saw her shadow on the wall. She was pacing again.

"All right," she said. The phone slammed down. "Damn it to hell!"

She came back into the room and threw me a fierce look. "You have to leave."

"I'm going with you," I said.

"You can't."

"You have a backup?"

She shook her head. "It's not your concern."

I went to her and grabbed her shoulders, shaking her. "Damn it, Marion! I'm making it my concern. I'm going with you."

"Why?"

"Because I want to see you do this," I told her. "Maybe if I watch you I'll get some idea of what I should do from here on."

She was hoping for more, I think, but she was backed into

a corner. It would be foolish to meet whoever she was supposed to see alone.

She got the briefcase from her room and hefted her bag to her shoulder. She reached into it and took out a small .38, snapping off the safety. "Do you carry a gun?" she asked. "I only have one of these."

"I do sometimes, but not today. I don't want one anyway."

She slipped the revolver into her bag and eyed me sardonically. "You'll be a big help."

Marion had a car this time, a rental. She drove, heading across town towards Somerville. We drove through Porter Square and headed for the eastern edge of the town, where the old Boston stockyards use to be. This was the lowlands, a broad floodplain at the foot of Winter Hill, where all the northern rail lines merged into a massive steel network of train yards and, years ago, cattle pens and slaughter houses. Rows of tenements for the railroad men and the slaughterhouse workers, along with their dark, narrow pubs and drinking houses, ringed the yards. The rail traffic had shrunk to a few trains a day and the cattle yards were gone, but as we drove past block after block of squat, shabby factories the lowlands felt like an old, used prostitute grown ugly and unwanted after the city had had its way. The earth, soaked with diesel fuel, industrial oil, the blood and manure of gutted animals, still reeked from a violated past.

I said to Marion, "This is a good place for a meeting."

"In broad daylight," she said.

I stared out the window as we rolled past the dirty brick warehouses, the scruffy abandoned lots that hatched broken bricks like petrified eggs, the rail lines sprouting weeds between rusting rails.

"Who are these guys?" I asked.

"I've never met them," Marion said. "I've been directed to them by somebody who knows somebody who knows someone else."

"That's comforting."

"That's the way it is," she answered, too casually.

We came to the intersection in Union Square and Marion slowed the car. There was a policeman directing traffic around a group of gas workers digging yet another hole in the street.

"Are you going to keep pretending that this is just business? When are you going to let go of Dunn County and Chicago?"

"I've tried, Derek," she said. "I've tried to write off everything as just unfinished business. Bad debts. But I keep coming back to, 'Why should I? Why should I sit back and watch the power brokers, the money men have *their* way?' I have to keep moving, keep active, feel I'm doing *something*, anything."

"Abstract nouns. 'The power brokers, the money men.' What the hell is that?"

"You want me to name names?" she asked. "I can give you names. I can list people, companies, to Doomsday if you want."

"Doesn't matter," I said. "What you're doing is just the same old shit. Business as usual."

"Maybe," she said. "Maybe it is."

We drove under the rusting girders of the elevated McGrath highway and turned down a service road to an industrial complex. All around us low buildings surrounded by blacktop parking lots and dried out lawns hugged the ground like Quonset huts on the moon. The complex was nearly empty except for a few warehousemen loading a semi at the Kravitz Wholesale Produce Company. They cast bored glances at us as we passed by, and for a moment I thought about Spenser, thinking I should call him.

We bumped over a set of railroad tracks and Marion swerved around some deep potholes in the street. We were driving to the back of the complex, the low rent district, where the buildings were smaller and shabbier, with windows boarded up and trash cans spilled on their sides, with no one bothering to pick them up.

Marion said, "I don't expect trouble from these people, but keep your eyes open."

"Look," I said, "if these people have set us up, Marion, we're cooked. No chance. But they've called you here at," I looked at my watch, "seven o'clock. That tells me they have nothing but the noblest of intentions."

"You're probably right."

"I hope I'm right," I said, "but if I'm not we're not going to have much to say about it."

Marion finally pulled up beside a windowless single-story brick building that stood by itself like an industrial-strength mausoleum. There was just one door. Walking in there would be comparable to entering a lion's cage at the zoo and locking the door behind you.

Marion had put on her blank, business face.

"Are you sure you want to do this?" I asked.

Again she gave me that resigned smile of hers that I was getting used to. It seemed to be her answer to everything.

"Too late now," she said, opening her door.

As we walked towards the building the lone door opened and a man in his early thirties stepped in front of us. He was medium height with a wiry build and didn't look particularly dangerous. He had short blond hair and a soft, pampered face.

"Miss Wilson?" he asked.

Marion nodded.

"Who's your friend?"

"A friend."

The man thought about that for a second and then said, "Come on in."

If the building looked like a mausoleum from the outside, inside it felt like one, cool and dark. It consisted of just one room with a high ceiling and with the steel structural girders exposed along concrete block walls. The floor was cement, sloping off to a drain at the center. The room was empty except for a folding card table set up almost exactly in the middle, as if someone had paced off the measurements of the room and had determined dead-center. Five wooden crates, about four feet long and two feet wide, were stacked beside it. Standing beside the table was another young man, a little taller than the first, but with the same neat blond hair. He stood formally erect and wore an apologetic smile.

"I'm sorry for the change in time, Miss Wilson," he said. "It was more or less a precaution. In case anyone was aware of what we're doing."

Marion nodded. She crossed the room and stood on the opposite side of the table. She put the briefcase on the floor. I lagged behind, placing myself between the men and the door.

"Let me introduce myself," the young man said. "My name's Smith and this is Mr. Jones."

Marion laughed.

"Another precaution," Smith said.

"You don't trust me?" Marion asked.

"It's not you," Smith said. "It's the circumstances. We're not from around these parts." He glanced at Jones. "So we have to be careful." He rushed on, "But we want to do business with you."

"Great," Marion said.

Smith gestured to the wooden crates. "We have access to more where these came from." He smiled confidently. "Lots more."

"You do?" Marion asked, leading him on. She seemed to have relaxed a little. "From where?"

Smith glanced at his friend. "From a Brother in the Army."

Marion tensed. "A Brother?"

Smith ignored the question. He motioned to Jones, who produced a crowbar from behind the crates. Jones jammed the blade into the top box and ripped it open, nails screeching.

"Take a look," Smith offered. "Fine stuff. Lots more where this came from."

Marion seemed to be digesting what he'd said before. She hesitated, then crossed to the box and pulled out a Beretta 92 automatic, the kind used by the military.

I watched uncomfortably as Marion expertly looked the weapon over, knowing the details to look for, feeling for weight, balance, checking the firing mechanism. Her cool appraisal struck me like a heavy fist in the chest, as if I'd thought all along that Marion would not be involved this deeply, would

—— 174 ——

not be able to handle a gun as calmly as a shopkeeper reviewing his stock for a year-end sale.

She put the automatic back and dug out another, repeating the inspection. A careful buyer.

"This is U.S. Army materiel," she said.

Smith nodded. "We can get you an unlimited supply."

"You're anxious to accommodate us," Marion said.

"Anything to help out."

"Help out?"

Smith glanced at Jones again, who stood like an eager assistant ready to suggest additional merchandise, or to measure the proper fit, a tailor's helper learning the trade.

Smith said, "These are going to South Africa, right?"

"Maybe." Marion took a cigarette from her bag.

"Well, then," Smith went on, "that's okay with us."

Marion paused for a moment, bringing the cigarette to her lips.

Smith couldn't gauge her reaction. He went on cautiously. "We want to keep the fat in the fire . . . like you."

"Who's 'we?'" Marion asked.

"They didn't tell you who you're buying from?"

"No."

Smith looked to his partner and smiled. "We're members of the Aryan Nations, Minnesota chapter," he said.

I watched Marion slowly light her cigarette. It was a good trick . . . her hand barely shook. I asked, "You're with the Klan?"

Smith nodded again, "Dedicated to the supremacy of the white race," he said, as if reciting the preamble to some constitution.

"This is priceless," I said. "Fantastic."

"Quiet, Derek," Marion said. She turned to Smith. "I don't understand what's in this for you."

"You don't?" Smith wore a polite look.

"Well . . ." Marion seemed lost for a moment, ". . . I just want us to be clear . . ."

"About what?"

Her voice sounded weak, unsure, "Where these pieces are going . . ." The room fell into an awkward silence. Smith inclined his head slightly to one side, like a good host encouraging his guest to continue, still wearing his polite smile. Jones glanced at his watch.

Smith urged her along. "They're going to niggers, right?"

Marion winced. "They're going to blacks, yes."

"Fine," Smith said.

"But why do you . . . would you want . . ."

"So that we do understand each other," Smith interrupted. "We expect trouble in South Africa. We want it. The more trouble the better."

Marion stared at him, confused. "What's in it for you if Pretoria is overthrown?"

Smith looked over to his partner and laughed. Jones grinned back. Smith said to Marion, as if addressing a very slow child, "Do you really think the U.S. will let a bunch of left-wing niggers control the major diamond and gold reserves for the entire world?"

"Beautiful," I said.

Marion turned to me angrily. "That's enough," she said.

"Marion, you're going to deal with these people? What's with you?"

"Leave it to me," she spat out.

"Shipping Italian-made guns, stolen from the U.S. Army, to African terrorists to use against whites who the U.S. will step in to support," I said. "I like it, it has a certain feeling of symmetry, closure."

"What's with your friend?" Smith asked.

Marion exhaled a cloud of blue smoke and watched it mushroom toward the dark rafters.

Smith, disturbed, said to her, "I don't think we can deal with you." He made a sign to Jones that I couldn't interpret.

"Wait," Marion said. "Don't mind Derek." She picked up the briefcase and opened it up on the card table.

Smith considered her a moment, then glanced at me. He

wasn't sure what he should do. Marion turned the case toward him so he could count the bills.

"Okay," he said finally, "but don't bring him next time. All right?"

Marion nodded, keeping her eyes on the briefcase.

They packed the five cases in the trunk of the Ford and Marion and I drove away into a purple sunset. Streetlights were coming on randomly. Cars drove with their running lights on. Marion steered silently, her face rigid.

"Did you see what you wanted?" she asked.

"No," I answered. "I wanted to see a particular Marion I had in mind. The one who was having second thoughts. Wanted a better life. Whatever that is. The Marion I saw was just running by rote, following a well-worn path. She was so blinded, so calloused that she was willing to deal with people who stand for everything she hates."

"You don't understand," she said, a note of desperation in her voice. "You don't understand the trade-offs I have to make." She'd driven out of Somerville the wrong way, without thinking, and we were heading toward Boston. She noticed her mistake and turned down Memorial Drive. "Look," she said, "I hate those people. But I'm trying to make a difference and I'm fighting the tide the whole fucking way. I want to exert pressure and to do that I have to use pressure."

"Where will it get you? What's the end?"

"I don't think there is an end. Just process. A constant bettering."

"How can you make anything better using the same old methods?"

She looked at me across the darkened car. It was now night-time and the shadows made dark circles under her eyes.

"That's why I said process," she answered. "No one has come up with a new idea in two thousand years. Just old ones dusted off and changed the slightest bit. That's what history is, just a slow distillation. I'm part of it, an agitator. A catalyst."

"You're just perpetuating the worst part of us all. The myth we all hate but really believe in our hearts, that only the strong survive."

"Isn't it true?"

"Maybe it is now, but we're the only ones who will make it different."

"Then that's it," she said, staring dully ahead. "I guess there's nothing more for us to say."

"I want you to give me one chance," I said.

"To do what?"

"Leave here with me," I said. "Let's try it differently. Just you and me. I want what Bill and Margaret have. Working on life day to day. You want it too. I saw you on Castle Island with Amy."

"You have to compromise too much for that kind of life, Derek, like my father did, like everyone does. I don't compromise."

"Who says you have to close your eyes? Is it engraved in stone somewhere?"

She smiled again. "It's not engraved in stone, but that's the way it is."

"So you won't give me one chance?"

She thought a minute, which was more than I'd expected. Her answer surprised me more. "I'll think about it, Derek."

"Now. Decide now. We'll dump this shit in the river."

We'd come back to the Brighton apartment. Marion pulled up behind my car, shifted to neutral, then turned to face me.

"Don't ask for too much, Derek, please. Don't you pressure me too. I need room. Let me decide myself. Okay?"

I didn't want to give her any room at all, but what could I do? I was certain if I pushed her she'd turn and run.

"Decide soon, Marion."

"Tonight. I'll call you tonight," she said.

The next question was what she was doing from now till then, but I didn't ask it. Maybe if I had I would have saved us a lot of grief. Instead, I let it pass. I got out of the car and watched Marion drive away.

XIV

⸻

I DROVE HOME AND PARKED MY CAR, placed the FBI transmitter back under the rear bumper, then went into my house and poured myself a quick drink. Before I had time to settle down, two phone calls came in that put an edge on the evening.

The first was from Bill Stacom. He was drunk. He said he was being forced to move.

"Me and my family have been condo-minimized," he said, slurring his words.

"You're being kicked out?"

"Sent to the hinterlands, or wherever the poor folk go."

"They can't do that. You're ordinanced."

"I guess the bastards finally found the right palms to grease. Got a variance."

"How much time did they give you?"

"Oh, they're being very gracious about it. They've given us three months. But where is a social services schmuck like me going to find a decent place for Marion and Jody?"

"We'll find a place. I'll help you look in Waltham."

"Rents start at six hundred over there. For studios for god's sake."

"We'll find a place."

There was a breathy pause and I heard Bill take another slug of whatever he was drinking. "How are the schools over there? I had my heart set on sending them to Matignon."

"The schools are fine."

"'Fine', he says."

"Bill."

"Don't kid me, Derek," he said. "I know what I'm getting my girls into. You need a good town and a good neighborhood with hard-working kids. You start your girls off in an ass-backwards school and they have two strikes against them."

I didn't answer. He had to let it all out.

"I wanted the Seven Sisters for Jody," he said.

"She's a smart girl, Bill. No matter where she goes they won't be able to hold her back."

"I always thought I'd send her to a private academy. Concord or Madeira." He let out a short laugh. "What a dreamer. I'm a fool, Derek. I've got no money and anyone who wants to can slap me around."

"You're a good man, Bill." Even though the words were true they sounded limp and forced.

"I make sixteen thousand a year. I'm a fool."

"Salary doesn't mean anything."

"No, it doesn't, it doesn't," Bill said with false conviction. "It just means a decent house and car and food on the table and nice clothes for Margaret—"

"Margaret doesn't give a damn about clothes."

"What?" he said. "Well, she better not, because she can't afford to be choosy, can she?"

"Go ahead, cut yourself down, Bill, get it over with. Try to convince me what a bum you are. I've got all year."

There was a sullen silence at the other end.

"Where are you calling from?" I asked.

"The Cosy Bar. Nice name." he said. "There are all these young studs in baseball uniforms with their pretty girl friends celebrating their game. I guess they won."

"Do you want to come over here?"

"No," he said. He was starting to wind down. "I better get

home. I stormed out on Margaret. She's probably worried."

"Go home then. I'll start looking tomorrow. There're some possibilities on my street."

"How are the schools?"

"They're good."

"Great. Fine. Everything's wonderful. No problem. Isn't that what they say? No problem."

I told him I'd be in touch and we hung up. I poured myself another drink. The glass was almost empty when the phone rang again.

"Derek? This is Mike MacDonald. Have you seen John? I mean, has he been in touch with you?"

"I talked to him a couple of nights ago. What's up?" I felt the Scotch in my stomach start to sour.

"Nothing, I hope. I've been calling him for the past two days and there's been no answer."

"Maybe you've just been missing him," I said, although I didn't believe it myself.

"He hasn't been into work. Hasn't even called in sick."

"I don't like it."

"Neither do I," he said.

"Do you know what he had in mind?" I asked.

"What do you mean?"

"Skip it. Did he mention if he was going to see McGuiness?"

"McGuiness? What for?"

"I don't know, it was just a thought."

MacDonald persisted. "John seemed strange lately. Did he have something going with McGuiness?"

I ignored his probing. "Not that I know of," I said, "but he didn't tell me everything."

"Are you sure?" MacDonald asked. I thought, now you want to help him, when it's too late.

I ended the conversation as quickly as I could, telling Mac-Donald to call me with any news. Dropping the receiver cut me off from MacDonald and anyone else whom John Spenser might have asked for help. Instead Spenser had asked me and I'd refused. The McGuiness thing had blown up in Spenser's face, that meant he'd probably already made the arrangements to confront McGuiness the last time I'd spoken to him and he hadn't mentioned it. He'd already given up on me. And why shouldn't he? I hadn't given him any reason to believe I'd help. I poured my third drink of the night and sat down. There was still a chance for a simple answer. Spenser might be somewhere thinking things over. But I didn't believe in it.

I spent an hour trying to convince myself that I'd done all I could for Spenser. He was committed to a wrong and dangerous course that I'd tried to talk him out of. There was nothing more I was responsible for. But the argument didn't take. All I could feel was that I'd let the young man down and that Richard McGuiness was the person I'd helped. The established powers benefit most from inaction. One thing was certain: if I heard nothing from John Spenser I would lay the blame on McGuiness's door. With that late, futile resolve, I occupied myself waiting for Marion's call.

She said that if all went well she'd phone me by midnight, and by two A.M. I knew there was trouble. It was a feeling as heavy as the electric charge that precedes a thunderstorm. The air in my living room grew thick and the corner shadows seemed to creep out and surround the pools of lamplight like animals outside the safety of a campfire. All the cars that passed on my street and the distant sounds that slipped through my windows caught my attention, and I packed each with useless meaning. The car crawling past observed my house, the dim siren rushed to a scene where Marion lay injured. My muscles tensed with each passing minute and I drank mechanically, the alcohol having no more effect than the melted ice cubes.

At three-fifteen the phone rang and I jumped at the instrument, answering before the second ring.

I heard Marion's voice, strained, tightened almost beyond recognition. "The intersection of 128 and III. Will you come?"

"Twenty minutes," I said.

"Think about it," she said.

"Twenty minutes." The line went dead as she hung up the receiver.

I went to my closet and took out my Colt Lightweight and an extra clip. From the bathroom cupboard I grabbed a roll of cotton gauze and some medical tape. I didn't know what I'd find when I reached Marion but I knew the supplies I had probably wouldn't do that much good and that if I used the Colt it would be against federal agents or local police. I thought about that for a minute and put the gun back.

The transmitter was still on my car and I put it back in the row of hedges, wondering if the FBI was really falling for so simple a trick. I thought they might, only because they weren't working me over very hard, despite what Newman said. Whatever information they had on Marion's whereabouts was most likely very sketchy and their surveillance halfhearted. At least that's what I told myself as I drove off, with one eye glued to the rearview mirror.

At three-thirty Rt. 128 is an eight-lane graveyard. It's wide and empty and you could land a jumbo jet on the hardtop and roll it all the way to Gloucester without disturbing anyone except a few long-distance freight haulers. I felt exposed and an easy mark for any cops keeping watch from the bridges overhead. Whatever Marion had started would bring out the State Police, and they would have this highway covered. I kept looking for them but didn't see one and that made me nervous. They weren't in the truck stop by the Mass Pike and they weren't in the rest area in Lexington. They had to be out somewhere and they were doing a good job of keeping it a secret.

The intersection Marion directed me to led to Rt. 111, a small road that headed north into the rural reaches of Massachusetts. When I got there I took the northbound exit and curled around over the bridge that crossed 128. The road wound quickly into thick forest and I drove north for about a mile before I realized I must have passed her already. I turned around and made another run over the highway, then retraced my route north. A half-mile past the interchange I saw Marion step out of the woods into my headlights. I pulled onto the soft shoulder and rolled down the passenger's window.

Marion's face was haggard and the lines around her eyes seemed to have deepened in the past few hours. She glanced quickly up and down the road and leaned against the window frame.

"You don't have to help," she said. "I'll understand if you drive away."

"Just answer one question."

"What?"

"Were any policemen wounded?"

"No. Just Robert."

"Robert? Robert Glazier?"

Marion nodded. "He keeps saying you can't be trusted. Can I trust you, Derek?"

"To a point, Marion. I want you safe."

She smiled. "It's strange how good that sounds. Even if it's not possible for you to make me safe."

"Get in."

She slipped into the car. "There's a dirt road up about a hundred feet."

I drove slowly along the shoulder and saw a path filled in with grass and weeds, an old farmer's lane that had once led to a pasture. It led through a stone wall that had been overtaken by forest. We headed into the dark, under red maples and pin oak and I was conscious of the raucous sound of crickets and the stray call of night birds.

The lane ended in a small copse of silver birch. Marion's rental car was parked facing us, and as my lights played over it I saw Robert's head slumped against the front seat. Even at this distance I could see how bloodless his face was. Marion was out of the car before I stopped. I shut off my lights and grabbed a flashlight from the glove compartment and the gauze from the back seat.

Marion had the passenger door open.

"Let me see him," I said.

She stepped aside and I leaned in. "Hold the flash," I said.

His mouth was open and he looked like a man in a deep sleep. His breathing was shallow, but steady. There was a gash along the right side of his head. His glasses were snapped at the bridge and hung crazily on his face. His right eye was pushing out against its socket and the right side of his shirt was caked in dark blood. When I leaned over him his left eye fluttered open.

"Derek," he said. "She called you. I told her not too."

"That night at Bill's," I said, "I didn't trust you, you didn't trust me. So it goes."

He smiled faintly. "You had your turn in Brighton," he said. "Looks like it's my turn tonight."

"I guess so," I answered. "A round gave you a shave up here," I told him. I reached for his glasses. "Let me get these off. Looks like you'll finally have to get a new pair." His eye looked bad, swollen nearly out of its socket. There was nothing I could do there. I moved to what looked like a shoulder wound. "Let me have a gander at this."

"I don't feel a thing," he said. "I feel like I'm on downs. Remember that night on Day Street?"

I tried to pull the fabric of his shirt from the wound. The blood had dried and the material was glued to his skin. "You mean the supposed Darvon that turned out to be horse tranquillizers?"

"Yeah," he said. "I spent the whole night remembering to breathe."

"Why don't you practice that now," I said. I left the shirt where it was. The wound had stopped bleeding. I told him that. "You've lost a lot of blood but you're going to be all right."

He nodded and seemed to drift off.

I stepped out from the car and faced Marion. In the dark I could just make out her pinched and worried face.

"Do your friends have a safe doctor we can bring him to?" I asked, surprised at the bitterness in my voice.

She shook her head. "They might, but almost everyone was arrested. It was a setup. A fuck-up from beginning to end." She looked sadly at Glazier. "We have to drop him at a hospital. It means jail, but there's no choice."

."Giving up on another soldier," I said.

She gave a sad, forlorn look. "Am I? I don't know what else we can do."

"Nothing, there's nothing else you can do. You've done enough."

She turned abruptly and started toward the rear of the sedan. "Don't start, Derek. He knew what he was getting into."

"What the hell was he doing with you, anyway?"

She said angrily, "He was fed up. Tired of putting out his useless newspaper and running a few candidates for office—when they could get enough votes to qualify for the ballot. I told him he didn't belong on this trip, but he insisted. At least he hasn't just given up like you."

She went to the trunk, inserted her key and opened it.

"We'll have to leave him in the car," Marion said. "I want to move these to your trunk."

I shook my head. "I'll help Robert. I'll help you, but I won't help you in what you're doing. Leave them."

Marion's face sagged as I refused. I don't know what disappointed her most, my refusal or the fact that she couldn't get the guns to wherever they were going. She stood holding the trunk open, her eyes searching my face for any sign of giving in. She saw that there was no way I was going to help her and she wavered for a moment, then she began pulling the crates out and moving them to a spot under a tree a few yards away. She slammed the trunk.

"Let's take him to Emerson Hospital. We can get there on back roads," she said.

"I'll lead," I said.

We pulled out onto the dark, winding strip of asphalt and slipped through sleeping neighborhoods and past quiet town greens. We followed roads Paul Revere galloped down, racing ahead of advancing British regulars who'd come looking for rebel guns. We passed Lexington Green where, every April, brave dentists, lawyers, and car salesmen, decked out in period costumes and carrying vintage muskets, trade blanks with accountants, computer programmers and industrial engineers. We went through Concord and crossed the Concord River within sight of the rude bridge. And I knew, as we quietly parked the black sedan in the hospital's lower parking lot, leaving Robert, who was unconscious, alone; as we drove to the Citgo station in West Concord, where Marion telephoned the emergency room; I knew that Robert wouldn't be treated as any kind of hero but as a criminal, as he was, if only because he was two hundred years too late, in a country where people believed they had left violence behind. Perhaps it was not so much a belief as a hope, a hope that I realized I too had been trying to keep alive ever since that night fifteen years ago in Brighton.

XV

"TELL ME WHAT HAPPENED," I said to Marion.

We were parked in an overlook in a small town about thirty miles west of Boston. I could see the lights of cars on a highway below and the stars were thick and cold above us. It was hard to tell where the land and sky began, except for a suggestion of light on the horizon.

Marion took a deep drag from her cigarette. She'd been chain smoking since we dropped Robert off.

"It was one of those deals that are simple and yet tailor made for a setup," she began. She let out a plume of smoke. "One leak and you walk right into a trap. I guess that's what happened. Robert and I were supposed to meet a lobster boat in Gloucester. Buy a bunch of lobster and exchange boxes in the process. Three other people that I have contact with were supposed to be on hand to keep watch. When I got there only one was visible and he didn't look right. We had driven into the parking lot that leads to the pier, so I turned around immediately, just as a car was moving to block our exit." She sucked on the cigarette. "I got around them and two men jumped out and started shooting. Some rounds—one or two—caught the rear window and hit Robert. I lost whoever they were on the back streets and wandered around for a few hours until I called you."

"Robert could have bled to death by then."

"I needed someone to help me drop him off. I couldn't very well walk away from the hospital."

"Even if it was a choice between him dying and you walking?"

She let out an exasperated sigh. "I had to make sure I could get away, Derek. It was a chance I had to take. That he had to take. He knew what he was getting into. He was glad to do it. He begged me for the opportunity."

"Why?" I asked. "I don't understand. It's not like Robert."

She took a last drag from her cigarette and stubbed it out, looking at me from the corner of her eye. "I told you, too much frustration for too long."

I looked out over the valley and watched a tractor-trailer inch along the distant highway. "I hope he's satisfied."

"He's not satisfied, dammit! He was looking for results. And who are you to talk? You're a detective, a bodyguard, and you're preaching to me and anyone who'll listen."

"It's not the same, Marion. I'm a free agent. I get to choose whatever I stand for."

"So do I."

We were at a standstill again.

Marion lit another cigarette. "I don't care anymore, really." She took a drag. "Christ, I feel like someone's sitting on my chest." She expelled the smoke and coughed. "I just don't care about anything."

This was the opening I'd been waiting for. The low ebb where I hoped Marion would be most willing to give up her fight. Go after that life she'd dreamed about the first night we'd spent together in Ron's apartment. I had my chance, but hesitated. I remembered the telephone calls from Bill Stacom and Mike MacDonald and they seemed to sap my energy. I felt responsible for the two men in some abstract way. Marion was right: there was no difference between us, no matter how much I tried to argue. Only matters of degrees. Nuances that I could no longer juggle and dissect.

Marion coughed—a rough, grating smoker's cough. The muscles in her face were slack and her eyes showed exhaustion. She was the one person I had it in my power to help.

I said, "Let's get out of here. I have a friend in Maine. Way, way up in Maine, in a small town on Deer Island. It's all the way up near Bar Harbor, a secluded island with just one bridge to the mainland. He can put us up until we get settled."

Marion laughed. "We can join all the other fugitives skulking in the north country. Can you see me?"

"Why not?"

"Darning socks."

"Come on."

"Puttering in the garden. Tomatoes. Lettuce. Keeping a sharp eye out for mealy bugs."

"I'm serious."

She looked at me dubiously. "I should just leave the shipment back in the woods?"

"Yes," I answered, "leave the goddam guns under the goddam trees to rust in the goddam rain."

"It's not possible," she said, but I saw in her eyes and heard in her voice a trace of curiosity like, This could happen?

"Anything is possible," I said, "even happiness, or peace. Contentment. Try contentment, it takes a little work but . . . it's possible."

"Happiness and peace?" she said, as if I'd just proposed a complex formula of physics, like the wedding of gravity to quantum theory.

"It's not possible," she murmured.

"Give it a try," I said. "We'll leave Boston behind . . . and Oakland. And Chicago."

"And Newark?"

"And Detroit and Los Angeles."

"Is it possible?" she asked.

I started the car. "It's not only possible, it's probable." I was full of it, watching her waver, waving impossible possibilities before her eyes. I put my hand on the shifter, my foot on the clutch, looking at her, waiting for one brief moment of assent.

Marion laughed and slid down in the seat. "Deer Island? Maine? Is it near the shore?"

"It's smack dab on the ocean. He'll put us up in rooms that sit right above the water."

I put the car in gear. We started forward. "We can look out over Kings Bay, clear out into the Atlantic," I said.

"Kings Bay," she repeated. She laughed in exhausted, giddy release. "Yes. Deer Island."

Part Two

I

WHERE I TOOK MARION was the summer home of a friend of mine, and I was leery about bringing her there for two reasons. First, the place was not just a house, but an estate that occupied the top third of a peninsula jutting out into Kings Bay. It didn't take much imagination to guess how she'd feel about that. Secondly, my friend was Butler Burgess, a lawyer, more specifically, the lawyer who had represented me after Brighton. Butler would be useful to me in figuring out what we were going to do next. Rich man, rich lawyer—a snake oil combination to Marion, but it was a place to go.

I trusted Butler, even if I wasn't sure I could convince Marion to. Butler was the man with the *Mayflower* pedigree who gave me an in with Charles Street, but, more importantly, he hung in with me through all the years I was getting back on my feet. When I left prison I was just another body on the streets. I had half of a college education, a criminal record and the kind of past history that employers don't particularly greet warmly.

At that time Butler was a very visible media figure, the long-haired, rumpled lawyer who took on every radical, controversial case that came along. When we were marching against the war we would write Butler's telephone number on the back of our hands so we could call him after the inevitable arrest. I remembered a plaque in his library that he'd been given by his Harvard classmates, a highly sarcastic number in ornate Latin, crowning him the King of Lost Causes. That was Butler.

He was there when I walked out of prison, having anticipated my dilemma and the chip I had on my shoulder.

He said to me, in characteristic frankness, "I'm a very visible personality. You're a pariah. You can get a job as a janitor or you can work for me. Watch my back for me."

He wasn't being entirely serious but I got the message, and took his offer. For three years I trooped around the country with him, the shadow just outside of the TV cameras, the man standing by the open door of the limo, while Butler defended Indians, migrant farmhands, striking auto workers. I found that standing on the fringes suited me—I enjoyed watching the circus while feeling detached from it all, the just causes seeming just, but having nothing to do with me. I grew attached to detachment, felt like a man breathing free, with no concerns. Butler noticed this and took exception. As our third year together went on he started to give me research assignments, got me working with his clerks writing up briefs. These were jobs intended to get me thinking again. I went along with him for a while, but when he started dropping hints about law school I balked. Or rather, I walked, starting my own office with contacts I'd made while working for him.

He was concerned about me and said so. "What are you doing? Is this it?"

"This is it," I'd said, amused that he was worried. "Watching you work has taught me one important lesson," I said, "that there are two types of people. Those like you, who can't do enough, and those like me, who have had enough. You can go out and storm the barricades, Butler. I'll stay here and man the fort."

He was a hefty, bulky man, and he'd shaken his great gray head, with his face as craggy as the Old Man in the Mountains, and claimed I was turning my back on him. He'd been wounded, but over the years we'd worked it out, and it was Butler who'd helped me convince the police that I should have a detective's license, to "facilitate," he'd said, my "reintegration into society."

Now I was hoping he'd help me "reintegrate" Marion.

She slept most of the way up through Maine, but she woke up as soon as we turned into the long driveway that led up to Butler's manse. The road wound leisurely through a pine forest so thick that the ground was a mat of orange pine needles. The blacktopped lane continued circuitously.

"This is a private road?" Marion asked.

"Well, it's not a road, actually, it's just a driveway."

"A driveway."

"Right."

She looked from me to the road, and back to me. "We've been driving for five minutes."

"Yes, well, it's a long, winding approach."

She was silent for a while as we trundled along. We passed an opening in the forest where a field ran to a cliff that overlooked the bay. The hay in the fields had recently been cut and stacks of drying grass sat stolidly in the early morning light like druid temples to the God of Sweat and Labor.

"Do we get to see picturesque serfs tilling the soil?" she asked.

"It's a lot of land," I said, as an answer, "but it's not like Butler bought all of it. He inherited most. He could never afford this . . . at least I think he couldn't."

"Butler? Butler Burgess?"

"That's who we're going to see."

"What have you got in mind, Derek?" Marion asked, her voice growing urgent.

I told her I had nothing planned. That Butler was just someone to trust. "We couldn't just run off into the hills," I argued.

She seemed to accept that reasoning, but still looked uncomfortable.

She looked more uncomfortable when we broke out of the

forest and got a view of Butler's house on a high outcrop of rock. It was a Frank Lloyd Wright design, all planes and glass, and it stood audaciously facing the sea, right above waves that crashed against the granite shore. I always thought that Butler's house had the feel of a man pointing his chin into the teeth of a hurricane. One of these days a good nor'easter was going to pick it apart and leave the foreland barren again. That's what the locals said, anyway, and I suspected they were right. For his part, whenever Butler heard a strong blow was coming he hustled back here to sit through it. I sat with him through the hurricane of 1978, sitting right in the seaward picture windows, downing Johnnie Walker straight-up and watching white foam sail over our heads. The ocean was all white caps, salt spray streaming into the thin window glass, which shook ominously with each gust. We whooped and hollered like kids at a sideshow.

"You're taking me to the lap of luxury," Marion said. It sounded like an accusation.

"I'm taking you to see a good friend, okay?"

"Okay, Derek," she answered, not convinced.

"He's probably not even here," I added.

He wasn't, but he was expected in three days, that weekend. The housekeeper, who answered the door, remembered me. She was used to people dropping in unexpectedly on Butler, that is, on Butler's summer home, and since I was an old, old friend, she showed us in. The maid, named Brigit, was a local woman about thirty years old who had been a caretaker for Butler a long time, and was living pretty well off him too, so she didn't have any qualms about other people taking advantage of her employer. No animosity there, it's just that wealth should be spread around.

Brigit gave Marion, who was dressed, again, in jeans and a gray sweatshirt, the once over, and showed us to the first-floor rooms. These had French doors that opened onto a broad patio. Beyond the patio gray granite dropped straight down to the waves. I opened the doors and let a fresh salt breeze sweep in.

"What now?" Marion asked. She stood in the middle of the

room looking lost. It was a big room, with a sitting area separated from the two king-sized beds by a waist-high mahogany counter. There was a refrigerator set under the counter along with a well-stocked bar.

"Fix yourself a drink," I suggested.

"It's eleven o'clock in the morning."

"You're right. Well, then, sit down and relax, take off your shoes. I'm going to have a shower."

Marion didn't make any move to sit.

"What's the problem?" I asked.

She shook her head. "I don't know. I feel strange. I think I'd be more comfortable in a motel."

"Well don't let it throw you," I said, starting to take off my shirt, "we're better off here."

There was a polite knock at the door. When I opened it Brigit stood outside.

"Have you got any suitcases, Derek?" she asked.

I told her our visit was so spontaneous that we hadn't packed. I went on, "Is anyone else here other than you and the groundskeeper?"

"No," she answered and considered me thoughtfully. "If anyone should happen to call for you, should I tell them you're here?"

I smiled. Brigit, I realized, was more used to strange and tense arrivals than I'd remembered. "Absolutely not. Except Butler."

She nodded. "You'll take care of your meals?"

"Yes."

She looked over my shoulder at Marion. "If you'd like to take a swim there are suits in the cabana by the pool." She pursed her lips, thinking again. "And I think I have a change of clothes for your friend. Would that be all right?"

"That would be great. Got some shorts for me?"

She looked at my waist and smiled. "We have some of your old ones, stored away somewhere. Do you think you'd still fit them?"

I sucked in my stomach. "Of course I could."

"Right," she said, and she went to see what she could find.

"She seems to take everything in stride," Marion said.

"Comes from working with Butler." I went in to take a shower.

When I came out there was a pair of my old cut-offs lying on the bed and Marion was sitting in a lounge chair by the French doors, sipping a drink. She had on white shorts and a red sleeveless blouse.

"Does he keep a whole clothing store in the cellar?" she asked.

"Butler takes pride in anticipating all his guests' needs. It's a personal thing with him."

"Sort of like a competition."

"No, sort of like enjoying seeing people comfortable." I squeezed into the shorts. They were tight, but I could still breathe.

"You said he inherited this place?"

"His father had it built. He was friends with Wright."

"The old boy network."

"Yes, the old boy network." I fixed myself a drink at the bar and took a chair beside Marion. The sun was high overhead, crossing the noon meridian, but the room was cool. The ocean before us sparkled.

"This Butler is Boston Brahmin, isn't he?" Marion asked.

"That's true."

"Bloodlines all the way back to the *Mayflower?*"

I sipped my drink. "What's the point, Marion? Are you trying to tell me that because he's rich and his family is rich and everyone around him is rich that he's not a good guy?"

"Never mind."

"He's going to give us a place to stay—he's not going to kick us out, he's going to try and help us. He's worked his entire life for causes you would have sympathy with. So what's wrong with him that he doesn't pass the Marion Wilson test?"

"You're right, he's wonderful."

"Tell me."

"Forget it. Let's just sit here in our private room on the coast and look out at the water. It's beautiful, isn't it?"

"Give it a rest, Marion. Suspend judgment for a while. This day is just R & R, okay?"

"Okay."

"You had a close call yesterday. Can't you relax today? Do you have to always be in the politically correct place doing the politically correct thing?"

"That's the way I am Derek. If I brought you to a whore house to stay overnight, how would you feel?"

"That's a stupid comparison."

"To you."

We were definitely headed on the wrong track. Marion sat swirling her drink and staring at me grimly. She was more upset than I'd expected. I'd underestimated her again.

"I guess I don't understand you," I said.

"I'm not that hard to understand," she answered, and continued in slow, measured tones, "I am completely committed to equality for all people; men, women, races, colors, creeds. Tall people, short people. Fat, thin. Got it? And now, not in some distant future. I will do all that has to be done to see this come about. Simple enough?" She motioned to take in the whole room, the house and its fields. "And this place is a symbol of everything I stand against."

"Should we leave?"

She shook her head. "You wanted me to see Burgess, didn't you?"

"Yes."

"Then I'll see him."

We idled away the afternoon, walking along the rocky coast, swimming in the olympic-sized pool, making our own lunch down in the huge country kitchen. But where I saw peace and comfort, Marion saw extravagance and unwarranted privilege. She relentlessly disliked everything about Butler's house, from the private property signs down on the shoreline to the silver butter knife in the silver butter dish. I started to get jumpy, wondering what small detail would finally set her off; the brass door handles, the heat lamp in the shower, the recessed lighting behind the bed. I realized anything I appreciated, simplemindedly, purely for its convenience or design, Marion would detest as a matter of principle. She carried it too far, but that was how she lived. Attention to comfort above and beyond basic needs was anathema to her.

Things were better the second day, though, because we found out that Robert was doing okay. I risked a call to Emerson Hospital, saying I was a reporter from a newspaper in Connecticut, and found that he was in stable condition and out of intensive care. Later we found out that Butler had the Boston *Globe* delivered to the house, and I read, with relief, a very short story on the Gloucester arrest. Neither Marion nor I was mentioned. It didn't seem right, as though there was some kind of news blackout, but we decided to look at it as a good sign.

We decided to celebrate by taking our first excursion into the bay. There were three islands out there: Lamb's Head, Big Back and Little Back; and we'd decided to head for the largest island, Lamb's Head. It was a treeless hunk of granite, coated with a green swath of indomitable long-blade grass and a thick mat of wild flowers: yarrow, butterfly weed, Queen Anne's lace. The island was home to thousands of cormorants. From the patio we watched them wheeling above the island in thick swarms.

We loaded sandwiches, fruit and a thermos of iced tea into a pack and brought it down to the short dock where a seventeen-foot Mercury sailboat was tied up. The boat was a sorry sight. It had once been painted white, but the paint had long since worn off and patches of dried wood stared out forlornly at us. Brackish water lolled under the wooden seats and fermented some healthy brownish life form.

"Doesn't look very promising, does it?" Marion said.

We stared down at the boat like two natives observing some technological wonder beyond their grasp.

"We'll have to bail first," I said.

Marion looked out over the bay. Lamb's Head was only a quarter-mile of gentle, open water away, but now she looked at it like we were crossing the Bering Straits in a rubber raft.

"Are you sure you want to do this?" she asked.

"I'm sure. Don't worry, I've sailed before—even if it's been a while."

She looked at the bright blue sky overhead.

"We'll need hats," she said. "Do you have a hat?"

"There must be some around here somewhere."

We dug some baseball caps out of the boathouse. Marion looked down at the beat-up old boat.

"How do we bail?" she asked.

We monkeyed around slopping the dirty water from the boat and then climbed in with the awkwardness of confirmed landlubbers. Marion held on to the gunwales as I set the lines and ran the sail up the mast. I untied the bow and stern lines and pushed off from the dock, then grabbed the main sheet and tiller and steered out from shore.

We sailed out from the shade of the shore trees and felt a wind that had been blowing unnoticed across the bay. Marion wore a cap that had MERCURY stenciled on it and the wind flipped the free ends of her black hair. She smiled out from the shadow of the brim, still holding onto the gunwales for dear life.

I laughed at her as I remembered something. "You don't know how to swim, do you?"

I thought I saw a blush spread under the tan on her face and she smiled sheepishly.

"I never had time to learn," she said.

"I'll teach you."

"Not now, please," she said, looking fearfully out into the deep water.

"Put this on," I said, throwing her a life vest. She'd seen it lying there in the boat but was too proud to put it on.

We slipped away from the shore out into open water, and the house was soon lost in the trees. The whole shoreline of the island swept behind us, a green wall of trees and gray rock, broken in places by the dim outline of another cabin or summer cottage. To the south the island coast blended with the mainland, encircling us in a green wall. Northward, two headlands marked the bay's entrance, and beyond them I saw the low outline of ocean waves, deep blue water that raced to a dim, hazy horizon. We slipped across the broad bay and it seemed as though we were scarcely moving at all, that it was the sweeping coastline that turned behind us like a theatrical backdrop on a carousel. The water gurgling under our feet was a current running in a river. I steered on a port tack, the boat inching forward, the coast turning behind. Marion leaned back against the bow and turned her face to the sky with her eyes closed. I watched her sink into a warm lethargy and I sailed her farther from shore, farther still from the past. We could have been sailing through a Force 9 gale, and if Marion had had that peaceful look on her face I would have been happy.

We approached Lamb's Head with the wind to port and I fell off to run with the wind, under high cliffs of granite. The sheer wall facing us was pock-marked with crevices, and I saw as we drew closer the army of cormorants perched on their nests. They were sleek, black birds with sharp, pointed heads and they stood silent and attentive, watching our approach like sentries. It was like sailing to a well-defended fortress. I was watching the birds when I heard Marion say, "Hey, fella."

She was sitting in the bow looking off to starboard, where a harbor seal had surfaced, poking his tawny head above the waves and regarding us with grand indifference. He gave us no more than a casual look, ignoring Marion's reaching hand, as she said, like a kid at the zoo, "Come here seal, over here." Instead, he rolled over on his back, let out a brief snort and floated. With his stiff whiskers and brown fur matted to his skull he looked like a burgher condescending to share his swim with the peasants.

"We're on his turf, now, aren't we," Marion said, more as a statement than a question.

"He doesn't seem to mind," I answered.

"I wish we had something to feed him."

"Don't give him my sandwich," I said.

We swept on with the wind and I pointed to the cliffs. "We've got a welcoming committee," I said.

"They look grim," she said.

"Tough life."

"Very tough. Fly around a little. Snag a few fish. Survive."

We drifted with the wind. Marion lay back, the very picture of the vacationer at ease. There was no sound except for the light rap of the halyards, the slap of water against the hull.

"This is seductive," Marion said, speaking with her eyes closed, her face to the sun, "the thought of staying here. Some place on the coast. Get a simple job. One of those small cabins hugging the cliffs."

I tacked to port, rounding the island's southern edge. I watched an occasional breeze ripple the coarse grasses.

"But what then?" Marion went on. "The thought of every day just passing by scares the hell out of me. I'm not that type of person. I need a reason to get up every day."

"Are you talking to me or just out loud to yourself?"

"Jump in anytime you want."

"I'd ask why it scares the hell out of you."

She opened her eyes and looked out from under the cap brim. "Why do you think?"

I thought about it a minute before answering. "I'd say that part of it is that you don't know who you are outside of what you do. The thought of having to be Marion without being Marion, 'the little people's Joan of Arc,' leaves you entirely at sea. No pun intended."

"I hear your sarcasm."

"It wasn't too rough, was it?"

"I can handle it, but go to hell anyway." She smirked, looking out from down under.

Around the lee of the island the wind dropped down until there was barely a tug on the mainsheet. I stood up and motioned to Marion. "Time for your first sailing lesson."

Marion protested, but I prevailed. She stumbled to the tiller while I explained what she had to do. Holding the mainsheet in her left hand and the tiller in her right, she looked comically uncertain.

"Why are you doing this?" she asked, voice high pitched.

"Think of it as Outward Bound. A nature lesson. Get in touch with the wind."

"The wind, hell, we'll be swimming soon."

"Not enough of a blow. Concentrate. Feel the pull on the mainsheet?"

A brief gust came up and the boat heeled slightly. As soon as Marion felt the pressure on the sail she turned windward.

"Don't bail out so fast," I commanded. "Hold the tiller steady and let's pick up some speed."

"It feels strange. When the sail fills it's like I'm driving a team of horses." She was having difficulty operating both the sheet and tiller at the same time.

I pointed in the wind's direction. "Keep an eye on the water. You can see a gust coming by the dark ripples on the surface."

Marion stared out over the water. Catspaws came towards us. She tightened her grip on the sheet and her face lit up in a smile when we heeled.

"I saw it coming!" she yelled.

"You're learning. Watch out, here comes another."

We sailed behind the island for an hour while I taught Marion how to tack, run with the wind, how to sight the best windward course. She was a fast learner, as always, and she didn't want to quit when we had to start back home.

"We come out again tomorrow," she insisted.

"Absolutely," I said, "we'll turn you into an old salt in no time."

The sail home was perfect, with a following wind that made the keel rumble and shake, the sail belly out tight as a drum. Marion was sunburned and weary, but running, like a kid, on nervous energy when we tied up at the dock. We stripped the boat together and put the gear in the boathouse. She ran up to the room to shower while I was stowing the sail.

When I got to the room she was singing operatically in the bath. I climbed in with her and soaped her back.

"Turn around," I said. The water was cold when we finally left the shower.

I was awakened by the sound of a car door slamming closed. Marion dozed comfortably beside me and I shifted my weight, careful not to disturb her. When I got to the front of the house I saw Butler unloading his maroon Jaguar.

"You're early," I said.

He looked up, startled. "Derek!"

Butler had gotten older, and not gracefully. He had a round, basketball paunch, and his face, never exactly handsome, was mottled, either from too much drink or ill health or both.

"Derek!" he exclaimed again. He dropped the bag he was carrying and wrapped me up in a bear hug, giving me a killer squeeze.

"What the hell?" he said. "This is wonderful. Great. When did you get here?"

The car had a passenger who now climbed out and stood patiently off to one side. He was thin, almost anemic, and completely bald. Butler remembered him and introduced us.

"This is Reverend Hugh Williams," he told me. "He's my latest mission of mercy."

Williams offered me a mild, shy hand. "Butler's trying to keep me out of the hands of the government."

"Hugh's involved with the Sanctuary movement. The government wants to bag him for breaking the immigration laws," Butler explained.

"I'm not the only one involved, of course," Williams added with what seemed an attempt at modesty. "My congregation is helping the refugees, too. I'm the example."

"Butler will take care of you," I said.

He gave me a cheery smile full of false bravado, "Let's hope so."

We brought their bags into the house, Butler loudly filling me in on his latest courtroom exploits. I took his suitcase to his room and threw it on the bed. He snapped open the locks and started unpacking.

"I've got a surprise for you," I said.

"What?" He took some folded shirts and tossed them carelessly into a bureau drawer.

"Remember Marion Wilson?"

Butler stopped in mid-stride. "Yes?"

"She's here."

The smile he'd been wearing faded. The Burgess professional scowl took over.

"I need some advice," I continued.

He dumped the rest of his shirts into a bottom drawer. "You don't want advice," he said, "you want legal assistance. There's only one thing for her to do. You know that."

"Help me convince her."

He nodded. "This is a tricky situation."

"No one knows we're here."

"I do."

"Attorney-client privilege."

Butler smiled, a hundred deep lines engraving themselves on his face. There was an anticipatory look in his eye.

"She's my client, then?" he asked.

"She doesn't know it yet. But assume she is."

He nodded again, his mind already at work. "Bring her up for dinner. Six o'clock. I'm going to crash for a while." He straightened his heavy frame and patted his enormous sloping stomach. "The old boy isn't what he used to be."

"Six o'clock." I headed for the door, then stopped and turned back. Butler was staring absently at the floor. "Thanks, Butler." He grinned and waved vaguely, his mind elsewhere.

Dinner was in a broad, screened porch that had a cathedral ceiling arching fifteen feet over our heads. Salty breezes filtered off the ocean, which we could hear dimly as rolling surf. Butler put on chamber music and set up candles on the table. He rolled a wheeled liquor cart beside him and sat down, esconced for the evening.

"I dream about this place wherever I go," he said to us— Marion, Rev. Williams and me, sitting around the table like an expectant audience. He fixed himself a double black Russian, then settled back and beheld us, a father surveying his brood. "What a group," he said, chuckling. He took a long slug. "I see before me all of radical America. Malcontents every one. American refuseniks. The best and the brightest . . ." He paused, nibbled his drink, continued, "Well, the bravest, at least. We'll withhold judgment on the brightest."

Butler loved holding court, and I could tell he was going to be in rare form tonight. He waved his drink at me.

"Derek, you slouch, you missed out on some good cases, some real Donnybrooks."

"I followed them in the paper."

Brigit came out and started making drinks for the guests. Marion waved off the service and noisily got her own. Butler watched her annoyance with amusement.

He asked me, "Did you read about the dogfight that almost killed me?"

"Which one was that?"

"The doctor in New Hampshire. They had a very gifted, ambitious prosecutor down there with the euphonious name of Salvatore Ciccariello." He let the name roll musically off his tongue, then said, "We called him Chicklets. Had a great smile. He wanted to be DA so he courted the pro-life group by charging Doctor Jessup Homer with murder for an abortion he'd performed."

"How'd you do?"

"I played this one cagey, Derek, very cagey." He shook his head, pleased at his own chicanery. "I knew I was going to take a tanning on this one because the issue is pure emotion—it'll never be settled by reason. So I opted for a jury trial."

"Why a jury trial?" Williams asked. He didn't look comfortable with the talk of abortion.

"Because with an issue like this you want to make sure you get an appeal. A jury trial leaves more margin for technical errors on which I can base an appeal. If I just had some ornery judge, some backwoods old fart presiding over the case, all my eggs would be in one cantankerous basket. Judges hate to overrule another judge's decision."

"Did you get your tanning?" the minister asked.

"You betcha." The attorney gulped the last of his drink and made another, rattling ice cubes. "We brought in our experts and they brought in their experts, but our experts, of course, were dry, academic types. Theirs were committed to the cause, gladly willing to hype the emotionalism. For instance, they had a cool customer in Emily Pierce, the president of the local right-to-life group. She was this wonderfully austere, upright woman who insisted on calling the fetus 'the unborn child.' We'd already agreed in chambers that this was not an applicable term, but she had me objecting over and over. I got knees like Carlton Fisk, bobbing up and down like a yo-yo. 'I object, your Honor,' 'I object, your Honor.' It was quite a performance."

Reverend Williams shifted self-consciously in his seat. Butler noticed and said to mollify him, "Abortion is a terrible issue, but we're a pluralistic society, that's why it should be free choice. Anyway, Chicklets put on a great show, too. He trotted out pictures (one basis for appeal, by the way), he ridiculed my frigid experts, he made the jurors feel like the last bastion of decency in a corrupt world. He said, 'What are we talking about here? A piece of dirt? Some sputum? A blob of mucus? This is a child!' I got up wearily, 'Objection, your Honor.' When he was through with them there was no way they could face their families without having found poor Homer guilty."

"You lost the trial?" Marion asked.

He nodded, "I lost the battle, but not the war. We won on appeal, as I expected."

"What's this about it almost killing you?" I asked.

"I can joke about the trial now," he answered, taking a deep breath, "but at the time it was rough. It was a media circus. It caused hard feelings on my staff, divided my friends. And no matter what I felt about the issue technically, I couldn't help feeling that I could just as easily be defending the rights of the only claimant that had no say in the trial. But anyway, midway through the appeal process I had a heart attack." He chuckled, his heavy shoulders bouncing, "The right-to-lifers called it divine retribution. Maybe it was."

"Was it bad?" I asked.

"I survived. I can't play tennis anymore, but I survived. And I've had to cut back on my case load. The Reverend here is my only cause right now."

Williams gave the attorney a half-hearted smile. "I have to admit, Butler," he said apologetically, "that I have mixed feelings about your defense of Dr. Homer."

Butler stopped him with a wave. "Just because I'm defending you doesn't mean we're joined at the hip, so to speak. I don't have to hold dear all that you do either. I only have to believe you have a right to do it."

Here Butler stopped and looked pointedly at Marion. "Or, if I believe that you meant well by your actions, I can help you make an accommodation without extreme consequences."

I caught an intensity passing between Marion and Butler, as they calmly regarded one another, and as Marion considered what he'd said.

"Nicely done," she said, finally, "I get the parable."

"You do?" Butler looked pleased.

"Yes."

"I'm sure there is plenty about me that you don't like," Butler went on. "This house for instance. But I'll tell you I'd never give this place up, because it's my island of sanity after dealing with the heavy hitters month after month."

Marion shrugged. "Don't we all wish we had someplace to run? Except most of us don't."

"Did I miss something?" Reverend Williams asked.

"We were coming to an understanding," Butler told him.

"I see," Williams said. "You are a tolerant man, Butler. I could never in good conscience defend Miss Wilson."

"I'd never ask you to," Marion said.

"I'm sure you wouldn't," the Reverend answered, angry despite himself. "Perhaps some pastoral counseling would help you."

"I doubt it," Marion said.

The Reverend looked as if he were going to give another short answer, then caught himself.

Butler watched the exchange, waiting for it to run its course. He refilled his glass. Around the Burgess table, yelling, screaming and hurled epithets were nothing new, as likely a part of the meal as a salad or ice cream.

The Reverend's eyes remained fixed on Marion. He seemed to be gathering his thoughts. "There is a pervasive element in all the major religions that I've always found disturbing," he finally said. "It's a pessimism, really—a lack of faith in man's ability to establish a just life here on earth. I see this same lack of faith in you, Miss Wilson. It's what prevents you from renouncing violence against other humans. You could learn something from the Anabaptists. One of their spiritual leaders, Dirk Philips, refers to *lijdsaemheit,* yielding without resistance. A fascinating and terrifying concept. The only defense the Anabaptists have against aggression is to move on, actually uproot their lives and flee, or to rebuff the offender by 'witness,' forcing him to do whatever he's doing before the eyes of the community. Despite its impractical aspects, I see in this the only redemption for the world."

"We tried that one, Reverend," Marion said, "and found out first hand that it doesn't work."

"It works, you just gave up," the Reverend answered, his impatience rising again.

"Then what are you doing with your Sanctuary movement?" she pressed.

"Passive resistance. Bringing witnesses to U.S. policy in Central America up north to spread the word.

"It's futile, Reverend."

"The common view."

"I never thought of myself as common," Marion said.

"You are," Williams answered, heatedly now, "more common than you think. You are a typical American with a typically American response to power."

This made Marion laugh. "Wonderful. Can I join the middle class now?"

"You already have," Williams replied. He took a deep breath and worked visibly at calming down, saying to Butler mildly, "I just don't have your tolerance, I'm afraid. I want too much to achieve real order, peace."

Butler held up his hands, pointing to Marion and Williams together. "Listen to you two. You both are really after the same ends, but couldn't be more at odds. You both need to make room for the various and sundry ways, within reasonable limits, people of good intentions stumble toward their goals. It's those 'reasonable limits' *I* concern myself with because, collectively, they constitute the law." Butler held up a hand to ward off Marion, who had leaned forward to interrupt. "Law is created every day, by right-wing legislators, by left-wing legislators; by right-wing district attorneys, by left-wing district attorneys; by right-wing judges, by left-wing judges; you catch my meaning. We are a nation of laws that are interpreted *every day*, case by case. And where there is daily interpretation, there is the possibility for constructive change."

"No, not constructive change," Marion objected. "Laws are almost always refurbished at the expense of the most defenseless. Take, for example, workers on strike. When the courts finally intervene, it is always to, in some way, shackle the union . . . when courts intervene they are almost always ordering the strikers back to work or allowing nonunion people to take their place. The ultimate goal of the courts is always to preserve the wealth, the property, the company—not the people, not the union."

Butler took a deep breath and planted his elbows on the table. "Often, but not always, Marion," he answered, "and that's why I keep the faith. Your generalities are too general. They ignore the specifics. I operate on a case-by-case basis and take the victories with the defeats. That, as the song goes, is life."

"Don't quote Sinatra to her," I said.

Butler smiled sheepishly. "One of my few lapses in taste." He turned to Marion again. "But all of this is beside the point. What about you? We want to get you the lightest possible sentence, the most just resolution to your longstanding dispute with our legal system."

He caught Marion off-guard. "What do you mean?" she asked.

Butler feigned surprise, badly, "Surely you came here to ask my advice on a possible rapprochement with the authorities?"

"I've thought about it," she answered, "but . . ."

"Don't think too long," Butler said. "You really don't have a choice."

" 'Rapprochement with the authorities,' " Reverend Williams repeated. From across the table I could see his face flush red. "My God, Butler, you countenance barbaric acts. The woman should be sentenced for what she's done."

"Made to say Hail Mary's every day?" Marion snapped back.

"People, please," Butler said, "there's enough justice for all. Have faith. Trust me. In the end, Marion, you simply have to choose to believe that our courts, clumsy as they are, produce some kind of equal justice, that it is a country where, with all its prejudices, anyone can still get ahead. In the end you have to realize that the real, cruel dirty work is not the fight, but the day-to-day maintenance of fragile values.

He didn't expect an answer from Marion and he didn't get one. She gave him a nearly imperceptible nod, thinking more, I felt, about the Reverend's outburst than what Butler had said. Around midnight we decided to call it a night and I followed Butler to his library on the second floor. I took another drink from him even though I'd had enough. He seemed to have a limitless capacity. We sat in overstuffed leather chairs and I watched Butler brood, staring down at the oak floor.

"What do you think?" I asked, after he'd had enough time to collect his thoughts.

"I'll keep her away from the press, that's for damn sure." He took a gulp of his drink.

"You should watch that."

He considered his glass as if seeing it for the first time. "It's just habit." He rattled the ice cubes. "Because that boy was killed—funny, I forget his name now—we'll have to get her off on the felony-murder charge, like we had to with you."

"Richard. His name was Richard," I said.

"Richard, right." Butler nodded his head, remembering. "It seems like a very long time."

"Seems like yesterday to me."

The lawyer smiled sympathetically. "I'll bet. I'm sorry, I didn't mean to seem callous. At my age you realize you've forgotten more than you'll ever learn in the time that's left. I hope I didn't offend you."

"No offense taken, Butler. If you'd asked me two weeks ago I would have said that was another lifetime. Turns out it wasn't."

Surf boomed against the granite shore, caught Butler's attention. He tilted his head as if listening to music.

"Sometimes in my apartment in Boston I can hear the trucks on the Expressway," Butler said. "Their air horns remind me of the lighthouse up by the Point." He listened again. "Can't hear it tonight." He winced, head angled, straining for basso tones.

"We took your *Merc* out today. Don't you ever look at the thing? It needs work."

"I expect to come back some day and find it in the mud, barnacles roosting on the mast." He shrugged his big shoulders, half frustrated, half resigned. His mind went through some convolution and came to a different point. "Marion's right, half right. People like her always are. I know that my life is charmed. I suppose my career has always been an apology for that."

"So much the better for us."

He dipped his head, humble, accepting the accolades of cheering multitudes. "The fact remains it isn't enough. Never is, never will be. Every human being enters this world hungry, hoping for, expecting, the best in life. We claw each other's eyes out for it." Preoccupied, his eyes wandered the library, taking in the mahogany bookcases that were arranged neatly, alphabetically along the wall.

"Marion's going to be tough to convince, I think," he went on, "because of that small grain of truth she clings to. She can always make herself believe that she's more right than anyone else. She believes she sees the world more clearly." He took a huge deep breath and let it out slowly through pursed lips. "In the end, Derek, she has to decide for herself."

"You're right," I said, adding, "but I was hoping we could gang up on her."

Butler grinned conspiratorily. "Well, I think we'd better keep her away from the good Reverend. He's a shade too rigid to mix with her."

We agreed to meet for brunch the next day (Butler was going to sleep in) and I went back to the first-floor bedroom.

When I returned I saw that the French doors were open and that Marion was sitting on the patio. I left her alone, to consider by herself what had gone on that evening, and climbed into bed. When I awoke sometime before daylight, she was lying beside me, with her head on my chest, and she was still awake, her eyelashes brushing my skin as she stared out into the soft, cool night.

Hot beams of sunlight streaming into the room told me it was late morning when my eyes opened again. Marion murmured something under her breath, tossed restlessly, then came awake with a start. Her eyes searched the room, confused.

"What a dream," she said in a husky morning voice.

"I didn't sleep well either."

She closed her eyes, drifting, half-awake, "I didn't want to come in last night."

"Make it last forever."

"Yes."

We got going slowly, rising from bed in stages, running the hot water cold in the shower. When we made it upstairs Butler was at the table on the porch, with brunch spread before him. He looked up from his paper when we came in.

"I thought I got up late," he said. His voice, I noticed, was oddly restrained.

I brought Marion a cup of coffee and sat across from Butler.

Marion said to him, "You'll represent me?"

He put his cup down carefully. If he was surprised he didn't show it. "You'll have to do everything I say. Trust me."

"I understand," Marion said.

Butler nodded and again I thought he was holding something back.

"This will be a long haul, Marion," he continued. "The trial will be harder than anything you can imagine. I want you to avoid reading the sensation-seeking newspapers, not listen to the vitriolic talk shows, to ignore the prosecutor who will do his best to make you out to be the devil incarnate. Your life will be in the hands of 12 strangers. Do you know what that means?"

"No, I don't think I do."

"You're right. You'll have to be ready for that. For accepting the judgment of your peers."

Marion's lips drew tight. She nodded slowly.

"And you'll have to deal with this first." Butler unfolded his newspaper and handed it to her.

In a column on the bottom of the page a headline ran, "Suspected Gun-runner Dies."

A sharp-winged cormorant swept over us, its shadow skipping across the room, leaping to the wall, sailing over the roof and away. Marion put the paper down carefully, as if the letters could be dislodged from the page and sent tumbling to the floor.

"We checked. He was all right." Her voice had no tone, was flat, as distant as a voice leaking out from a wireless radio.

"I'm sorry," Butler said, carefully.

"The hospital said he was out of intensive care," I told him.

Butler just shook his head, staring at Marion. "This doesn't change anything," he said to her.

"Sure it does," she answered quickly. "Of course it does. It changes everything. What the hell do you think?"

Butler made a face. "Let me be blunt. Your friend is dead. This is very sad. But you knew and he knew the risks involved. That's changed for you now, Marion. You've chosen a different path."

Marion stood abruptly and paced the room again, the way she did that day in Ron's apartment. "Everytime I try to make peace with myself and this frigging country of mine something screws it up."

"What do you expect?" Butler asked, annoyed. "You bring it on yourself. You live a self-fulfilling prophecy."

"Maybe so," she replied. She stopped in the middle of the room and gazed around with the same confused look I'd seen that morning. "This is not where I belong," she said.

"Marion . . ." I began, but she cut me off.

"This isn't my place, Derek," she said. "We all find what we were supposed to do, by accident maybe, but we're stuck with it." She headed for the door.

"Damn it!" I yelled, rising.

Butler grabbed my arm. "This will show us what she really wants. I need to see what she does."

"To hell with that." I jerked my arm away and followed her.

I got to the room just behind her and saw her grab the car keys.

She turned on me and said, voice clipped, full of the anger she was creating, "Butler can give you a ride back, can't he?"

"He says this is what you really want, this is what you're most comfortable with. It's true, isn't it?"

She made her face impassive, emotionless. I realized that it was true, that she felt more sure, more safe, when it was essential that her feelings be checked tightly. That the sense of urgency, immediate crisis, was a buffer between her and everything outside of her.

"Believe whatever you want," she said.

"I will."

She stepped past me and started down the hall.

"Marion," I called after her, "don't look for me again."

II

B UTLER KEPT TELLING ME that Marion would be back, so I stayed on in Deer Island for two more days. He kept telling me that she was playing out the last of her illusions, whatever that means, and even though I thought he was spouting grand phrases like a good lawyer, I listened to him. There was nothing else to do.

On Monday he had to get back to the city and I hitched a ride down with him. We didn't say much in the funereal atmosphere of the car. Reverend Williams sat in the back seat with his arms folded and an air of having been proven right, that Marion was hopeless, and headed for a bad and well-deserved end.

Butler pulled up in front of my house and left the car idling. "Will you be all right?" he asked.

"Sure." I stared at my house, feeling strange for having left so suddenly, with no word to anyone. Mrs. K and the Harlows must have been wondering where I'd gone and rumors were probably flying up and down the neighborhood. I didn't feel like going back there but I couldn't think of an alternative. Not a logical one anyway.

"Call me if there's any word," Butler said.

"There won't be. I told her not to contact me again."

"Since when has Marion listened to what anyone else tells her?"

"That's a thought. I guess I'm just hoping she won't."

"Balls." Butler gave me a knowing smile. He was two steps ahead of me.

When he drove off I stood on the sidewalk like a man who had just dropped in from another century. He was right on one score, if Marion showed up I'd do anything for her again, and I wondered for a moment just how much of fool I was, and why.

I wasn't in the mood for explanations to neighbors, so when I finally snapped back to reality I hurried up the walk to my house. I probably would have made it inside, too, if I hadn't glanced back and seen my car parked by the curb, looking for all the world like a faithful horse returned to the stable. I was thinking that Marion was up to her old tricks, risking a dropoff like that, when Mrs. K, walking down from Orchard Street, spotted me. She was pulling her two-wheeled grocery cart behind her, walking slowly in her stiff-hipped, painful way, as if she was hauling the weight of the world behind her. She was the last person I wanted to see.

"Derek Anderson!" she called out. "Where have you been? We were worried about you."

I gave her a smile while working my key into the lock. "Just a short sabbatical, Mrs. K." I opened the door.

She stood the cart by her front walk and continued to my place, hauling her plump body slowly, as if she wasn't at all curious about my absence, but with the clear intention of getting to the bottom of things.

To head her off I said, "I took a well-deserved vacation."

She took that without answering and continued all the way to the bottom of my steps. Her dark brown eyes surveyed me critically. "There were some men looking for you."

"Encyclopedia salesmen?" I said, mustering a smile.

She didn't think it was funny. "They were very rude. Especially the young one with a movie star name, Oldham or something."

"I'm sorry if they bothered you." I put one foot in the door.

Mrs. K remained fixed at the bottom of the steps. "They came by several times. To the Harlows too, and the Druzbinskis next door."

I stepped towards the front of the porch, letting the screen door close with a pneumatic hiss. Mrs. K looked at me sternly but her eyes were watery.

"I'm sorry you got involved in my problems, Mrs. K."

"They said they just wanted to talk with you but I didn't believe them."

"Well, that's probably all it was. If they bother you again send them to me." I turned back to the door.

"Are you in trouble, Derek?" Her voice had a quaver in it. "I told them you were a good young man. A nice young man. The Harlows told them, too."

"The Harlows?"

"We all did."

When I turned to look at her, her face was set hard, defiant against some threat she wasn't even sure of. I didn't know what to say.

"You watch out for that young one. He's trouble."

"Thanks, Mrs. K. Don't worry about me. I'm fine."

She wasn't convinced and gave me a look to show it, saying, "Well, you let me know if you need anything," before turning and working her way back down the walk.

"Thanks again," I called after her.

The house was musty and cold, like an underground cave, and the first thing I did was throw open all the windows. I left the front door open and the back door too. Standing in the living room, surveying the place, with the benefit of perfect twenty-twenty hindsight, my run to Maine with Marion seemed all the more crazy, more doomed from the beginning.

I didn't know exactly where to start over. The answering machine was topped out with twenty minutes of messages. The machine at my office would be, too. There would be mail to answer and people with all kinds of questions. Crazy. Everything. Running away, coming back. The house, solid and patient, told me I'd been irrational again and I couldn't remember any time in my life where, if I was given the ability to go and do it over, I'd do it the same way. I had just stumbled from one delirium to the next, until something woke me up from my dreams.

There was nothing to do but jump in with both feet. I looked up Bill Stacom's office number and gave him a call.

"Jesus Christ, Derek, where have you been?"

"I've been away."

"No kidding . . ."

"Have you found a place?"

"Never mind that," he said impatiently. "The FBI is going crazy looking for you . . ."

"Why?"

There was a pause on the other end. "Are you going to bullshit me? You know what happened."

"What happened?" I asked, trying to be convincing. "I told you, I've been away."

There was another pause, this time accusing. "Okay. Fine."

"What happened?" I asked again.

"Right, fine, Derek." He was angry. "The FBI broke up some kind of arms shipment in Gloucester. They said it was Marion—and Robert Glazier was with her. He was shot, supposedly killed."

I tightened my grip on the phone. "What do you mean, 'supposedly'?"

"Then you haven't heard the update. No probably not. You were probably in transit. Why? A sudden attack of conscience? After leaving him?"

"What the hell are you talking about?" Since I'd started the charade I had to keep it going, no matter how bad it felt. Bill was having none of it but I had to keep lying to him. "Robert was shot?"

"Fuck you."

"C'mon, Bill," I said, and added to myself, give me a break. Trust me.

He hesitated a minute. Then, good friend that he was, went

on. "The *Globe* ran a story this morning saying that the report of Robert's death was an FBI scam. To get Marion back. They figured she'd come back to the funeral or something. They were going to stage a fake service, funeral, the whole bit. Can you believe that?"

And it worked, I thought. Marion had done just as they'd expected. It wasn't surprising, really, because they were all following a pattern as well choreographed as a ballet. Your move, my move. Action, reaction. Retribution, revenge.

"Well? Did she come back?" Bill asked.

"I don't know. I told you I was away."

"Okay, Derek," he said, disappointment in his voice.

It wasn't right, lying to him, but I didn't have any choice—he probably knew that, but it didn't help.

"What have they done with Robert?" I asked.

"He's been moved to Walpole. Christ, Derek, he lost an eye. He's still in bad shape. They shouldn't have moved him."

"The fuckers will do whatever they want."

"Why not?" he said bitterly. "Marion'll do whatever she wants. All's fair."

"Maybe she has to."

"You're defending her now?"

"No, but why defend them?"

"I'm not. I think they're all a blight on the face of the earth. I wish they'd all go to hell."

"They won't, so there's no use hoping."

"That's too bad, isn't it?" he said.

"Maybe."

We were both mad and didn't have much left to say. Bill cut the conversation short.

"I suppose you have catching up to do. People to see. I won't hold you up."

"I do," I said. "Stay in touch."

"Right," he said. The line went dead.

I put the phone down, annoyed by the bitter turn the call had taken, and worried because Marion was in Boston and Newman and company were waiting for her. There was only one place—Ron's apartment—where I might be able to contact her, and I turned from the phone, shut up the house and headed for Brighton.

I stood in the poorly lit hall, waiting. I knocked again. I could hear someone moving quietly inside Ron's apartment, but he hadn't made up his mind to answer the door. I thumped my knuckles against the dirty wood. The stealthy movements stopped. I pounded harder.

Finally he made up his mind. The lock clicked rapidly and the door swung wide. Ron stood a little back from the opening, steeling himself for whatever came next. He was about six feet tall, thin, with a bald head fringed with grey hair.

"What do you want?" he asked.

"We have a mutual friend, Ron. I want to talk to you about her."

That put him on guard and his eyes narrowed. "Who?"

I stepped into the threshold. "It would be best not to talk about it in the hall."

He put a hand against my chest. "I didn't say you could come in."

I slipped sideways into his hallway, the one between the back bedroom and the livingroom. "I've been here before, Ron. You have an old railroad conductor's lamp. I used it with your roommate."

"My roommate moved out. She's gone. Period."

"Let's close the door."

He hesitated and I took the opportunity to reach for the door and ease it shut. Quietly. His nerves were on edge and I didn't want to make any sudden moves.

"Let's go into the living room," I suggested. I put my hand on his shoulder and directed him through the archway. He didn't resist, walking slowly, lowering himself carefully, like an old man, onto the covered couch. I took the ragged armchair. The room was dark, still shadowed by the elm in the courtyard.

Ron looked like he hadn't been sleeping well. Having been

associated with Marion was too much for him. He sat with his elbows on his knees, working his hands nervously.

"So you're one of her 'friends,' " he said.

"I know her."

He wasn't listening. "What have you gotten me into?"

"I think you got yourself into it."

"Not this." He waved his hands, disclaiming all responsibility. "I thought I was just helping out someone . . . I don't know who . . . but not someone who gets into this heavy shit."

I tried to calm him down. "You're pretty clear, Ron. No one's going to trace her back here."

"Sure."

"It's a long shot, anyway."

"A long shot I don't need." He looked at me angrily, as if it was all my fault. "Do you know what this could do to me? I mean, not just me, all I've worked for? Do you know what I do?"

"Something with projectionists."

"Not just 'something,' " he said. "I'm building a union here. I've trained a whole generation of projectionists and taught them—not just how to run machines, but what a union is all about. They're all union people. They'll live and die by it. Every theater in this whole city," he made a sweeping motion with his hand, "every one of them will *have* to hire union help."

"Don't worry, it's not in jeopardy."

"Yes it is, man, it's all hanging by a thread. The owners would just love this. They'd have a field day. 'UNION LINKED TO UNDERGROUND.' It'd all go right down the tubes."

"Do you know where she is?"

"No."

"Any ideas?"

"I don't want to have any idea, understand?" He pointed at his chest. "I am the projectionist's union in Boston . . ."

"Okay, so you're a very important person."

He let his hand fall limply into his lap and his lips turned into a sour scowl. "You don't care. So what. You're one of those people who only think big. Only world movements interest you. The little things you pass over. Fine. Movie houses are no big deal, you're right. Forget about . . ."

"Hey, slow down a minute," I said.

He gave me a surprised look, as if he'd just noticed I was there. " 'Slow down,' he says. Right now the FBI is probably snuggled up next to that little shit Glazier, half out his mind on pain killers, and they're asking the same questions you are, 'Where's Marion? Where's fucking Marion?' The little bastard will cut a deal with them and he'll tell them my address. Everything'll go all to hell. They don't give a damn about me, they'll just screw up my life looking for her. They'll stomp on me to get at her."

"Look," I began patiently, although he was beginning to grate on my nerves, "I feel for you. You have a lot at stake. Fine. Just ride it out."

He smirked. "All you care about is Marion."

"Not for the reasons you think."

"I don't care what your reasons are." He shut his mouth tight, cutting himself short. A heavy silence fell between us.

It was useless to continue. I got up slowly and stood over him. "You're wrong about me—I hope it works out for you."

"Thanks."

As I walked to the door he called after me, "If you see Marion, tell her to go fuck herself for me, will you?"

Outside, on Chestnut Hill Avenue the midmorning sun was too bright. There wasn't a trace of humidity in the air, so the hot rays blasted through the atmosphere, making the sidewalks shine like metal ribbons and reflecting daggers of light off the windows of passing buses. I sat in my car, sweat rolling down my back, trying to figure out where else to look for Marion. Glazier's place was out. His offices too. The more I thought about it the more hopeless the possibility of finding her seemed. The morning's urgency began to dissipate. I was one person, with no useful contacts, trying to find a woman who had evaded the FBI for fifteen years. Unless she contacted me, there was nothing I could do for her.

I drove aimlessly, through Brighton, around the reservoir by Boston College, across town to Jamaica Plain, just scanning sidewalks with no hope of turning anything up. It was a useless exercise and I gave it up around one o'clock when I decided to switch gears and answer another nagging question—whether John Spenser had finally turned up.

The place where he'd lived was a row of brick apartments on a noisy street in Allston. About as far away from the Mystic Lakes as you can get. I had a sudden image of him in his running getup, gliding down the worn, dirt paths beside the first basin, his feet barely making a sound as he dipped into the hollow across from the yacht club. The image came on so strong I could almost hear him breathing, gulping the air, then it was gone. When I found the right address I mentally crossed my fingers, hoping I'd find him home, surprised to find me looking for him, amused that I'd been worried. But when I rang his apartment no one answered. That didn't mean anything, he might be out. I buzzed the super.

"What do you want?" an impatient voice called out of the intercom.

"I'm looking for John Spenser."

I listened to the static crackling from the speaker.

"You a friend of his?"

"I'm looking for him."

"I want to talk to you." He buzzed the door and I went up.

The super stood in his doorway on the second floor, his body blocking the entrance with the practiced caution of someone used to handling trouble on his own—angry tenants, unsolicited solicitors. He was short and fat and wore brown polyester pants and a white undershirt. His eyes gazed over me suspiciously.

"You know John Spenser?" he asked.

"I do and I'm looking for him," I said. I showed him my detective's license. "Is he around?"

He pulled some bifocals from his pocket and used them to

read my license. When he handed it back he said, "He seemed pretty straight. I didn't think he would do this to me."

"Do what?"

"Take off. Month and a half behind on his rent. Hasn't come in, hasn't come near the place. You know, they usually sneak back for a few things before I change the locks. He's too late, I changed them already." The super shook his head. "Too bad, I thought he was a nice kid."

"Don't give up on him yet," I said. "I mean I don't think he just took off because he wanted to."

"Is he in trouble, then?"

"Could be. Not with the police. At work."

The super wasn't surprised, or he didn't show it. He looked like someone who couldn't be surprised anymore.

I added, "Not drugs, either. He just got involved with the wrong people."

The heavy man nodded, although what I'd said must have raised a bunch of questions in his mind. He seemed willing to settle for the little I'd told him. He probably didn't want to know more.

"So what can I do for you?" he asked, swinging the door open slightly wider. "I told you all I know."

"I want to see his place."

He thought about it for a moment and then said, "Sure. Why not? Hang on."

We walked up three flights to the top floor, the super sorting through a ring of keys as we went up.

"I changed the locks," he repeated when we came to the door. He gave the tumbler a twist and swung the door open.

The air in the apartment was stale, lifeless. We walked down a short hallway, me following the super, and entered a small kitchen. Light filtered in from a small window over the sink. There was a plate and a couple of cups filled with stagnant water sitting in the basin. A few pieces of mail—bills—sat on the counter, unopened. The super eyed the dirty cups and pursed his lips. We went through an archway into an equally small living room where there was just enough room for a couch, a low table and one end chair. Two windows on the rear wall looked out onto an airshaft.

"How much did he pay for this place?" I asked.

"Four hundred."

"For two small rooms and a bedroom?"

"And a bathroom. The going rate. It's a tight market."

The walls were bare except for an old movie poster advertising "On The Waterfront." Marlon Brando stared soulfully out at the room. Next to the poster a couple of wall shelves were crammed with books. I scanned the titles: Studs Terkel's "Working"; O'Casey's "Selected Plays"; Commoner's "The Politics of Energy." Spenser's only nod to light reading seemed to be Kundera's fiction, and even his work is driven by politics.

The super spoke up beside me, "It says right in the lease, 'No shelves attached to the wall.' I'm going to have to redo this whole section."

"Where's the bedroom?"

"Through that door."

There were no windows in the bedroom.

"Was this place built from another apartment you chopped up? I thought you had to have windows."

"Not when this complex was built," the super answered.

"It's great. Where's the light?"

Spenser had tried to make the room more liveable—he'd stretched a blanket across the overhead light to cut down the glare, to add some color to the tiny cramped space, and he'd built a bunk bed with a writing desk below it. I snapped on a lamp. The desk was strewn with letters, piled with newspapers, sheets of paper. There was a plastic filecard box that I poked through. I shifted through the papers, finding nothing much: an unfinished letter to a friend in California ("The union campaign is going along, slow as hell . . ."); a page of notes for the speech I'd heard at Kiernan's; a stack of quick copy notices for some rally. There was nothing incriminating, no notes on a pad of paper: "Meet McGuiness at . . ." Nothing. The apartment felt like someone's tomb.

"Is that it?" the super asked.

"That's it." Spenser was gone and I knew he'd never be back here.

"What'd you think?"

"How long are you going to keep it vacant?"

"Another month and a half. That's the law. Then I clean it out."

"Let's get out of here."

I leaned against the wall while the super locked up. "I want to pay his back rent," I said.

The super gave me a puzzled look.

"And I'll pay one in advance," I added.

"What the hell for? I mean, sure, great, but why?"

"Humor me," I said.

I drove home and paced the house again. I had a job that night with Joanne and I was anxious to get started, to climb into another stretch limousine and gulp martinis or whatever depressant that would be passed around. To pass the time I hauled myself up to the top porch. It was not yet dark, although the sun was down; the blue sky was deepening towards black. Jupiter was just climbing over the horizon, shining bright like some important idea just remembered. If I'd had the energy I could have pulled out the Meade, but instead I just imagined the planet: hot-red, seething with clouds; its moons circling according to precise forces, forces that could be calculated, measured, tested. If I could start again, go back to Vermont and that Sunday nearly two decades ago, I wouldn't board that bus. I would stay and study medicine or some science where the world has order—predictability. Where the electron's spin and the planet's spin and the galaxy's spin can be divined with reassuring accuracy. Instead I found myself on a porch in Watertown, staring at Jupiter, one friend dead and another heading for trouble, and not able to do a damn thing about it.

III

———

I LEARNED NOTHING FROM my search of John Spenser's belongings—I hadn't really expected that I would. Looking back, I think I went to his apartment to try and fill the void left by his disappearance. He had vanished too quickly; without the slightest disturbance. He had simply been removed from the picture. All that remained of his life was dust collecting on books and stagnant water in a coffee cup. That's too harsh—I remembered him; the few people who loved him would remember him, be confused, worried, would press the police for an investigation. It would come to nothing, of course, because it was too small a case, without the backing of a public uproar.

So as that first day back from Maine went on I found myself getting tighter and tighter; saying to myself after arguing with Bill, "Relax, we'll settle this later"; saying to myself after not finding Marion, "Relax, be patient"; saying to myself after not finding Spenser, "Relax, there's nothing to do"; and all the while feeling my stomach muscles tighten, my neck muscles stiffen, feeling a nervous energy inside me building up to overload.

It was a relief when the time finally came to get back to work, and I left early to meet Joanne at the airport. She was dressed in a sleeveless black jumpsuit with a silver belt and a heavy silver buckle that sat low on her belly. Her eyes were rimmed in black and her blond hair was streaked with purple dye and held stiffly awry with mousse. She looked smug and self-satisfied, cool and *au courant,* and the sight of her tightened my stomach another notch. I started a fullblown argument with myself, one side sarcastic, a what-the-hell voice saying, "Go for it—have some fun;" the other side sensible, mature, "Ignore her, it's not her problem, it's yours—"

She snapped a wad of bubble gum as I approached and said, "Back down to it, huh Derek?"

"I'm on the job if that's what you mean."

She cast a scathing glance over my suit.

"Why don't you relax a little? Ditch the tie. We're not going to the Chateau, tonight it's the Centrum."

"Great—down and dirty tonight, Joanne?" I asked, taking off my tie.

"Yeah," she said, "rock n'roll."

"Fantastic," I said. The two Derek's seesawed up and down. I felt the hellion rising, ready to kick ass.

The band we were escorting came out of the terminal, three men in their mid or late thirties (it was hard to tell), dressed extravagantly in silk shirts and leather pants and high boots. They weren't punk rockers, they were heavy metal, which meant their hair was chopped and layered, pretty-boy style, and they wore gold anywhere it was possible: gold chains, rings, ear rings, nose rings, wristlets, anklets (probably), gold on their bodies, gold on their guitars, on their cars, on their girlfriends, gold on their records and up their nose. My hellion levitated, stuck out his tongue and waggled it at me.

Up close the band looked beat, with tired, lined faces that said they should have quit the business years ago. But on stage, bathed in colored lights, producing a crushing sonic noise from thousand watt amps, they'd look like gods, or close enough for the promotors.

Joanne whispered to me, "Two years ago these guys were playing the bars in central Pennsylvania. Now I have to make sure they have individual suites at the Plaza."

She introduced them to me, pronouncing Pennsylvania-German names that didn't go with the creatures hulking before me—Hans, Reinhart, Helmut. Their stage names were Stiff, Backer and Poison. There was some kind of joke in there but I never figured it out.

"Jesus, what a flight," Hans said. "Fucking turbulence from New York to Boston." He rubbed his paunchy stomach as if to calm the airline-dinner beast that was threatening to return.

"I've got something to soothe your nerves," Joanne said.

"Forget my nerves, my stomach is killing me," he said, and he belched loudly, his cheeks bulging out.

"Hans doesn't fly too well," Reinhart said. He was the tallest of the three, with coarse black hair starting to show streaks of gray. He had crows feet around his eyes deep enough to grow corn.

We hustled into the waiting limo and Joanne opened up the courtesy table above the bar and pulled three grams of cocaine from her purse.

I waited for her to measure out the lines and chop the bright crystals into a fine powder. Distance was what I was looking for. A far away place from John and Marion and Bill and the whole fucking mess. Joanne set up some lines on a small square mirror and held it out to me with a questioning look. Five years ago I would have accepted the offer, but I've lived long enough for it to have sunk in just how stupid it is to add another vice to my self-destruction repertoire. The boys in the band obviously hadn't caught on, and they expertly downed the stuff. They did two lines apiece and Joanne lined up more. My hellion watched and harrumphed, rubbing his stomach, so I fed him a straight Scotch. By the time we'd hit the turnpike they'd gone through the three grams and I'd made a dent in the limo bottle. Joanne dug into her black alligator bag for more coke.

"Good stuff, Jo," Helmut said.

"Watch out for him," Reinhart warned her, "when he get's fired up . . ." He made a spinning motion with his finger pointed upward.

I fed them some Scotch while they waited for Joanne to set them up again, and by the tollbooths in Brighton the five of us were feeling no pain.

"That's more like it," Hans said, sinking into his seat. "I thought for sure we were going down over New Jersey."

"Plane must have dropped a thousand feet," Helmut said. "Imagine dying in fucking New Jersey."

"It's as good a place as any," I said.

Hans was tugging at Reinhart's sleeve. "Let's do the bus, like Billy suggested."

Reinhart shook his head and said, for our benefit, "Billy's our New York accountant." He pronounced it, "Jeww Yawwk."

Hans persisted, "We spend fifty, another ten to fix it up. Two baths, separate rooms, video. The works. Nice smooth roads. The hum of rubber on the highway. No more fucking vertical takeoffs through the mountains."

"Man, we'd spend forever driving from date to date," Helmut said. His eyes half closed, he was inching across the seat towards Joanne. She wore a fixed smile.

Reinhart said, "If we're going to do anything it's a Lear. We get our own pilot and we," he pointed his finger to his chest for emphasis, "we, say when to fly."

Hans groaned. "We'd still have to take off, land. Fly through those . . . what do they call them? . . . bumps, air pockets."

"Drafts, vertical drafts," Reinhart told him.

"Air pockets," Helmut chipped in. He leaned against Joanne, started to massage her shoulder and said, "How're you doin?"

"Vertical drafts," Reinhart repeated. "There are up drafts and down drafts. But with our own Lear we can choose our route, our arrival time and everything. Plus we get a huge write-off."

"We get a write-off with a bus," Hans said.

"No way we're going to do a bus. What do I look like, some Negro honky-tonk player? B. B. King? He rides a bus. Not me." With a trace of annoyance, Reinhart reached out towards me, signalling for the Scotch. "We lose four gigs if we take a bus. That's two hundred. Enough for two goddamn Lears. Doesn't make sense. Do I look stupid?"

Helmut was almost in Joanne's lap.

"Whoa, take it easy," she said. Her voice shaky, wary. "I'm your rep, not a groupie."

"Don't be so up tight," he said.

"If you're so hot, Derek'll find a girl for you at the show. Won't you, Derek?" She looked at me, her eyes imploring. Her mascara had started to run.

"Sure," I said. "What's your poison, Mutt?" Joanne thanked me silently. It must have seemed a fair trade, some Worcester girl for her Back Bay virtue.

When we had parked behind the Centrum and I stumbled from the limousine, I felt like my shoes had rubber soles a foot thick. No contact with the ground. Cool as a cucumber. Floating. My sensible man was prostrate, the hellion doing a tap dance on his chest.

I cleared the way through an anxious crowd of teenagers waiting at the stage door. As we waded through them, Helmut caught my eye and nodded at a blond in three-inch heels. I led the band to the dressing room and went back outside. Prepubescent girls formed a circle around me like hopeful minnows. The blond was dressed tough in some kind of hard-bitten uniform, but her eyes were bright with inexperience.

"Do you want to meet the band?" I asked her.

She nearly jumped with excitement. "Yes!"

"Say you don't."

"But I do," she said breathily.

"No, say you don't." She was puzzled at first, her mind racing to figure out what was expected of her, and then she got the idea that this was the game, this was what the rock star wanted.

"I don't," she said.

"Good, go home," I said, and I went back in, slamming the door behind me.

"She chickened out," I told the Mutt.

"Then get another," he said. "I'll see her after the sound check."

The band went to the stage and left Joanne and me in the dressing room, which was outfitted in the usual concert opulence, as though for a head of state—full buffet with shrimp and lobster tails and soups and five kinds of meat. A well-stocked bar. I wandered in a daze, unable to contemplate forcing food down my throat. I ordered a drink from a white-suited bartender.

Joanne came up and put a hand on my shoulder. "Thanks," she said, "I never get used to fighting those guys off."

"Hazards of the trade," I said.

"I get so sick of it," she said. "Someday I'll give them a swift kick."

"Careful. Unless you don't mind modifying your employment situation."

"Maybe I don't."

I turned on the stereo. "Let's dance."

"You're in a strange mood tonight."

"I need to cut loose."

She gave me a puzzled smile and said, "Me too. Do some coke with me."

"I'll stick to this," I said, shaking my glass. I lead her out into the middle of the floor and we began to move together.

The room began to fill up with press, roadies and guests of the promoter. Joanne and I got the party going and everyone dancing. I found myself talking to the rock critic from a Boston weekly. He wore a gray pork-pie hat, a gray shirt, a gray tie, a gray sports coat, gray pants, gray socks, gray shoes. He said he was breaking away from the tiresome black that everyone was wearing these days.

"I don't like to march in that fashion lock-step, you know?" he said.

He explained to me the significance of the band, which represented, he said, the "dissatisfaction and outgrowth of rural America."

"Their sound is hard like the pre-Cambrian granite that forms the valleys and ridges of central PA." He said, swirling a hand, grasping for words. "It's a groan like the warping of earth, the neolithic crashing together of continents that bent the land, built mountains. You see, they come from dark valleys and high hilltops, and their psyche, whether they know it or not, evolved from this environment." He smiled apologetically. "I'm big on the importance of environmental influences, you know, as opposed to social influences. I mean, their sound is different from a big city band sound."

"But it's all electric . . ."

"Don't say it all sounds the same." He waggled a finger at me. "You're just not listening. They're much different than, say, a band from Boston, or New York. It's because of the environment. Boston bands can never sound really hard because it's too soft a place, with the ocean next door and the Charles flowing serenely through the city." He sniffed and bent over a table, snorting up a line. "This band is hard. Real hard." An idea occurred to him that he thought was brilliant, and he pointed his finger at me for emphasis. "Their sound is hard, but desperate too. The desperation of the land-locked, the person cut off from the sea . . ."

"The man afraid to fly . . ."

"I beg your pardon?"

"Hans is afraid to fly."

The reporter looked at me blankly. "Oh. Well. That would add to it, wouldn't it?"

The band came back in from the sound check and the Mutt hunted me down right away asking where his girl was.

"No takers, I guess you're losing your touch," Joanne said, coming up behind him. She looked like she'd been waiting for him to come back, so she could be the one to break the news.

"Say what?" Helmut didn't believe her. He looked from Joanne to me and then got the picture. He walked away mumbling, "Stiffs . . ."

Joanne laughed behind his back as he trudged away, and

then, triumphant, pulled me to where the dancing was, in front of the five kinds of meat.

"I think he was bent out of shape," she said.

"He'll get over it."

"Probably call my boss."

"He'll forget about it by morning."

She shook her head, with its absurd purple dye. "You don't know these people. I had one jerk raise hell because there were three cases of beer instead of four."

"The world must have stopped turning."

"Apparently it took him a whole case just to get himself lubed up."

I stopped dancing and took her by the arm to a quiet corner. She stood close to me and brushed her hand lightly over my chest. A smile turned up the corners of her mouth.

"We've worked together a long time, Derek. I always thought you were something of a stuffed shirt."

"I keep to myself."

"That's all right, I guess." Her fingers found their way to my skin. I pulled gently at the light hairs on the nape of her neck, toying with the idea of sex with Joanne Smythe. Since we were both high, it was possible, bordering on probable—highly likely. It wouldn't take much to get us started. Somewhere in my brain some last remaining cell of reason squeaked out a warning, but I didn't listen. I bent over and kissed Joanne, and her mouth opened, her tongue darting between my lips. She leaned against me and the fabric of her jumpsuit stretched against the contours of her body. I ran my hands down her waist and along the tops of her thighs. Her eyes had a liquid, sensual depth when she looked at me and said, "Let's get a cab and leave these boys to their own devices."

"What about the boss?"

"I feel a family emergency coming on. Hold on a sec." She went off to talk to another agency rep. When she returned she grabbed my arm. "Let's ditch these jerks. If I stay here another second I'll hurt someone. Or myself."

She lived in a Back Bay apartment, in a building where

three-quarters of the rent you pay is for its "wonderful, central location." Six hundred dollars gets you a studio, a corner kitchenette and a cramped bathroom. The rumble of traffic is loud only until three A.M. There was a couch against one wall, a bed against another, an expensive stereo system spread out on the floor, and little else, hardly anything that would tell you who lived here. It could be a man, a woman, a teenager or an adult. It felt as if the girl didn't know how to fill the free time in her life between work and sleep. An overhead fixture gave out a harsh light. The only object that gave the room a sense that some one lived there was an old doll propped on the bed, sitting upright against the pillows. Joanne threw her bag on the couch and waved her arms to encompass the room. "Here it is," she said apologetically.

She draped her arms over my shoulders and gave me another long kiss. It felt just slightly theatrical—overdone to help bridge the initial awkwardness. "Well, Derek," she said, huskily, "want a drink?"

"I don't think I need it," I answered. The barren room was depressing and I felt an urgency to get this going. Already I was beginning to feel the morning-after regrets. I backed her slowly against the wall and began to lower the zipper on her suit, the emptiness of the room working against my desire, as if a vacuum was drawing the heat from my body. So I sought her to ward off the chill. As she sought me. She tilted her head back, exposing her soft throat, and I ran my lips down to the taut skin on her chest, to the soft mounds of her breasts. She moaned and worked her shoulders free from her clothes, the jumpsuit sliding to the floor. I threw off my coat and undid my fly as she grazed my neck with her teeth, biting my shoulder through the cloth of my shirt. I entered her, pressing her against the wall as she wrapped one leg around me. We moved together, our mouths hot and wet, our tongues darting. She slipped down and put her mouth to my sex, licking my shaft and pulling me into her, sucking hard and insistently. I pressed my head against the wall and closed my eyes to the harsh light, concentrating to shut out the blare of automobile horns, the roar of engines, working to forget the image I held in my mind of the spare room, the single couch, the lonely bed.

Joanne stood up and her eyes were glazed with passion, nearly closed from sensual intoxication. "Let's lie down," she said, pushing me to the bed.

As I turned and stumbled forward I saw the doll propped against the bed pillows. For one moment it looked like a child, sitting with an expectant look on its sewn-on face, happy that Mom's home. It threw me, and I stopped dead in my tracks. It's hair was a rich yellow yarn and it was dressed in brilliant colors: red, blue, green. The doll brought the room to sudden life, but it wasn't a life that had anything to do with Joanne's Back Bay or her entertainers or her constantly changing outfits. The doll sat against the pillow like a memory of another time and place. Joanne spread herself out on the bed and, too carelessly, threw the toy on the floor, turning her naked body towards me expectantly. I stood immobilized, wondering what she thought every morning as she meticulously made up her bed, straightening the sheets, fluffing the pillows, tucking the cover in a neat line along the mattress, then placing the doll carefully, sitting upright, with a clear view of all she did during the day; and what went into that careless toss as she wrenched the doll from its place.

"What's the matter?" she asked.

The desire drained from my body and I lay down slowly, a short distance separating me from Joanne.

I smiled. "I'm having a sudden moral crisis."

She looked puzzled. "Why?"

There were wet tendrils of sweaty hair matted against her forehead and I reached out and brushed them gently aside.

"I hardly know you, Joanne. I sometimes think I can make love to someone and have it mean nothing, nothing at all. But I can't."

Her eyes roved my face distrustfully. Did I find her unattractive? Was she performing badly?

I took the edge of the cover and spread it over her, then cradled her head in my arm.

"I've got a lot going on, things you don't know about," I said. "I think what I really needed tonight was just someone to hold."

She didn't say anything, still looking put off, but she let me pull her into the crook of my arm and lightly brush her forehead. We were both breathing heavily like runners after a dash.

"Sorry," I said, "I know my timing stinks."

She allowed herself a smile. "That's the understatement of the year." And then, "I don't know whether to be hurt or angry." She thought about it. "I'm angry." She thought about it some more. "I think. I'm not sure."

"Want me to leave?"

She reached up and squeezed my arm, "Not yet."

Outside a truck shifted gears, slowing down for the lights at Mass. Ave.

Joanne said, "It's funny how this can turn to feeling cheap, dirty, so quickly."

"I think we avoided cheap."

"Did we?"

"By a hair's breath."

She was stroking my arm. "I'm not really good at pickups. I've got to be stoned to the gills."

"Now that's cheap."

She looked up, hurt. Then she smiled again. "I was right, you are a prude."

"Didn't I tell you?" I answered, "I'm a member of the God Squad. I've got to go and say a thousand 'Our Fathers' now. Kneel all night."

Joanne laughed. "It's not enough for the letdown you just gave me." She looked up and I noticed that the intoxicated glaze had left her eyes, that the fabricated flush of passion on her face had cleared and that they had been replaced by something else—curiosity, the bright spark of interest.

IV

―――

I LEFT JOANNE ON GOOD TERMS, after thrashing out what had happened, a short time later. Sex can be a substitute for real intimacy and what we'd ended up with instead of the usual bumping and grinding was a moment of disclosure, albeit brief and superficial . . . we didn't pour our hearts out—we weren't ready for that—or even sure we wanted to go further—but she knew something more about me and I'd seen beyond the surface of Smythe, the cool professional. I hadn't bargained on getting to know her better, but that's what I'd gotten myself into. And although I felt better for my loss of verve, in the back of my mind there was a disgruntled hellion who couldn't get Derek to ease up and just have a "good time."

I went home to bed and the next morning awoke with a start, heart pounding, senses alert. But the room was quiet and still; sunlight lolled behind the window blinds. I listened, wondering what had shattered my sleep, mentally bending an ear to each room of the house. It felt empty. Somewhere down the street someone was banging with a hammer. I closed my eyes and drifted, hearing the methodical thud, the intermittent rumble of a car passing. Sleep wouldn't come.

After fifteen minutes I sat up and threw my legs over the

edge of the bed, sitting hunched over like a boxer who'd just gone ten rounds. My ribs ached and my head was in a fog. There was a feeling of dread in my chest that I couldn't put a meaning to. The house creaked, expanding at the joints.

"Get up, Derek," I mumbled, and stood, stiffly, like an old man. Cold water on my face cleared some of the mist, so I followed it up with a chilling shower followed by a vigorous rubdown with the towel. A little better. Blood flowing more steadily. The energy level kicked up just enough to get me into the living room, but ran dry by the couch, where I plopped down and dozed.

The telephone snapped me awake.

"Derek? It's Margaret."

Even groggy as I was, the tone of her voice shook me.

"What is it? What's wrong?"

"It's Marion. They finally got her."

My mind cleared before Margaret had finished talking. "Where? When? How did you hear about it?"

"It's in the paper. They stopped her in Lexington. That's all I know, what I read. Do you have the paper?"

"It's outside," I said, standing up.

"What can we do?" she asked.

"I don't know, Margaret. Can I call you back? Later?"

"Okay. You know, it's probably for the best."

"Maybe," I said.

"It is, Derek."

"Whatever you say." I said I'd call her later, then I went and grabbed the *Globe* from the front steps. The story was on the front page. Big news. Newman would be happy. It read:

MARION WILSON, BRIGHTON BOMB SUSPECT, ARRESTED

Marion Wilson, member of the 60's radical group, the Day Street Commune, wanted for the 1970 bombing of a Brighton bank, was arrested yesterday in Lexington.

Wilson, age 37, has been underground since the attack on

the bank, which was staged at the height of the Vietnam War era protests. She is wanted in connection with several other terrorist incidents, including the 1972 robbery of a Wells Fargo depot, a 1975 bank holdup in Ohio, and a shooting incident on the Pennsylvania Turnpike in which State Trooper Roland Ames was seriously wounded.

FBI spokesperson William Duggan said Wilson was arrested following a routine traffic violation on Rt. III in Lexington. A subsequent search of her automobile uncovered a shipment of automatic weapons. Duggan said the guns are thought to be part of an arms transfer that law enforcement officials foiled earlier this month in a raid that resulted in the arrest of five men. Day Street Commune member Robert Glazier was wounded in that raid.

When I'd finished reading I was shaking with frustration. I'd been hoping that Marion would decide to turn herself in, hoping that she would decide to set her life straight, forget the endless retributions. She couldn't do it.

I went out onto my porch. A housewife drove by on her way to the market. Overhead, a jet roared into high gear, heading for Europe. My phone rang. I didn't answer it. Through the leaves of the maples I saw the jet's vapor trail, white and pure, cutting a diagonal across the sky. I thought, but didn't really believe it, that Margaret was right, that this was for the best. No, it wasn't for the best at all, because in Maine Marion had had a choice to make, and she'd made the wrong one. Now she wouldn't have that chance again, not for a long time.

V

THE ROOM SMELLED OF SWEAT and stale cigarette smoke. It was a small room on the fifth floor of the Women's Correctional Institution in Framingham. Dim sunlight filtered through a window high up on the wall and the bars cast a pattern on the lone table at which I was sitting. I wasn't alone. There were two FBI agents with transcription pads so they could take down everything Marion and I said. Standing behind me was the director of the Boston bureau, James Avery, and Paul Newman. When I'd arrived Newman had put on a triumphant look that I ignored. Beyond that, no one spoke. There was a single ash tray on the table.

I stared at the scarred metal door across the room. Avery bent over and whispered something to the stenographers. I heard the metallic rustle of keys and the door swung open. The entry way was dark and I couldn't see into the rear hallway. A plump matron came through the door. There was a pause. I strained against the table. Marion came through the door and took two steps into the room. She was dressed in a gray, shapeless uniform and her wrists and ankles were shackled. She looked around, her face impassive, taking in the stenographers, Avery and Newman, the high window, the spare table. Her gray eyes rested on me without emotion. She sat in the chair opposite me.

"It's over," I said.

She was holding a pack of Winstons and she pulled out a cigarette. She looked at the stenographers. "Did you get that?" she barked at them.

They stared at her. One of them wrote down her question.

"Bastards," she said. They wrote that down too. Marion lit her cigarette.

She let out a plume of smoke. "Failure to signal for a lane change. Can you beat that?" she said. She took another drag.

"I said, 'It's over.' "

She looked at me from the corner of her eye. "I heard you," she said. "Have they been giving you a hard time?"

I shrugged. "Just a few preliminary questions. They say I'll be subpoenaed. How about you?"

"They've got me in isolation." She glanced at the matron. "So I won't infect the rest of the population." She inhaled from her cigarette and gave it a disgusted look. "And all they have are these horrible Winstons."

I watched her, noticing her sallow pallor and her tense movements. I'd expected to find her resigned, almost relieved, but she was bitter and frustrated, at least that was the act.

She looked at the stenographers again. "Did you get that down? The cigarettes stink. They're stale." She turned to me again. "I'm sorry, Derek. I'm wound up." She lifted her hands. "They keep me in these, as if I could break out one of those windows." She nodded at the barred opening above. She turned to the matron. "I get an hour's exercise a day, alone. I eat, alone. The only time I see anyone is when I have visitors, then I'm surrounded by guards."

"Take it easy," I said.

She smiled for the first time. "I know. I'd better get used to it." The smile vanished. "But I don't like being treated like a leper." She looked accusingly at the matron. "I'm not contagious."

—— 246 ——

The matron stared back without speaking.

Marion smiled again. "They never say anything except 'Come here,' or 'Go there.' It gives me the creeps."

I reached out and took her free hand. It was the stiff hand of someone fighting for control. "I'll give you some pointers," I said, "I've had some practice at this."

"I see what you went through a little better," she said, trying to be sarcastic.

"Maybe you'll appreciate me more."

"I always did, more than you thought."

It was difficult, painful, not to be able to say all I wanted or to talk about the time we'd been together. I couldn't speak of it for fear of incriminating myself and that fear felt traitorous, disloyal, like a denial of all she meant to me. She knew all this, I could tell, and she was just glad that I was there, no matter what happened or what we said. She was going to need help, more than she'd probably admit.

"I'm here," I told her, "and I'll be here through it all."

A smile turned up the corners of her mouth. "I wish I'd come to you before, Derek," she said. "Maybe you could have steered me better."

I shrugged, "Maybe keep you from making bad choices."

"You would have tried, you would have done your best. The best anyone possibly could." She fixed her eyes on mine and squeezed my hand. "Maybe it's starting to sink in. A little too late, but it's sinking in nonetheless."

This was new. She stared at me intently, with an ironic look on her face, because it *was* too late, too late for what I'd been trying to get through to her, what Butler had tried, and succeeded for a while, to get across, and this had to be the first time in her life Marion had taken too long to make up her mind.

"It doesn't matter," Marion said.

It did matter, of course, but we left that unspoken. Instead I said, "My lawyer, Butler, has offered to take your case."

"Your lawyer, Butler, would be a good choice."

"Excellent choice. Harvard connections, you know."

"Fabulous," she said. She was looking better.

"You're going to be all right here." I made it a statement. "A couple of years, bingo, on the streets. You'll be fine."

Marion looked at all the blank faces around her, her own face becoming impassive again. "I can take it. I can handle what they throw at me. They can't do anything that isn't done to millions of people in the world every day. They'll do less. We live in a civilized society." She said this last sarcastically.

"We do, you know," I said.

She gazed at me, her gray eyes cool lenses. "I suppose we do. The society is civilized, it's just the people who aren't."

"Time's up," Newman said.

The matron came over and put a hand on Marion's shoulder. Marion gave my hand one last squeeze.

"Will you come again?"

"Of course."

"Good." She stood up and the matron clasped her arm. Marion gave her an annoyed look. "I'm coming," she said. She picked up her cigarettes. "Could you bring me some decent cigarettes next time?"

"They're bad for you."

She smiled. "I suppose I'll have plenty of time to work on quitting."

"It's a good project."

"And after a few days I'll be able to rip the bars right out of the wall."

"Okay. What kind?"

"Kools."

They led her out and I sat staring at the door, watching as it shut with a heavy bang. I heard the stenographers talking, comparing notes. Newman came over and tapped my shoulder. He wasn't exactly gloating, but he looked pleased with himself and the general state of things.

"Well, we did get her," he said, voice full of vim and vigor.

I stood up and started to go past him, but he put a hand on my shoulder.

"That was touching there. I've very moved—" he went on.

"Watch yourself," I interrupted.

He feigned hurt, "No, I'm serious. The two lovers reunited after so long. Years and years. The last time they saw each other was a night long-g-g ago. Way back when. And now, to see each other again in such tragic circumstances—"

"You're pushing it," I said.

"Sorry," he said, and for a moment he caught himself, taking a mental step back, but he was excited. "You made me think of something, in the kitchen there. You said, 'You'll keep doing what you're doing' . . . etc., 'eventually you'll bump into each other.' I thought, why not make sure? The death notice was my idea."

"Brilliant."

He tapped his forehead, "I knew she'd come back."

"Good for you." I pushed past him and headed for the door, but he caught my shoulder again.

"That part about the 'few years and out on the streets,' I'm sorry but that's a little off." Newman looked to Avery before continuing. "We've got a lot on Marion Wilson. All kinds of charges. Years' worth. She's not going to get two years," he shook his head, "she's not going to get ten years . . . we're going for thirty, maybe fifty. She's going to get very old here."

"Why are you doing this?"

"Because it's my job."

I looked over Newman's shoulder to Avery, who'd been watching the scene impassively. "You keep guys like this on your staff?" I asked him.

He shrugged. "He's got the spirit. He's young." He shrugged again.

Newman smiled with false sympathy, or maybe it was real. "Nothing personal, Anderson. Believe me. It's my job. I do it well."

There was plenty I could say to that, but I didn't. He was lying; this case was very personal to him and a hell of a lot more than just his job, and I couldn't figure out why. I had a feeling it was one of those questions I'd never get an answer to, that its solution was somewhere in the unseen grudges passed between generations, lost in Freudian Oedipal/Electra complexes or explainable more simply by the need of each new crop of humans to impose themselves on those who came before them. Whatever it was, Newman was going to make it as bad as possible for Marion and there was nothing I could do about it. Again, nothing I could do to help her—except chew my fingernails while Butler did his work and hope that he did a better job than Newman.

VI

T HE NEWSPAPERS MADE A BIG PLAY of Marion's arrest, running retrospectives on the antiwar movement and the Day Street Commune. My name came up often and my client load fell in direct proportion. This had happened once before, when a *Globe* series had cut into my business for a few months. But the public has a short memory. After the newspapers end up in the trash heap people remember my name but not where they first heard it. In the long run the notoriety helps. But during the initial furor it was Joanne Smythe who stood by me. When I was a pariah she neglected to tell her employers that I was still freelancing for them and most of my income still came through her. That one night when I called time out made me more real to her than any sexual gymnastics could have. Joanne felt it had created some kind of bond between us and she began calling me on days we had off. We went out a few times but my interest in her was simply platonic. (Is there any such thing as 'simply' platonic?) I was seeing Marion in Framingham twice a week and when, following a visit, I met Joanne, her vacuousness annoyed me. She had only a superficial, 'Liberal Arts' knowledge of everything: politics, history, science. Her vision of the civil rights movement was one of cheating welfare mothers, her vision of the Vietnam war was simply that we'd 'lost.' For Joanne, two decades of struggle that I'd lived through had been reduced to slogans—Bring Home Our MIA's. I couldn't fault her, we were just raised in two different times. But the facility with which she changed her whole image for her jobs bothered me. She hid behind masks every day. She was like a living copy of the ads on TV where Wall Street accountants chuck off their Brooks Brothers suits and become "real people" on the weekends, wild and crazy, water skiing on the lake, drinking "the real thing." As if personality were transferable. Her apartment, with its minimum of furniture and bare walls, seemed a reflection of her soul and it reminded me of a cell, made more horrible because, unlike Marion, she wasn't confined there against her will—this is how she chose to live. I told myself, as I drove from visiting Marion to a job with Joanne, that any comparison was useless, but I couldn't help thinking that it was Marion I understood, who, I thought, at least had tried to live beyond herself.

On a Saturday in the second week of September I went with Bill to do some work on his new apartment. He was moving in on October first and wanted to fix up the place. I followed him over to a street in Medford lined with hundred-year-old three deckers. The houses butted right against the sidewalk with postage stamp lawns. There were no trees on the street, just raw telephone poles with electric lines sagging loosely between the homes. There was a factory at one end of the street and a main boulevard at the other. Bill got out of his car and stood, a massive form with drooping shoulders, before his new apartment. He had the third floor.

"This is it," he said, looking up without enthusiasm.

"Looks like a quiet street," I said.

"It is when the factory's closed." He pointed to the house beside his. "That worries me." The house was run down. The front porches had been removed and you could see where the main support beams had been. It was sided with crumbling asphalt shingles that must have been twenty years old. There was an old Ford Fairlane set on blocks in the driveway. It looked like it hadn't been moved in years.

"Come on," Bill said.

We went up through a musty hallway to the top floor. There was a note tacked onto Bill's door that read, "Mr. Stacom. The previous tenants owe me two months' rent so I've changed the locks. Come to me for new keys."

"Great," Bill said.

We ended up climbing from the hallway onto the porch and entering through a side door.

The apartment had a side hallway off of which was a living room, dining room and bath. The kitchen was in back with two bedrooms. The previous tenants had left in a hurry. There were a few odd pieces of furniture remaining and some clothes still hung in the closets.

"Everything looked cosy with the tenants when I saw the place," Bill said.

"I guess it wasn't."

There was a loud roar out in the street and we went to window and saw a black GTO with its rear end jacked up and a chrome air scoop on the hood screech into the driveway across the street. Stenciled across the trunk in white letters was the legend, "Flirtin' With Disaster." A kid in his teens jumped from the car and sauntered into the house.

"Beautiful," Bill said. "Come on, I'll show you what needs to be done."

In the living room a water leak had started the ceiling paint peeling and two of the walls needed a lot of spackling to fill in holes. The dining room had a linoleum floor that was coming up that Bill wanted to replace. A panel in one of the bedroom doors had been kicked in. The kitchen cabinets were stained with grease, and the faucet let out a steady flow of water. In the bathroom the shower tiles bulged away from the wall and maybe twenty of them had fallen off. The rest of the tiles were stained with a black fungus.

"Why don't you get the landlord to fix all this?" I asked.

Bill gave me a hard look. "I made a deal in lieu of the deposit. I couldn't really pay it," he said. He looked around at the disarray. "Can you believe this place is six hundred a month? That's without heat."

We heard yelling from across the street. A door slammed.

"Fuck you! I don't have to tell you where I am every fuckin' minute!"

"You're out all goddam night . . ."

"Big fuckin' deal!"

"You walk in here like it's a goddamn restaurant . . ."

"I gotta eat!"

They went back and forth like this for a couple of minutes. A few times it looked like some punches would be thrown. The boy would storm down the driveway, fists tight, then storm back. They looked like a nice family.

"Come back here!"

The kid raised a finger at his father and marched away, slamming the GTO's door. The engine started up, all eight cylinders banging. There was a screech of spinning tires as the car shot from the driveway, then a long wail of burning rubber as it charged up the street.

Bill had gone pale. "I can't bring my girls up here."

"Why? Because of one muscle head?"

"I know the kids around here, Derek. I work with them."

"You're talking like an elitist now, Bill."

He watched as blue exhaust smoke filtered up from the street. "Listen, I feel for them, but I've got to think of Marion and Jody." He began an agitated walk around the living room. "I had bad feelings about this move. Why didn't I keep looking? Now there's only two weeks left." He gazed around him like a stunned man. "What was I thinking? This won't do."

"It'll work out."

"It won't! It won't work out!" He waved his arms in a disgusted motion. "Jesus, Mary and Joseph!"

I tried to calm him down but he was too agitated. He said, "Just leave everything here, just leave it." He hurried to the door and opened it. "Come on, I've got to find another place."

"In two weeks?"

"In two weeks. I don't care if I have to pay a thousand a month. My kids are going to be in a good neighborhood."

"C'mon Bill, don't panic. You don't even know anybody here."

But there was no talking to him. He was in a sweat over protecting his daughters, imagining all the years ahead of them, tough schools and tough, rough-edged boys, with no interest in college and the white collar, and somehow this move, at this point, was crucial—one slip altering the course he'd dreamed for his girls. He grabbed my arm and ushered me through the door, leaving it wide open in disgust, hustling me downstairs as if I was to blame, because I was the nearest live body he could rail against. It was like being thrown from a bar by a bouncer.

On the sidewalk he cast a relieved glance behind him, like a man who'd just escaped a house fire. "Christ," he said.

I let Bill go off on his own, and drove back to my place. When I got there Mike MacDonald was sitting on the front steps. He stood as I parked my car and came down the walk.

He looked nervous and I thought if he'd worn a hat he would have taken it off and held it humbly in his hands. I knew what was coming, and, following on the heels of my experience with Bill, I wasn't in the mood.

"Hi," he said quietly.

"What do you want?" I went past him, opened my door and went inside.

"It's about John."

"What about John?" I snapped.

He followed me into the living room. "We've got to do something."

" 'We?' 'We've got to do something?' You mean me, don't you? You want me to do something, don't you?" I spun around and glared at him. "What do you want me to do? Take on the union myself? He's dead, you've figured that out, haven't you?"

MacDonald stared at me, his face white. He hadn't admitted to himself that Spenser was dead. He probably didn't know what he expected of me, he just wanted help. His face went slack and his hands dropped to his side. He looked around numbly, saw the couch and wearily lowered himself into it.

"Look," he said, "I don't know what's been going on. I don't know what John's done or what he was up to. I've just been sitting around stupidly waiting for something to happen. Nothing has. I can't believe it. John's gone, the contract's been passed, the TOU is falling apart, nothing's changed." He said this slowly, as if recounting a dream. "Everything's happened and nothing's happened." He looked up at me with wet eyes. "I don't get it."

I went over to the liquor cabinet and poured myself a drink. "You don't get it?" I said. "What don't you get? What did you expect when you took on the Teamsters? Did you expect McGuiness to walk over, shake your hand and give you the keys to the union hall?"

He waved his hands in confusion. "I didn't expect this."

I sat across from him, counting to ten to calm down. I wasn't being fair to him and I knew it. "Okay, Michael," I said, "how much do you know?"

"I told you before, I just knew that John was acting strange. You were the one who said something about McGuiness."

I nodded. "You don't know what he had on the president?"

"No."

I told him everything I knew.

"That's absurd," MacDonald said, his eyes wide with disbelief. "You can't play games like that with McGuiness. Why didn't he tell me about it?"

"Judging from your reaction he probably knew you wouldn't help him."

"So he went to you for help."

I couldn't decide if there was any recrimination in what MacDonald said. I shrugged, "He came to me and I advised against it. Several times. That's all I could do."

"You could have gone with him."

"I thought you just said the idea was absurd."

"For someone like me or John."

"Why am I any different?"

MacDonald's face got a shrewd look. "I've been reading about you in the *Globe*. You know about these things. You're a detective. He would have stood a fighting chance with your help."

"You're reading ancient history. I was a kid then. I don't think that way now."

"But you knew John would go ahead anyway. You knew how determined he was. But you let him go alone."

I was starting to get mad. MacDonald had somehow managed to turn the blame on me. I had enough guilt from myself, I didn't need his help in making me feel worse.

"That was his choice," I said, "I'm not responsible for that."

"And now you're just going to let McGuiness get away with whatever he's done."

"I'm not letting him get away with anything. I have nothing to do with it."

"Yes you do, now." MacDonald said. "You know what's gone down."

"It's a police matter."

He shook his head. "That doesn't mean anything. You and I have nothing but a suspicion of what's happened. The police couldn't do a thing with it. I've already filed a missing person report. It's collecting dust somewhere. You're the only one who can do something."

"What about you?"

MacDonald raised his hands, palms up, helplessly. "This is out of my league. I'll help you if I can, in whatever you do."

I smiled grimly back at him. "In whatever I do. How is it that all of a sudden it's my business?"

"Because you know what happened. You made it your business when you became a private investigator. Why'd you do that? You put yourself in a position where people come to you for help."

"Not illegal help."

MacDonald nodded. "Okay, maybe it's all right that you didn't help John. But now you have certain knowledge that he's been murdered. You've got to do something about it."

I went and refilled my glass. "I'll never pin anything on McGuiness," I said.

"Have you tried?"

I smiled. "I know better than that. This isn't a TV show. I haven't anywhere to start. Not a thing to go on."

The shrewd look came back. "You have what John told you."

I felt something knot up in the pit of my stomach. Mac-Donald thought of himself as a peaceful man who was now being clever. I said, "You're not talking about justice, now, MacDonald, you're talking about revenge, and you want me to do it for you."

MacDonald leaned forward, a gleam in his eye. "You can finish what John started," he said. "You can salvage all his work for the TOU."

"I don't give a damn about the TOU."

"Then do it for John."

He was still leaning forward, anxiously, and I saw him for the conniving bastard that he was. His neat brown hair was freshly combed. His shirt had a polo player stitched above his heart. His pants were chinos from L. L. Bean. He drove a new car and lived comfortably in a home of his own. Bill Stacom would give his right arm to live in MacDonald's neighborhood.

"Get out of here," I said.

His face paled. "What?"

"Out!" I slammed my glass down on the coffee table and some liquor sloshed out. I went to MacDonald and grabbed him by his shirt, pulling him to his feet.

"I don't owe you anything!" I yelled into his face. I pushed him towards the door.

"Wait a minute," he protested, "you've got to do something. McGuiness is going to get away with it!"

I pushed him out onto the walk.

"If I do anything, it won't be for you, do you understand?"

He stood blinking in the sunlight, dazed. It took him a moment to collect himself, and then he started to get mad. "You're a coward, Anderson. You're useless!" he shouted.

"To you, yes," I yelled back. I slammed the door. I heard his rapid footsteps on the cement walk. He'd come very close to getting me to help him. I knew very well that a murder had been committed and felt obligated to do something. But Mac-Donald was the species of man who created trouble and paid others to do the hard work while he stayed far away, neat and clean. I could picture him egging on John Spenser in some subtle way; bemoaning their lack of success against the union, talking bitterly about the apathetic membership. He would always be pessimistic, cynical, and an organizer like John would keep trying harder and harder. Had I been just as bad? I tried to remember how I'd talked to him. Had I encouraged him as well as discouraged him? Had I been optimistic about his alternatives? Not enough, not enough.

I dropped down into the couch and grabbed my drink, staring dully at the white sunlight that filtered without conviction through the curtains. I felt limp, numb, without even the energy to berate myself for the way in which I'd failed John Spenser. I sat there for a long time, until the window was dark.

VII

W HEN MARION AND I STARTED working in the Day Street Commune we believed that we could change the world through peace, love, harmony and all those large, vague, nouns. Even after our disappointment in Dunn County we were still committed to nonviolence. Marion thought that we had failed in the South simply because we finished working before the job was done, and so we formed the commune as our way of life and as a symbol of the way others should organize their lives. It was our small encampment on the frontier of human trust, cooperation, peace. From that center we would branch out, the plan had it, to take on other large nouns, like injustice, racism and imperialism. Our first target was the war in Vietnam and at first we continued as nonviolent activists. But for all our marching and sit-ins the war kept going, escalating, the numbers of troops stationed in Da Nang, Hue, and Na Trang, growing monthly. We started working with Vietnam vets who told us what was really going on with our troops, the drugs, the racial battles, the fragging of officers. One black sergeant told us how he landed in Da Nang on April 4, 1968, the day Martin Luther King was assassinated. The first thing he did in

Vietnam was to disarm all the blacks in his platoon. The war became an absurdist piece, more befitting of Genet or Sartre than real life; General Lyn Kao Ki, the little man with a gun strapped to his hip; the My Lai massacre; the unceasing body counts ticked off nightly on the national news. Yet the harder we demonstrated the more terrible the war became. The mining of Haiphong harbor on Christmas Day—can something so cynical happen outside of fiction?—the incursions into Laos. In the end Marion and I were just as determined not to fail this time as others were determined to defeat the North Vietnamese, and our tactics escalated with theirs. Call it failure of principles, nerve, frustration or whatever; after the riots in Chicago, when Richard dragged me, stunned from a concussion, through Grant Park, I came to believe that force could only be met by force. King was dead, Robert Kennedy was dead, and yet American forces raided Cambodia.

So Marion, Rich and I began to plot on our own—excluding Stacom and Margaret, Priscilla and Glazier—and the commune began to go bad; it became a fetid soup, invaded by a poison virus. The closeness soured, as if some fermentation process were under way. We were torn: Bill and Robert kept urging peaceful demonstration. Richard, Marion and I urged action. That's how it happened that it was just the three of us who fashioned the primitive explosive device, the faulty timer, that tore through the Brighton National Bank as Richard walked toward me, smiling his crazy smile, with his square white teeth shining in reflected street light.

"You know about these things," Mike MacDonald had said. I got up the next day and sat before my toast and coffee, reading in the paper "Sikhs Bomb Temple," "National Guard Clears Picket Line," and heard in the back of my mind Newman's words, "She's going to grow old here." We spend our lives trying to live up to a set of values, finding it increasingly hard to do so as we knock up against the practical world. The strongest of us persist; the rest of us make excuses and live as less than we want to be. That morning I surveyed all that happened since Marion had reappeared, since Spenser leaned beside me in Kiernan's. I came to a decision. It was Friday. McGuiness would be heading for the club. It was already too late to help Spenser, but if I could get McGuiness where I wanted him, it might not be too late to help Marion.

Part Three

I

I DROVE UNDER THE BARE MAPLE TREES, their limbs forming a fine tracery against a deep blue sky. The last time I had taken this road John Spenser sat beside me, talking about the Mystic Lakes as though they were some grand metaphor for American life. It was now a warm early Fall day, but the lakes were still alive, sailboats skimming the water, swimmers lolling on the beach. I made a loop around the three basins, staring at the houses Spenser had admired. I saw college kids painting the trim on one of the Dutch Colonials and Mexican gardeners tending thick, bushy rhododendrons. I passed the yacht club, the small bungalows, the sprawling colonials with deep green lawns, the sturdy two-family houses. John had marveled at his luck, how his daily jogging route had crossed paths with McGuiness. He'd been amazed at the coincidence that had drawn them both to this string of blue water. Driving now past the homes clustered against the shore, I thought it was not a coincidence but inevitable, that in our hunger for the good life we would all eventually end up driven in masses, fighting for the last small square of green, the final breath of clean air, cool water.

I parked my car by the pumping station and took a camera with a telephoto lens from the trunk. The path John and I had followed was slippery with leaves. I slid down the steep embankment to the low hollow where we'd stopped and watched McGuiness. There were three couples seated at the tables on the club's rear deck. A waiter moved unhurriedly among them.

I stood there a half hour before the realization hit me. It should have occurred to me before. McGuiness wouldn't show. John Spenser would have driven him somewhere else. His Friday rendezvous would no longer be safe here and that's what would concern him most, safety, security from knowing eyes.

I took one last look around. Spenser had stood under those birches and said to me, "I should let him get away with what he's been doing because he's got the power and isn't afraid to use it?" I wondered if he'd approve of the use I was going to put his information to. Probably not. I went back to the car and drove from the lakes, heading to the one place I might be able to pick up McGuiness.

The union hall sat in an old warehouse district of Chelsea, surrounded by the remnants of flattened buildings, their cement foundations peeping out of the rubble. The hall looked like the survivor of an air raid. It was a hard, dirty, brick building in which the first floor windows had been boarded up. Totally appropriate for the union headquarters. After circling the block I spotted McGuiness's black limousine parked in back. I situated myself across the street underneath the steel girders of the central artery and slid down in the seat, prepared for a long siege. Long-bed trucks rolled down a nearby off-ramp and wound their way through industrial lots. From one the girders above the roadway a sign was hanging: Support The McGuiness Team. I drove forward a few feet until the sign was out of sight. At three o'clock McGuiness exited the building. He was preceded by two men, one of them Packy; the other I didn't recognize. Packy held the door for his boss and then climbed into the driver's seat. They sped around the block and then climbed onto the artery, headed towards Boston. I followed them easily, a few cars behind. Packy drove in a slow, almost stately manner, as would befit the king of the union. We got off at the Storrow Drive exit and headed west for a short time, then got off at Beacon Street. We circled the Public Gardens, wound past the State House and headed downhill to Tremont Street. The limousine pulled into the parking garage for a new condominium, Common Gardens. The union president was doing all right for himself. The condominium had double bronze and glass doors that opened onto Tremont Street and I positioned myself outside. McGuiness came from the garage by himself and entered one of the four elevators in the lobby. I went inside and watched the numbers. He stopped at 20. Top floor. Top drawer. I went to the desk. There was a dark, Middle Eastern-looking young man there with an economics book spread open before him.

I asked, "Is Mr. McGuiness in?"

His hand reached automatically for the tenant book. "What apartment?"

"20–C"

He skimmed a page. "Mr. McGuiness is in the Teamsters hospitality suite, 20–B. I'll ring for you."

I put up my hand. "I want to surprise him."

He gave me a cool, apologetic look. "I have to announce you."

I tried to look flustered. I looked at my watch. "Maybe this isn't such a good idea. I'll try later." I hurried back outside. My car was parked illegally on Tremont and when I got back there was already a ticket on the windshield. The only efficient department in the whole city bureaucracy is the traffic department. I climbed into my car and thought over the situation. What I needed was information—information about who McGuiness's mistress really was. Compromising photographs would help, too, particularly if I were going to threaten McGuiness and his mistress with exposure. I wasn't sure yet whether that would be necessary, but it would help to have options. I decided to start by working both ways at once.

The condominium parking garage had a booth off the sidewalk with an attendant. I went over to it.

There was a sallow-faced, middle-aged man inside. He wore

Dacron pants that needed washing and a sweater with seams that were pulling open. He looked like he was one step away from sleeping on the Common, or in the vents of the Public Library.

"Is there public parking in this garage?" I asked.

He raised his eyes from the *Herald*. "No, sir."

"Parking for guests of the tenants?"

"Yes, sir," he said, "they have to sign in."

I made a show of slowly taking my wallet out, parting the billfold so he could see the green bills inside. His eyes followed me carefully.

"I'd like to know the plate number of one of the guests," I said.

"Sorry, sir, we can't do that."

"I understand," I said. I took out a twenty, starting him out slowly, giving him a chance to push up the fee. "It's a private matter," I said, folding the bill and handing it towards him.

"Sorry," he repeated, with less conviction, "the list is private."

"I understand," I said. We were singing an old duet, a love song with currency for the melody. I brought out another twenty. I folded this one and put it beside the first.

He tried to keep his eyes off the bills but the money drew his attention seductively, like a beautiful woman alone at the bar on Friday night. "What apartment would that be, sir?"

"20–B."

He pulled out a guest book from the shelf behind him. When his eyes found who owned the apartment he hesitated.

I slipped out another twenty and nestled it beside the others. "Utmost discretion is ensured," I said.

He paused a moment, his eyes flicking from the book to the money. Finally, he said, "Mrs. Regis, Brown Mercedes. Mass. plates, 270 NJN." His hand darted out and grabbed the money. Then, a nervous twitch jerking his upper lip, he went back to his newspaper, trying to act as though nothing had happened.

I called the Nashua Street registry, got the main desk, and

asked for complaints. A woman with a hard-edged Dorchester voice answered.

"I got a ticket yesterday," I bellowed, the irate citizen, "and I had time left on the meter."

She ignored my heavy wind and asked calmly, "Plate number?"

I told her, accenting that the car was a Mercedes. The light tap of a keyboard came over the wire.

"Your name, sir?"

"Regis."

"Sixteen, Lincoln Road, Wellesley?"

"Yes, yes," I said impatiently.

"Mr. Regis, that ticket hasn't been entered into the computer yet. You'll have to wait three days or mail in the ticket with a note requesting a hearing."

"I don't want a hearing, I want the damn thing erased." I argued with her for a while, as any self-respecting businessman would, then hung up. I had a name and address.

I went back to my car. There was another ticket on the windshield. On Tremont Street the metermaids work in swarms, like killer bees.

If I wanted to, I could now put some pressure on Mrs. Regis—something I was inclined to do. But I was working fast and hot, so I decided to explore the photographic possibilities.

The only entrances to the condominium complex were a doorway directly to the garage from the sidewalk and another past the main desk. The garage door was locked and I'd have to sign in at the desk, so I circled to the rear of the building and found a service bay that was open. There was a maintenance man shuffling boxes around.

"I live in 16–C," I told him. "I thought I saw a couple of roaches darting around in my kitchen."

"We'll have to spray, sir," he said.

I frowned and shook my head. "That's so inconvenient. Taking everything from your cupboards and all that. Do you have some kind of trap I could use?"

"Sorry, sir, you have to buy them yourself."

"That's too bad." I spotted a door that led into the building. "Is that open? I don't want to walk around again."

"You could have come here through the back hall," the maintenance man said, reaching for a ring of keys on his belt. He let me in.

I was in a rear hall, with an elevator that probably went to the garage, where Packy was waiting for his boss. A short distance down the hall was a locked door that opened to a small room with mailboxes. I waited for a few minutes, until an older woman with silver hair and a pinched face came in walking an elaborately coiffed poodle. I knocked politely on the door and she opened it.

"Forgot my keys," I explained. I picked out a mailbox and peered into it. "No mail, again."

The woman looked into her box and I saw a disappointed look cross her face.

"Discouraging, isn't it?" I said.

When she answered I caught a whiff of Scotch on her breath and she talked with a gravelly voice. Too many cigarettes, too many long afternoons. "Depressing. Four children and two grandchildren and they never write."

"Shameful," I said. I walked with her into the lobby and put her between me and the front desk. It didn't matter, the desk clerk was deep in debits and credits.

The hallway on the twentieth floor was long, narrow and quiet. I stood outside of 20–B and just for fun put my ear to the door. Nothing. Besides the elevators and the uniform row of apartment doors, there was a laundry room, but no windows, no access to the outside from which I could observe the floor. I went back to the elevator and descended to the tenth floor, where a sign told me I would find the pool.

The pool stood on a rear deck, with apartment balconies rising ten floors above it. Across the alley where I'd found the service bay was the blank wall of the Opera House. The theater's roof was only six stories high, too low for what I had in mind. A short distance behind it I saw the new hotel/shopping plaza of Lafayette Place rising a full eighteen stories. It would do as an observation post. The wonderful thing about high-rise apartments is that the occupants don't feel the need to draw their blinds. From Lafayette Place I could train a long lens on McGuiness's love aerie. But it would have to be a very long lens and any pictures would be grainy and rough, which offended my professional pride. I decided it would be better to focus on Mrs. Regis.

I returned to my car and sat watching the traffic crawl, bumper to bumper, down Tremont. I already had Mrs. Regis's address, so I could look her up anytime. If my plan were to work, though, it would have to be put into action soon, so I decided to take a chance and follow Mrs. Regis's Mercedes when it left the garage.

As I sat there in the front seat, absently drumming my fingers on the steering wheel, I thought about McGuiness. He had done all right for himself. In his day you moved up through the union by starting at the bottom, working the ware-houses and trucks, taking on the difficult job as shop steward, then business agent, then any one of the Local's offices. Being a Local president meant a position on the board of the national organization, like moving from state senator to Congress. McGuiness had spent his adult life working for the union and I guessed this affair with Mrs. Regis, a refined woman who wore expensive perfumes and discreet but valuable jewelry, was his reward to himself—a kind of summation. Had John Spenser realized he was attacking not just an office, but a man's life? Spenser wouldn't have cared. McGuiness had abused his trust, the faith of his men. Spenser wouldn't be interested in excuses.

What was in it for Mrs. Regis? It could be anything, from actual interest in an ambitious man with rough hands who'd risen through an infamous organization, to simple revenge on a wayward husband. Or, like the poodle's mistress with her Scotch, she could be escaping long afternoons and an empty home. The reasons weren't really important. What was impor-tant was finding some way to leverage McGuiness.

I almost missed the Mercedes when it finally slid past me at nine o'clock. Mrs. Regis drove carefully down Tremont and headed through the theater district to the Mass Pike. We got off at Route 95 and headed south to Route 16. From there we went west to Abbott Road, and then turned toward the country club. The street instantly became a country lane, threading quietly under oaks and maples. The houses were far apart here and hidden from the road. Mrs. Regis turned into an unmarked drive and I pulled onto the shoulder, watching her red taillights disappear.

I sat for a few minutes, thinking. Common sense argued against confronting Mrs. Regis in her own home. It was easy to imagine Mr. Regis taking exception to a stranger barging in at nine-thirty P.M. and demanding a private audience with his wife. But that could throw her off balance too, which was good. I decided to risk it.

I turned the car up the private lane, which followed what looked like a golf course to my right. Past the course the drive took a sudden left and headed deep into a quiet wood. Without warning it led into a wide opening in the forest and just ahead was a sprawling, modern house, with large windows and broad flat walls that intersected in clean, sharp angles. In front of it was an intricate, contemplative Japanese garden. The drive ended in a circle set off to the side and I parked and stepped out into the cool night. The stars seemed unnaturally bright, and for no reason at all I remembered that Jupiter and Saturn were sharing the sky. They'd be in the southeast, shining with no regard for what was about to happen.

A small, plump woman with white hair and a round, pleasant face answered the bell.

"Is Mrs. Regis in?" I asked.

She smiled politely. "She just returned home. May I tell her who's calling?"

I gave her a calling card that was printed with just my name. She looked at it briefly and then opened the door for me to enter.

"I'm Christine's mother-in-law, Mrs. Alberts," she said, still smiling warmly. "Follow me, please, Mr. Anderson, and I'll tell her you're here. She's freshening up."

Mrs. Alberts led me to a sitting room that had floor-to-ceiling windows looking out over the garden. When she left I glanced over the room. There was a Frankenthaler original on one wall, a couple of Miro prints on another and several pieces of sculpture I didn't recognize. There was a comfortable L-sectional couch and two chrome-and-leather Vassily chairs. Along each wall were waist-high book shelves and I wandered over to one, where a group of family pictures were spread out. They were shots of typical family outings; in one I saw Mrs. Alberts when she was much younger, with a woman I took to be Mrs. Regis—a strawberry blonde with a healthy complexion and a generous smile. Beside her was a man I assumed was her husband, who looked remarkably like Mrs. Alberts, with the same round face and frank smile. Later pictures showed two children, and as I walked along the bookshelf I watched them grow from toddlers to high school to college. In the final pictures they had children of their own.

"Christine will be right down," Mrs. Alberts said as she returned. She saw me by the pictures. "You're admiring our brood?" She stood beside me and pointed to the man beside Mrs. Regis. "That's my boy by my first marriage, Christine's husband. He was killed in an auto accident on that horrible Route 2. That dangerous section in Lincoln."

"Oh," I said, unable to mask my surprise. "I'm very sorry." It had never occurred to me that her husband might be dead.

"Thank you," she replied. She regarded the pictures thoughtfully. "I moved in with Christine four years ago. She's been very good to me." She paused as some memory occupied her mind. She seemed to shake it off and pointed out the children for me. "This is Reese with his wife Nancy and my great-grandchildren. Excuse me," she smiled, "their children, my great-grandchildren. How possessive an old woman gets, and this is Ruth with her husband . . ."

"Mother," a voice behind us chided gently, "I'm sure our guest doesn't want the grand family tour."

She was standing in the doorway, wearing a white blouse and a tan cotton skirt. Her hair had faded to a light gray from her early years, but her face was still open and warm. She advanced across the room and extended her hand.

"I'm Christine Regis, Mr. Anderson. I don't think we've had the pleasure of meeting before."

I felt my mouth go dry. "No, we haven't," I said.

Christine Regis turned toward her mother-in-law. "I think we should have a few moments to ourselves, Mother," she said.

Mrs. Alberts said to me, "Sometime I'll take you through the rest of the tour." I mumbled some reply and she excused herself.

"Let's sit down," Mrs. Regis said. She was a tall woman and she moved with a casual grace. She sat on the couch and I sat beside her. This was not what I'd intended to do. I had planned to come in and confront her roughly, with a hard edge, hoping to panic her into calling McGuiness with a request to "give Anderson whatever he wants." But Mrs. Albert had started to shake my resolve and now Christine herself made me pause. I began to wonder if there was a gentler way I could do what I'd come to do.

"May I get you a drink?" she asked.

"No thanks."

"Fine," she said, folding her hands in her lap. "What can I do for you?"

I took a deep breath and met her eyes. They were a light green and regarded me with frank curiosity.

I launched right in, not in the gruff voice I had planned to use, but quietly, like an insurance man discussing the very important benefits of an expensive plan. "It's about Richard McGuiness," I said, "and you."

Her back stiffened perceptibly. "Oh dear," she said.

I looked down stupidly at my hands.

"Oh dear," she said again. There was a pause. I was tongue tied and searched for some way to continue.

"He is married, you know," I said finally.

One of her hands had crept up to her breast bone, as if she

—— 274 ——

was short of breath. She rose slowly and walked to a cabinet across the room. She opened two doors and brought out a glass and a bottle. "I think I'll have a drink," she said.

Her back was to me. After she filled a glass she stood gazing into the cabinet. "Do you represent Deborah?" she asked.

"No."

She thought about that and then collected herself, turning and taking her place beside me with some hidden resolve.

"Is this some dirty little union business, then?" she asked.

"No."

"Blackmail?"

"Not for money," I said. "It doesn't really concern you, Mrs. Regis." I went on, aware in the back of my mind that the words sounded strikingly like those Newman had used on me, "I just think you should stop seeing him."

She sat with her back straight, her shoulders firm and square. "But you don't know what you're saying," she replied. "It does concern me, very much. Richard has been very good to me." She sipped her drink. She continued in a rushed voice, "He and Peter were friends, they got to know each other through business, and when Peter died Richard came to the funeral, and then here. He helped me through a terrible time."

"He's married," I said. I almost said, "And he killed a friend of mine," but that was something I didn't want getting back to McGuiness.

"So what are you? A religious fanatic, making the world safe for the righteous?"

Her lips had begun to tremble as she fought for control. This exposure, this late-night visit by some creepy little man was something she'd lived with for a long time. Now the bad news had been delivered and I was the messenger.

As if on cue in a farce, Mrs. Alberts appeared in the doorway. "Can I get you two something?" she asked. "Some hors d'oeuvres?"

"No, mother," Mrs. Regis almost shouted, then she controlled her voice. "Nothing, thank you."

"Are your sure? Mr. Anderson?"

"Nothing, thank you."

"Oh, really, come on now Christine, it's so rare that we have guests." Mrs. Alberts hustled busily into the room and crossed to the cabinet. "We have some cheese here, and a spread." She worked up a tray of snacks. Mrs. Regis and I sat in a composed and uncomfortable silence. Mrs. Alberts brought a glass tray over and placed it on the coffee table. "Mr. Anderson, you don't have a drink," she said, "please, let me get you something. A Scotch perhaps?"

"Nothing, really."

"Soda water and lime?"

"I'll be leaving soon, thanks."

Mrs. Alberts looked from me to Christine and saw that all her efforts were failing. "That's too bad," she said. "Christine doesn't get out enough. All she has is this charity on Fridays. I keep telling her to—"

"Mother," Mrs. Regis interrupted, her voice tight, constricted, "Mr. Anderson is *not* interested in my social life."

The elderly woman stopped and finally realized that my visit wasn't what she'd hoped it was, something good for her daughter-in-law. She became cool and correct. Nodding to me, she said, "Mr. Anderson," and quickly left the room.

Mrs. Regis and I stared at distant points, avoiding each other's eyes.

Finally, she said, "I suppose it had to come to this. The whole situation was untenable. It just happened. I'm against adultery, really. I think a husband and wife should remain faithful, through everything. The vows say, 'through sickness and health, for richer or poorer till death do us part.' They're beautiful words. I've always believed in them, despite what you might think."

"Mrs. Regis, I—"

"No," she said, holding up her hand. "You're right. I helped a man break his vow. It was wrong—terribly wrong."

The situation had gone awry—not at all what I expected—and I found myself wanting to comfort her. I said, "Your mother-in-law is right. You should get out. There are other men."

She shook her head. "I'm too old to start again."

"No you're not."

She looked at me with red-rimmed eyes and a weak smile. "Believe me, I am. That's probably why I've clung to Richard. I need that magic and I'm afraid I'll never feel it again. It's a horrible thing to lose, that first love. Everything that follows is so mannered and careful. I've been fooling myself that my feelings for Richard were the same passion. They weren't, they can't be. Those passions only happen when you're young and stupid and still believe in magic. When you're older and have seen life you can try to force that feeling again, but it's never the same. Never."

I stood up, anxious to escape what I'd started. "Try," I said. "He's not a good man. You can find someone better."

"You're wrong, Mr. Anderson. He's been very good to me."

There was a lot I could say to that, but I didn't. I'd already upset her enough. "I'm sorry, Mrs. Regis, but this is how it has to be."

She sat staring down at the carpet and didn't answer. I walked quietly from the room.

Outside, I took a deep breath and looked up at the sky. Through waving branches I saw Jupiter and Saturn climbing in the west—the god of Innocence following the Roman King of Gods, the heaven's supreme power, like a dog on a leash. It struck me then that I'd started my own grab for power and it seemed somehow fitting—or sadly predictable—that the first person hurt in the struggle was the most innocent.

II

I DIDN'T EXPECT I'D HAVE to wait very long for McGuiness's response to my visit with Christine Regis, and I didn't. The next morning I was reading the newspaper ("President Calls Star Wars 'Our Best Hope For Peace' ") when there was a brief and very firm knock on my door. I was wearing my Colt in a shoulder holster and before answering the door I slipped the safety catch off.

It was Packy. Behind him, the black limousine idled by the curb.

"Mr. McGuiness wants to see you," he said.

I looked pointedly over his shoulder. "Oh? Where is he?"

He nodded towards the car. "We'll take you to him."

"I have regular business hours. Do you know where my office is?"

He eyed my Colt and made a quick decision. "You didn't listen to me. We don't want trouble with you. Why cause problems?"

"There won't be any trouble."

"No?" He seemed surprised. Relieved. "Good. Just don't push your luck."

"Luck has nothing to do with it."

He answered with a long stare. "Ten o'clock. Be there."

"Aloha." I waved at him.

I went back to my paper and tried to ignore the loose feeling in my stomach. I dug into my grab-bag of cliches to buck myself up: Derek makes his move; he who acts is right; might is right; power rules; Derek reenters reality.

My office had the strange feel of an empty set in which a play was about to unfold. But no matter how normal I tried to act, I was waiting for the big hand on the clock to reach twelve and the little hand to reach ten. The sounds of traffic on the main street had a distant, detached quality, as if I was hearing them out of sync with a movie track. The whole day had an unreal, theatrical feel to it. I rehearsed the variables in my mind.

By going to Christine Regis first, I'd sent Richard McGuiness a message. If he hadn't been sure before, he knew now that I was a person who could hurt him. Unfortunately, how much I could hurt him was still open to question. As long as he cared what his wife thought or what Christine Regis thought, he had a reason to negotiate. But if the unintended effect of my visit to the Regis home was to prompt Mrs. Regis to break things off immediately, and if McGuiness cared nothing about what his wife might think, I had no leverage at all. And that worried me.

There were good signs, though. McGuiness had sent Packy to my door alone. That suggested conciliation. The fact that McGuiness had agreed to come to my office at an appointed time also suggested conciliation. So there was reason to hope.

McGuiness arrived right on cue. I heard his car drive up to the curb, the driver's door open and close, the rear door open long enough for someone to disembark. Then a pause as the door was closed and Packy hurried to open my outer door, my bell ringing as it opened. Feet in the anteroom and then silence. I stood up. House lights.

They were impatient. Packy knocked on my office door.

I opened it. "You're supposed to wait quietly until I open it myself," I said.

Packy stood regarding me with the look of a man trying to identify a strange bug. Behind him was McGuiness.

I'd never seen him up close and I was surprised by him. He had a rough edge to him as you would expect, but there was a calm about him too, a quiet presence. He had a full head of silver-gray hair with a regular cut like you see on the golf course or Johnny Carson. His face was angular and he had a slight hook nose. His skin was leathery, but almost translucent, as if he spent much of his time indoors. He had blue eyes that seemed to look at you from a faraway place. He was my height, a little over six feet, in good shape, and he wore a white shirt with the cuffs rolled up and chino pants. He seemed to be considering the significance of my remark. He brushed it off as flippancy.

"Wait here," he said to Packy.

I held my door for him and watched him pass, entering the room coolly, surveying the decor casually. He saw the visitor's chair and sat down. I rounded my desk and sat across from him. I waited for him to speak. A heavy truck rolled by in low gear.

"You've hurt me very much," he said, the wounded lover.

"Sorry."

"You struck out at me from the clear blue," he continued. This wasn't true and he knew it . . . he was just feeling out his role. Starting slowly. He'd stay love-crossed until he was sure what I was about.

"It wasn't out of the clear blue," I said. "I need something from you and I needed leverage. Be sure that I'll expose your affair if I have to. Then the damage will be irreversible."

"What makes you think it isn't already?" he asked.

"It isn't," I said. If he said it was, the deal was off.

He eyed me, wondering perhaps just how extensive my knowledge of his relationship with Christine Regis was.

The silence between us lengthened and he let me hang, waiting for his answer as he glanced around the room like a man who has lost everything and is numb, beyond caring. The air conditioner across the alley kicked in with a loud whoosh. McGuiness folded his hands limply in his lap.

"Christine isn't like you and me, Anderson," he said, finally. "She has a conscience. She's never been happy with the arrangements, our meeting secretly. It grates against her up-bringing. She's a very refined woman." He stopped just short of admitting he was lucky to have her.

He let another long interval pass. The man knew how to control things. He must have studied with the Japanese, who use silence like a blunt instrument. I wanted to shift my position but sat rock still instead, trying to match his solid calm.

McGuiness took a deep breath and picked at an imaginary piece of lint on his trousers, then looked like he was going to speak, then stopped again. Another interminable silence fell in the room and it started to get to me. For a panicky moment I wondered where Packy was and I looked quickly toward the back door, to the dark alcove at the back of my office. Nothing.

When I looked at McGuiness again he was staring at me with a faint smile on his lips. It disappeared quickly and his features went slack again, his direct gaze drifting to something faraway. He considered something and then went on.

"Christine has stayed with me through a great deal," he said. "She sees something in me, I don't know what it is, but she sees something that makes her want to be with me. Me, Richard McGuiness, who grew up in Southie and worked in a ware-house when he was seventeen. I never finished high school. I drove trucks till I was thirty-two. Christine—she went to Wellesley, and her son went to Harvard. She eats off of bone china, *bone china*, every night. She reads the New York *Times* on Sunday and goes to the ballet. I used to laugh at people like her because I thought they were soft and arrogant, but they're not, they're better than us. They have better lives and they take advantage of it. Still, she wants me, she sees something in me that's better than all those rich, smart men she's known and I have a chance to keep her. So what do you want, Anderson? How do I keep your mouth shut?"

I let out a silent breath. The deal was on. I stared McGuiness down for a few seconds, then said, "I need your help."

He gave me a questioning look.

"Let's get this straight," I went on, "I'll back off from Chris-tine if you lend me some men for a morning's work."

"For what?"

I sat forward in my chair. "I need to save someone who's important to me, too." I told him what I had in mind. The scene played itself out without a hitch; we worked our parts like real pros. The whole time we kept up the pretense that it was Christine Regis we were discussing when actually the actor on whom the play really centered, the silent player on whom the whole story turned, was John Spenser.

III

———

I T WAS A BEAUTIFUL CLEAR MORNING, which was not what I was hoping for. I was hoping for heavy rains and low clouds. You can't have everything. What I had was a sawed-off shotgun resting on my lap, Packy beside me, and a man named Streak behind the steering wheel.

"How'd you get your name?" I called out to him from the back seat.

He looked at me through the rearview mirror. "I'm the slowest guy on the dock," he said. "I've perfected slowness to a fine art." His eyes flicked to Packy.

McGuiness's man stared out the side window, ignoring us. He had a Remington 870 on the seat beside him. The barrel had been chopped off that one too.

"Amazing how you can get illegal firearms at a moment's notice," I said to Streak. "You ever use these before?"

He didn't answer. I could only see his thin, I've-been-through-hell-and-back face in profile. He seemed to be studying the high cattails growing in the marsh beside us. We were on a side road a half mile from the Women's Correctional Institute in Framingham. After a week spent observing the police vans departing from the prison I figured out that the wagon transporting Marion to court would pass by here at about 7:10 A.M. A few miles further, on Route 9, it would pick up a State Police escort. This short stretch of back country road was the van's only, to borrow a phrase, "window of vulnerability."

Packy wasn't at all happy with the arrangements and you could almost see his second thoughts rolling past his eyes like screen credits. He'd do a lot for the union but this was close to the limit. I wondered what kind of convincing McGuiness had to go through to get Packy to help me. He would be glad to take me for a final ride to the salt marshes of Revere—that he could understand. But helping spring a Federal prisoner on trial for crimes against her country—that was hard to swallow. He hadn't said two words to me.

"This shouldn't take long," I said to him.

He grunted, still looking away.

I nudged him with my elbow. "Lighten up. Now you're going up against some real big boys. Not some unarmed scab."

Streak looked at me through the mirror. "Packy doesn't like you much, pal." His eyes smiled.

"Shut up, Billy," Packy said.

"How'd you get your name?" I asked him, just to keep the words moving, cut through the nerves. "Packy . . ."

Billy, or Streak, answered again, "His name is Elliot Packard Cummings the . . ."

"I said shut up!"

Billy laughed. Packy twisted and went back to staring out the window, disgruntled.

I felt the shotgun's weight on my knees. "The help these days," I said. Packy threw me a nasty glance.

There was another car with just a driver, Jimmy, parked off the road a hundred yards from us on a piece of dry ground in among the weeds. In between our two cars was a stalled tractor trailer, its hazard lights blinking, a set of triangular warning markers spread behind it as if by a conscientious driver—who'd unfortunately left his truck in the middle of the road. Very little room to pass by on the soft shoulder that dropped off to marsh. This would slow, or stop the police wagon . . .

create confusion and give me the time I needed. Time was particularly important because the shotgun on my lap was empty. A hollow threat. Packy hadn't liked that and I knew he wouldn't. That's why I was going to have to pull off the first part of the operation by myself.

A sparrow flitted from stalk to stalk, looking harried, rushing under the constant search for food, shelter, safety from predators. This was marsh hawk country. Not far from here, at the Long Meadow Sanctuary, I'd done some spotting for hawks with a pair of binoculars and a telephoto lens on my Pentax. I looked up into the clear blue sky and saw a black form, a spread of wings with the serrated ends like fingertips, floating casually before preparing to dive. Watch out, sparrow.

Packy cleared his throat and looked at the back of Streak's head. He wouldn't look at me when he talked. "We drop off the truck and make two car changes together," he said. "Then we split up." He looked out the window again.

"Sure, chief," I answered.

"Don't call me chief," he said, "and stop the jokes."

"I'm nervous," I said. I called to the front seat, "You nervous, Streak?"

"Shit sure," he said to the mirror, "this is big time."

"It'll be a piece of cake."

"The grab? Yeah," he said. "But the whole state's gonna go ape shit. There'll be Smokies and uniforms and Feds on every street." He talked with a kind of lust for the sheer danger of it.

"That's my problem," I said. "You'll be out of it by then."

"What are you going to do?" Packy asked.

I smiled. "You'd like to know, wouldn't you? After you've done your bit, you could just stop and make a phone call."

Packy's mouth opened in a brief smirk. I saw yellow canines.

"I'm just curious," he said.

"Stay curious."

I looked out and saw the sparrow take off in a flash of brown and white. In the sky the hawk floated serenely. I said to Packy and loud enough for Streak to hear, "If my name ever comes up in connection with this I can still make life miserable for McGuiness, never mind you two. Is that clear?"

Streak nodded, "Hey, I know man, my lips are sealed."

"Packy?"

"I hear you," he said.

It was 7:05. As the time drew closer I felt a calm settle over me. The kind of peace that comes with accepting anything that comes next, when you're doing what you want. I wanted Marion free again. Away from Newman's revenge. I dusted off some more cliches: If everyone else can get what he wants, so can I; No more Mr. Nice Guy, etc. I tried not to think that in a few minutes I would turn against everything I'd stood for (more or less) over the last ten years. I'd read the morning paper ("Vt. Minister Trial Begins") and I told myself I was just doing what seems to come naturally to men and beasts. It was time to move.

"Good luck, gentlemen," I said, stepping from the car.

"I thought you didn't believe in luck," Packy called after me.

"I do now," I said. Streak started the car and backed down the road, out of sight around a bend. It suddenly got very quiet. Except for the pounding in my ears.

I stepped off the roadway into ankle-deep marsh water, sloshing my way into tall cattails. When I got a good view around the back of the stalled truck I squatted down. A bird cheeped in protest behind me and took off in a diversionary flight from its nest.

In the distance I heard the rumble of a truck at low throttle. I pulled down my ski mask and whistled a low, meaningless tune through it.

The blue and white police van rounded a bend two hundred yards away, moving unhurriedly. It reached the straightaway and slowed as the driver saw the truck. He kept coming and I smiled, thinking what was going through his mind, calculating road width and shoulder strength. Behind the truck he stopped and I saw his partner craning his neck and gesturing. "You can make it," he was saying. The van moved forward and tried to pass on the opposite side of the truck from where I waited. When the front tire hit the shoulder the van's hood started to sink. The driver stopped with a jerk. More talk. My breath began to condense on the inside of the ski mask and I smelled wet wool. Everything stopped for a moment, the universe held poised.

The passenger door of the police van opened and one of the guards stepped out. I watched his feet as he walked to the front of the truck. They disappeared as he hoisted himself up on the step and peeked into the cab. That's when I slipped from the marsh with the truck as a shield, and stationed myself behind the tires.

"I don't like it," the guard said. "Call the barracks."

I stepped out quickly from behind the truck. "Too late," I said. I didn't stop moving, walking directly at the guard on the road. He made a move toward his gun and for a moment I thought he'd call my bluff and I saw twenty-five more jail years before me. Then he changed his mind and raised his hands.

The driver jammed the van into reverse as soon as he saw me, but before he got off the shoulder Jimmy was behind him. When the guard I was watching pivoted toward me I kicked him in the knee and knocked him to the ground. Then I poked the empty shotgun in the still open passenger door and yelled at the driver, "Slide out this way. Move. Fast." To my right I heard car doors slamming as Packy and Streak ran toward us. Packy grabbed the fallen guard's pistol and Streak ran behind the trailer, pulling open the back doors. He dragged two wide, thick planks and set them up as ramps. I motioned to the driver, "Inside the trailer." I followed him up.

Packy yelled at me, "You kicked him in the knee, idiot!" He and Streak picked up the injured guard and threw him into the truck like a sack of laundry. Packy climbed in and dragged him back to where I covered the driver.

Jimmy had already pulled his car off the road and let the air out of one of the tires. Then he ran to the police wagon and set the engine racing, throwing dirt in reverse. He lined the wagon up with the ramps and then flew forward. All of us in the back of the truck shrank back as the van roared towards us.

Jimmy was out almost before the van jerked to halt. He jumped to the ground and the trailer's doors closed.

By the inside lights Packy and I handcuffed and gagged the guards, the four of us staggering like drunken sailors as the trailer lurched forward. We sat the guards down in front of the police van and tied their feet to the axle.

"Let's get the cargo," Packy said.

Most police vans aren't meant to hold up under an all-out attack and this one was no different. There was nothing more than a dead bolt holding the two doors closed. Packy grabbed a crow bar we'd stashed in a corner, wedged the blade between the two doors and yanked once. The doors sprang apart with a snap and flew wide open.

Marion was in the rear, left corner, bruised from all the bumping and sudden jerks, staring at us goggle-eyed. "What the hell . . . ?" she said.

I smiled at her, feeling a flush of triumph. All I needed was a white horse. "Let's take a powder," I said to her.

But something happened that I wasn't ready for. Marion sat looking white faced, ashen, bloodless, a person in shock. She didn't seem capable of moving. She said, "No." That's all.

"What?"

"No," she repeated. "Not again. No more."

Packy looked at me. "She doesn't want to be sprung?"

I ignored him. "Marion, let's go." The trailer truck was moving fast now and I stood unsteadily as it bounced from side to side. Marion didn't move.

"This is no time for moral choices, we've got to hustle," I said. My voice sounded a little desperate.

"What's the problem?" Packy asked me.

"I don't know."

"Perfect," Packy said.

I jumped into the van. "Come on, I've got the whole thing arranged," I said.

The van jerked as Packy followed me. He took Marion by the right elbow and heaved her up. "Time to go, honey," he said.

I took her left arm. There was a length of chain between her ankles and she had to take short steps.

"You don't understand," she said.

"Shock," I said to Packy.

"Sure."

"She doesn't know what's happening."

We lifted her and brought her to the rear of the van, sitting her down on the back steps. Packy looked at her chains. "The fucking tools are in the car," he said.

"We'll have to carry her," I said. "Where are we making the switch?"

"Behind a supermarket."

"I hope no one's there."

"Jesus, this is insane," Marion said.

Packy sat down beside her. "Your buddy here is nuts," he told her. He pulled up the bottom of his ski mask and got out a cigarette, offered them around and then lit up.

We pulled to a stop behind an out-of-the-way grocery store and waited until no one was around. Then Marion was hustled into another car, driven by Jimmy, this one a snazzy Toyota Celica. Factory air, FM stereo. Borrowed for the morning. We put Marion in the back seat and I got in beside her. Streak took the other front seat and Packy climbed in the back with Marion and me. "Take a left at the end of the street," Packy called to Jimmy.

"I know," he answered. He said to me, over his shoulder, "We drove right by the Smokies. It was great. They were checking the time, getting worried. I laughed."

"Wonderful." I twisted in the seat and watched the trailer recede behind us, then said to Packy, "Don't tell the cops where the truck is for at least two hours."

"I hear you."

I turned to Marion. "Are you okay? What's the matter?"

"You don't understand," she said. Her color had come back and she seemed more composed.

"Marion, they were going to bar no expense, throw the book, use you as an example . . ." I said.

"I was going to bargain," she said. She slid down and laid her head on my shoulder.

We made the first change on a back road two miles away, switching to a Buick LeSabre. The men put on suit coats and ties. Three men and a woman car-pooling to work. We drove towards Sudbury.

"You gonna work on those?" Packy asked, eyeing Marion's irons.

I took out a small jimmy set and bent down to Marion's ankles. I got the ankle irons off and went to work at her wrists. She watched the operation without speaking.

"You're a fucking pip," Packy said to me, "saving someone who doesn't want to be saved."

"A domestic squabble," I said, "we'll work it out." I got the wrist cuffs off. Marion rubbed her sore skin.

We were in heavy traffic, commuters inching east and west, north and south, hurrying through that brief period where the parking lots of massive, impersonal buildings, fill with employees who scurry to their appointed tasks. At Sudbury Center we took a left onto Route 20 and then a quick left onto a country lane where suburbanites parked their cars and doubled up for the ride to Boston. There were six cars parked on the soft shoulder—two of them were ours.

Before we got out and split up Packy said to me, "We're square now, correct?"

"For now, yes," I said.

"What do you mean, 'for now'?"

I gave him a steady look. "Just what I said."

His gray, washed-out eyes gazed at me. I thought I saw some anticipation in them. "I'll be seeing you," he said.

"Thanks for all your help in these difficult times," I said. We didn't shake hands.

"Who were they?" Marion asked.

"Just folks," I said.

We headed down narrow back roads towards Marlboro, where there's a small airfield.

"We've got to talk," Marion said after a while.

"So talk."

I heard her sigh. She said, "I felt free for the first time in years. Can you imagine? Everything was out of my hands. I'd done all I could and I'd been stopped. Halted. Arrested."

"Marion, I'm burning all my bridges here. Get to the point."

"Okay, Derek. I was ready to do my time and get it over with. I *wanted* to start over."

I was speeding. The roadside trees flicked by and I took a corner way too wide. I took my foot off the gas and slowed the car.

"There's something else, too. When we heard about Robert I was furious, right? Shaking my fist at the injustice of it all. Vowing to get back for him." She slipped down in her seat. "Well, when I was driving down to Boston I realized I felt good, very good, happy, you could say." She looked at me to see if I was following her. "And I wondered what that was about. Robert is dead, I'm leaving you in Maine, heading to Boston where most likely the police are waiting for me, and I just feel charged up. Eager. I know who I'm going to see and what each step has to be. I'm going to identify who shot Robert. I think over a few possible responses. I'm driving down the Maine Turnpike, feeling I have a purpose, a strong purpose and I realize that I feel good because I'm on *familiar ground.*" She twisted in the seat and put her hand on my shoulder, demanding attention. "All that talk in Maine scared me, Derek. I felt adrift. Facing something unknown. I'd always thought that I was being courageous, but I was just doing, in a way, what was expected of me, conforming, filling in one role society has always expected. That minister was right, which is surprising. I'd always thought I was someone dedicated to change, but real change scared me, and the first chance I had in Maine I ran from it."

"You sure did."

"Are you mad?" she asked.

"Not mad. Disappointed. I expected more from you."

"I expected more too. All my life I had a high opinion of myself, what I was about. It turns out to be all delusion. Fear of facing what really matters. Your own life lived well. Is it too late for me to try for that?"

"You're not afraid of the monotony? The routine?"

"I embrace the routine. Simple tasks. Cleaning the house. Watering the plants."

"And injustice? Poverty? Human rights? They're no longer important?"

"They're important," she said, "but I'm starting here," she pointed at her chest, "with me. I'll do it your way. It's sanity, hope."

I shook my head. "Now I'm doing it your way."

"Slippage," she said, "a moment's indiscretion."

"What about Newman?" I asked.

"I'll deal with him," Marion said. "I can tell him things that'll make his hair stand on end. Routes, places, routines. Make him feel like he's king of the heap."

"You'll do that?"

Marion smiled. "It won't matter. The underground is not cast in concrete. Nothing stays the same. It's an element in constant flux, a gas that seeps through the infrastructure. It's as much a part of the country as Exxon and General Motors. Nothing I can tell them will change things. As long as there are countries, separate entities, ways people try to exclude each other, there'll be people like me."

We were on a larger road now, a main artery from one town to the next, another vehicle in a long chain of single-occupant cars, their drivers hunched over the wheel. I pulled onto the shoulder. Automobiles whizzed past. Shush. Shush.

"This time I'm going to do it myself," Marion said.

"It'll look good."

"ESCAPEE RETURNS—*Globe.*"

"GUN MOLL: 'I GIVE UP'—*Herald.*"

"Judge cites change of heart."

"Prosecutor cites cooperation, okays leniency."

"Are we dreaming?" Marion asked.

I watched the cars pass by. They all looked new, like current models, which seemed to indicate the economy was healthy, robust. Housing starts are up, rents are soaring in high tech Massachusetts. "We're dreaming," I said.

"I haven't dreamed in years. It seems so . . ."

"Innocent."

"Naive."

"You always were a tough nut."

I felt Marion's fingers brush my hair, stroking softly.

I said, "You were going to ask?"

"What'll you do?"

"I'll be here," I answered. "This is my state. I've got things to do."

I dropped Marion off on the south side of Marlboro, about a mile from the police station. She asked for some money and I gave it to her without question. She told me later she got a bite to eat, then sat for a while in a park near the square. Then she walked the two blocks to the station.

IV

THE LONG COUCH WAS WEDGED awkwardly in a turn in the stairwell.

"These hallways were built wide for easy access," Bill Stacom said, "it should be easy. We must be doing something wrong." Sweat beaded on his forehead and his breathing was labored, his heavy chest heaving from the unaccustomed work.

"Next time hire movers," I grunted, holding up the rear of the couch.

"If you lift up your end a smidgen more, you can get the leg over that step," Margaret suggested, "then Bill can swing his end around."

"What? Press this couch over my shoulder?" I said. "What am I, a weight lifter?" I pressed the couch up towards the ceiling.

"That's it," Bill yelled. "Here it comes."

We staggered into a bright living room with shining hardwood floors. Bay windows looked out onto a shady lawn.

Bill caught his breath. "Let's get the refrigerator before we poop out altogether."

"Refrigerator?" I asked.

"Where does this go?" Jeremy stood in the doorway holding

a small, lightweight box. He kept it away from his body, afraid of messing his white shirt and clean pants.

"The boxes are all marked," Margaret said.

"Glad you dressed for the job," I said to him.

He looked down at his clothes. "I've got a date later."

"Then you'd better take off the shirt when we move the refrigerator."

"Refrigerator?" he said.

"Don't worry, I've got a dolly," Bill said.

The three of us humped the unit, grunting, stumbling, down a long hall to the kitchen in back.

"Look out this window, Derek," Margaret said, after we'd pushed the refrigerator into an alcove.

There was a view of a long yard that ended in a copse of birches, their crowns brilliant orange.

"There's a stream just beyond the treeline," Margaret told me, nodding to indicate distance.

"Come on, come on, I'm renting the truck by the hour," Bill said. "Time is money."

"I'm going to get all sweaty," Jeremy complained.

"Then what'd you come for?" Bill asked.

"I know, I know, I'm just squawking so you'll be even more in my debt."

Bill put his arm over Jeremy's shoulder and led him towards the door. "I'm so grateful, so grateful," he said, his voice an exaggerated whine, "I'll never be able to repay you."

Margaret watched them go, then said to me, "He's still hurt. Confused. He feels like you betrayed him somehow."

"I know. I did in a way."

"He doesn't know why he feels that way. He just does."

"We'll work it out. Over time."

"I hope so." She put on a bright smile to cheer herself up. "What do you think of the place?" she asked.

"I'm speechless. Ma and Pa Kettle move to Concord."

"Who'd've thunk it? We're right over the highway from Walden Pond. Thoreau's backyard."

"I feel a quote coming on," I said. " 'There are a thousand hacking at the branches of evil to every one striking at the root.' "

Margaret smiled, a real one this time. Sunlight from the window draped over her like a soft cloth, catching the strands of gray in her hair. "Remember when we read him religiously? 'Civil Disobedience' was my bible. 'Law never made men more just . . . even the well-disposed are daily made the agents of injustice.' "

"That was another life time."

Margaret leaned against the counter and stared out towards the birches. "Do you think it was? I don't, I feel like I haven't changed a bit." She laughed. "There must be some Freudian name for that. 'Post-adolescent Adjustment Delay,' 'Adult Attitude Denial,' or something. I don't know, but I still carry the torch for that love we had, that belief that this can be a good world, a good life. I just didn't know it would be so hard, be such a constant struggle. Bill works with his kids and seems to get nowhere and meanwhile every day brings another little crisis, an overdue notice, the car, a leaky faucet. We haven't done anything earth shaking, but we've tried. We've done our part, don't you think?"

"I think you two deserve an A+ for effort," I said. I rubbed her shoulders. "How are you two going to do, with you working?"

She shrugged. "We'll have to thrash it out. It was time for me to get out of the house anyway."

"Really?"

She looked out over the yard. "We both wanted this. Needed this. We'll just have to see what happens. One step at a time. What about you, Derek?"

"I've got some waiting to do," I said, "and a friend I owe a favor to. I'll be around. I'm here for the duration, like you, taking one step at a time."

"That's all we can do," Margaret said. "Rub my neck, will you? This move is taking its toll on my poor body."

In the front hall we heard bumping and scraping, stumbling feet, as Bill and Jeremy fought with some piece of furniture.

"We better get out there and help them before they kill themselves," Margaret said.